seek me darling
Maree Rose

seek me darling

by Maree Rose

Copyright © 2025 by Maree Rose

First Edition: May 2025

Published by Maree Rose

This book is a work of fiction. Names, characters, places and incidents (outside of those clearly in the public domain) are products of the author's imagination or are used fictitiously. Any resemblance to actual events, locales or persons, either living or dead, is entirely coincidental.

Foreword

Hello little darlings!

Thank you so much for choosing up my book!

Although not necessary, I strongly advise reading book 1 and 2 of the Darling Games before this. All books in the Darling Games are standalone books and can be read individually though as I keep spoilers to pretty much non existant...

Please be aware that this book is a MFM romance, meaning our leading lady Seanna will not have to choose between her men, because #whychoose.

Warning, this book is a dark contemporary romance. It contains very explicit 18+ dark, sexual content, and straight-up smut.

The male leads are not prince charming, they are the opposite with psycho tendencies and therefore there is stalking, obsessive and possessive behavior, unaliving people, and lots of dark and twisted content. All the characters are 18+

Proceed at your own risk...

Thank you and I hope that you enjoy seek me darling

Content Warnings

If you don't have any triggers and feel like taking a gamble on the content then just skip the next page completely.

For those who do need to check the warnings then they are listed on the next page for your reference.

Content Warnings

Please be mindful of triggers when going into this story...

Mask Play

Knife Play

Blood Play

Primal Play

Mild Breeding Kink

Stalking

Abduction

Dub con

Somnophilia

Shibari

Bondage

Voyeurism/Exhibitionism

Forced Sedation

BC Tampering (IUD Removal without her knowledge)

Graphic Violence

Murder/Unaliving

Explicit Language

Explicit Sex Scenes incl rough sex scenes and DP

Obsessive/possessive and psychotic behavior

Some may consider there to be a mild amount of Stockholm, though Seanna would disagree...

Apologies if I missed any, please reach out to me on social media if that is the case.

Playlist

I know how much you all love a
good playlist to set the mood...

For your listening pleasure:
https://tinyurl.com/seekmedarling

PLAYLIST

Twisted - MISSIO
Sacrifice - Black Atlass, Jessie Reyez
Prisoner - Raphael Lake, Aaron Levy, Daniel Ryan Murphy
Secrets - Omido, Ordell, Rick Jansen
Black Hole Sun (Acoustic Version) - Sofia Karlberg
Throne - Saint Mesa
Hide and Seek Reimagined - Klergy, Mindy Jones
Desire - MEG MYERS
Dark Side - Ramsey
Pretty In The Dark (Slow + Reverb) - Ashley Sienna, Ellise
Storm - Honors
way down we go (slowed + reverb) - badkarma
Mine - Sleep Token
Fight for Survival - Klergy

Hush Hush -Klergy, Mindy Jones
The Sound of Silence - Lexxi Saal, NOCTURN
Scary People - Georgi Kay
Heart of Darkness - Steelfeather
Straight For The Kill - UNSECRET, Anna Renee
Insane - Monelise
Whisper (Slowed) - Able Heart
Dangerous Hands - Austin Giorgio
Deeper - Female - SATV Music
Welcome To The Jungle - Tommee Profitt, Fleurie
I Lose Control - Lee Richardson, Jonathan Murrill, Tom Ford, James
Cocozza, Alex Francis

*For the ones who fall hardest for masked men with
filthy mouths and darker intentions—
This is for you.*

I hope the story Rule's your mind, while the smut Ruin's your body...

Here is to the final unmasking...

Prologue

Some people fear the darkness.

Me? I welcome it.

Not the night. Not the absence of light. I'm talking about the kind of darkness that lives inside you—the kind that curls around your spine and whispers sweet nothings when you're thinking things that wouldn't normally be acceptable in society. The kind that doesn't beg to be tamed, but instead demands to be fed.

Most people spend their lives pretending it doesn't exist. I don't have that luxury. I never did.

My name is Seanna Darling, daughter of the infamous Agent Alexandra Darling and her two obsessively devoted husbands. Sister to the golden girl, Detective Hydessa Darling. Everyone always assumed I'd follow in my mother's footsteps—become the next profiler prodigy or head up some elite task force of my own.

And sure, I work with the DEA. I have my own team. I hunt monsters. I dismantle cartels. But I don't do it to be the hero. I do it because I understand what lives in the dark. Because I am not afraid to go there. Because sometimes, to take down the worst of them, you have to become something worse.

Others flinch at the horror of murder scenes, at the blood and broken bodies. I lean in closer. I examine the angles and look for the artistry. And if that makes me fucked up? Good. Let them think I'm unhinged. If they can't handle the storm I bring, they should stay the fuck out of my path.

My family is made up of legends, warriors, and shadows. Mom walks through crime scenes like a ghost of judgment, unraveling motives with a single glance. Hydessa chases justice like it owes her a debt, chasing truth through the ruins of her own restraint. And me?

I don't chase, I lure. I go where the monsters live and I walk into the fire without flinching. Because deep down, I am just as twisted as the men I hunt—I've just chosen a different outlet. A different target. A different set of rules.

The world taught me early on that monsters don't always hide under the bed. Sometimes, they sit in the boardroom. Sometimes, they run billion-dollar drug empires. Sometimes, they stare back at you in the mirror and dare you to blink first.

I didn't become this way on accident. I became this way because I had to.

Growing up in the Darling household meant survival was never just a metaphor. It was drilled into our bones between target practice and coded language lessons. We were never told fairy tales. We were told facts. The world is cruel. The system is broken. And sometimes, justice doesn't come with a badge—it comes with blood.

My sister still believes in things like purpose, and fate, and maybe even love. Me? I stopped waiting for love a long time ago. If someone ever wants me, they'll have to be as obsessed with me as my dads are with my mom. They'll have to crave every broken piece of me—and sharpen their edges just to keep up. Because I won't play nice. I won't soften for anyone. I won't shrink to make someone else comfortable.

I know who I am. I'm the storm, the fire, the razor-sharp edge. I'm the woman who doesn't just stare into the abyss— I make it beg for mercy.

So go ahead. Seek me, darling. But be warned: once you find me, there's no coming back.

Chapter 1
Seanna

Men are only good for one thing. Okay, maybe two—if their aim doesn't completely suck. Which, let's be honest, it usually does.

I watch the faint, unmistakable red dot lazily trace patterns across the chest of Diego Alvarez—mid-level cartel trash who clearly thinks he's hot shit because his boss tossed him out here as a sacrificial lamb. Poor bastard doesn't even realize he's already screwed. He's too busy stripping me naked with his eyes, probably deciding whether I'm his next big mistake or his future fantasy girl. Spoiler alert: I'm absolutely both.

I lean casually against the hood of the sleek black SUV parked smack in the middle of this god-awful parking garage—a charming spot filled with rust-stained concrete, oil-slick floors, and a potent bouquet of piss, mold, and despair. Romantic, right? Honestly, I couldn't have picked a better place to watch Diego squirm.

Beside me, Eli and Jensen are doing their best "bored muscle" impersonations. Eli's dark hair falls carelessly around a smirk that promises trouble, while Jensen stands like a human brick wall, inked arms crossed loosely, somehow looking both bored and murder-ready. They might fool Diego, but I know better—they're wolves just waiting for the chance to rip someone apart.

Matteo's hidden somewhere above, watching quietly from his sniper perch. He's exactly the type I trust—silent, precise, and capable of turning someone's head into confetti at a moment's notice. I bet he's up there right now, mentally laughing his ass off at the disaster unfolding below.

A few other agents are stationed close by, silent and ready to move if things go sideways.

"I already told you, sweetheart," I drawl lazily, voice dripping honey-coated venom. "I'm here for business. But blind dates aren't my style. If I'm dropping serious cash, I expect to see your boss face-to-face. Got it?"

Diego's jaw tightens. Good. Angry men fuck up fast, and I don't have all night.

"The boss doesn't waste his time with random bitches flashing cash," he snarls, puffing his chest like he's auditioning for alpha asshole of the year.

Internally, I roll my eyes so hard it hurts. Typical macho bullshit. "Cute. You really think real threats come with a resume and a fucking billboard? Honey, your intel sucks harder than your fashion sense. Less posturing, more research next time."

His nostrils flare like an irritated bull, fingers twitching nervously toward his jacket. Bingo. God, men are predictable.

"You're asking too much," Diego growls, eyes darting between me, Eli, and Jensen. "How do I know you aren't some cop bitch playing games?"

I laugh sharply, making sure every note drips with pure disdain. "If I were a cop, Diego, I'd be choking down shitty coffee behind a desk, not standing here inhaling your insecurity and the lovely aroma of motor oil. Trust me, if I was undercover, I'd pick a target far less pathetic than your sorry ass."

He doesn't smile. Diego glances toward Eli and Jensen, sizing them up again. "Maybe. Maybe not."

His fingers twitch near his side, and I wait, my breathing steady, my heart calm. "Look," I continue smoothly, "I came here in good faith. I'm just here to do business. You want the deal, you make the call. If not, I'm sure someone else would happily take my money."

He hesitates again, clearly torn. The seconds stretch long and tense between us. Finally, something shifts in his eyes—something subtle but unmistakable. Suspicion wins out.

His hand moves, slipping inside his jacket.

Wait. My hand taps two fingers on my bicep where my arms are crossed, my signal to the team.

He tenses, his gaze shifting downward, hand hovering with uncertainty. Gun or phone. Fight or call. Life or death.

Wait.

My heart beats steadily, counting off the seconds.

Wait.

He jerks his hand free, a gleam of dark metal catching the dim lighting of the garage.

Wrong fucking choice, Diego.

Matteo's shot echoes through the empty concrete space, sharp and decisive. Diego jerks violently, screaming out in agony as the bullet slams into his right arm making him flail like a broken puppet on a marionette string. He howls like the fucking coward he is, his gun skidding uselessly across the filthy floor.

Jensen moves forward in a flash, kicking the weapon away as Eli forces Diego down to his knees, swiftly cuffing his wrists behind his back. Diego struggles uselessly, spewing curses in spanish between cries of agony. The wound won't kill him.

I stride forward slowly, deliberately, savoring the echo of each sharp click of my heels against the grimy floor. Crouching in front of Diego, I grip his jaw roughly, forcing his bloodshot, terrified eyes up to mine. "You really should've chosen the easy way. Now we're going to have to do things *my* way."

"You fucking bitch, you don't scare me!" He spits, glaring up at me.

I smirk coldly, gripping tighter. "Oh, sweetheart, we're just getting started. You haven't even begun to experience just how fucked you really are."

I stand, waving Eli and Jensen to drag his sorry ass away. Matteo's amused voice crackles through my comm. "Well, that was fun. Bet he'll regret his life choices when he tries jerking off to your memory later."

I snort softly, rolling my eyes. "No shit. Nice shot, Matteo. Wrap it up—we're done here."

Diego's panicked wails fade into whimpers. I breathe deep, adrenaline thrumming deliciously through my veins. Eli and Jensen haul Diego off toward the other agents stationed just outside. They will take him to where he belongs.

The thought of getting Diego back to interrogation sends a ripple of anticipation down my spine. Breaking him will be half the fun—and I have no doubt he will break. They always do.

"You good?" Eli asks lightly as he comes back to our car, already knowing the answer.

"Fucking fantastic," I reply, flashing a dangerous grin. "Time to celebrate."

Jensen groans dramatically, swiping a hand over his face. "Whiskey, dancing, and shitty life choices?"

"You know me too well," I smirk, sliding gracefully into the passenger seat. Matteo emerges from the shadows, slipping smoothly into the back seat, looking annoyingly smug. "Nice of you to finally show, Matteo. Drinks are on me tonight."

He grins, eyes glittering with amusement. "Wouldn't miss it for the world."

As the vehicle purrs to life beneath us, my smile widens. We're one step closer to the big fish—the cartel boss who thinks he's untouchable. Tonight didn't exactly go as planned, but with Diego secured and spending the night on edge waiting for us to come in and break him is the next best thing. And I've learned to savor every victory, no matter how small.

Besides, there's something deeply satisfying about a man who chose the hard way. Breaking him will be delightful.

I lean my head back against the seat, closing my eyes for a brief moment as we speed out of the parking garage and into the neon-lit night.

It isn't long before we are at the club, pushing through the crowd toward an empty booth having shed our DEA persona's back at headquarters. The music pulses around us, neon lights slicing through the haze, the bass vibrating in my chest. It's our ritual—each victory means whiskey and bourbon, laughter, and enough sarcastic banter to make it all worthwhile. After what we pulled tonight, we deserve it.

Sliding into our usual booth, I watch as the others settle in around me. Eli drops down on my left, his muscular frame filling out his black leather jacket in a way that turns more than a few heads as we pass. His dark hair still hanging around his face, a faint scar slicing through his left eyebrow—courtesy of an earlier bust gone sideways—and he catches me watching, offering a cocky smirk.

"See something you like, boss?" he teases, nudging me lightly.

"Hard pass," I reply smoothly, sipping my whiskey. "I've seen enough of you for two lifetimes, Eli."

He laughs, utterly unfazed as he reaches for his bourbon glass, eyes sparkling. "Your loss."

Jensen snorts, shaking his head as he stretches out comfortably across from us. Jensen's the oldest, mid-thirties, built as solid as a mountain, his dark skin inked with tattoos that map out his entire military and undercover history. He's grinning at me, clearly entertained. "Ever get bored of rejection, Eli?"

"Adds spice," Eli retorts, raising a brow.

Matteo scans the crowd, responding dryly, "Your idea of spice seriously concerns me." Matteo is tall, and muscular with an intensity that rarely fades, his dark eyes constantly scanning the room, taking in every detail. Tonight his thick brown hair is messy from the wind. He catches my glance briefly and offers me a tiny, crooked smirk.

"Enjoying the view, Seanna?" Matteo asks.

I roll my eyes and raise my whiskey, savoring the slow burn as it slides down my throat. "Don't flatter yourself. Just wondering if you ever smile wider than that."

He scoffs, but the corners of his lips curve slightly, eyes dancing. "Not likely."

Eli chuckles again, leaning back comfortably. "Leave Matteo alone, Seanna. If he smiled any bigger, he'd scare away the locals."

I grin into my drink, relaxing into the rhythm of our easy banter. Tonight my long black waves are braided down my back, keeping them away from my face, fully exposing my bright blue eyes. I've noticed a few stray glances already; I know my looks draw attention, but tonight I'm not interested in playing nice.

We're halfway through our second round when I feel a presence beside the booth. Turning my head slowly, I see a younger man hovering near me. He's attractive enough in that clean-cut, overly-confident way, probably used to charming his way into whatever he wants. He runs his hand through his blond hair, offering me what I suppose he considers his best smile as he leans in closer.

"Hey there, gorgeous," he says, trying to pitch his voice over the music. "Wanna dance?"

I tilt my head slightly, slowly letting my gaze drift over him from head to toe, openly appraising. Then I meet his eyes again, smile colder than the ice in my glass. "Sweetheart, I'd snap you like a twig before the chorus even starts. Save yourself the trouble."

Matteo snickers into his drink, Jensen bursts out laughing, and Eli whistles low, amused. Humiliated, the frat-boy stammers something incoherent and quickly vanishes into the crowd.

"Did you have to crush him that hard?" Jensen chuckles, shaking his head.

"Better shattered pride than false hope," I say coolly, taking another sip of bourbon. "Fragile egos bore me."

Eli grins, swirling his drink. "That was cold."

I arch an eyebrow playfully. "You expect anything less?"

He shakes his head, a warm chuckle escaping him. "Never."

Matteo shifts slightly, glancing down at me, his voice low enough only I can hear. "You do seem to enjoy breaking spirits."

I look up into his dark eyes, matching his subtle smirk with one of my own. "Only the weak ones."

Eli raises his glass suddenly, cutting into the moment. "To Diego—may he realize quickly just how badly he fucked up."

"To Diego!" Jensen echoes, laughing again as we all clink glasses, the sharp sound lost in the club's loud music.

I lean back comfortably, the warmth of the bourbon settling nicely in my chest. Nights like these remind me exactly why I do what I do. The danger, the power plays, the thrill—it's intoxicating. But the bond with this team, forged in fire and sealed in whiskey, makes it worth every risk.

Tonight, we celebrate. Tomorrow, the real work begins again. After all, breaking arrogant men is absolutely the best part of this job.

Chapter 2
Seanna

The night air is cool, a sharp bite as I pull into the gravel driveway, tires crunching beneath me like bones under pressure. My cabin sits at the edge of my parents' sprawling estate. It's just far enough to pretend I've carved out my own slice of solitude, but still close enough to remind me that I'm never truly alone, no matter how secluded the property is.

I park and step out, the stillness immediately wrapping around me like a cold, comforting blanket. Another night, another bullshit victory that doesn't actually mean anything. I was hoping for more progress toward Javier Reyes, that elusive bastard who's been slipping through my fingers like smoke. Instead, it's just another loose end, another damn riddle in a never-ending game.

It would have been better if Diego had brought me directly to his supplier. While tonight wasn't the win I was hoping for, in this line of work I have learned that I need to take a win when I get it.

Inside, the quiet of my cabin greets me with its familiar whispers—the wooden floors creaking beneath my boots, the faint rustle of night air slipping through an open window. My gaze shifts toward Hydessa's cabin—dark and silent. Good. She's asleep, probably tucked away safely, blissfully oblivious to my restless presence. I don't want company tonight. Hell, most nights I don't.

The past weeks blur, days chasing nights in an exhausting cycle as I hunt the goddamn cartel. Diego Alvarez was supposed to be my light at the end of the tunnel, my way closer to Javier Reyes. Instead, he's just another frustratingly insignificant puzzle piece. Reyes is still out there, safe behind layers of security thicker than my fucking patience. Every day inches me closer—just not close enough. One step at a time, I remind myself bitterly. Always one damn step at a time.

Hydessa finds peace in order, paperwork, safety. Good for her. Me? I thrive on chaos, adrenaline, the constant itch of danger. She sleeps easy, her demons neatly tucked away. I invite mine to dance.

We may look nearly identical, but how we see the world and ourselves couldn't be more opposite.

I kick off my boots and step into the living room, a space designed like a cinematic crime scene—vivid reds, stark blacks, unapologetic as fuck. It's me, splashed onto the walls. I exhale a slow breath, collapsing onto the couch as the residual warmth of the whiskey still pulses through my veins. The club was loud, chaotic, filled with faces I didn't want to know, bodies I didn't want to touch. We've been making it a ritual, going out after each victory, but even that loses its appeal with time. Tonight, thankfully, no bad decisions were made. Not enough whiskey in the world to make some of those idiots seem attractive.

Yet the restlessness inside me remains. Frustration coils tight, pushing me off the couch, pacing through the room like a caged predator. Diego's capture was a victory, sure, but if he'd grabbed his damn phone instead of his gun... I'd be a step closer to Reyes right now. He had one simple fucking choice, and he chose wrong. Men always do. Now, I'm stuck playing hide-and-seek with a ghost—one shielded behind walls, security, and more secrets than the fucking Pentagon.

Fuck patience. I'm tired of being patient.

I've come close—so close—to catching him twice before, only for him to slip through my fingers like smoke. Each failure feels personal, a scar etched deeper into my pride. Reyes has harmed too many innocent lives, destroyed too many families. Capturing him would mean justice for the voiceless, a message that no matter how big the monsters, they don't always escape into the dark.

A sudden prickle of awareness crawls across my skin. My pulse quickens, my instincts sharpening to a razor edge. Dangerous work breeds paranoia, or so I've been told. But I've learned to listen to my instincts, experience has taught me to never ignore that feeling. The feeling of being watched.

I stride to the window, peering out into the night, but the dark expanse offers nothing except my own reflection. My long, black waves are still neatly braided down my back, even tidier than my thoughts. I stare, unflinching, daring the night to reveal something more. Let whoever is out there look—they can watch all they want. I don't hide, and I don't fucking run. If they try to interfere, they'll soon learn they're the ones making a mistake.

With a huff, I switch off the living room light, casting the cabin into comforting darkness. I linger by the window a moment longer, my eyes adjusting to the dark, then turn toward the hallway and head for my bedroom. In our family, the idea of being watched isn't new; if someone wants to stalk me, let them. I'm no damsel in distress. Fear isn't an option. Never has been, never will be.

Inside my room, I leave the door wide open behind me with a defiant smirk, fuck modesty. I cross to the window, lifting the blinds, letting the moonlight spill in, and cracking it open just a bit. Might as well give them a decent view. Enjoy the free fucking show, assholes.

Methodically, I peel off my clothes until I'm stripped bare. The bedding is cool against my already heated skin as I lie down in the center of the bed. I sink into their embrace, savoring this rare moment of quiet dominance. Alone, powerful, unapologetically in control.

I trail my fingers slowly down my body, savoring the buildup of anticipation. Each light touch sends shivers along my skin as I trace lazy, deliberate circles over my breasts and across my stomach. My fingers glide lower, finally brushing against the sensitive swell of my clit. A soft gasp escapes my lips as the pleasure begins to stir—familiar, electric, undeniable.

I continue, unashamed, letting my hand explore with confident, practiced motions. I stroke myself in slow, teasing circles around my clit, gradually building tension. My other hand wanders up to gently pinch and roll one of my nipples, a deliberate contrast of sensations that makes me arch my back slightly. I think of all the men who've come and gone—those foolish enough to think their touch was enough to sate me. None of them knew how to truly bring me to the edge. They left me wanting, always, until I was forced to finish the job on my own.

I move faster, strokes more insistent as I spread my legs wider, my other hand teasing my clit, a symphony of sensations that draws a ragged moan from my lips, unfiltered by shame or pretense. Two of my fingers slip inside me, curling in to stroke that perfect spot. My hips rock in rhythm with my self-stimulation, a private dance of pleasure that is as much an act of defiance as it is indulgence. The room is lit only by moonlight, but if anyone were watching through that window, they'd see a woman in complete command of her desire—unapologetic and fierce.

My breath comes in short, heated bursts as I move closer to release. The sensations build, wave after wave of pleasure cresting until, with one final, desperate touch, ecstasy crashes over me in a cascade of raw, unbridled intensity. My body shudders, and I cry out, riding the wild pulses until I'm left trembling and spent.

Eventually, my breathing slows, body heavy and sated. I stretch lazily, basking in the lingering afterglow. If someone got a show, congratulations—I don't charge admission, but maybe I should. I take exactly what I need. I am in control and I am my own master of pleasure.

I sigh, thoughts inevitably circling back to Reyes, to the hunt, to the chase that consumes every waking moment. My life is built on shadows and secrets, endless puzzles and twisted paths. Hydessa's world might be safer, cleaner—but safe bores the hell out of me. She might sleep soundly tonight, but peace has never been my goal. Justice is messy, violent, and relentless. And I'm exactly the woman for the job.

I close my eyes for a moment, trying to quiet my racing mind, but it won't be silenced. The faces of the cartel, the men I've yet to take down, the twisted paths of lies I have to untangle—they swirl together in a dizzying whirlpool. I think of Javier Reyes. The man is more myth than flesh. He hides behind his empire, his walls. It's maddening, not being able to reach him. But that's the game, isn't it? Every layer of his life, every guard dog, every bit of information, it all feels like another riddle I'm supposed to solve. But I won't stop until I have the answers. Until I have him.

I sigh, pushing myself up from the bed. I know I won't get any sleep tonight like this, not with everything on my mind. I glance at the clock. It's already late, heading toward midnight.

Moving over to the window, I look out at the empty expanse of the property. The trees stretch tall in the moonlight, casting long shadows that seem to go on forever. I think about how different everything feels when I'm alone here. When I'm not surrounded by the noise of my team, or the constant chatter of family and friends who can't understand me. This cabin—this sanctuary—is the only place I feel like I can breathe freely, even if that freedom comes with its own weight.

I press my forehead against the cool glass. What am I waiting for? Validation? Certainty? Fuck it. This is my life—chaotic, dangerous, real. Chasing shadows is what I do best.

A soft sound from outside catches my attention—something moving in the distance. I freeze for a moment, but then, nothing. I'm paranoid. A result of too many years on the job, always watching, always waiting for something to jump out of the dark.

Let them watch, I think again. Let them come. They'll find out soon enough I'm not someone to be trifled with.

Shaking my head, I step away from the window and move into the connected bathroom, the cold tile grounding beneath my feet. The shower's hot spray beats down on me, washing away superficial stress but never quite touching the chaos inside. I towel off, slipping into loose pajamas, grabbing a glass of whiskey before sitting on the edge of my bed. Tomorrow, the world spins again—more battles, more bullshit.

I sip the whiskey slowly, savoring the burn as my mind reminds me that Reyes will still be out there tomorrow, hiding behind his fortress.

I'll continue hunting, inching closer with every step. Nothing worth having ever comes easy. Hell, nothing in my life ever has.

My eyes drift to the window, shadows dancing across the moonlit landscape. Maybe someone really is out there, watching, waiting for me to show weakness. They'll wait a long damn time. Let them underestimate me. Let them think I'm reckless, unhinged. Maybe I am. But I'd rather embrace my demons than pretend they don't exist.

I exhale slowly, glass now empty. Tomorrow, it begins again—the chase, the hunt, the dance with darkness that keeps my blood racing and my heart alive. For now, I'll enjoy this quiet rebellion, this rare peace that feels anything but peaceful.

Because in my world, calm is just the silence before the storm—and I'm always ready to strike.

Chapter 3
Seanna

Sleep is overrated anyway.

At least, that's the lie I feed myself as I stride through my cabin just before dawn, yanking on boots and shrugging into my jacket in the near-darkness. Restlessness kicked me out of bed long before sunrise had a fighting chance, my mind tangled in knots, refusing even the briefest respite. Sleep? Not today—not with all the chaos swirling relentlessly in my brain.

Catching a glance in the mirror, I smirk at my reflection. Even with minimal sleep, I still look ready to cut someone down—long, dark hair piled into a tight bun, blue eyes sharp enough to pierce steel. Good enough. Hell, better than good enough.

The rich, bitter scent of coffee fills the kitchen as I pour the steaming dark roast into my travel mug, inhaling deeply. Coffee isn't a luxury; it's survival—especially when the job involves dragging information out of reluctant cartel assholes like Diego. I'm practically buzzing with anticipation at the thought of breaking him.

My phone buzzes suddenly, startling me just enough to annoy me. My mother's name flashes across the screen, and I sigh—she always manages to call precisely when I'm at my edgiest. Must be some twisted motherly sixth sense.

"Morning, Mom," I say, leaning against the counter and bringing the phone to my ear.

"Good morning, sweetheart," she replies, voice warm, soothing, entirely too pleasant for this ungodly hour. "Your dads and I were wondering if you'd join us for breakfast at the main house."

I glance at the clock, already knowing my answer but making a show of pretending to consider it. "Thanks, but not today. I've got a date with an interrogation room and a stubborn bastard who doesn't know when to quit."

She laughs softly, knowing better than to argue. "Everything okay, Seanna? This case seems to have you wound pretty tight."

"I'm always wound tight," I quip dryly, swirling the coffee in my mug. "You should worry more if I'm calm. But yeah, it's been a pain in the ass. How are things at home?"

"Good. Actually, we're heading to Chicago today—just a routine investigation," she adds quickly, preempting my instinctive worry. "But there's something else—about your sister."

My brows lift sharply, instantly suspicious. "Hydessa? What's she done now? Alphabetize the file cabinet wrong?"

Mom chuckles, amused. "She found something online, a blog we think is worth investigating. Honestly, it would be good for her to handle it personally—get her out from behind that fortress of paperwork."

I snort, skepticism practically radiating from me. "Have you told her this grand idea yet? Because we both know she'll wiggle out of it faster than you can say 'fieldwork.'"

"Not yet," Mom admits with a resigned sigh. "But maybe she'll actually listen if you talk to her. She might take it seriously coming from you."

I roll my eyes dramatically, even though she can't see. "I'll talk to her, but I'm not holding my breath. Knowing Hydessa, she'll just delegate it to one of those eager newbies—like Bodhi or Thorn. She loves handing off responsibility."

Mom hums thoughtfully, clearly planning her next move. "I'll figure something out. It's time she steps up—she's hidden behind reports long enough. Besides, Max found the blog is being posted from a small island, she could do with the holiday."

"Good luck with that," I mutter dryly, lips quirking into a smirk. "We both know stubbornness runs deep in this family."

"Definitely inherited," she counters, laughter coloring her tone.

"Guilty," I retort, finishing my coffee in one swift gulp and grabbing my keys. "I'll nudge—or shove—her in the right direction. Whatever works."

"Thank you, Seanna," she says softly. "Be careful today."

"Careful is overrated," I tease back, heading toward the door. "But I'll stay alive, at least. Love you, Mom."

"Love you too, sweetheart."

Sliding the phone into my pocket, I step outside, greeted by crisp air scented with pine and damp earth. Climbing into my car, I can't help but dwell on Hydessa. My sister's always been too cautious, content hiding behind routine. Maybe Mom's right—it's time she learned to embrace a little chaos.

The car roars to life beneath me, headlights slicing through mist as I race away from the quiet sanctuary of my cabin. The conversation with Mom gets tucked neatly away for later—right now, I have a stubborn asshole named Diego to break. Javier Reyes won't topple himself, and today's interrogation will bring me one step closer to finally nailing the bastard.

A satisfied smirk curls my lips as I slam the pedal down, road stretching endlessly ahead.

The day's just getting started, and I intend to make it count.

The drive to the DEA offices is mercifully quick at this time of morning, the familiar route letting my restless thoughts settle into something resembling clarity. Headquarters looms ahead, a sleek, faceless building blending seamlessly into the mundane corporate landscape. Unremarkable from the outside, but within these walls, we hunt monsters and tear entire worlds apart—my kind of place.

I flash my ID badge at the guard, who nods with practiced indifference, waving me through without a second glance. Parking my car in my usual spot, I step out, savoring the briskness of the early-morning air against my skin as I head toward the entrance.

Inside, I breeze through security on autopilot—badge, metal detector, brief nod—and immediately get hit by the scent of cheap coffee, paperwork, and crushed dreams. Phones ring, voices chatting, and for some twisted reason, it feels like home.

Striding into the bullpen where my team congregates, I nod to a few familiar faces, murmuring greetings as I pass without inviting conversation. I'm halfway to my desk when Eli looks up from his mountainous pile of reports and flashes a grin.

"Morning, boss," he drawls, lifting a steaming mug in mock salute. "Bright-eyed and ready to ruin someone's day as usual, I see."

I raise an eyebrow at him, smirking faintly. "Someone has to pick up your slack, Eli. That coffee isn't going to fill out your paperwork for you."

Jensen snickers from the desk behind Eli, leaning back in his chair with arms crossed, his grin wide and lazy. "Ouch. You really gotta cut him down first thing, Seanna? Can't you let the poor guy finish his caffeine first?"

"Where's the fun in that?" I retort lightly, draping my jacket over my chair and pulling out my notes from yesterday's bust. "Besides, I prefer him slightly terrified. Keeps productivity high."

Matteo strolls past, dropping a fresh cup of coffee onto my desk without looking away from his phone, dark brows furrowed in concentration. "Remember, she likes to break men's spirits before breakfast," he says dryly, moving toward his own workspace. "Keeps her young."

"Careful, Matteo," I warn lightly, not bothering to glance up as I shuffle through paperwork. "You could be next."

He snorts, finally lifting his eyes to meet mine, a spark of amusement dancing in their depths. "I've survived worse."

I laugh under my breath, slipping easily into the familiar rhythm of our banter. My team might be a chaotic collection of misfits, but I trust these men with my life.

Just as I've started mapping out Diego's interrogation strategy, my phone buzzes sharply against my desk. I glance at the screen, rolling my eyes dramatically at my dad's name.

DAD

Your mom, Papa, and I are leaving for Chicago soon, so we won't catch you today. Can you call into the organization HQ at some point? Uncle Max needs to talk to you about your case.

Of course Uncle Max wants to talk. If it's not my parents poking around, it's Max's paranoid hacker brain digging into every digital breadcrumb. Still, irritation aside, I can't ignore him. Max has a sixth sense and the uncanny ability to find things that even the DEA can't.

Mentally bookmarking a visit to HQ later, I stand up smoothly, sliding my phone into my pocket.

"Leaving us already?" Eli feigns disappointment, pressing a hand dramatically to his heart. "You just got here."

"Some of us actually have work to do," I shoot back, heading toward interrogation. "I've got a date downstairs with our stubborn cartel asshole."

Jensen pushes away from his desk with a stretch, a grin spreading across his face. "Perfect. I love a good intimidation session before breakfast."

"Better than TV," Eli quips, trailing after us eagerly.

Matteo shakes his head with mock resignation, falling silently into step beside us as we head toward the interrogation rooms downstairs. "Remind me again why I spend everyday with you three?"

"My charming personality, obviously," Eli says smoothly.

Jensen snorts loudly. "Yeah, let's go with that."

Stepping into the elevator, silence settles around us as we shift from banter to cold focus. Jensen straightens, a wall of muscle radiating quiet menace. This dance is one we've perfected—me leading the charge, Jensen playing executioner, and Eli and Matteo dissecting every twitch from behind the glass.

Interrogation is in the basement, buried beneath layers of concrete and secrets. The hallway echoes quietly under our footsteps, tension rising. Outside Diego's room, Eli and Matteo veer toward the observation area. When I take a deep breath, Matteo pauses briefly, offering a small nod.

"Go get him, boss," Eli whispers with a smirk, slipping inside.

I glance up at Jensen, who cracks his knuckles menacingly. "Ready?"

"Always."

Pushing open the heavy metal door, I step inside with deliberate calm. Diego snaps his head up sharply, eyes bloodshot, his arm wrapped tightly from Matteo's well-placed bullet yesterday. His jaw tightens immediately.

I smoothly pull out the chair opposite him and settle gracefully into it. Jensen takes up a position slightly behind me, towering in silence, massive arms crossed over his chest. His shadow alone seems to swallow the room whole, and Diego visibly shrinks under his icy stare.

"Good morning, Diego," I greet calmly, placing my notes in front of me. My tone is pleasant, bordering on friendly. "I trust your accommodations were comfortable?"

Diego spits something colorful in Spanish, glaring daggers. "Fuck you."

Behind me, Jensen's deep chuckle vibrates dangerously. "Wrong answer."

"Remember Jensen?" I ask sweetly, leaning forward slightly. "Six-foot-five, zero patience, capable of snapping you like a toothpick? Might want to reconsider your attitude."

Diego swallows hard, eyes darting nervously between Jensen's unforgiving scowl and my calm gaze.

"Now," I continue, leaning forward slightly, "Let's try again, Diego. Tell me what you know about Javier Reyes. I want names, locations, meeting points—every single thing."

His mouth tightens stubbornly, though the fear flickering in his eyes betrays his façade of defiance. "If I talk, Reyes will kill me."

I lean back slightly, letting out a soft sigh as I shrug. "Sure, that's a possibility. But Jensen here?" I glance briefly over my shoulder. "He's a certainty. You really want to gamble with certainties, Diego?"

Jensen takes one slow step forward, his eyes narrowing. He looms silently, every inch of him dangerous, but even Jensen's quiet menace doesn't seem to hold a candle to the invisible threat of Reyes in Diego's mind.

"You think you scare me more than Reyes?" Diego scoffs weakly, defiance lingering stubbornly in his voice despite the faint tremor betraying his fear. "You have no fucking clue."

Jensen's muscles tense visibly, danger rolling off him in waves. Diego flinches slightly, but Reyes clearly terrifies him more. The realization settles unpleasantly—Reyes is even worse than we thought. He must truly be a monster. Even locked safely away with Jensen's imposing bulk hovering over him, Diego clings to silence as if it's his only lifeline.

"Think carefully, Diego," I say softly, drumming my fingers on the cold metal tabletop. My voice lowers, velvet-edged and deceptively gentle. "Reyes isn't here. We are. You should be more worried about what we can do."

Diego's jaw tightens again, eyes flicking nervously between me and Jensen. I see him mentally weighing threats and fears against each other. "If I give you Reyes, I'm a dead man. Worse than dead."

I sigh softly, leaning back and exchanging a meaningful glance with Jensen. He shifts his weight subtly, arms still crossed, a silent wall of intimidation behind me.

"You don't want to talk about Reyes himself, fine," I concede lightly, offering Diego an out. "Give me something else. Names. I want to know who else we can reach out and touch. You're mid-level, Diego—you're disposable. But I bet you know a few names that are a step or two above you. People who might be useful."

He hesitates, still trying to balance the consequences. "You promise protection?"

"No promises," Jensen answers coldly before I can respond, voice rumbling with dark authority. "But talk now, and we might consider it."

I offer Diego a small smile, the kind that doesn't reach my eyes. "It's the best offer you're going to get. Reyes won't make you any offers at all."

Diego's shoulders slump slightly, resignation slipping through the cracks in his stubborn façade. "Fine. But I don't know how much it'll help you."

My smile sharpens. "Start talking."

Chapter 4
Seanna

We grill Diego for hours.

Bit by painstaking bit, we squeeze out names, locations, and fragments of Reyes' meticulously crafted empire. Diego coughs up Sebastián Cruz, the person he would have called had he chosen currently and went for his phone, the next line up the food chain from him. He also gives us Valeria Mendoza and Rafael Navarro—each name dropping like coins into our growing collection. He even throws in a handful of disposable foot soldiers who handle daily tasks outside Reyes' direct orbit. Every scrap of intel nudges us a step closer to the elusive Javier Reyes himself.

Eventually, Diego clamps down, silence settling stubbornly as exhaustion and fear outweigh our relentless prodding. My sharp questions and Jensen's cold, calculated threats eventually hit a wall. Diego's eyes glaze over, focusing on nothing, clearly more afraid of Reyes' ghost than Jensen's very real presence. For now, Reyes wins this round.

With Diego left to marinate in his own fears, we head upstairs to regroup. I drop into my chair with a tired sigh, massaging my temples. Matteo is already buried in data, fingers flying across the keyboard, dissecting every crumb Diego spilled. Eli collapses theatrically into his chair, kicking his feet up with exaggerated relief, while Jensen slumps wearily, rubbing his eyes.

"Got something useful," Matteo announces without looking up. "Cruz's nightclub—the Silver Orchid—is likely a front. Drugs, trafficking, probably money laundering too. Mendoza and Navarro will take more work, but it's a start."

I stretch my arms above my head, joints popping satisfyingly. "We didn't sign up expecting this to be easy. Reyes isn't hosting a damn open house."

The afternoon drags while we sink into the monotonous slog of chasing down leads, sifting through endless surveillance footage, bank records, and criminal profiles. Hours blur, and boredom threatens our sanity.

I lean back in my chair, stretching my shoulders and glancing around the room. Eli is sprawled lazily, spinning a pen between his fingers and muttering to himself while his other hand flips through files. Matteo sits stoically at his desk, eyes narrowed in concentration as he pours over data, completely oblivious to Eli's theatrics. Jensen hunches over his screen, scowling at something he's reading.

"If I have to look at one more bank transaction," Eli groans dramatically, leaning back until his chair creaks dangerously, "I'm gonna stab myself in the eye with this pen."

"You're welcome to," Matteo replies without even looking up, voice dry as sandpaper. "Would be the most exciting thing you've done all day."

Jensen chuckles quietly, shaking his head. "Keep whining, Eli. Maybe Matteo will let you help with cross-referencing traffic camera footage instead."

"On second thought," Eli mutters quickly, snapping upright, "these bank records sound delightful."

I smirk faintly, shaking my head at their endless banter. It's the only thing keeping us from losing our minds while hunting ghosts.

My eyes blur as names and faces flash across the screen, connections forming frustratingly slow.

Eli's chair scrapes loudly as he pushes away from his desk. "That's it. I'm going out to get coffee."

"We have coffee in the break room," Jensen says absently.

Eli snorts, grabbing his jacket. "I said coffee, not pond sludge. Anyone want anything?"

Jensen makes a vague gesture, either agreement or dismissal—it's unclear. Matteo nods distractedly. I look up at Eli, mouth twitching into a smirk. "Bring me back something strong enough to dissolve paint, would you?"

He salutes sarcastically. "Consider it done, boss."

Matteo finally glances up as Eli exits. "You think better coffee will improve his attitude?"

I arch a brow. "No. But he might complain less if he takes himself for a walk, he's like a puppy."

Jensen laughs softly, eyes flicking briefly to Matteo. "Wishful thinking, Seanna."

"You know me—eternal optimist," I reply dryly, rubbing my temples lightly, trying to ease the ache building there.

The room falls back into a rhythm of clicking keyboards and sighs of frustration. When Eli returns triumphantly, holding steaming cups aloft, the rich aroma of genuine coffee fills the bullpen.

"This, gentlemen," Eli declares smugly, passing cups around, "is coffee. Take notes."

Matteo rolls his eyes but takes a careful sip. "Not terrible."

Eli gasps dramatically. "Did Matteo just give me a compliment? Quick, Jensen—take his temperature."

"Don't push your luck," Jensen warns mildly, hiding a smirk behind his cup.

I chuckle softly, savoring the bitter, strong taste of my drink. This, at least, helps ease some of my frustration over Diego's fucking stubbornness. Our progress is slow at best, but we're getting closer to Reyes. One layer at a time, we'll strip away his protections until he has nowhere left to hide. Reyes' carefully built fortress will crumble.

My gaze drifts momentarily to my phone, remembering Dad's earlier message. I sigh quietly—soon enough I'll need to head over to the organization's headquarters to see what Uncle Max has uncovered.

We fall back into our tedious rhythm, each of us buried alive in a digital avalanche of endless data. The hours drag painfully slow, my eyes glazing over as I stare at screens filled with intel I've already branded permanently into my memory. My patience frays dangerously thin, restless tension coiling beneath my skin until I just can't fucking take it anymore. I abruptly shove myself to my feet, stretching my arms overhead until my spine cracks satisfyingly, loud enough to announce to the room that my tolerance has officially died.

"You good, boss?" Eli asks cautiously, peering over his monitor with wary curiosity.

I ignore him, pacing purposefully toward the oversized whiteboard dominating the room—our chaotic altar to Javier Reyes, covered in mugshots, tangled aliases, maps cluttered with colored pins, and scrawled notes. Each desperate scribble is a testament to months of frustration. Folding my arms tightly, I stare down the mess, irritation simmering dangerously beneath my surface.

Behind me, chairs creak subtly as the team senses the shift, their attention snapping to me with cautious alertness.

"We're missing something fucking obvious," I snap sharply, voice hard and edged with agitation. "There's another angle here—some crack we haven't forced open yet."

Matteo lifts his head slowly, dark eyes moving methodically over the board, revisiting trails he's walked too many damn times. "We're thoroughly examining everything Diego provided. Nothing stands out yet, but we're getting closer. Something will break soon."

"What about Reyes' family?" I pivot sharply to face them, eyebrow raised in challenge, daring any of them to argue. "Have we made any actual progress there, or are we still chasing ghosts?"

Jensen exhales heavily, frustration carved deep into his typically unreadable expression. "Just smoke and shadows, Seanna. Reyes obliterated every digital record—medical, marital, birth certificates. Even school transcripts vanished overnight. If we didn't know better, I'd swear the asshole was a fucking figment."

"Indulge me," I insist sharply, arms crossed tighter, eyes narrowing. "Give me the rundown again, Jensen."

He sighs again, visibly exhausted by repetition but obediently rattling off the intel he knows I need to hear. "Rumors put Reyes as married, three kids—two sons, one daughter. Eldest son would be pushing thirty by now, groomed from birth to take over daddy's criminal empire."

"Daddy's little monsters," Eli mutters sarcastically, leaning back lazily in his chair, disdain coloring his tone. "How charming."

"Unconfirmed," Matteo reminds softly, pressing fingers against his temple, clearly also at his patience's end. "Anyone digging close enough gets permanently silenced."

I glare at the board, frustration nearly boiling over. Reyes leaves nothing but shadows, but even shadows fade eventually. Every kingpin slips. Every criminal fucks up. It's inevitable.

"We don't drop the family angle," I mutter defiantly, more to myself than them. "Eventually, they'll surface. Deals, meetings, appearances—something. We just need to be ready to pounce."

Jensen nods slowly, thoughtfully. "I'll lean harder on informants. Someone always cracks under pressure eventually."

"Careful," I warn sharply, pinning him with a look. "Push too hard and they'll scatter faster than cockroaches in daylight."

Eli rocks his chair back dramatically, balancing precariously, the perfect portrait of exaggerated boredom. "No pressure, right?"

I fix him with a narrowed stare, my tone dripping venomous sarcasm. "Bored, Eli? I can happily arrange a cozy desk job filing tax returns if you need entertainment."

He flashes a cocky, unapologetic grin. "Hard pass, boss. I'm allergic to boredom."

Matteo smirks, exchanging a knowing glance with Jensen. "Explains a lot."

I turn back toward the board, barely suppressing a frustrated growl. We're close—I feel it in my bones—but Reyes still has the upper hand. Every day he's free, innocent people suffer, more blood stains his hands.

"We keep pushing," I declare firmly, steel in my voice as I meet each of their gazes directly. "Every lead, every whisper, every *fucking* breadcrumb. Reyes will slip eventually—they always do."

A ripple of determination moves visibly through the team. Eli's chair hits the ground solidly as he straightens, suddenly dead serious.

"When he slips," Eli promises darkly, voice low and dangerous, "we'll bury the bastard."

I step back slightly, forcibly releasing the building tension in my shoulders. Staring at dead-end leads won't magically conjure some of Reyes' secrets tonight. We've hit our limit, and stubbornness won't change facts.

"Enough," I finally sigh, pivoting back to my team. "We're spinning wheels. Pack it up and go home. Rest tonight, we'll attack this fresh tomorrow."

Matteo nods swiftly, already closing his laptop with quiet efficiency. Eli stretches dramatically, his yawn obnoxiously loud and intentionally irritating. Jensen stands slowly, relief briefly softening his stoic mask.

"You too, Seanna," Jensen warns pointedly, giving me the protective look he reserves for my most reckless moods. "Rest isn't optional."

"Yeah, boss," Eli echoes smugly, grabbing his jacket. "We all know you'll just stand here staring at the board until sunrise otherwise."

"I'll leave when I'm damn good and ready," I retort dryly, but a slight grin betrays my amusement. "Trust me, I'm as done with these dead ends tonight as you."

Matteo eyes me skeptically but wisely stays silent, packing up quietly. The familiar evening routine offers slight comfort amid the collective frustration.

"Bright and early, boss," Eli calls cheerfully, mock-saluting as he and Matteo step into the elevator.

Jensen pauses at the door, glancing back briefly. "Call if anything happens."

"I will," I promise quietly, waving him off firmly. "Now go."

As the elevator doors close behind them, I exhale deeply, finally allowing the rigid tension to ease from my frame. The bullpen feels eerily silent, haunted by lingering frustration. Reluctantly, I grab my jacket and keys, knowing my night isn't close to finished yet. The team doesn't know about my extra obligations to my family's organization—and it's safer that way. Secrets layered within secrets, a Darling family tradition.

The bullpen lights flicker off as I step into the elevator alone, descending quietly through the building's suffocating silence. Uncle Max had better have something worth my fucking time tonight. Because after today, my patience is gone—and god help whoever tests it next.

Chapter 5

Seanna

The organization's headquarters aren't far from the DEA offices, but stepping inside feels like entering an entirely different universe—one governed by secrecy, shadows, and blunt, unapologetic purpose. Nestled discreetly within an industrial park, hidden behind layers of security and strategic obscurity, the nondescript building fades seamlessly into the background. Exactly how my family prefers it. No bullshit, no fanfare, just ruthless efficiency.

I park swiftly and stride inside, exchanging only the barest nods with guards who know better than to question or delay me. The hallways here hum quietly, sterile and cool, the air punctuated only by the steady drone of ventilation and the faint buzz of hidden machinery. This isn't some flashy government office; it's a nerve center for vigilantes who gave up waiting on a broken justice system years ago.

My parents founded this place right around the time I was born, fed up with the corruption and incompetence poisoning every branch of law enforcement. They built it for one reason alone—to hunt down predators that the system fails to touch. The ones hiding behind badges, wealth, or political connections. Over the years, the organization has grown into an intricate web, recruiting operatives at all levels. Some joined already embedded in well-placed positions, jaded and ready to fight from within. Others—like me and my sister—were brought in young, trained carefully, then strategically placed where we'd do the most damage.

I head straight to the back, toward Uncle Max's personal sanctum. One of the largest rooms in the building, it's been transformed into a digital war room—a fucking fortress of screens, wires, and data streaming ceaselessly from every corner of the globe.

Max's domain is unique to him. Opening the door, I'm bathed in the neon glow of monitors stacked in precise tiers from floor to ceiling. Every screen displays a different torrent of information—video feeds, satellite imagery, databases, encrypted communications scrolling endlessly. More computing power sits crammed in here than NASA would probably use for a damn Mars mission, powered meticulously by generators, solar panels, and backup batteries carefully arranged so no one outside suspects a thing. Data servers take up an entire wall, lights blinking all over the place.

"Good evening, Seanna," Max greets without turning, his gravelly voice laced with dry amusement. He makes a quick adjustment on one keyboard before swiveling in his chair, meeting my gaze over thin-rimmed glasses. "Took your sweet ass time."

I smirk, folding my arms as I lean casually against the doorframe. "Hello to you too, Uncle Max. Still obsessively stalking my whereabouts?"

"Unnecessary," he shoots back, dry as dust, spinning briefly to type something into a terminal. "Your Dad let me know you'd be coming tonight."

"How considerate of him," I deadpan, stepping further into the room and scanning the screens. My gaze locks onto familiar faces flashing on the largest monitor—Reyes's known associates, surveillance stills, financial flows, everything my DEA unit has scraped together and then some.

"You've been busy," I comment quietly, eyes narrowing. "Find anything worth my time?"

Max raises an eyebrow. "Define 'worth your time.'"

"Something that helps me get my hands around Reyes's throat," I answer bluntly, moving closer. "We're stuck chasing Diego's breadcrumbs. I need a breakthrough."

Max nods thoughtfully, tapping a finger on the desk before pulling up a fresh wave of images. "I've been probing Reyes's operations for vulnerabilities. Your informant, Diego—he gave you Sebastián Cruz, Valeria Mendoza, and Rafael Navarro?"

"Yeah," I confirm, watching closely as profiles fill the screen. "Mid-tier, careful assholes keeping their hands mostly clean. Right now, it feels like spinning wheels."

"That's intentional," Max mutters, contemplative. "Reyes built layers of disposable assets between himself and exposure. But you're right—family might be his weak point."

My pulse quickens slightly, interest sparking. "You have something solid?"

"Possibly," he says slowly, adjusting his glasses. "Still verifying, but some names keep resurfacing. He's wiped nearly every digital trace, but not perfectly."

"Names?" I prompt impatiently, taking another step closer.

"His wife's name might be Elena," Max reveals, tone cautious. "Still verifying that. His children are even tougher to pin down—but I have one name that keeps popping up. Kingston, I believe it's his eldest son."

I test the name silently, tasting the weight of it. Kingston Reyes. A new player on this deadly chessboard, someone Javier would have been carefully grooming from birth. My mind churns with possibilities, threats, and strategic moves.

"What else do we have on Kingston?"

"Not much," Max admits, obvious frustration crossing his features. "His digital footprint is virtually nonexistent. Encrypted conversations suggest he's intimately involved in operations, yet careful enough to remain completely invisible."

A slow, predatory smile curves my lips. "Age?"

"Late twenties, maybe early thirties," Max estimates. "Hard to confirm exactly. Tread carefully—if he's half as dangerous as Javier, he's lethal."

"Good," I murmur unapologetically. "Dangerous beats boring every damn time."

Max shakes his head slightly, but amusement tugs at the corners of his mouth. "You inherited your parents' twisted definition of fun."

"It runs in the family," I fire back smoothly. "Keep digging. I want every detail you can rip out about Kingston. If he's Javier's heir, he's exactly the opening we need."

Max turns immediately back to his screens, fingers flying with renewed intensity. "Already on it. I'll update you the second I have more."

"Thanks, Uncle Max." I hesitate briefly, remembering Mom's earlier conversation. "Do you know anything about Hydessa's upcoming mission? Mom mentioned it."

Max pauses briefly, glancing up. "I do. She's heading undercover tomorrow. Not my place to spill specifics—you know the rules—but it'll be good for her. She needs this."

I nod slowly, satisfied. "Just wanted to confirm someone's watching her back."

"Always," Max assures me quietly. "She'll be fine."

With a final nod, I accept the gentle dismissal. "I'll see you soon, Max."

"Stay safe, Seanna."

I step back into the hall, closing Max's door behind me with a quiet click. The muted echo of my boots on polished concrete keeps me company as I head toward the exit, but my pace slows when I notice unexpected noise spilling from the training room. Usually, operatives stagger their schedules to keep suspicion at bay, yet tonight the mats buzz with restless energy.

Pausing in the doorway, I lean casually against the frame, crossing my arms and absorbing the scene. In the center, Bodhi and Thorn are locked in fierce, unyielding combat—two alpha males equally as broad, powerful, and brimming with ego, neither willing to surrender an inch. Fresh-faced recruits surround them, wide-eyed, laughing, and heckling the spectacle unfolding in front of them.

Bodhi moves with dangerous grace, ducking smoothly beneath Thorn's heavy strike. Thorn mirrors him, solid muscles rippling beneath a thin sheen of sweat, matching Bodhi's cocky grin with a calculating smirk. The raw, competitive energy between them fills the room, barely restrained beneath their playful façade.

Bodhi's eyes flicker toward me, his grin wolfish and teasing. "Look sharp," he calls out suddenly, his eyes sliding toward me. "Boss's kid is watching. Can't let Seanna report back that we're slacking."

Oh, perfect—someone to take my frustration out on.

Thorn straightens slightly, offering an equally cocky grin. "She's just jealous she missed all the fun."

I roll my eyes dramatically, stepping forward from the doorway. "You two enjoying your little show for your fan club?"

"Always," Bodhi drawls lazily, eyes glittering with amusement and challenge. "Think you could handle a round, princess?"

Thorn chuckles darkly, arms folded confidently across his chest. "Careful, Bodhi. She bites."

"Only if you beg nicely," I reply, arching an eyebrow, lips curving into a slow, wicked smile.

The recruits erupt in amused cheers and whistles, encouraging the challenge. Thorn gestures arrogantly toward the mats. "Prove it, sweetheart. Unless you're worried about ruining up your pretty little outfit."

"Cute," I retort smoothly, slipping my leather jacket off my shoulders and tossing it aside without hesitation. "The only thing I'm concerned about ruining here is your fragile male egos."

Laughter roars through the room as I step onto the mats, rolling my shoulders slowly, adrenaline already pumping like liquid fire. They both regard me with matching cocky grins, clearly confident that I'm no real threat. Let them underestimate me—it'll make victory all the sweeter.

Bodhi steps forward first, theatrically cracking his knuckles, eyes gleaming mischievously. "Alright, princess, let's see if you're more than just talk."

"Funny," I reply sweetly, adopting a fighter's stance. "I was about to say the same to you."

The recruits laugh louder as Bodhi feigns hurt. "Ouch. And here I thought we were friends."

"We are," I smirk playfully, eyes glittering with challenge. "I just like reminding you of your place."

Thorn chuckles. "Better watch yourself, Bodhi. You might lose your dignity here."

Bodhi lunges swiftly, aiming to catch my wrist. "Predictable," I tease, sidestepping effortlessly and driving an elbow sharply into his ribs. "Maybe try something original?"

He pivots quickly, retaliating with a low kick I barely dodge. "Better," I admit sarcastically, circling him, eyes locked in challenge.

He charges again, feinting high and attempting a quick sweep to my legs, but I leap back gracefully. I immediately return fire, striking swiftly with rapid jabs. He blocks expertly, grinning widely as he lands a glancing strike to my shoulder.

"Not bad," he concedes, eyes gleaming. "I almost felt that."

I smirk back, breath quickening slightly. "Then let me make sure it sticks this time."

He lunges again, gripping my forearm firmly. "Gotcha," he taunts.

"Think again," I retort sharply, twisting free and spinning behind him to land a solid strike between his shoulders. Bodhi stumbles forward, quickly recovering and closing the gap, his powerful arms encircling my waist. I drive my knee upward sharply into his thigh, forcing him to loosen his grip.

"Careful, Bodhi," I purr mockingly, "you're starting to sweat."

He growls playfully, tightening his hold again, nearly pinning me. I twist sharply, throwing us both off balance. We crash onto the mats, wrestling furiously, each maneuver calculated, intense. I finally gain leverage, pinning him down firmly.

"Yield," I pant victoriously, eyes shining with triumph.

Bodhi laughs beneath me, surrendering graciously. "Fine, princess. You win this one."

I stand gracefully, offering him a hand. "Better luck next time."

"Next time," he agrees with a smirk, accepting my help to pull him up.

Turning smoothly to Thorn, I flash a challenging smile. "Ready for round two?"

"Bring it," Thorn responds confidently, ignoring Bodhi's amused groan.

Thorn charges without hesitation, his power and precision impressive. "Eager, aren't we?" I taunt, ducking swiftly beneath his strikes, retaliating with quick, focused blows. He blocks smoothly, retaliating immediately, the exchange fierce and rapid. He grips my wrist, pulling me close, his arrogant smile hovering inches from my face.

"Had enough yet?" he breathes smugly.

"Oh, honey," I shoot back breathlessly, eyes flashing tauntingly, "I was just getting warmed up."

He chuckles darkly, suddenly sweeping my legs from beneath me. We crash onto the mats, grappling fiercely. These are the moments I love, I wasn't made for a desk job, my body always craves the action. I drive my knee into his ribs sharply, eliciting a satisfied growl from him before he flips me expertly onto my back. "You're getting predictable," he murmurs.

"Careful what you wish for," I warn, twisting sharply to escape, delivering a swift kick that knocks him off-balance. He recovers instantly, tackling me forcefully, finally pinning me beneath him with an infuriatingly smug expression.

"How about now?" he asks softly, eyes bright with triumph.

I glare defiantly, dramatically sighing in defeat. "Fine, you win—this round."

Thorn helps me gently to my feet, admiration clear in his gaze. "You fight damn well."

"I know," I reply confidently, raising my chin. "Don't underestimate me again."

"Never do, but the reminder is always damn fun," he murmurs respectfully.

Bodhi claps loudly, commanding attention. "Alright, kids, show's over. Let's wrap it up before Seanna bruises more than our egos."

The recruits laugh and disperse back to their training. Bodhi tosses me my jacket effortlessly, eyes glinting with humor. "Impressive moves, princess. Consider me humbled."

"Glad to meet your impossibly high standards," I reply dryly, slipping into my jacket.

Thorn nods quietly from the sideline, appreciative and amused. "Next time we'll see if that was beginner's luck."

"Anytime," I promise, mock-saluting them both. "See you around, boys."

Their laughter echoes behind me, leaving a rare warmth in my chest.

That was what I needed, the fight, to remember how good it feels to let the adrenaline take over for just a few minutes. To let it clear my head and fill me with fresh determination.

Chapter 6
Seanna

It's late by the time I pull up to my cabin, the engine softly rumbling to a stop, headlights slicing aggressively through the dense darkness, scattering shadows across the gravel driveway. I cut the engine and step out, boots crunching on gravel as the night air fills my lungs with its familiar blend of sharp pine and damp earth.

My eyes automatically drift toward Hydessa's cabin. Dark again. Either she's already deep into that undercover mission, or she's out getting herself into something messy. A flicker of curiosity briefly surfaces—wondering just what trouble my careful, methodical sister might have found—but I brush it off immediately. Hydessa's tougher than people think. Still, an uneasy prickling creeps down my spine, irritatingly persistent.

Halfway to my door, I freeze, muscles instantly coiled tight, eyes narrowing sharply. Resting innocently on my doorstep is a small, matte-black box. Neatly placed, unmistakably deliberate.

"Well, isn't this cute," I murmur sarcastically, scanning the shadows. The surrounding trees whisper mockingly in the breeze, but otherwise offer nothing. If someone thinks leaving creepy packages is enough to frighten me, they're in for a rude awakening.

Cautiously, I approach, crouching down to inspect the box. No markings, no shipping labels—just pristine black cardboard with a crisp white envelope sitting precisely on top. Carefully crafted and unnerving.

I pick it up, testing its weight. Light but solid. No obvious threats inside. I let out a soft, humorless laugh. Whoever's playing games tonight clearly didn't do their homework. I've built my entire life around chasing monsters—an anonymous box isn't about to spook me.

Once I'm inside, I lock the door behind me out of habit and flick on the lamp, bathing my living room in warm amber tones.

Settling onto the couch, I set the box on the coffee table and slide the note from its envelope. My jaw tightens as I read the blunt, printed words:

> Stop looking.
> You're messing with
> something you shouldn't.

I let out another cold laugh, tossing the note aside dismissively. Really? That's the best threat they could muster? I've gotten more intimidating notes from drunk idiots at bars. But my pulse quickens slightly—not from fear, but from the exhilaration of knowing I'm clearly closer to my target than ever.

Cautiously lifting the box lid, I'm half-expecting something grisly—some twisted token. Instead, resting on plush black velvet, is a single vibrant red flower. It's unlike any flower I've ever seen—bright crimson petals arranged in graceful clusters, exuding an unsettling beauty. The delicate blossom looks freshly picked, as if someone took great care in choosing it specifically for me.

The sight startles me, making me frown slightly in confusion. A flower? Seriously? It doesn't match the ominous vibe of the note at all. Are they trying to confuse me, or just being annoyingly cryptic?

I lift it gingerly, rolling the delicate woody stem between my fingertips. Its fragrance is faintly sweet. Whoever picked this out knows exactly what they're doing—trying to get under my skin.

I place the flower back into its velvet coffin, leaving the box open with a show of defiance. "Cute," I mutter sarcastically, eyes narrowed. "But if this is your big play, you'll have to do better."

Before I can muse further, my phone buzzes harshly against the coffee table, shattering the silence. Glancing down, surprise flickers through me as Hydessa's name flashes across the screen. It's late, unusual even for her, and given what Mom said earlier about her leaving for the undercover assignment, a flicker of concern hits me sharply.

Quickly, I move to the window facing her cabin, lifting the phone to my ear as I scan the dark expanse outside. My pulse jumps again when I see a light, faint but unmistakable in the darkness. Hydessa's home—and something tells me this isn't just a casual check-in.

I answer immediately but wait, the silence stretching just a heartbeat before her quiet voice whispers the familiar words we've shared since childhood.

"If I hide..." Hydessa murmurs softly, her voice smaller, shakier than usual, carrying a heaviness that instantly tightens my chest.

"Then I'll seek..." I reply automatically, my voice sharpening with protective concern. "Are you okay?"

She sighs deeply, hesitation clear when she finally answers. "No, I'm not," she admits quietly. "I... I went to the club tonight."

"The club?" My eyebrows rise in genuine surprise. Hydessa doesn't do clubs. Crowds, noise, forced social interactions—not her scene at all. "Why?"

"I'm leaving on an investigation tomorrow," she explains softly, vulnerability bleeding into her tone. "It was just... a distraction. I needed to escape, even if just for a moment."

Her confession stabs deeper than I'd like, unsettling my usual cool exterior. I lean against the window frame, eyes narrowing in concern as they drift toward her cabin again.

"And did it help?" I prod gently, keeping my tone intentionally casual. "Pretending to be someone else for a while?"

"No," she breathes, there is a bitterness there that makes my chest tighten. Quietly, she recounts an awkward encounter she had tonight—clearly meaningless, leaving her emptier than before. "It just made everything... worse. I feel so lost, Seanna."

I let out a slow breath, my heart aching slightly for her. "You know I'm here for you, right?" I remind her gently. "Our parents already told me all about you heading out tomorrow. Maybe this investigation is exactly what you need."

There's a brief pause. "What do you mean?"

I chuckle softly, hoping to nudge her sadness away. "Think about it. It's a small island, right? And you need to be discreet. When in Rome, as they say..." I trail off, smiling to myself. "Take the time to live a normal life for a little while. You're technically on vacation, so act like it. Obviously, you'll have to handle things your way at night, but still... you get my point."

Silence follows. Finally, her voice softens. "Yeah, maybe you're right," she concedes quietly. "Thanks, Seanna."

"Anytime," I say warmly, allowing myself a relieved breath. "Now, get some rest. You've got a big day tomorrow."

"I will," she promises softly. "Goodnight."

"Night, sis," I murmur gently, ending the call.

Moving away from the window, I glance once more toward Hydessa's cabin, the shadows of the tall pines looming protectively around it. A brief pang of worry passes through me, mingled with irritation. She's stronger than she realizes, yet still so vulnerable sometimes. I shake my head slightly, reminding myself she'll be fine. She always is.

My thoughts quickly shift back to the unwanted gift waiting on my coffee table. That damned flower still sits there, bold and disturbingly beautiful. Its vibrant petals and sweet-yet-sharp scent now seem pointedly sinister, an intentional contradiction to the blunt threat of the note. Someone wants me off-balance.

Too bad for them, that's never worked on me.

Driven by irritation and curiosity, I grab my phone again, quickly scrolling through my contacts until Uncle Max's name appears. Without hesitation, I hit the video call button, needing his unique expertise to decode whatever cryptic game is being played tonight. Max answers after barely two rings.

His face appears instantly on the screen, illuminated by the harsh glow of multiple monitors behind him, casting stark blue and silver shadows across his features. As always, he looks more at home behind those screens than anywhere else.

"Do you ever sleep?" I ask dryly, lips quirking into a teasing smile. "Or have you just moved permanently into the Batcave and started mainlining caffeine intravenously?"

Max snorts, his mouth twitching into a fleeting, rare smile, though his eyes stay sharp, unreadable. "Sleep is overrated," he responds flatly, leaning back slightly in his chair. "Besides, the criminals we chase rarely take a night off."

"True," I concede, studying him thoughtfully. Max has always been elusive, a mystery even within our tightly-knit organization. The sudden thought occurs to me that I've never really known anything about him beyond these walls even with how close he is to our parents. "Don't you have a family to go home to?" I prod gently, half-curious, half-teasing.

Something flickers briefly in his gaze, a shadow crossing his face for just a second before it's gone, carefully masked behind professionalism once again. He nods slowly, cryptically. "They understand," he says quietly. "This work isn't exactly safe, Seanna. Keeping them hidden ensures their protection."

His admission surprises me, and I lean forward instinctively, eyes narrowing with intrigue. "You do have a family, huh? You've been holding out on me, Max."

Max gives a subtle shake of his head, amusement fading quickly into seriousness. "There's a reason I keep them hidden," he repeats more firmly this time, the message clear: boundaries exist for a reason.

I exhale slowly, realizing no matter how curious I am, I won't get anything else from him right now. "Fair enough," I concede quietly, shifting gears to why I called. "I actually have a reason for bothering you this late. Someone left me a... present."

At his questioning look, I angle my phone toward the table, carefully aiming the camera toward the red flower and note resting on the dark velvet. His expression instantly changes from mild curiosity to intense focus, eyes narrowing sharply as he leans closer to the screen.

He's silent for a long moment, his eyes darting carefully over the vivid petals, his brows furrowing deeply in concern, adjusting his glasses as he leans closer.. I watch his reaction closely, an disconcerting feeling creeping along my spine at how intently he studies the bloom.

"Uncle Max?" I prompt softly, my voice tight. "Max?"

He blinks abruptly, shaking his head slightly as if trying to clear his thoughts. "Sorry," he mutters, clearly rattled, though trying hard to mask it. "That caught me off guard." He clears his throat, his voice dropping to a lower, more cautious tone. "That flower—it's a rhododendron, Seanna."

"A rhodo-what?" I raise a eyebrow. "English, please?"

I look again at the flower, its delicate beauty seemingly innocent. But Max's reaction tells me there's more to it.

"Rhododendron," he emphasizes slowly, tension heavy in his voice. "Flowers aren't chosen randomly. Every bloom has meaning. Someone picked this one deliberately, Seanna. A rhododendron symbolizes danger. Caution. It has a clear meaning and message: beware."

My jaw tightens, irritation flaring. I glance back at the flower, the vibrant red petals now seeming sinister. "Great," I drawl sarcastically. "So my secret admirer is a florist with a flair for drama. Should I be worried about touching it?"

His mouth tightens briefly before softening with a reluctant chuckle. "Touching it is fine, but I wouldn't recommend randomly nibbling on it. Rhododendrons are poisonous when ingested. They can be deadly if consumed in large amounts."

"Good to know," I deadpan, rolling my eyes. "I'll make sure not to toss it in my next salad."

Max sighs, his expression solemn. "I'm serious, Seanna. Someone is sending you a direct warning. They're watching you, and they don't want you looking into whatever it is you've found. They chose that flower specifically to communicate that threat."

A fierce, reckless smile curls at my lips. "Then they clearly don't know me very well, do they?" I challenge quietly, adrenaline beginning to pump steadily through my veins. Threats have never deterred me—they only heighten my determination, sharpen my resolve.

Max stares at me silently for a moment before shaking his head slightly, resigned. He knows me well enough to understand that arguing caution is pointless. "Just promise me you'll be careful."

A wicked, defiant grin slowly curves my lips. "Careful has never been my style."

"I've noticed," Max mutters wryly, shaking his head. "Just promise you'll at least pretend to think before you act."

"No promises," I retort smoothly, smirking openly. "Thanks, Max. I owe you."

"You owe me a lot," he replies dryly, though affection softens his tone. "Stay alive, Seanna."

I disconnect and lean back on the couch, eyes fixed defiantly on the flower still mocking me from its velvet coffin. Whoever delivered this clear-cut warning has drastically miscalculated if they think I'll back down from a fight. I've built my entire life around hunting monsters like Javier Reyes. Danger isn't a deterrent—it's my fuel.

Pushing off the couch, I place the flower and note purposefully on my desk, my own symbolic message that I'm far from intimidated.

Javier Reyes just showed his hand.

Big mistake.

Game fucking on.

Chapter 7
Seanna

The afternoon sun slices mercilessly through the blinds, streaking harsh golden lines across the chaos of files littering my desk. Frustration throbs just behind my temples, threatening to break loose. Jensen mirrors my agitation, scowling at the reports as though they personally offended him.

Eli groans dramatically, leaning so far back in his chair I briefly wonder if he'll crack his skull on the linoleum floor. "We've been spinning in goddamn circles all day. My brain is about to dribble out of my ears if we don't make a move soon."

"Not sure you'd miss it," Matteo says without glancing up, dark eyes scanning his monitor, still deep in thought. "But Eli's right. Diego gave us Cruz, Mendoza, and Navarro. Three leads, but Cruz and the Silver Orchid nightclub remain the most viable first step."

I nod slowly, picturing the neon-lit facade, the heavy beats thumping through expensive speakers—a beacon of luxury and filth. "Agreed. Cruz values money and power. Flash enough cash in front of him and his eyes might glaze over. Still," I say, leveling my gaze at each of them, "we can't just walk in cold. Cruz isn't a fool. We need an 'in', something concrete."

A beat of silence hangs as Jensen finishes a phone call and he straightens slightly, eyes sparking. "Actually, as luck would have it, that was our local PD contact. Their narcotics team picked up one of

Cruz's footmen early this morning. A low-level dealer named Carlos Rivas—easily spooked."

"Perfect," I say instantly, grabbing my keys and jacket. "Jensen, call them right fucking now. Tell them to hold Rivas and keep their mouths shut. That guy is ours, end of discussion. Eli, Matteo—move. We're leaving five minutes ago."

They surge to their feet, phones out, jackets in hand, the lethargy evaporating instantly. Jensen's voice is low and commanding as he calls the local PD. I hear him bark quick orders, giving them just enough to keep them cooperating. By the time we hit the cars, he snaps his phone shut and grimaces at me.

"Local narcotics are being pains in the ass," he says tightly. "They're making noise about turf and jurisdiction. They want in on Cruz if they're giving us Rivas."

I sigh, rolling my eyes sharply. "Fine. Tell them whatever bullshit they want to hear. Just get us to Rivas—now."

"On it," Jensen mutters, rapidly sending a text to smooth feathers. "We're set."

We hit the precinct hard and fast, our reputation clearing a path for us. The local narcotics captain eyes me warily as I pass, and I flash him a dismissive smile, cold enough to warn him off speaking. He doesn't dare follow.

"Interrogation room three," he grumbles to Jensen. "Don't break our suspect."

I turn sharply, narrowing my gaze at him. "Don't fucking test me. Your little fish is helping us catch a shark—play nice, and I'll let you tag along when we hook him."

He backs off, raising both hands in surrender. "All yours, Agent Darling."

I give a curt nod, motioning Eli forward. The interrogation room is windowless, starkly lit, and intentionally oppressive. Carlos Rivas sits cuffed, twitching nervously as we step inside. Eli closes the door firmly behind us.

It always surprises me how utterly Eli changes when we step into an interrogation room—like flipping a switch. Gone is the playful, flirtatious man from earlier; in his place is someone cold and sharp-edged, lethal as a blade. He stands silent and deadly beside me, a clear warning etched in his gaze.

Rivas squirms in his seat, sweat beading at his temples. "Who are you? I already told those cops—"

"I'm DEA, sweetheart," I interrupt calmly, sliding slowly into the chair across from him, meeting his panicked stare evenly. "And I don't give a damn what lies you spun to the locals. Here's what's going to happen: Tonight, you're introducing me to Cruz at the Silver Orchid."

Rivas's eyes widen in terror, his breath catching audibly. "Are you fucking insane? Cruz? He'll slit my throat and yours too—he doesn't meet strangers."

Eli shifts slightly, the subtle movement somehow more threatening than if he'd shouted. His voice comes out cool, controlled. "Trust me, Rivas, we're far more dangerous than Cruz on his worst day."

I lean forward slightly, locking eyes with the trembling dealer. "You have two choices. Play nice and introduce us convincingly tonight, then walk away free. Or refuse—and I pick out the nastiest federal hole imaginable to stick you in. Five years minimum, surrounded by every violent psychopath I can find."

His Adam's apple bobs, fear warring with self-preservation. "I—I can't—"

"You can," Eli interrupts smoothly, softly lethal. "And you will."

I lean back, smiling coldly. "Better practice that 'yes', sweetheart. If Cruz smells your fear, you're dead before you blink."

He slumps in defeat, shoulders dropping. "Fine. I'll do it."

"Good boy," Eli murmurs, voice edged with faint mockery.

We leave Rivas sweating, defeated. Outside, Jensen and Matteo wait, alert and watching. I give a curt nod.

"He's ours. Narcotics can shadow in their surveillance vans tonight," I say, glancing at the local captain who now stands at a cautious distance. "They get credit. We get Cruz."

The captain nods in grudging acceptance, clearly unhappy yet too intimidated to protest further.

"Let's eat," Matteo suggests quietly, breaking the tension. "We can finalize our covers before the meet."

Ten minutes later, we're at a food truck outside, grabbing quick meals to steady nerves and clarify our plan. Matteo leans casually against the table, eyes sharp as he outlines our next steps.

"Covers are simple," he says, voice calm. "Seanna and Jensen negotiate directly. Eli hangs back as our driver and surveillance. I'm security—silent muscle. We're independent buyers looking to expand distribution, flush with cash and ambition."

I nod thoughtfully, scanning each face. "And remember—Cruz isn't stupid. Confidence and consistency matter more than anything."

Eli cracks a grin. "Don't worry. Jensen's got the confidence, and Seanna definitely has the attitude."

Jensen nudges Eli, eyes glittering. "Keep it up, Eli. She might make you sit on surveillance in a trash bin."

"Rude," Eli chuckles lightly, eyes warm and teasing again now we're outside the interrogation. "Just don't fuck it up."

Matteo raises a brow. "Coming from the guy who almost broke his chair leaning back this morning, twice."

Eli scoffs. "That was tactical reclining, Matteo. Advanced skill."

I roll my eyes, amusement slipping through the tension. "Can it, children. Remember, tonight has zero room for mistakes."

They sober instantly, nodding firmly. My team. Irreverent one moment, deadly serious the next—exactly why I trust them implicitly.

"We'll regroup at the usual spot, fully prepped. Jensen, give PD the heads up on where to be and when," I say finally, standing and glancing at my watch. "You've got two hours. Clean up nice, gentlemen."

"Don't worry," Eli says with exaggerated seriousness, slinging an arm around Jensen's shoulders. "We'll make Jensen pretty."

Jensen rolls his eyes, shoving Eli away gently. "Get off, idiot."

We split smoothly, the mood shifting again into steely determination as we prepare for the dangerous game ahead. Cruz and the Silver Orchid await—and we're going in ready to rip apart his world from the inside out.

Rather than waste precious time trekking back to my cabin, I drive straight to the organization's headquarters. As usual, headquarters is mostly quiet at this hour, the silence broken only by the faint, rhythmic sounds of operatives training somewhere deeper within. I nod curtly at the guards as I breeze past security.

I make a beeline for the wardrobe room, a sprawling temple of transformation built over twenty-five years of undercover missions and operatives who understood that a good disguise is sometimes more lethal than a gun. Gowns. Suits. Combat gear. Streetwear. Wigs. Jewelry. Accessories arranged with almost religious precision. It's a shapeshifter's paradise—and tonight, I need to look like sin dipped in diamonds and power.

My fingers trail across satin and leather, silk and sequins, until I land on the perfect black dress. Sleek. Body-hugging. Sophisticated enough to own any room, and seductive enough to make Sebastián Cruz forget how to spell his own damn name. The fabric is cool, expensive, and screams danger wrapped in temptation. Exactly the kind of energy I bring when I want to be unforgettable.

In the changing area, I strip down and slide into the dress. It clings to my body like it was stitched with my sins in mind. Stilettos—sharp enough to stab a man if the conversation turns south. Silver jewelry that whispers elegance, not screams it. Makeup comes next: bold eyeliner sharp enough to cut glass, contouring to carve my cheekbones into something feral, and a swipe of deep crimson lipstick—the kind that warns you not to get too close unless you're ready to burn.

One final glance in the mirror and I barely recognize myself. I don't look like a federal agent. I look like the kind of woman you beg to ruin you.

As I step into the hallway, I nearly bulldoze a group of rookies loitering outside the training room. Their conversation halts. Eyes widening.

"Looking fierce, Seanna. Going hunting tonight?" One of them teases lightly.

I smirk back, head cocked. "A girl's gotta eat."

Their laughter trails behind me as I move down the corridor, quickly drawn to deeper, familiar voices echoing from around the corner. A moment later, I spot a group standing in casual conversation near the training room—Bodhi and Thorn are there, along with Kayla and Jaxon, both highly skilled operatives at around the same level as the two men. Kayla's red hair gleams beneath the overhead lights, her green eyes sharp and perceptive, while Jaxon's calm demeanor contrasts nicely with the energy radiating from Bodhi and Thorn.

Thorn clocks me first. "Well, well," Thorn drawls warmly as his eyes sweep appreciatively over my attire. "Look who decided to grace us with her presence again tonight."

Kayla whistles low, eyes glittering. "Hot damn, girl. I hope that's for work, or someone's about to have a very, very good night."

"Undercover op," I say with a lazy smile, leaning into the sass. "Thought I'd dress like someone who doesn't ask for permission."

"Shame you two missed yesterday," Thorn says, nodding toward Kayla and Jaxon. "You would've witnessed Seanna wipe the floor with Bodhi."

Bodhi snorts, crossing his arms loosely. "Funny. I remember things differently."

"Selective memory," Thorn counters lazily. "It's okay, Bodhi. We still respect you."

Jaxon smirks, interest lighting his dark eyes. "What happened? You two finally get shown up?"

I laugh softly, leaning back against the wall. "Bodhi gave me a decent run—managed to tire me out just enough for Thorn to swoop in afterward and claim victory."

Bodhi grins faintly, clearly enjoying my subtle compliment. "See? Told you she'd admit it eventually."

Thorn rolls his eyes, scoffing good-naturedly. "A win's still a win. Don't let him downplay it—I pinned her fair and square."

"After I did most of the heavy lifting," Bodhi interjects with dry amusement. "You barely had to break a sweat."

Kayla laughs warmly, shaking her head in mock disappointment. "And here I thought missing out meant missing drama. Turns out it was just the usual testosterone-fueled circus."

"You're jealous," Thorn counters immediately, eyes sparkling with mischief. "It's okay to admit it."

Kayla snorts, eyeing him skeptically. "Of your ego, Thorn? Not likely."

Jaxon chuckles, nudging Thorn's shoulder. "Careful, Thorn—Kayla fights dirty. You'll end up losing next."

"I'd pay to watch that," Bodhi mutters with a sly grin.

"You know," Kayla drawls, her green eyes dancing with humor, "I might take you all up on that challenge. Maybe tomorrow."

I shake my head, amused. "You're all impossible."

Thorn steps forward, his grin cocky. "So what's the op? Want backup? I could wear something tight, too. I'd volunteer my exceptional services."

"Exceptional?" Bodhi asks, his voice incredulous. "Now you're just lying to her face."

I laugh. "Appreciate the enthusiasm, boys. But the DEA team's already in place. This one? It's personal."

Jaxon leans in, voice sly. "One day, you'll slip and tell us who you're after."

I lift my brow. "If I do, check the skies. Pigs will be flying."

Kayla shrugs. "Can't blame us for being curious. You certainly look ready to take someone down."

Bodhi glances briefly at me. "I doubt whoever it is stands a chance."

"Careful, Bodhi," I tease lightly. "Keep flattering me and you'll give me an ego as big as Thorn's."

Kayla chuckles, elbowing Bodhi lightly. "Impossible. There isn't enough room in this building for another ego of that size."

Thorn rolls his eyes good-naturedly, holding up his hands in mock surrender. "I'm feeling very attacked right now."

"Poor baby," Kayla says dryly. "You'll survive."

Laughing, I take a step back, prepared to leave. "Behave yourselves."

Kayla smirks mischievously. "We make no promises."

I offer a final amused wave, leaving their comfortable, teasing banter behind as I slip outside into the crisp night, the air electric with tension. I inhale deeply, the weight of the evening settling across my shoulders.

Cruz is the kind of man who confuses wealth with power and power with untouchability. That's the fun part. He won't see me coming until I'm already slicing through his empire.

Tonight, I walk in smiling.

He'll never see the teeth underneath.

Chapter 8

Seanna

The night air hits me like a promise of trouble—cold, electric, and full of secrets. I pull into our secondary rendezvous, a scrap of asphalt tucked just out of range of the Silver Orchid's glaring neon. Eli, Jensen, and Matteo wait beside Eli's sleek black sedan, the street lamp glow slicing across Matteo's tense stance and illuminating Eli's smug grin.

Another dark vehicle sits nearby—the local PD surveillance van, engine idling quietly. Two narcotics detectives lean impatiently against it, badges glinting, their faces pinched with irritation. Between them stands a very nervous-looking Carlos Rivas.

Stepping from my car, the cold air bites into my bare shoulders, sharpening my focus. Jensen greets me with a low whistle, eyes openly appraising the tight black dress hugging every dangerous curve.

"Damn, boss. You clean up *very* well." His mouth twists into an amused smirk, as if inspecting a particularly impressive weapon that just landed in his hands.

Eli arches a brow, leaning casually against his car with a teasing glint. "Still trying to figure out how you flip from lethal DEA agent to lethal seductress. Ever gonna share your secret?"

I snort, tossing him a playful, dismissive glare. "Trade secrets, Eli. Maybe after you hit puberty."

Jensen chuckles, clapping Eli's shoulder in mock sympathy. "Sorry, buddy. Sounds like never."

"Brutal," Eli mutters good-naturedly as he slips into the driver's seat, shaking his head with exaggerated disappointment. "Let's move."

Detective Harris pushes off the van, crossing his arms over his chest as his partner shifts uneasily beside him. Harris eyes me with a mixture of irritation and grudging respect.

"We agreed—Rivas is yours, but when you move on Cruz, we're in," he says, attempting firmness but failing to mask his discomfort at losing control of the situation.

"Sure," I reply dismissively, flashing a humorless, razor-edged smile that makes his jaw tighten. "We'll keep you posted."

He hesitates, clearly dissatisfied but smart enough to pick his battles. With a reluctant jerk of his chin, Harris motions toward Rivas. Jensen steps forward smoothly, gripping Rivas by the upper arm, steering him forcefully toward our vehicle.

I step close, locking my icy gaze with Rivas' wide, frightened eyes, my voice low and merciless. "Make this convincing, Rivas, or that deal we discussed earlier vanishes—along with you."

Rivas swallows thickly, nodding vigorously. "Understood."

We pile into Eli's sedan, Jensen pressing Rivas firmly between himself and Matteo, who sits silent and intimidatingly calm beside him. Eli guides us smoothly into traffic, tension crackling like static electricity inside the car. Jensen finally breaks the silence, his voice dangerously quiet as he leans toward Rivas.

"Remember your lines, Rivas. Fuck this up, and tonight's your last taste of freedom."

Rivas shivers visibly, but manages a weak nod. "I won't screw it up."

The Silver Orchid soon comes into view, its garish neon pinks and electric blues slicing through the night, a beacon of temptation and sin. Eli pulls us smoothly to a stop at the valet, turning slightly to meet my eyes, voice deceptively casual. "I'll be out here. Don't do anything too stupid."

I let a slow, predatory smile curl my lips. "If it's stupid but works, we'll celebrate later."

I step out into the chaotic rhythm of the night, Jensen and Matteo flanking Rivas protectively. Rivas straightens his posture as best he can, clearly terrified but holding together. Jensen leads with unapologetic confidence, slicing through the envious whispers and hopeful glances from patrons waiting behind velvet ropes.

The massive bouncer eyes our approach, taking in Jensen's lethal stance, Matteo's quiet menace, and Rivas' nervous compliance before finally settling his gaze on me—cold, confident, deadly. Without hesitation, he unhooks the velvet rope, letting us pass.

Inside, music crashes into me, bass pounding through my bones as lights strobe hypnotically, shifting from blue to violet to red. Bodies twist and sway, sweat and alcohol scenting the air with reckless abandon. Jensen moves purposefully, leading us upstairs toward the VIP area, every step silently asserting dominance.

In moments, I spot Sebastián Cruz lounging arrogantly in his private booth, tailored suit perfectly draped over his lean, predatory frame, flanked by two enormous bodyguards with sharp, assessing eyes.

I nod subtly to Rivas. "Showtime, Carlos," I murmur, my tone brooking no argument.

Taking a deep breath, Rivas straightens slightly, preparing himself as I lean toward Matteo. "Hold back," I instruct quietly, my voice low and firm. "Keep your eyes open. I want no surprises."

Matteo's dark gaze flickers, sharp and assured. "On it." With practiced ease, he melts seamlessly into the dancing crowd, disappearing instantly, but still somehow present, a deadly ghost in the shadows.

With Jensen flanking close behind, Rivas guides us directly toward Cruz's booth. Jensen maintains a subtle proximity, his presence unmistakably protective yet unobtrusive.

Cruz notices immediately, curiosity arching one dark brow. "Carlos. Wasn't expecting you tonight."

Rivas clears his throat, voice shaking only slightly. "This is Samantha," he says, indicating to me with a nod. "She's the buyer I mentioned earlier. She's serious, Cruz. Thought you should meet."

Cruz dismisses Rivas with a lazy wave. Carlos disappears, leaving me alone beneath Cruz's piercing gaze. He pats the seat beside him, a faint smirk pulling at his lips. "Sit. Let's talk."

I slide into the booth across from him with practiced grace, meeting his gaze calmly, my pulse accelerating. He eyes me skeptically, guarded beneath his charm.

"So, Samantha," he drawls smoothly. "Carlos tells me you're looking to buy. Why should I trust you?"

"Because I have money," I reply bluntly, leaning closer so my words pierce through the music. "Lots of it. My suppliers can't keep pace. Yours can. Your reputation is the only guarantee I need."

Cruz stiffens slightly, suspicion clouding his features. "Are you a cop?" he demands, eyes searching mine for cracks. "Entrapment isn't my kink."

I laugh humorlessly, arching one brow mockingly. "If I were a cop, would I come to your club dressed like every bad decision you've ever dreamed of making? Cops have rules. I don't. But hey, if you want me in cuffs, that's another conversation entirely."

He pauses, clearly wavering. Jensen shifts subtly closer. Cruz notices immediately, eyes narrowing slightly before finally nodding.

"Words are cheap. Show me you're worth my time. Three days from now, noon—the club's closed. Come alone, and we'll talk business properly."

I smile slowly, satisfaction spreading like heat through my chest. "Three days. Noon. I'll be here."

He leans forward slightly, voice edged with threat beneath velvet charm. "Don't be late."

I rise smoothly from the booth, locking eyes one final moment. "Wouldn't dream of disappointing you."

As I turn to leave, Jensen falls into step with me silently. The exit beckons, but a rough hand suddenly seizes my hip, yanking me roughly backward against a hard chest. Hot breath, thick with entitlement, washes over my ear.

"I thought it was you. You slipped away from me last night without your number," he murmurs smugly, fingers digging possessively into my hip. "Not that I mind the chase, but damn, I'd really like to fuck you again."

Disgust boils hotly inside me, recognizing him instantly as the creep who'd touched Hydessa. It's not that he had sex with her, it's that he is a selfish pig who didn't even make sure my sister came. With vicious swiftness, I whirl around, one hand gripping his neck tightly, the other seizing his cock through his pants, nails pressing in mercilessly.

"You just made a grave mistake," I hiss sharply, voice venomous. "That wasn't me you screwed—it was my sister. And she found you lacking, so walk away before I do permanent damage."

His eyes widen in pain and shock, humiliation darkening his expression, but before he retaliates, Jensen smoothly twists his arm behind his back with brutal precision.

"You heard the lady," Matteo growls coldly as he steps back up to us. "Walk away."

Cursing bitterly, the man storms away, swallowed by the crowd. Jensen's eyes briefly flicker toward mine, silent reassurance passing between us.

"I'm fine," I assure quietly, heart pounding with adrenaline.

Outside, we slide into Eli's waiting car, victory burning fiercely beneath my skin.. I lean back, satisfaction settling in my chest for what I know is going to be an extended drive to make sure we didn't pick up a tail.

Game fucking on.

Eli eases us away from the pulsing neon chaos of the Silver Orchid, guiding the car onto quieter streets draped in shadows. The lingering thrill of confronting Cruz still simmers beneath my skin, mixing with the residual irritation of dealing with the asshole who dared put his hands on me.

Jensen shifts forward slightly, curiosity etched clearly in his voice. "How'd things shake out with Cruz in there?"

I exhale sharply, leaning my head back against the cool leather seat. "Better than expected. Cruz bought our cover, thanks to Rivas. He wants another meet—three days from now, noon, when the club's closed."

Matteo's brows draw together subtly, concern flickering in his dark gaze. "He'll probably insist you come alone."

A quiet scoff escapes me as I meet Matteo's cautious stare. "Oh, he insisted. But I don't give a damn what he thinks. I'm not walking into that meeting without at least one of you watching my back. I'm a woman—going in alone screams vulnerability. I'm not handing Cruz that kind of advantage."

Eli glances back through the rearview mirror, his teasing smirk already in place. "Seanna, you might be a woman, but you could still kick his ass."

I arch a brow at him, my lips curling in a slow, challenging smile. "Yeah, but he doesn't know that."

Jensen chuckles deeply from beside me, relaxing into his seat. "Cruz won't know what hit him."

"True," I murmur, eyes flicking toward Matteo, then Jensen, assessing silently. "I'll decide who's going in with me closer to meeting time. We'll play it by ear."

Eli groans dramatically, glancing back at me with exaggerated dismay. "Great. That means we're stuck babysitting our PD friends for another three days."

I smirk at his irritation, arching an eyebrow playfully. "Consider it community outreach, Eli. Builds character."

He rolls his eyes, lips twisting. "I'd prefer the kind of character built over drinks, but fine."

My laugh cuts softly through the tension as I lean back, closing my eyes for just a moment. Cruz might think he's calling the shots, but he has no fucking clue about the storm he's just invited into his world.

Chapter 9

Seanna

Somehow, I'm not surprised to find another sleek black box waiting for me on my doorstep, almost perfectly centered, as if carefully placed by meticulous hands. Moonlight spills across my cabin porch, outlining it with an eerie, silvered glow. Whoever's behind these twisted little gifts clearly wants my attention. Unfortunately, they're also getting irritation—mixed with a dash of grudging curiosity.

I pause, gaze sweeping carefully over the shadows between the trees, assessing the night's silence. The property sprawls empty and isolated around me, the woods pressing close, whispering quietly in the darkness. With Mom and my dads deep in Chicago chasing a new lead and Hydessa submerged in an undercover op she barely discussed, I'm alone here. It's rare, a stillness I normally savor, but tonight there's a subtle edge to it, sharp enough to keep my senses heightened.

Sighing softly, I lean down and scoop up the box, its smooth, heavy surface cool against my fingertips. Turning to unlock the door, I carry it inside, kicking the door shut behind me with a decisive bang. I toss my keys onto the entry table, hearing them skid briefly across the polished wood before coming to rest. The entire cabin feels too quiet, every familiar creak and rustle amplified in the night's hush.

I set the box down carefully on my kitchen counter, tapping my nails impatiently against the sleek surface before flipping the lid open. Nestled against midnight velvet, a single black rose stares up at me, hauntingly perfect, dark petals glinting softly beneath my kitchen's overhead light.

"Charming," I mutter dryly, picking it up delicately between two fingers. The petals are impossibly soft, too beautiful to be anything but a warning—a promise that someone out there is watching me closely.

With a low sigh, I set the flower aside, pulling out my phone. Scrolling swiftly through my contacts, I tap Max's number, pacing slowly back and forth across the polished wood floor as it rings. He picks up on the third ring, his voice calm and alert, clearly expecting trouble.

"Seanna. Everything alright? I don't normally hear from you this often."

"I got another delivery," I tell him bluntly, irritation threading through my voice. "This one's a black rose. What does it mean?"

He exhales slowly, thoughtful for a moment before he answers. "Black roses mean many things—the end of one era and the start of another, defiance, resilience, even transformation. Could also represent deep, enduring love, though I doubt that's the intent here. Unless whoever left it is obsessed with you. Was there a note?"

"Nothing," I reply sharply, staring at the rose's dark beauty as I shift the topic. "Any progress from your end on Reyes or his people?"

Max lets out a frustrated sound. "I'm still coming up empty. They're ghosts, Seanna. Better at hiding and being invisible than even I am—and trust me, that's saying something."

I shake my head, sighing. "I had a meeting tonight with Cruz at the Silver Orchid. He's suspicious but interested. I go back in three days to finalize negotiations."

Max lets out a short laugh, humor tinged with genuine concern. "Maybe I should send in one of the recruits to watch your back. Considering Thorne's particular dislike for federal agents, maybe that's not the smartest idea—though I do think you're the exception."

A laugh slips from my lips, lightening some of the heaviness in my chest. "I appreciate the thought, but I'm good. I can handle Cruz. And I'm definitely not worried about some prick sending me roses in boxes."

Max's voice softens, genuine affection slipping through the gruffness. "Just watch yourself, kid. If it is obsession, that doesn't usually end well."

I grin faintly, my voice confident and unwavering. "You worry too much, Uncle Max. I've got this."

Ending the call, I set the phone aside, glancing again at the rose resting on the counter. Let whoever sent this watch me—they'll quickly learn I'm not someone they should've fucked with.

They'll find out soon enough.

Slipping my shoes off I pour myself a generous whiskey. I savor the burn as it slides down my throat, chasing away the remnants of tonight's tension and the nagging irritation from whoever's playing this twisted little game. The familiar warmth spreads smoothly, easing my nerves just enough to regain control over the restless storm simmering beneath my skin.

Glass cradled loosely in hand, I wander down the hall toward my bedroom, the wooden floorboards creaking softly beneath my bare feet. My cabin usually feels like a sanctuary, a fortress nestled deep within solitude—but tonight, every familiar shadow seems sharper, every silence heavier.

I step into my bedroom, taking one lazy sip of whiskey, but my muscles instantly snap to attention. A sharp spike of adrenaline overrides the whiskey's comforting burn, and I freeze mid-step, eyes locked on yet another goddamned box—this one perched boldly in the *center. Of. My. Fucking. Bed.*

Seriously? The audacity of this asshole.

I exhale slowly through my teeth, eyes narrowed at the larger black box adorned with the same annoyingly meticulous satin ribbon as the first. An envelope rests conspicuously atop it—the note I'd anticipated with the black rose, finally making its unwelcome appearance.

Setting the whiskey carefully on the nightstand, I move cautiously toward the bed. My skin prickles, awareness heightened, senses strained to catch any hint that I'm not alone—but the stillness in the air is as thick and stubborn as my growing irritation.

"Someone clearly has too much fucking time on their hands," I mutter, snatching the envelope from the box with deliberate impatience. I rip it open with exaggerated annoyance, eyes quickly scanning the message inside:

> If you're going
> to put on a show,
> at least dress the part.

A derisive snort escapes my lips, and my eyes roll toward the ceiling. *Really? That's the best this mystery admirer—or stalker—can come up with?* I'd almost hoped for something more original. But clearly, originality isn't their strong suit—creepy persistence, however, seems to be their specialty.

This does confirm they have been watching me, at least.

Flipping open the lid of the box, I brace myself for more cliché theatrics—only to have the breath punched from my lungs by the stunningly provocative lingerie inside. This isn't some tacky strip-mall lace bullshit; no, this set screams expensive taste and dark, dangerous elegance. Supple black leather interwoven seamlessly with delicate lace, tiny crystals shimmering wickedly under the soft lamplight, every carefully placed strap and cutout clearly designed by someone who intimately understands the power of suggestion.

And probably costs more than some people's cars.

My fingertips drift cautiously over the luxurious material, heart hammering with irritation—and, admittedly, reluctant fascination. Whoever chose this knows exactly what they're doing, and the audacity of it makes me equal parts furious and impressed.

"Fucking hell," I whisper to the empty room, shaking my head even as curiosity digs in deeper, a stubborn thorn beneath my skin. Of course, the asshole behind these gifts would think expensive lingerie would throw me off my game, maybe intimidate me, or worse—seduce me into playing along.

Too bad for them, I'm not easily intimidated, and I sure as hell don't bend to anyone's twisted fantasies—not without making them earn every damn inch.

But as I stare at the lingerie again, a slow, rebellious smirk curves my lips. If they really want a show, maybe it's time to teach this mysterious admirer exactly what happens when you push Seanna Darling too far.

My pulse quickens, heat pooling deep in my core as defiance and reckless impulse merge into something irresistible. A thrill courses through me as I realize I can practically feel their eyes crawling over my skin, their pathetic attempt at control sparking something primal and savage within me.

Fuck that. Fuck their games, fuck their power trips, and fuck their delicate attempts at intimidation.

If they're out there right now—and I'm sure they are—let them watch. Let them realize just how little control they have over Seanna Darling. I'll show them exactly what happens when they try to pull my strings.

Ignoring the ridiculously expensive lingerie they've chosen for me, I turn on my heel and stride purposefully toward the French doors at the end of my hallway, leading to my private deck. My hand curls around the polished brass handle, flinging the doors wide, and the cold night air rushes in, caressing my heated skin, whispering promises of danger and rebellion.

Stepping out onto the wide wooden planks, I tilt my chin up defiantly, daring the darkness to test me. The moonlight bathes my skin, illuminating every curve and bare inch I reveal as I deliberately peel away my clothes. First the dress I wore to the club, then my bra and panties, sliding them off until there's nothing left but smooth skin and an unwavering challenge.

The chilled night breeze teases goosebumps across my naked body, nipples tightening to sharp peaks, but adrenaline and bold rebellion keep me warm. I smile coldly into the night, heart racing as I imagine their eyes on me right now—watching from some hidden spot in the shadowy tree line.

Fuck them.

Slowly, I run my fingers down my throat, across my collarbone, lingering at the swell of my breasts before slipping lower, teasing myself just enough to send sparks shooting through my nerves. I shiver, the sensation a mixture of cold night air and my own fiery determination.

But this isn't about gentle teasing or subtlety tonight. I'm not here to give them the submissive show they want. No, tonight they get the truth—the aggressive, fierce side of Seanna Darling who refuses to yield, who takes pleasure on her own fucking terms.

Glancing around the deck, my eyes settle on the large, sturdy chaise lounge, illuminated faintly by moonlight. Perfect.

Without hesitation, I stride to the chaise, my movements confident. I sink onto the cushioned surface, spreading my thighs shamelessly wide, offering a bold, unobstructed view of every intimate inch of me. It's not like anyone else should be on this property right now, so if they are, let them fucking look. I hope it drives them insane.

My fingers dive lower, circling aggressively. I'm rough, impatient, deliberately harsh, taking my pleasure rather than coaxing it gently.

I'm not here to be controlled or dictated to—my pleasure belongs entirely to me, and tonight I'm making damn sure whoever's lurking in the shadows knows it.

Every stroke is fierce, relentless, my breathing ragged as I arch into my own touch. I imagine their frustration, their helplessness at realizing I'm not theirs to command, and that image only heightens the white-hot pleasure surging through me. Teeth sinking into my lower lip, I let out a fierce moan—raw and unapologetic, echoing through the night air.

This is my moment, my body, my rules. The orgasm hits me like lightning—hard, brutal, and intense—tearing through my body until I'm shuddering and gasping beneath the moonlight, every nerve raw with satisfaction.

Chest rising and falling, I let my head fall back against the cushion, breathing in the sharp night air as I slowly regain control of my body.

"Hope you enjoyed the fucking show," I murmur darkly into the night, my voice dripping with venomous satisfaction.

If they think tonight makes me vulnerable, they've never been more wrong. I rise slowly, body still humming with aggressive satisfaction, and step back inside without a glance back, slamming the door behind me. Whoever they are, whatever twisted plans they have in store—let them try.

Because Seanna Darling doesn't play by anyone else's rules.

Chapter 10

Seanna

The bullpen feels like a cage today, constructed from stale coffee, unanswered questions, and the aggravating tick of a clock marking every wasted second. Being stuck at our desks, hands tied, waiting for Cruz to play nice is its own special brand of fucking torture. Patience has never been my strong suit, and right now it's practically non-existent.

The PD narcotics team drew the short straw–well the only straw there was really since I gave the order–now tasked with babysitting Cruz and making sure Rivas keeps his mouth shut. Better them than us. The last thing I need is hours trapped in a surveillance van with nothing but stale donuts and cheap coffee.

Unfortunately, the other two names Diego coughed up—Mendoza and Navarro—aren't exactly offering us gold either. Jensen scowls at his screen, clicking through endless surveillance notes before finally shaking his head with frustration.

"Still nothing firm on Mendoza," he mutters, rubbing his temples. "His people are too spread out, and every lead circles back on itself."

I sigh heavily, glancing toward Matteo. "Anything better on Navarro?"

Matteo meets my eyes evenly, lips pressed thin. "Same story. He's cautious. Low-level enough that he's off most radars, but high enough that taking him down would make a decent fallback if Cruz goes sideways. But nothing we can actually act on right now."

I lean back, fingers drumming impatiently against the edge of my desk. "Great. So we sit here spinning our fucking wheels."

Just then, a sharp voice cuts through the space. "Agent Darling, my office."

I glance over to find Assistant Special Agent in Charge Everett Ford standing in his doorway, his severe expression focused entirely on me. He jerks his head sharply, indicating I need to follow him immediately, before disappearing back inside.

Behind me, Eli quietly sings a dramatic little "dun-dun-dah," grinning into his coffee mug.

Jensen murmurs a sympathetic yet amused "good luck," his eyes twinkling mischievously.

"Shut it," I mutter back, pushing out of my chair and feeling every set of eyes in the bullpen follow my steps across the room. Ignoring them, I stride forward with purpose, forcing a composed mask onto my face even though my gut tightens with uncertainty at what Ford might have waiting for me.

I step into his office, closing the door quietly behind me. His space is a study in meticulous order—files stacked in perfect alignment, not a single stray paper or pen out of place. Ford himself mirrors the strict orderliness of his surroundings, seated rigidly behind his massive oak desk, fingers steepled beneath his chin, piercing gray eyes locked onto me with laser precision.

"Take a seat," he says curtly, motioning to the chair opposite him with the barest flicker of his hand.

I settle into the stiff-backed chair, holding his gaze steadily as I wait for him to speak. Ford studies me silently for a moment that stretches just a little too long, a deliberate test meant to unsettle me. I keep my expression neutral, refusing to give him the satisfaction.

Finally, he breaks the silence, voice clipped and professional. "Give me an update on Reyes. What do you have?"

Taking a careful breath, I deliver a swift, clear rundown of the current state of the investigation—detailing our progress on Cruz, our limited intel on Mendoza and Navarro, the setup with Rivas, and our next planned moves. Throughout, Ford remains perfectly still, his gaze never wavering, absorbing every detail like a seasoned prosecutor waiting to cross-examine a witness.

When I finish, he sits back slowly, assessing me with cool calculation. Silence hangs thickly in the air before he finally nods once, decisively.

"I put a lot of trust in you with this, Seanna," he says, voice low but razor-sharp. "There are a lot of eyes watching this case—important eyes. Don't make me regret giving you your own team this early in your career."

I hold his stare evenly, letting the weight of his words settle between us without flinching. "Understood, sir. I won't."

His expression softens just a fraction—barely enough to register, but enough to feel like a subtle acknowledgment of approval. "Good. Now get back out there and make sure we get results."

I rise from my chair smoothly, offering a single nod before exiting his office. As I step back into the bullpen, I feel the charged anticipation in the air, the guys all watching and waiting at their desks.

I'm barely sitting when my phone vibrates insistently in my pocket. I pull it out to see Hydessa's name flashing across the screen, and a brief stab of worry tightens my chest until I realize it's been two days since our last check-in. Damn, how quickly worry has become my default setting with her off chasing shadows on that fucking island.

Stepping away from the bullpen, I quickly move toward a quiet corner near the windows, glancing over my shoulder to make sure Eli isn't listening in—nosy bastard. Finding enough privacy, I answer the call, my heart rate already slowing at the sound of her breathing on the other end.

"If I hide..." comes Hydessa's soft whisper, our familiar greeting instantly calming my nerves.

"Then I'll seek..." I reply automatically, relief loosening the tension in my shoulders. Her voice always grounds me, even when we're both stuck knee-deep in bullshit. "You know I worry about you, especially with you on this mysterious island. How's the investigation going?"

I hear her pause and know she's gathering her thoughts. It's so typical of her—careful, thoughtful, everything I struggle to be. I fight the urge to shake answers from the phone.

"It's progressing, slowly. I've met some interesting people, but there are lots of pieces to this puzzle," Hydessa admits. Her hesitation makes me grit my teeth; she's onto something, I can tell. "There's something here, Seanna, something beneath the surface. I can *feel* it."

Her determination makes my chest tighten with pride and anxiety in equal measure. *Damn, we're both too stubborn for our own good.* "Trust your instincts, Hydessa. You've always had a knack for finding the truth. You are so much smarter than me, believe in yourself. Have you even reached out to our parents or Uncle Max to help?"

She hesitates again, and I roll my eyes. Stubborn Darling pride.

"I don't want to involve them," she finally admits quietly. "They're busy, and I want to do this on my own. I feel like I need to get to the bottom of this myself, to prove that I can handle it."

Her reasoning hits too close to home, and I sigh softly, understanding her fierce independence all too well. "I get it. Just promise me you'll be careful, okay?"

"I will," Hydessa assures warmly, sincerity evident in her voice. "And I promise to keep you updated."

I can't resist shifting the conversation to lighter territory, needing to distract us both from this endless, anxious spiral we tend toward. "Good. I'll be waiting for your updates. Now, back to the island life. You're surrounded by beaches and handsome men—please tell me you're having a little fun at least!"

She scoffs, exactly as expected, and I smile despite myself. Always so damn cautious.

"There are plenty of good-looking men here, but knowing my luck, I'd end up sleeping with the killer and he would stab me before I even climax."

I burst into genuine laughter, her dark humor perfectly matching my own twisted sensibilities. "Hey, you never know. You might have a knife kink and get off on being stabbed," I tease, my voice dripping with mischief. "We both know our parents are deviant as fuck, maybe you inherited some of it."

Her laughter echoes through the phone, lifting my spirits immediately. "You're terrible," she says through giggles.

"I know, I know," I chuckle warmly, savoring this rare moment of levity between us. "But seriously, Hydessa, take a breather when you can. Don't let this mystery consume you completely. Enjoy the island while you're there."

"You're right," she agrees, finally sounding a bit lighter herself. "I'll try to unwind a bit, too."

"Good. Now, go get some rest or do something fun. You've earned it," I encourage, knowing she needs it more than she'll admit.

"Thanks, love you Seanna," she says gratefully.

"Love you, Hydessa," I reply softly, ending the call with a lingering sense of relief and warmth. Sliding my phone back into my pocket, I return to my desk, feeling just a little steadier, even if just for now.

Sliding back into my chair, I find Jensen, Matteo, and Eli staring at me with varying degrees of curiosity and amusement. I was far enough away that they *shouldn't* have heard the conversation.

"What?" I snap, arching an eyebrow at them pointedly. "Anything useful happen while I was gone, or are you all just hoping I'll magically solve this clusterfuck myself?"

Jensen chuckles softly, shaking his head as he swivels his monitor toward me. "Actually, we might have found something." His voice turns serious, a welcome change from the frustrating lull we've been trapped in.

Interest piqued, I lean forward to study his screen. Jensen points to a series of surveillance images, timestamped from yesterday. "We've been combing through Navarro's known spots again—mostly dead ends, but Matteo noticed something interesting here."

Matteo steps up. "Navarro met someone new last night—unknown face, not on any watch lists. But look at the timing." He taps the timestamps. "Navarro shows up late when no one else is around, waits around almost an hour, then this guy arrives, and they talk for exactly two minutes before splitting."

"Looks like a drop or instructions being passed," Jensen adds quietly. "Whoever this guy is, Navarro clearly trusts him enough for direct contact, which means he could be a valuable weak link."

I study the grainy footage, narrowing my eyes thoughtfully. "Do we have an ID on this mystery guy yet?"

"Working on it," Eli pipes up, spinning his own monitor toward me. "I ran facial recognition—nothing local, but I'm broadening the search. Fingers crossed he pops up on someone else's radar."

"Make it a priority," I instruct sharply. "We're running out of patience. If Navarro won't give us an opening, maybe his friend will."

"Already on it, boss," Eli replies confidently, fingers flying over the keyboard. "I'll shake every digital tree until something useful falls out."

"Good," I say, nodding firmly. "And Jensen, Matteo—keep monitoring Navarro closely. If he meets this mystery man again, we need ears on that conversation."

"We'll handle it," Jensen assures, his gaze unwavering.

As they get back to their work my mind races, turning over Ford's stern warning alongside Hydessa's determination to solve her own mystery. Between Ford's expectations and my sister's stubbornness, my drive to close this case burns hotter than ever.

Jensen catches my eye, leaning in slightly. "You alright? Ford looked intense."

"Ford's always intense," I say dryly, shaking my head. "But he's right—we need results, and we need them fast."

Matteo lifts his chin slightly, eyes fierce. "Then let's get them. Reyes is careful, but careful men get complacent."

I smile, sharp and dangerous. "Exactly. Cruz, Mendoza, Navarro—all roads lead back to Reyes. Somewhere there's a gap he thinks we've overlooked, a vulnerability he's forgotten. That's where we strike. So, let's tear these assholes' lives apart. Find me something we can exploit."

Eli spins back around, grinning wickedly. "You know how much I love it when you talk dirty, Seanna."

"Focus, Eli," Jensen mutters, though amusement gleams in his eyes.

My lips twitch, fighting a smile. "Dirty talk later. Right now, get to work."

They all nod, determination clear as they dive back into the fray, keyboards clattering furiously as we chase down every lead. I lean back for a moment, letting the bullpen's chaos wash over me. Ford's warning rings in my ears again, mixing with Hydessa's cautious determination.

We're so damn close, I can feel it—one slip-up, one mistake, and Reyes's whole world will come crashing down around him. And when it does, I'll be standing right there, watching it burn.

Game on, indeed.

Chapter 11

Seanna

Pulling into my driveway, the first thing I notice tonight is the emptiness on my doorstep. No sleek little box, no flower tucked neatly inside with a cryptic note. I should probably feel relieved—maybe my secret admirer finally figured out their creepy little gestures weren't having the desired effect. But weirdly, irritation spikes instead. Clearly, I'm more fucked-up than I realized—missing my nightly dose of unsettling affection.

I step inside, locking the door behind me even though I know damn well it's pointless. I don't normally bother—what's the point when locks mean fuck-all to the type of people I hunt? But tonight, I crave the illusion of control. Between the weight of Ford's judgment at the DEA, the crushing expectations of my family, and the constant, underlying pull of the organization, my grip on normalcy feels dangerously tenuous. Sometimes it feels like I'm caught between worlds—respected agent by day even if I do step over the line occasionally, shadow operative by night, and always a Darling. Always living in someone's legendary shadow, always expected to perform. And I'm fucking tired of performing.

My mission, though, is clearer than ever: burn down every last scrap of corruption, drag every smug bastard out of the shadows, and hold their sins against the innocent up to the light. I might be twisted, but even I have lines I refuse to cross. Protecting those who can't protect themselves, making those who think they're un-touchable suffer—it's a mission I've willingly taken on, and I'll see it through no matter what the cost.

Dragging my exhausted body down the hallway, half-expecting another sinister surprise, I push open my bedroom door. The empti-ness here is oddly reassuring. No black boxes, no sinister flowers. Maybe my stalker got bored. Maybe I've finally scared them off. Stripping off my clothes, I let them fall carelessly to the floor, too drained to give a shit about anything except sleep.

The mattress welcomes me, but my mind refuses to shut down. It churns relentlessly through every goddamn detail—the case, Reyes, Cruz's calculating gaze, and Hydessa off chasing her own monsters on some island that I hadn't even bothered to get the name of. A twinge of worry hits me, familiar and bitter.

I might be fucked up, but my protective streak toward my twin is undeniable. She's smart, methodical, and cautious—traits I envy. Traits that I never quite mastered.

Our family doesn't do casual; we obsess. We love dangerously, fiercely, possessively. Anything less would bore me to tears. Any-thing weaker would crumble beneath my intensity.

I roll onto my back, staring at the ceiling, my thoughts a tan-gle of twisted knots. There's something almost comforting about admitting my own darkness, acknowledging the parts of me that most people would find horrifying. I'm not a good person, not in the traditional sense—and I've never pretended to be. I just happen to direct my particular brand of ruthlessness at people who deserve it even more than I do.

I've gotten used to my own vicious cycle—work until exhaustion, fall into bed, stare at the ceiling until my brain finally surrenders to darkness. Lather, rinse, fucking repeat. Most nights I can at least fool myself into thinking I'm making progress, but tonight feels different. Emptier. Like I'm chasing ghosts that are always one step ahead, laughing at my futile attempts to corner them.

God, I hate feeling like this. Vulnerable. Uncertain. These moments when I'm alone with nothing but my thoughts are when the carefully constructed armor I wear starts to show its cracks. The fierce, un-apologetic agent facade slips, and underneath is just... me. The real Seanna Darling—messy, complicated, and perpetually unsatisfied.

"Look at you," I mutter to myself, "lying here feeling sorry for yourself when there's a fucking drug lord out there who needs to be destroyed."

But that's the thing about nighttime thoughts—they don't care about your to-do list or your vendettas. They dig deeper, unearthing all the shit you'd rather keep buried.

I roll over, punching my pillow into submission. The truth is, I'm not just frustrated about Reyes. I'm pissed at myself for being so goddamn obsessive about these creepy little gifts. Why do I even care? Why am I lying here actually disappointed that there wasn't another twisted present waiting for me?

"Because you're fucked up, Seanna," I whisper to the darkness. "Normal people run from danger. You fucking chase it."

And that's the real issue, isn't it? The adrenaline rush, the thrill of the hunt—it's become my drug of choice. The more dangerous, the more forbidden, the more I *crave* it. I've built my entire identity around being the fearless one, the reckless Darling who laughs in the face of death. Meanwhile, Hydessa is the careful one, the planner, the thinker.

Sometimes I wonder if we've both been typecast since birth—me as the wild child and her as the responsible one. What would happen if I tried to be cautious for once? Would the universe implode? Would my family even recognize me?

A bitter laugh escapes my lips. "Yeah, right. Like you could ever be anything but what you are."

I've never been good at lying to myself. I am who I am—relentless, fierce, and unapologetically intense. I don't do half-measures. I don't understand moderation. I throw myself headfirst into everything—work, fights, sex, life—with a reckless abandon that would terrify most people.

And yet... sometimes in moments like this, I catch myself wondering what it would be like to just... stop. To breathe. To not constantly be at war with the world and myself. To find peace in stillness instead of chaos.

"Bullshit," I scoff at myself, rolling over again and shoving the thought away. "You love the chaos. You'd be bored out of your fucking mind without it." Peace is for people who aren't me. I've tried stillness—it makes my skin crawl. I need the intensity, need the fight, need the danger. It's not just what I do; it's who I am.

I let out a soft, bitter laugh at myself. *How did I end up here, obsessively hunting monsters while battling the darkness within me?* Most people would probably be horrified if they could see the thoughts that flit through my mind on a daily basis—the casual violence I consider, the ruthless calculations, the complete lack of remorse when dealing with those I deem deserving of punishment.

But that's the thing about being a Darling—we were never raised to be normal. Normal was for other families, families who didn't understand the true nature of the world. Mom and my dads made sure we knew exactly how fucked up humanity could be from day one. They never sheltered us from the truth; instead, they armed us with it.

"Better to be the wolf than the lamb," Dad used to say. *He wasn't wrong.*

Growing up, I watched my parents move seamlessly between worlds—respected professionals by day, vigilantes by night. I learned to wear masks before I could even understand what they were for. The organization became our extended family, our purpose, our legacy.

And now here I am, continuing that legacy. DEA agent Seanna Darling, hunting Javier Reyes through official channels while simultaneously exploiting every underground connection the organization offers. It's exhausting living this double life, but I'd be lying if I said I didn't get a twisted thrill from it all.

"God, I'm fucked up," I mutter into the darkness, laughing softly at my own admission.

The worst part is, I don't actually want to change. There's something intoxicating about walking the line between light and shadow, between law and justice. Between what's legal and what's right. The rules that bind ordinary people don't apply to me—never have, never will. I've seen too much of the world's underbelly to believe in something as quaint as playing fair.

I close my eyes, willing my mind to quiet, but the endless loop of thoughts just keeps spiraling. Every time I edge toward sleep, some new theory, some hidden angle on Reyes or his operation jolts me back to consciousness. It's always been like this—my brain refusing to shut off until I've examined every angle, every dark corner where monsters might hide. It's what makes me good at my job, and it's also what makes me a fucking nightmare to live with.

Another hour of this bullshit, and I'm still wide awake, staring at shadows dancing across my ceiling. Perfect. Just what I need—sleep deprivation on top of everything else.

My phone buzzes on the nightstand, shattering my introspection. Jensen's name flashes across the screen, and I grab it with a mixture of irritation and curiosity. It's late, which means this is either important or he's about to get an earful.

"This better be fucking good," I answer flatly, not bothering with pleasantries.

"It is," Jensen's voice comes through, tense but excited. "Remember our mystery man from the Navarro surveillance? We got a hit."

I sit up immediately, sleep forgotten. "Talk to me."

"His name is Marcus Vega. Thirty-four, clean record—suspiciously clean, actually. Works as a private courier aka errand boy for several high-end clients in the city."

"A courier?" My mind races with possibilities. "Meaning he could be moving anything from intel, product samples, or cash for Reyes's operation."

"Exactly," Jensen confirms. "And here's where it gets interesting—he makes regular deliveries to an address just outside the city limits. Fancy neighborhood, very private. Property's registered to a shell company that took some serious digging to trace back."

"And?" I prompt impatiently.

"Matteo thinks it might connect back to Reyes's family. Not directly—there are about six layers of corporate bullshit between them—but it's the closest we've gotten to a potential residence."

Adrenaline surges through me. "Have we been watching this place?"

"Just started tonight. Eli's set up remote surveillance, but it's limited—too many security measures to get anything good without a proper team."

"Keep on it," I instruct sharply. "And Vega—I want everything on him. Where he lives, where he eats, who he fucks, his entire routine. If he's Reyes's messenger boy, he could be our way in."

"Already done," Jensen replies smoothly. "Also, local PD confirmed Cruz hasn't done anything out of the ordinary. Their surveillance is still in place and will be until our meeting day after tomorrow."

"Good," I mutter, mind already racing through scenarios. "Now, get some fucking sleep, Jensen."

I end the call and fall back against my pillows, the darkness suddenly less oppressive. A courier. Someone trusted enough to move between Reyes and his inner circle. Finally, a thread to pull.

As my mind churns with possibilities, exhaustion finally tugs at me, and I drift into a fitful sleep filled with fragmented dreams of roses and shadows.

The first thing I notice when I wake is something feels... off. The air in my bedroom feels disturbed somehow, like someone's been moving through it while I slept. My instincts flare immediately, that sixth sense honed through years of hunting predators screaming that something isn't right.

My bed is covered with polaroid photographs.

They're scattered across my sheets and comforter like playing cards dealt by some psychotic dealer. Some face up, others face down, dozens of them. My heart slams against my ribs as I bolt upright, fully awake now, adrenaline flooding my system.

"What the actual fuck?" I whisper, staring at the images closest to me.

The first one I pick up shows me sleeping—face relaxed, one arm thrown above my head, completely vulnerable. Last night. The angle suggests someone standing right beside my bed, looking down at me. I flip through more photos, each one stealing another piece of my composure. Me turning in my sleep. Me curled on my side. Close-ups of my face, my hands, my bare shoulders peeking from beneath the sheets.

But it's the next one that hits me like a physical blow.

There I am on my deck, completely naked under the moonlight, head thrown back. Every intimate detail captured with perfect clarity—my fingers between my thighs, my expression fierce and challenging. Picking up more, I can see the photographer varied their position, some shots close, others from a distance, documenting my deliberate display from multiple angles.

"Jesus fucking Christ," I mutter, my fingers trembling slightly.

I should be furious. I should be calling for backup, sweeping the house, filing reports, sleeping with a knife under my pillow. That would be the rational response. The correct response. But the burning in my stomach isn't just anger or fear—there's something else there, something dark and twisted that I refuse to examine too closely.

God, I'm fucked in the head.

Because part of me—a part I'd never admit to anyone—is fascinated. Impressed, even. They were in my fucking bedroom while I slept. Could have done anything. Could have hurt me, killed me. But instead, they left pictures. Evidence. A declaration. Whoever took these has serious balls—or a death wish. Maybe both.

Normal people don't get turned on by being stalked. Normal people call the police or keep a gun close. But here I am, some twisted part of me actually enjoying the dangerous thrill of... whatever is happening here.

I gather the photos into a stack, noticing several black roses arranged artfully on my nightstand that I'd initially missed in my shock. Nestled among them is a simple white card. I reach for it, flipping it over to read the elegant script and a laugh bubbles up from my chest, sharp and slightly unhinged. The absolute audacity. The sheer fucking confidence.

> Locked doors won't
> save you, darling.
> Nothing could keep us
> from getting to you.

Chapter 12

Seanna

After a hot shower that barely nudges away the lingering tension, I dress quickly, pulling on my standard dark jeans and a form-fitting black top. My badge and gun feel comfortably heavy at my hip as I grab my leather jacket and head out the door, locking it firmly behind me, even though part of me sneers at the futile gesture. Whoever's sending me those creepy-ass packages sure as hell doesn't care about locked doors or boundaries. Or even personal fucking space.

Traffic to the DEA is a nightmare—bumper-to-bumper, horns blaring, and my irritation spikes as I sit stuck behind a minivan moving at the speed of molasses. By the time I reach the office, my mood is firmly set to "touch me and lose a finger."

The bullpen today is a swirling cesspool of chaos—agents darting between desks, phones ringing off the hook, and everyone apparently trying to talk over each other like they're auditioning for a role in some shitty cop drama. I cut through it all like a shark, ignoring the sidelong glances and hushed whispers that follow me. Let them talk. I've got bigger problems than office gossip.

Jensen's already at his desk, surrounded by stacks of files and empty coffee cups, his usually immaculate appearance slightly rumpled. Matteo sits nearby, his dark eyes fixed intently on his computer screen, one hand absently tapping a pen against the edge of his desk in a rapid, inconsistent rhythm. But it's Eli who catches my attention—hunched over his keyboard, jaw clenched tight, none of his usual playful energy visible in the hard lines of his face.

"Morning, sunshine," Jensen drawls as I approach, raising an eyebrow at whatever expression is currently plastered across my face. "You look like you're ready to commit a few felonies before lunch."

"Only a few?" I drop into my chair, tossing my phone onto the desk with more force than necessary. "I've already mentally committed at least a dozen on my drive here."

Eli doesn't even look up, just grunts softly in acknowledgment. His fingers move aggressively across the keyboard, the clicking unusually sharp and impatient. This is the Eli few people see—the one beneath the jokes and flirtation, all sharp edges and cold efficiency.

"What's got you so wound up?" I ask him directly, narrowing my eyes at his unusual silence.

He finally glances up, and the intensity in his gaze catches me off guard. Gone is the carefree jokester, replaced by something harder, almost predatory. "Vega's good," he says, voice clipped. "Too good. Every time I think I've got a digital foothold, it slips away. Someone's scrubbing his tracks almost as fast as I can find them."

"Which means he's more than just a courier," Matteo interjects, leaning forward. "Someone's protecting him—someone with resources."

Jensen nods, sliding a folder across the desk to me. "Got the surveillance reports back from PD. They've been shadowing all our targets around the clock." He taps the file meaningfully. "Interesting patterns emerging."

I flip open the folder, scanning quickly through the neatly organized reports. Cruz has been behaving exactly as expected—running his club, meeting with his usual contacts, nothing out of the ordinary beyond our upcoming meeting. Mendoza's been spotted at several high-end restaurants, always with different companions, conversations kept casual but body language screaming business. Navarro's movements have been more erratic—never in one place for too long, constantly checking over his shoulder.

But it's Vega who catches my interest. The surveillance on him is the sketchiest of all—brief glimpses at traffic cameras, a few distant shots from storefronts, but nothing substantial. He moves like someone who knows he's being watched, using blind spots and timing his movements to avoid established patterns. Smart. Methodical. Dangerous.

"He knows exactly what he's doing," I mutter, tapping my finger against Vega's grainy surveillance photo. "This isn't amateur hour. He's been trained."

"That's what I've been saying," Eli says sharply, frustration evident in the tight line of his jaw. "Whoever Vega is, he's not just some errand boy. The digital countermeasures around him are professional-grade, military precision. Every time I think I've found a thread to pull, it vanishes."

Jensen leans back in his chair, arms crossed. "So what's the play here? We're spread thin trying to monitor all four simultaneously, and Cruz is expecting to meet with 'Samantha' tomorrow."

I drum my fingers against the desk, mind racing through possible next steps. "We stick with the plan. Cruz is still our best entry point. Matteo, I want you with me for that meeting—you'll play my silent backup. Jensen, you and Eli keep pushing on Vega. If he's as protected as he seems, he's the closest we've gotten to Reyes' inner circle."

Matteo nods, his dark eyes calculating. "Cruz will try to test you, see if you're legitimate. We should prepare for that."

"Let him try," I reply coldly. "I'm ready to play whatever game he wants."

Eli's phone buzzes, and he glances down, his expression shifting to something even sharper as he reads the message. "Interesting. PD just spotted Vega entering a private gallery downtown. Looks like he's picking up something—a package or artwork, they can't tell from their position."

"Art gallery?" That catches my interest immediately. "Which one?"

"The Obsidian," Eli replies, already typing furiously. "Very exclusive, very private. By appointment only."

My mind clicks pieces together rapidly. "Get me everything on that gallery—ownership, clientele, recent acquisitions. Art's a classic way to move money."

Jensen's already reaching for his phone. "I'll have PD maintain visual as long as they can without being spotted."

"Good," I nod, standing abruptly. I'm about to turn away to head to the break room when my phone vibrates against my desk. Unknown number. I almost ignore it, but some instinct makes me pick it up and open the message.

UNKNOWN

> *Did you enjoy the roses? Black suits you better than red, darling. Though, the other black gift would suit you even better.*

My heart stutters violently, heat flashing across my skin before being replaced by ice. I keep my expression neutral even as my pulse thunders in my ears. My eyes flick up, scanning the bullpen carefully, looking for anyone paying too much attention, anyone who doesn't belong.

Nothing. Just the usual chaos of agents hustling about their day.

With deliberate casualness, I type a response with steady fingers despite the rage boiling beneath my skin.

> *Cute. Real fucking cute. Next time you break into my bedroom, at least have the balls to wake me up. I'd love to show you what I do to people who invade my personal space.*

I hit send, watching the message deliver with vicious satisfaction. Let this creepy bastard know exactly who they're dealing with. I'm not some fragile victim that can be easily terrorized–I'm the night-mare that haunts other monsters.

My phone buzzes again, almost immediately.

UNKNOWN

> **Promises, promises. You're magnificent when you're angry. Almost as beautiful as when you come.**

I glance around at my team, all of them absorbed in their work, completely oblivious to the fact that I'm being digitally stalked by someone who was in my goddamn bedroom last night. And now they're texting me like we're fucking pen pals.

I force my expression to remain neutral, not wanting to draw questions from my team, but my fingers tighten around the phone until my knuckles go white. With considerable control, I type back:

> *Hope you enjoyed the show because when I find you—and I will—you'll wish you'd never laid eyes on me.*

I hit send, picturing the message landing like a slap across their smug, invisible face. Let them chew on that. Let them wonder if their little game has pushed too far.

My phone buzzes again almost immediately.

We both know you loved every second of it. The danger excites you. Why else would you put on such a performance on your deck? You wanted to be watched. You wanted to be seen. And you were. Beautifully.

My jaw clenches so hard I'm surprised my teeth don't crack. The worst part is, they're not entirely wrong—and that knowledge burns like acid in my veins. I don't bother responding this time, shoving my phone roughly into my pocket as I stand abruptly, nearly knocking my chair over.

"I need coffee before I murder someone," I announce flatly, voice cold as ice. "Anyone else want some, or am I drinking alone?"

Jensen glances up, his expression shifting from concentration to mild concern at whatever he sees on my face. "You okay?"

"Peachy," I snap, already halfway toward the break room. "Coffee? Yes or no?"

"I'll take some," Eli calls out, finally looking up from his screen. "And for the love of God, get the real stuff, not that pond sludge Wilson made earlier."

"Pond sludge it is," I shoot back over my shoulder, the familiar banter helping to ground me despite the rage still churning in my gut. "Extra sludgy, just for you."

After a brief internal debate—pond sludge masquerading as coffee from the break room versus something drinkable—I abruptly pivot toward the elevators.

"Actually," I toss over my shoulder, "I'm stepping out. There's no way I'm drinking whatever crime against humanity Wilson brewed today. Text me your orders if you want anything decent."

Jensen nods absently, already back to frowning at surveillance data, and Matteo murmurs a quiet acknowledgment without even looking up. Eli waves me off with a vague grunt, attention glued to his screen, his face still set in that hard-edged intensity that means he's barely tolerating the world around him. He might need the caffeine more than me right now.

I stride toward the elevator, ignoring curious glances from other agents. By the time the doors slide shut, my jaw aches from how tightly I'm clenching my teeth. My reflection in the polished metal surface is sharp, unforgiving—the dark circles beneath my eyes are more pronounced than I'd like. The stress and twisted games have been piling up, and I don't fucking like the evidence staring back at me.

In the quiet solitude of the descending elevator, my mind drifts back to that goddamn text message. Sneaking into my bedroom was a declaration of war. As much as the invasion rattled me, a twisted part of my mind buzzes quietly with anticipation of the chase—knowing someone dangerous has their eyes fixed solely on me.

And fuck if it doesn't piss me off that a part of me likes the thrill, gets off on the danger just a little too much. Maybe that's my biggest problem—I'm wired for chaos. Normal has never been in my vocabulary. Growing up a Darling saw to that. Raised by parents who walk a knife's edge between justice and vengeance, between the system and their own brand of morality, there's no chance I'd come out normal. Hell, Hydessa is the closest thing to normalcy in the Darling family, and even she thrives in the shadows, chasing down monsters in her own meticulous way.

Still, there's a difference between danger I choose and danger imposed on me without permission. Whoever this stalker is, they're crossing lines at breakneck speed. Lines I'm going to make them regret stepping over.

The elevator doors open, and I step out into the bustling ground-floor lobby. Sunlight streams through expansive glass windows, temporarily blinding after the artificial gloom of the bullpen. I cross swiftly to the coffee shop across the street, a trendy little place with more plants than furniture and baristas who look like they're auditioning for a fashion shoot. It's ridiculous and overpriced, but they know how to brew coffee that actually tastes like coffee, and today that's good enough for me.

I step inside, instantly assaulted by the aroma of roasting beans and freshly baked pastries. The line is short, thankfully, and I place orders for myself and the guys, reading their last-minute texts filled with increasingly complicated coffee requests.

"Long day already?" the barista asks with practiced cheerfulness, setting out paper cups and marking them with rapid, neat handwriting.

"Long fucking lifetime," I mutter dryly, handing over cash with a forced smile.

He chuckles nervously, obviously unsure if I'm joking. Good. Let him wonder. I'm not here to be friendly—I'm here because caffeine is the only legal substance keeping me sane today.

After placing our coffee orders, I move aside, impatiently tapping my fingers against the counter. My phone buzzes insistently from my pocket, and the irritation sharpening my features only deepens as I glance down at another message from yet another unknown number.

Careful, darling. That scowl might scare off your poor barista. Such a fierce look for someone simply ordering coffee.

Ice trickles through my veins, body rigid, a sense of exposure prickling sharply at the base of my spine. My eyes snap up, scanning the bustling coffee shop instinctively, heart kicking into overdrive as I seek out anyone out of place, anyone lingering too long with their gaze fixed on me.

Another message follows immediately, as though timed perfectly with my searching glare:

Don't bother looking, Seanna. You won't see us until we want you to.

Not the first time they've said 'us', subtly reminding me that this twisted game might have multiple players. Anger and unease swirl hotly together, punctuated by an unwelcome curl of excitement at the sheer fucking nerve.

My finger hovers briefly over Uncle Max's contact, the urge to call him for help fighting against stubborn pride and dark curiosity. But the thought quickly dissolves; even Max can't trace ghosts who hide behind burners and encrypted lines. Besides, something deeply possessive within me refuses to share this twisted dance, this secret chase, with anyone else.

Fuck this. With a surge of ruthless determination, I type back:

Who the hell are you? At least give me a name to add to my hit list alongside Reyes. It's only fair I know who I'm going to destroy once I find you.

I scan the coffee shop again, eyeing every customer with fresh suspicion. The young couple in the corner, the businessman scrolling through his phone, the woman with her laptop—any of them could be watching me. The vibration of my phone startles me because it comes faster than I expect. Almost like he'd been waiting. Like he wanted me to ask.

UNKNOWN

> *You can call me Ruin.*

> *Because that's what I'll do to you, Seanna.*

> *Body. Mind. Soul.*

> *And when I'm done, you'll beg me to do it again.*

I shouldn't be turned on. I should be furious—not standing in a fucking coffee shop with heat pooling between my thighs and my pulse hammering for all the wrong reasons. But there's something about the audacity, the sheer commanding confidence in those messages that hits a primal chord inside me.

Ruin. Even the name he's chosen drips with arrogance and dark promise.

What the actual fuck is wrong with me?

I almost laugh at the absurdity of it all. This fucker actually gave himself a supervillain name. As if we're characters in some twisted cat-and-mouse thriller instead of real people playing an increasingly dangerous game.

I slip the phone back into my pocket, outwardly smoothing my expression into bored disinterest, though adrenaline still drums a steady rhythm beneath my skin. The barista calls my name, voice cheerful, and I collect the tray of coffee cups with forced calm, heading back toward the DEA bullpen.

But as I push through the door, stepping into the cool air outside, the sense of being watched follows closely, as tangible as a lover's breath against my neck. Let them watch, let them think they've got the upper hand. Because sooner or later, these shadowy assholes will make a mistake.

And when they do, I'll be ready—waiting in the dark, exactly where I belong.

Pausing on the sidewalk, I pull out my phone again, typing one handed and with deliberate venom:

> *Cute attempt at intimidation. But you're going to have to try a lot harder than creepy messages and cheap theatrics. Reyes will rot in a federal prison, and there's nothing you can do to stop me.*

I send it off with a savage grin and continue walking, picturing their face—whoever they are—tightening with irritation at my defiance. But their reply is immediate, and the words hit me harder than I expect:

UNKNOWN

> *Oh, darling, you misunderstand us. No, we don't want Reyes locked away safely in some federal cage. We want him in the fucking ground.*

I pause mid-step, rereading the message carefully as confusion and intrigue wind together in a tight, uncomfortable knot in my chest. They're claiming they're not protecting Reyes—they want him dead. If that's true, the entire game might have just shifted, and

I'm suddenly not sure whether that thought thrills or unsettles me more.

Who the hell am I really dealing with here?

Chapter 13

Ruin

I see everything. Everything she does and every move she makes.

I always have.

Long before she joined the DEA. Before she set her sights on Reyes like it was a crusade she was born for. I saw her.

The girl who never flinched. Who didn't try to leash the darkness inside her, but danced with it like it was her favorite fucking song. Everyone else tried to dull her edges, soften her glare. But not me. I was obsessed with every blade she kept sharpened and ready. I didn't want her tame—I wanted her wild. Untouched by delusion. Unbothered by approval.

Seanna doesn't apologize for who she is. She never did.

And neither do I.

She walks through life like a goddamn storm, all fury and fire wrapped in a body made to destroy men. Not me, though. I'm no fool to be shattered by her—I want to stand in the onslaught of her storm, become a part of her chaos, and watch her writhe beneath me. Me—and the only other person in the world who could ever hope to truly handle her. My best friend. My shadow. My match in obsession. The day he saw her, really saw her, I knew she wasn't just mine.

She was ours.

She still doesn't know it. Not yet. But she will.

Right now, she's sliding into her car, her face set with the kind of quiet, lethal focus that would make weaker men piss themselves. She doesn't notice the camera tucked near the dashboard. She never will.

Soon enough I'm switching screens. From her car to the hallway of the building her parents turned into their headquarters a long time ago. I've been in the system for years. Their precious "Organization" is secure from the rest of the world—but not me. Their tech? Laughable. Max is decent, sure, but compared to me?

He's a fucking dinosaur.

I watch her stride through the corridors like she owns the place—and she does. Her boots echo like a metronome of violence, hips swaying with purpose, jaw tight. People part around her like she's royalty, and in a way, she is. The queen of carnage. The patron saint of vengeance.

Our Queen.

She heads straight to Max's office. I unmute the feed, listening as she updates him on Cruz. and the meeting tomorrow. The possibility she'll go dark. I already knew all this. But hearing her say it—hearing that tight rasp in her voice, like she's fighting exhaustion with sheer will—makes my blood stir.

She doesn't mention me. Not the notes. Not the flowers. Not the polaroids I left across her bed like a shrine.

Good girl.

Keep them secret. Keep us private. Because you know, don't you? This isn't just some stalker in the shadows.

This is personal.

Max rambles on about helping Hydessa, chasing ghosts, digital breadcrumbs—whatever. I tune him out. Hydessa isn't my concern.

She's not like Seanna. She hides from the shadows, like they aren't a part of her soul.

Seanna? She knows better.

She tells Max she'll check in when she can—if Cruz buys her cover. Spoiler alert, sweetheart: he won't. Not fully. Not the way she wants, and that's an even greater risk. Going after Reyes is a suicide mission, and we aren't going to let her continue on that path of destruction. If she doesn't stop, we'll be forced to intervene. She won't like it, but she'll understand eventually.

She leaves Max's office and heads down the hall. I follow her every step, eyes tracking her from screen to screen. She dips into the wardrobe room, selects her armor—something sleek, dark, dangerous. It'll make her look like temptation and wrath had a baby.

Perfect.

But she doesn't leave right away. She pauses near the training room, drawn by familiar laughter and the clash of combat. Bodhi and Jaxon spar aggressively, while Kayla sits nearby, offering sarcastic commentary that has the guys laughing even as they try to land hits. Seanna leans against the doorway, arms folded, observing with quiet amusement.

Thorn catches sight of her and grins, deliberately flexing and raising an eyebrow. "Come to see how it's done, Seanna?" he taunts playfully. Jaxon snorts, rolling his eyes as he tries to get the upper hand against Bodhi.

"Maybe she's scared she's lost her touch," Jaxon teases, barely dodging a punch from Bodhi. Seanna smiles faintly, clearly unimpressed but entertained by their attempts to provoke her.

Kayla shoots Seanna a conspiratorial look, silently encouraging her to join in the humiliation of their overly confident teammates. But Seanna merely shakes her head, effortlessly throwing back a sarcastic remark about not needing to embarrass them any further tonight. Her words spark laughter from Kayla and groans from Thorn and Jaxon, both feigning wounded pride.

I've seen enough. They don't deserve her attention or her quick wit. She belongs to us.

I send her a message.

UNKNOWN

> **Stop flirting with men who will never understand your darkness. They'll never deserve it the way we do.**

She pulls her phone from her pocket and goes completely still. Her eyes immediately dart around, scanning for something out of place, something unseen. Good. You can feel me, can't you?

She finds the camera easily, staring straight into it as though she can see me there.

Atta girl.

She types something back:

> *Tell me you're a delusional little voyeur without telling me... Cameras now too? Jesus fucking christ. Stroke your obsession a little harder, why don't you?*

Her words drip with playful venom, designed to challenge and provoke. I chuckle deeply, appreciating her defiance.

Bodhi notices her shift in mood, questioning if she's alright. She dismisses his concern casually, quickly regaining her composure and walking away as they watch after her curiously.

Hopefully she's starting to understand.

Nothing in her life will ever be the same.

Not now.

Not with me—us—in the picture.

She's walking toward danger, convinced Reyes is the endgame.

But Reyes is a footnote.

We are the real reckoning.

And she'll learn soon enough:

She doesn't get to choose how this ends.

Because Seanna Darling may be the fire...

But *I am her Ruin.*

Chapter 14

Seanna

The cabin is silent when I get back. Too silent.

The kind of silence that feels like it's holding its breath. Like it knows something I don't.

No gifts tonight. No little boxes and envelopes on the doorstep. But after this morning's polaroids—my face frozen in sleep from a camera I never heard clicking—tonight's silence doesn't feel like safety.

It feels like a fucking trap.

They've already proven they don't need to knock when they want to say hello. Don't care about doors or boundaries when they want inside. They just slip in like a thought I can't shake and leave like they were never there at all.

The only proof is the way my heart won't slow down every time I walk into a room.

I slam the door behind me harder than I need to. Let it echo through the bones of the cabin. Let them know I'm not scared—just pissed. My keys clatter against the counter, and I move through the space on autopilot. Kitchen. Living room. Bedroom. Bathroom.

All clear.

Which means absolutely nothing.

Paranoia used to be a professional edge. Now? It's just who I am. Wired into me like muscle memory. Like breathing.

I'm exhausted. My body aches, my brain won't shut off, and tomorrow I have to dance for Cruz and pray he doesn't smell the gasoline I've poured all over this cover. One wrong move and I burn.

But I've always liked fire.

I strip off my clothes and step into the shower. The water hits like a punch—hot enough to scald, loud enough to drown out the noise in my head. I brace my hands against the tile, steam curling around me like smoke. If only it could burn away the tension clawing under my skin.

But it doesn't. Because even here—especially here—he lingers.

Ruin.

His messages play on repeat, embedded behind my eyelids like a goddamn virus. Always watching. Always waiting. He speaks like he knows me. Like we're already in this together. Like every twisted thought in my head has a matching echo in his.

And the worst part? Some of what he says doesn't feel wrong.

That pisses me off more than anything.

I towel off, throw on a black shirt and underwear, and crawl into bed. The sheets are cool. The house is dark.

But none of it matters.

Sleep isn't something I fall into anymore—it's something I fight for. And tonight, I win.

For a while.

Then—something shifts.

My body jerks awake, lungs refusing to pull in air.

Because I'm not alone.

There's weight on me. Heavy. Unmoving.

A man straddles me, knees planted firm against the mattress, pinning me like I'm prey. One of his hands traps both my wrists above my head, fingers tight and unyielding. The other is over my mouth—hard and deliberate—muffling the scream that claws its way up my throat.

I can't see his face. But I can feel the certainty in his grip.

Moonlight cuts through the window, landing across the figure above me. He's covered head to toe in black tactical gear. No insignia. No identity. Complete with glasses that gleam with an odd light that hints at night vision and full head covering. Everything about him screams precision. Discipline. Purpose.

And something about the full tactical getup speaks directly to my dark fucking soul.

Like he came for war.

And if that's what he wants? I'll fucking give it to him.

"Don't bite," he murmurs.

The voice is filtered through a modulator, distorted and mechanical—just like the ones we use in our skull masks with the organization.

My body twists hard, hips bucking against his to throw him off-balance. I twist, push, strain against him, shifting all my weight to try and roll, throw him, anything—but he's heavier than me. Stronger. Built like he was made for this exact moment. My wrists ache in his grip. My muscles scream, but he never so much as flinches. All he does is hold me there—contained, restrained, completely under his control.

Once I wear myself out—my breathing ragged, chest heaving—he leans down. His mask brushes against the skin of my jaw, a cool scrape of hard polymer against flushed skin. I hear it then, clear and unmistakable—a breath. Inhaled deep, slow through some hidden valve in his mask like the fucker is savoring me. Drinking me in.

Jealousy flickers sharp and stupid across my thoughts—because our skull masks don't have that nifty little feature.

"You smell so fucking good," he breathes, voice modulated but thick with hunger.

His gloved fingers press against my mouth, not hard enough to hurt, but firm enough to make his point. I can feel the strength in his grip, the casual dominance that sets my blood on fire even as my mind screams in defiance.

"I'm going to move my hand now," he says calmly, that modulated voice somehow more unsettling in its evenness. "And it won't matter if you scream. In fact, I want you to scream for me, Seanna. I want to hear every desperate sound you make."

Slowly, he slides his hand from my mouth, trailing it down to rest against the column of my throat. The leather of his gloves is buttery soft, a sensual contrast to the unyielding strength I can feel coiled in his body above me.

"Ruin," I hiss through clenched teeth, glaring up at that impassive mask. "You sick fuck, what the hell do you think you're-"

A dark chuckle cuts me off, the sound distorted and mechanical. "Oh, darling. I'm not Ruin." He leans in closer, that blank facade filling my vision. "You can call me Rule. As in, you're going to follow my rules like a good girl."

Indignation flares hot and bright in my chest. "Like hell I will," I snarl, trying to thrash against his hold again. But he merely tightens his grip, pressing me harder into the mattress until I'm gasping for air.

"Ruin may indulge your defiance," he murmurs, a thread of cruel amusement winding through his words. "But I'm not as nice as him. You need to stop this foolish crusade against Reyes. No more meetings with Cruz. Because if you keep pushing, keep putting yourself at risk, you'll only have yourself to blame for what happens. So, the meeting tomorrow? It's not happening. Cancel it."

Fury lances through me, white-hot and blinding. How dare he try to dictate my actions, my choices? I open my mouth, a barrage of vicious insults ready to spill from my lips, but he cuts me off with a squeeze of his fingers around my throat.

"Careful, darling," he purrs, the endearment dripping with mocking condescension. "Wouldn't want to say something you'll regret."

I bare my teeth at him, anger and something darker, more primal, coiling tightly in my gut. "Fuck you," I hiss venomously. "I don't take orders from psychotic stalkers who get off on breaking into women's bedrooms."

His hand tightens fractionally around my throat, a warning and a promise. "You'll take my orders because you don't have a choice, Seanna. You're ours, you belong to us. The sooner you accept that, the easier this will be for everyone."

Despite the fury churning inside me, a traitorous shiver of heat slides down my spine at his words. Belong to them? Like hell. I'm Seanna fucking Darling—I don't belong to anyone.

"You're delusional," I snap, still straining against his unyielding grip. "I don't know what sick game you and Ruin are playing, but I'm not interested. Now get the fuck off me before I show you exactly why messing with me is a bad idea."

He laughs then, the sound dark and mocking even through the modulator. "Oh, I'd love to see you try, darling. But we both know you're not going anywhere until I say so."

As if to prove his point, he leans down, pressing his masked face against the sensitive skin of my neck. I feel his breath, hot and damp, as he drags the smooth surface of the mask along my thundering pulse point. Every muscle in my body goes taut, a mixture of revulsion and reluctant arousal warring for dominance.

"I could do anything I wanted to you right now," he murmurs, his free hand sliding down my body with deliberate slowness. "And part of you would love every second of it, wouldn't you? Because deep down, you crave this. The danger. The loss of control. Being at the mercy of someone strong enough to overpower you."

I clench my jaw so hard my teeth ache, hating the kernel of truth in his words. I've always been drawn to the darkness, to the razor's edge between pain and pleasure. But I'll be damned if I let this asshole use that against me.

"Get fucked," I hiss, pouring every ounce of venom I possess into the words. "You don't know a goddamn thing about me."

"But I do, Seanna," he counters smoothly, his hand dipping lower, fingers grazing the hem of my shirt. "I know everything about you. Every dirty little secret. Every twisted fantasy. And I'm going to use every single one of them to break you apart and put you back together again."

His hand slips beneath the fabric, gloved fingers dragging across the sensitive skin of my stomach. I suck in a sharp breath, muscles jumping beneath his touch. Hate and hunger tangle together, a sickening knot in my chest.

"Cancel the meeting with Cruz," he orders again, his voice a dark purr even through the modulator. "Be a good girl and do as you're told, and maybe I'll reward you."

His fingers dance teasingly along the waistband of my panties, dipping just barely beneath the fabric to graze the sensitive skin there. I suck in a sharp breath, hating the way my body responds to his touch, the traitorous heat pooling low in my belly.

"Fuck you," I hiss again, but there's less venom in it this time, my voice breathy and strained. "I'm not canceling shit. Cruz is the key to taking down Reyes, and I'm not backing down just because some psycho in a mask tells me to."

He tsks softly, his hand slipping lower to cup me through the thin fabric of my panties. I bite down hard on my lip, refusing to make a sound even as my hips twitch traitorously into his touch.

"So stubborn," he murmurs, fingers pressing harder, rubbing slow circles that make my toes curl. "But we both know you're only fighting because you're scared of how much you want this. How desperately you crave someone who can overpower you, dominate you *completely*."

I squeeze my eyes shut, trying to block out his words, his touch, the dark hunger unfurling inside me. But it's useless. *He's right, damn him.* Some twisted part of me is thrilled by this, turned on beyond reason at being so utterly helpless beneath him.

"Look at you," he purrs, satisfaction dripping from every word. "Already so needy for me. I bet you're soaking wet right now, aren't you darling? Desperate for me to touch you."

Shame and arousal war within me as he tugs my panties aside, his fingers grazing my slick folds. I can't hold back the choked moan that escapes me at the contact, my hips canting shamelessly into his touch.

"That's it," he praises darkly. "Don't fight it, Seanna. You need this. Need me to take control, to make you submit."

He strokes me slowly, teasing, leather-clad fingers gliding through the wetness he finds. I'm panting now, skin flushed and mind hazy with lust I don't want to feel but can't deny.

"So responsive," he murmurs appreciatively. "So perfect. My perfect little toy."

Toy. The word slices through the fog of arousal, and I grab desperately for the anger simmering beneath. I'm not a fucking toy, a plaything for him to use. The fury reignites, and I renew my struggles, bucking against him wildly.

But he simply rides out my thrashing, continuing his maddeningly slow touches until I collapse back against the sheets, chest heaving.

"Are you done?" he asks mildly, his voice mocking even through the modulator. In response, I simply glare up at him in defiance, my jaw clenched tight.

"Good girl," he praises patronizingly. Then, without warning, he plunges two fingers deep inside me, curling them just right to hit that perfect spot. A choked cry escapes my lips as my back arches off the bed, pleasure spiking through me like lightning.

He works me relentlessly, stroking and thrusting, building me higher and higher with ruthless efficiency. It's too much, too intense, and I can feel my orgasm hurtling toward me like a runaway train.

But just as I'm teetering on the knife's edge of release, he withdraws completely, leaving me empty and aching. I make a sound of desperate frustration, hips chasing his touch, pride be damned.

"Ah ah," he tuts, grabbing my jaw roughly and forcing me to meet that blank mask. "You don't get to come until you do what you're told. Cancel the meeting with Cruz. Say you'll do it."

"Fuck...you..." I manage to grind out, even as my body screams for completion.

He makes a sound of mock disappointment. Then, lightning quick, he thrusts his slick fingers deep into my mouth, pressing down on my tongue. I gag around the intrusion, the taste of my own arousal bitter.

"This bratty mouth is going to get you in trouble," he growls warningly. "Cancel the meeting tomorrow, Seanna. Or you *will* regret it."

I glare mutinously up at him, refusing to give him the satisfaction, even as my mind grows hazy with need. He holds me there a moment longer, fingers heavy on my tongue, before suddenly pulling back.

Then, without warning, he sprays something directly up my nose - a mist, sickly sweet. I cough and sputter, trying to turn away, but it's too late. Almost instantly, my head grows heavy, thoughts scattering like frantic birds.

"Wha...what did you..." I slur, tongue thick and useless.

"Shhh," he soothes mockingly, pushing me back against the pillows as my limbs turn to lead. "Just a little something to help you sleep."

Darkness creeps in at the edges of my vision as whatever he drugged me with drags me under. The last thing I feel is the ghost of his touch against my cheek, almost a tender caress, a cruel tease.

And then I'm gone, slipping into a thick, unyielding blackness.

Chapter 15

Seanna

I wake with a start, heart pounding and adrenaline surging, the memory of last night's twisted encounter still vivid in my mind. Soft early morning sunlight streams through the windows, a jarring contrast to the darkness that had enveloped me just hours before. I sit up slowly, half expecting to find some trace of Rule's presence—a lingering scent, a disturbed object, anything to confirm he wasn't just a fucked-up figment of my imagination.

But there's nothing. The room is undisturbed, exactly as I left it. If it weren't for the phantom sensations still ghosting across my skin—the bruising grip on my wrists, the press of leather-clad fingers against my most intimate places—I might be tempted to write it off as a bizarre, unsettling dream.

Except I know better. Rule was here, in my room, on top of me, his fingers inside me. And despite the violation, the fury at his audacity, some traitorous part of my body hums with remembered pleasure, craving his touch even as my mind screams in defiance.

Fuck. I'm so screwed up.

I drag myself out of bed, every muscle protesting the movement. Whatever he drugged me with has left me groggy and sluggish, like I'm moving through water. But as I stumble to the bathroom, splashing cold water on my face, a steely resolve settles in my chest.

Rule and Ruin may think they can control me, dictate my actions through creepy mind games and twisted seduction. But they've got another thing coming. I'm Seanna fucking Darling—I don't bend to anyone's will, no matter how darkly tempting their tactics may be.

And that meeting with Cruz? It's sure as hell still happening, mysterious stalkers be damned.

I shower quickly, washing away the lingering traces of last night, the phantom sensation of leather on skin. The hot water pounds against my shoulders, grounding me in the present, sharpening my focus to a lethal point. By the time I step out, I feel more like myself—razor-edged and ready for war.

I dress with deliberate care, each piece of clothing another layer of armor. Black jeans, tight enough to showcase every dangerous curve. A dark red top that dips low, hinting at the tantalizing swell of my breasts. Knee-high boots with a wicked heel, perfect for stomping on anyone who gets in my way. And of course, my leather jacket, the buttery-soft material like a second skin.

I look at myself in the mirror, taking in the woman staring back at me. She looks like sin and vengeance wrapped in one deadly package, eyes glittering with dark promise. Good. That's exactly what I need to be today.

I almost forget the dress for the meet, but detour to grab it from where I threw it over the back of my couch and find that's where they left their mark—the dress is ruined, torn and slashed in several places, intentionally destroyed. There's no way I can use this dress now. I curse under my breath, frustrated but not entirely surprised at just how devious they chose to play this.

Moving to the bedroom, I fling open my closet, searching for something else suitable to wear. That's when I notice the empty spaces on the racks, where all the dresses I keep specifically for nights when I want to prowl the clubs, looking for leads or a good time, are gone. I rifle through the hangers frantically, but no matter how thoroughly I look, those dresses do not reappear. That bastard Rule must have taken or destroyed them when he broke in last night, after knocking me out with that drug.

My phone rings, the shrill tone making me jump. I snatch it up, barely glancing at the caller ID before answering brusquely. "Yeah?"

It's Jensen on the other end. "Everything okay? You're on your way for the pre-meet briefing, right?"

Shit. In my anger over the ruined dress situation, I had lost track of time. "Sorry, I'm running a few minutes late. There's been a...co mplication. I'll be there in twenty."

"Everything secure on your end?" There's an edge of concern in his voice that I don't have time to address right now.

"It's fine. Just...have to make a stop first." I don't elaborate further, ending the call abruptly.

Fuming, I grab my keys and head for the door. If Rule and Ruin think destroying my clothes will be enough to derail me, they're gravely mistaken.

I'm fuming as I climb into my car and peel out of the driveway, tires spitting gravel. The drive to the Organization's headquarters is thankfully short, but my knuckles are still white from gripping the steering wheel so tightly.

I pull up to the nondescript office building and barely acknowledge the security as I make my way inside, brushing past the other operatives who quickly move out of my way. My boots strike the polished floors with sharp clicks, echoing my fury. How dare those bastards sabotage me like this? Breaking into my home, drugging me, destroying my clothes - it's a blatant challenge, one I have no choice but to meet head-on.

When I reach the wardrobe room door, I try shoving it open with unnecessary force, only to be met with unyielding resistance. Locked. I let out a frustrated growl between clenched teeth. This room is never locked - we're meant to have unrestricted access to gear and equipment at all times.

Stepping back, I glare at the keypad next to the door like it has personally offended me. We so rarely need to use these codes that I have to pause and actually think about the sequence of numbers. My fingers hover over the buttons as I mentally rifle through the memorized passcodes, finally punching one in with perhaps more vehemence than necessary.

The light blinks red. Denied.

"Are you fucking kidding me?" I snarl, resisting the urge to slam my palm against the unyielding metal. This is getting ridiculous. First my home is violated, now I'm being locked out of Organization resources? Just how far are Rule and Ruin willing to take this twisted game?

"You okay?" comes a voice from behind me and I turn to see Jaxon there with a frown on his face.

"Does it look like I'm fucking okay?" I snap, gesturing angrily at the locked door. "I can't get into the goddamn wardrobe room."

Jaxon arches an eyebrow at my outburst but doesn't look surprised. He's been on the receiving end of my temper more times than I can count. "Did you try your code?"

I shoot him a withering glare. "Obviously. It's not working."

He moves closer, tapping in a sequence on the keypad. The light blinks green and the lock disengages with an audible thunk.

"There, now stop raging before you give yourself an aneurysm," Jaxon says dryly, pulling the door open.

I brush past Jaxon without a word, stepping into the wardrobe room and scanning the racks with narrowed eyes. After a few moments, I spot what I need—a slinky black dress with a plunging neckline and thigh-high slit up the side. Skimpy but classy enough to pass for business wear if I accessorize right. Perfect for gaining Cruz's attention without being too obvious about it.

I grab the dress off the rack along with a pair of wicked stilettos and a slim jacket to complete the look. As I turn to leave, Jaxon is watching me with a bemused expression.

"You know, most people say 'thank you' when someone holds a door for them," he comments dryly.

I pause, reining in my anger with an effort. He doesn't deserve to be on the receiving end of my fury—not this time, at least.

"Thank you, Jaxon," I say evenly, meeting his gaze. "I appreciate you keying me in."

He smirks, clearly recognizing my restraint. "Anytime, darling."

The endearment makes me hesitate, a flicker of memory from last night—Rule's mocking tone as he pinned me down, calling me 'darling' over and over. I push it away, refusing to let my mind linger on the twisted encounter.

"Don't call me that," I say curtly, clutching my newly acquired outfit.

Jaxon arches an eyebrow, amusement playing across his features. "But it's your name," he points out with maddening logic.

For a moment, I freeze, wondering if the reason Rule called me 'darling' so mockingly was simply because it's my name. Jesus fucking christ, what the hell is wrong with me that I'm even analyzing this? Why do I care why that psychotic asshole used a particular term of endearment while he was fingering me?

I grit my teeth, struggling to regain my composure as unbidden flashes of last night flicker through my mind. The weight of Rule's body pinning me down. The rasp of his modulated voice against my skin. The exquisite torment as he worked me to the edge of release, only to cruelly deny me.

Heat blooms low in my belly at the memories, and I ruthlessly shove them away, appalled at my own body's traitorous response. I can't afford to lose focus, not now. Not with so much at stake.

"Thanks for the assist," I force out, the words clipped and terse as I brush past Jaxon toward the door.

He says something else, but I don't catch it, my mind already shifting gears, strategizing for the meeting with Cruz. Rule and Ruin may think they've rattled me, but they're about to learn just how unshakable I can be when properly motivated. Cruz is the key, and nothing—not deranged stalkers or twisted mind games—is going to keep me from exploiting that lead.

By the time I reach the briefing room, I've regained my focus. Jensen, Matteo, and Eli are already gathered around the central table, poring over intel files and surveillance stills. They look up as I enter, and the brief flicker of concern on Jensen's face tells me my chaotic energy is more obvious than I'd like.

"Everything good?" he asks carefully, holding my gaze in that way of his that says he won't accept any bullshit excuses.

I meet his stare levelly, daring him to push further. "Everything's fine. Just ran into a minor delay." My tone makes it clear the topic is closed for discussion.

Eli, ever the one to poke the bear, opens his mouth—no doubt to unleash some wisecrack about my mood. But Matteo cuts him off with a sharp look, his dark eyes assessing me.

"We should go over the plan one more time," he says evenly, dragging our focus back to the mission at hand.

Jensen moves things along before tensions can escalate further. "Right. Cruz is expecting to meet 'Samantha' at his club in"—he glances at his watch—"two hours. The place will be closed, just him and a few of his inner circle."

"Roger that," I confirm briskly, scanning the room to ensure everyone is dialed in. "Jensen, Eli—you two will be stationed nearby providing overwatch and backup in case things go sideways. Keep eyes and ears on Cruz's crew at all times. If anything feels off, you call it."

Jensen nods sharply. "We've got your back."

Eli shoots me a cocky grin, already looking a little too eager at the prospect of potential chaos. "Don't worry, boss. We'll be ready to blow this whole op sky high if your charms don't work their magic on Cruz."

I level a flat stare at him, unamused. "My 'charms' will be more than enough to keep Cruz occupied. But just in case, the PD narcotics team will be on standby two blocks out for rapid deployment if needed."

Matteo remains stoically silent, hands resting on the table as he studies the building schematics with intense focus.

"We go in tight but icy," I continue, tracing my finger along the blueprint. "Cruz is expecting an independent supplier looking to broker a deal, so that's the cover we sell. Hard, dismissive - make him work for any scrap of attention or validation."

I glance up to find Jensen watching me carefully. "Don't overplay it," he cautions in that low, even tone of his. "Cruz is too savvy to fall for over-the-top bravado. Walk the line—enough disinterest to stroke his ego, but not so much that you insult him. That's a very narrow target."

My lips quirk slightly at the hint of concern in his voice. The team knows how easily I can get carried away by the thrill of the game. Sometimes it's like there are two versions of me—the consummate professional DEA agent, and the adrenaline-fueled wild card who loves tempting fate a little too much.

"I know the drill," I assure him evenly. "Play hard to get, make him chase me. It's not my first time using my feminine wiles to reel in an arrogant prick."

Matteo huffs a laugh, muttering something about that being the understatement of the century. I shoot him a look that could cut glass, but there's no real heat behind it. My team know me—the good, the bad, and the recklessly impulsiveness that makes me such a nightmare to handle sometimes.

"All right, let's get this shitshow on the road," I announce, scooping up the slim folder containing my cover identity. "Cruz wants to tango? We'll give him one hell of a dance."

Chapter 16
Seanna

I'm already in the outfit I picked up from the Organization, every line of the sleek black ensemble designed to scream power, control, and zero tolerance for bullshit. It hugs in all the right places and conceals everything else. Samantha—the cartel queen I've become for this operation—doesn't walk into clubs. She *owns* them.

I sit in the passenger seat of Matteo's sleek black car as we glide through the late-morning traffic, the sun glaring off the windshield in bold, blinding streaks. The Silver Orchid isn't far now. The meeting with Sebastián Cruz is set for noon, and we're right on schedule.

We haven't spoken much since I got in. No need. The team's already locked in. Focused. Our comms are live, transmitting every breath, every shift. Words become distractions when the mission is this tight.

Still, a few blocks out, Matteo finally breaks the silence.

"You okay?" he asks, eyes still on the road. "You seem... tense."

I don't look at him. Just keep my eyes on the approaching skyline. "I'm fine," I reply flatly. "I'll be a hell of a lot better once we get to Reyes."

He nods once, no follow-up, no unnecessary sympathy. That's why I like working with Matteo—he doesn't push. He just shifts gears, fingers tightening subtly on the wheel as the car hums smoothly beneath us.

Three minutes later, we're pulling up to the side entrance of the Silver Orchid—Cruz's little playground disguised as a high-end club. Even in daylight, it looks expensive and dangerous. Tinted windows. Discreet security. Clean lines and sharper secrets.

Matteo steps out first, already slipping into his cover role. He circles around the front of the car and opens my door like it's second nature. His whole posture shifts, becoming the perfect picture of a man who works for *me*. Loyal. Submissive. Armed to the damn teeth beneath that suit.

I step out of the car with deliberate grace, every movement calculated to exude bored indifference. My dress clings to every curve, the thigh-high slit offering tantalizing glimpses of skin with each step. Matteo falls into step just behind me, the picture of a deferential employee escorting his demanding, disinterested boss.

As we approach the entrance to the Silver Orchid, the bouncer's eyes widen fractionally, sweeping over me in an obvious onceover before snapping back to professional neutrality. I pretend not to notice, barely sparing him a glance as I breeze past and into the dim interior of the club.

The place is deserted except for a few of Cruz's inner circle lingering near the bar, sipping drinks and watching our entrance with thinly veiled curiosity. I lock eyes with a brutish-looking man built like a brick shithouse, his gaze lingering just a little too long in a way that suggests he's picturing me on my knees. I arch an eyebrow coolly, letting my disdain show.

"Miss Delgado," a smooth voice greets. I turn to find Cruz emerging from a hallway, dressed to the nines in an impeccably tailored suit. He obviously looked into me and found the fake identity set up for 'Samantha', like we knew he would. "I've been expecting you."

His eyes rake over me with naked appreciation, and I fight the urge to roll my own in response. Men—so predictably easy to manipulate when you give them a tempting target for their lust.

"Cruz," I reply flatly, making no effort to return his overly familiar greeting. "I trust discretion won't be an issue? I don't like surprises when it comes to business matters."

His grin widens a fraction, clearly enjoying my brusque manner. The arrogant bastard probably thinks my dismissive attitude is all part of some coy act. Little does he know I have zero interest in playing demure little games—I'm here for one thing and one thing only: information to take him and his entire operation down.

"Of course, of course," he assures me easily, gesturing toward a secluded booth tucked away in a shadowy corner. "We have complete privacy. Please, make yourself comfortable."

I saunter toward the booth, hips swaying with just a hint of exaggerated swagger. Out of the corner of my eye, I see the man from before nudge one of his buddies, murmuring something that makes them both snicker crudely. Pathetic. Like they've never seen a woman who knows exactly how appealing she is before.

Matteo follows a few paces behind, slipping into the role of silent bodyguard with ease. I slide into the booth while he takes up a position a few steps away. I cross my legs intentionally to allow the slit in my dress to gape open even wider. Cruz's gaze darts downward, tracking the motion like a horny teenager, before he forces his eyes back to my face.

"Drink?" he offers with a wolfish grin, signaling to one of his men before I even have the chance to respond.

"Whiskey," I say coolly, tilting my chin up and letting a chill settle over my words. "Neat." It's what Samantha Delgado would drink. Strong and sharp—like poison dressed in silk.

Cruz seems delighted by this answer, barking out something in rapid Spanish that sends one of his lackeys scurrying behind the bar like an eager little rat fetching scraps for their master. Meanwhile, he leans back against the booth's plush leather with all the ease of a man who thinks he's untouchable.

The lackey returns quickly, placing a crystal tumbler filled with amber liquid in front of me. The glass clinks softly against the table, the sound barely registering over the thrum of my pulse. Cruz watches me expectantly, that arrogant grin still plastered across his face as he gestures toward the drink.

I let my gaze linger on the glass for a long, deliberate moment, considering it carefully. The whiskey swirls invitingly, the dim light glinting off the surface. Part of me is tempted to simply pick it up and take a sip, let the smooth burn of the alcohol slide down my throat and settle in my belly. But I know better. This is Cruz's domain, his playground - I can't afford to let my guard down, not even for a second.

Instead, I lean back against the plush leather of the booth. I let my fingers trail along the rim of the glass, tracing the edge with a feather-light touch as I hold Cruz's gaze.

"Shall we get down to business?"

Cruz nods, the playful glint in his eyes hardening into something more calculating. "By all means. You mentioned you were looking to expand your supply chain?" He leans forward, resting his elbows on the table as he regards me intently. "What kind of quantities are we talking about?"

I hold his gaze. "Significant. My client base is growing, and they demand reliability as well as volume." I pause, letting my eyes drift over to where his men are still loitering near the bar, pretending not to watch our exchange. "I trust your operation can handle that kind of demand?"

Cruz chuckles, the sound low and confident. "My dear Samantha, you underestimate us. We have the resources and the connections to supply even the most...discerning of clientele." He leans back, spreading his arms in a gesture of casual authority. "But I must admit, I'm curious. What made you seek us out, specifically?"

I allow a faint smile to curve my lips. "Word on the street is that your product is the best in the business. And I've grown tired of dealing with...unreliable sources." My gaze narrows slightly. "I need someone I can trust to deliver, no matter what."

Cruz's eyes gleam with something that looks dangerously close to triumph. "Well then, I believe we have the beginnings of a mutually beneficial arrangement," Cruz says, his lips curling into a predatory smile. He signals to one of his men, who hurries over with a leather pouch. "Here is a sample of our finest product. I think you'll find it exceeds even the lofty standards you've heard about."

Matteo steps forward and takes it, slipping it into his pocket without a word. I don't bother with it, simply observing the exchange. "I have no doubt your product is top-notch, Mr. Cruz. But as I said, I need reliable quantity and consistent delivery. Anything less and this partnership won't work for me."

Cruz nods, his expression turning thoughtful. "Of course, of course. Rest assured, my organization has the resources and the connections to meet your needs. All I ask is that you come back tomorrow with a firm order and the capital to back it up. Then we can discuss the details of an ongoing arrangement."

I arch an eyebrow. "I don't like to be kept waiting, Mr. Cruz. My client base is...impatient. I was hoping we could finalize the terms today."

He chuckles, clearly amused by my impatience. "Ah, my dear Samantha, good things come to those who wait. I must insist on taking the proper precautions. Tomorrow, with the funds in hand, we can hash out the specifics to both our satisfaction."

I press my lips into a thin line, feigning reluctant acceptance. "Very well. I'll return tomorrow, as you request." I pause, allowing a hint of warning to creep into my tone. "But I won't be kept waiting much longer."

Cruz's grin widens, clearly taking my veiled threat as playful banter. "I look forward to our continued negotiations, Ms. Delgado." He leans back, signaling to his men. "Gentlemen, please see our guest out."

As I stand from the booth, Matteo quickly steps up to my side. I catch the hungry looks the other men are sending my way and resist the urge to roll my eyes—these pathetic excuses for henchmen are nothing compared to the true predators I've faced. With a toss of my hair and a sultry sway of my hips, I lead the way out of the Silver Orchid, secure in the knowledge that I have Cruz exactly where I want him.

Once we're safely back in Matteo's car, I let out a long, slow breath, the tension in my shoulders finally starting to unwind. "Well, that went about as well as expected," I mutter, glancing over at Matteo.

He nods, his expression unreadable. "Cruz seems to have taken the bait. We've got him curious, at least."

"Curious, but still suspicious," I point out.

Matteo's grip on the steering wheel tightens as he navigates the winding roads, putting as much distance between us and the Silver Orchid as possible. We take the long drive through various streets and even a cemetery to make sure we aren't being followed. I glance periodically in the rearview mirror, searching for any sign we're being followed, but the streets remain clear. Good. The last thing I need is Cruz's goons catching wind of this little covert op.

I know that somewhere behind us at a safe distance are Jensen and Eli.

But, I can't help but feel like we're being watched. My skin prickles with the familiar sensation of eyes following our every move. I resist the urge to look over my shoulder, knowing it'll only feed that paranoia.

Instead, I turn my attention to the intel we've gathered so far. Cruz is intrigued, no doubt about that, but he's still playing it cautious. Typical cartel behavior—size up the new player, test their mettle, and then decide if they're worth the investment. I knew going in that it wouldn't be as simple as waltzing in, batting my eyelashes, and walking away with a direct line to Reyes.

But dammit, a girl can dream.

I clench my jaw, ignoring the faint throbbing in my temples. The last twenty-four hours have been a fucking whirlwind, from Rule's 'visit' then to the charged meeting with Cruz. And now, the constant awareness of being watched, hunted even, is wearing me down. I should be laser-focused on the task at hand, not letting my mind get sidetracked by twisted stalkers and their games.

"You're brooding," Matteo observes mildly, his eyes flicking to me briefly before returning to the road.

"I'm not brooding. I'm thinking."

The comms in my ear crackle to life, and Eli's voice filters through, dripping with his usual smug amusement. "Hey, Seanna, do you have that adorable little crease between your eyes right now? You know, the one that shows up when you're plotting someone's murder?"

"I swear to God, Eli, I will shoot you in the fucking kneecap," I snap, my fingers instinctively reaching up to smooth the space between my brows.

Eli's laugh echoes in my ear, unbothered by my threat. "You're not in the car with me right now, so my kneecaps are currently perfectly safe. Besides, that little furrow is cute. Makes you look all intense and deadly."

"I don't do cute," I growl, glaring out the window at the passing buildings.

"Everyone, focus," Jensen's voice cuts in, all business as usual. "We're approaching the rendezvous point. Let's keep the chatter to a minimum. Matteo, take the next right and follow the access road behind the industrial complex."

I straighten in my seat, grateful for Jensen's intervention. The playful banter evaporates instantly, replaced by the sharp, electric tension that always precedes an operation's critical phase. Matteo follows Jensen's directions without comment, taking the turn with smooth precision.

The warehouse district looms ahead, a sprawling maze of corrugated metal and concrete. Most of the buildings look abandoned or barely operational—perfect for our purposes. No prying eyes, no nosy civilians, just the quiet isolation we need to regroup and plan our next move.

We pull into the open garage of a nondescript building with faded numbers on its side, the paint peeling away like dead skin. Matteo kills the engine, and we sit in silence for a moment, scanning our surroundings with practiced vigilance. The air feels charged, heavy.

Behind us, Jensen and Eli pull their vehicle into the warehouse next. The rumble of the engine cuts off as Jensen steps out and moves to a control panel by the entrance. He presses a button, and the massive garage doors begin to close with a mechanical groan, sealing us in.

The moment the doors thud shut, the tension breaks. Time to debrief. And time to decide what the hell comes next.

Chapter 17

Seanna

Matteo kills the engine, and for a moment, the silence feels almost reverent. Sacred. Like we've stepped into some kind of confessional booth where sins aren't just whispered—they're cataloged.

I push open my door and step out, heels clicking against cracked concrete, the air inside this abandoned shell of industry stale and thick with dust. Eli and Jensen approach, their body language as tight and sharp as mine.

But it doesn't matter that I just walked out of a cartel nightclub in stilettos and a skin-tight dress without flinching. Doesn't matter that I've got three of the most dangerous men I know watching my six. The weight on my shoulders isn't Reyes, or Cruz, or the meet I have to finesse tomorrow. It's them.

Rule and Ruin.

The ghosts I can't seem to shake.

The warehouse smells like oil, metal, and secrets. Not the comforting kind—if those even exist—but the kind that rot from the inside out. The kind that cling to your skin like old smoke.

"Back room," Jensen says, breaking the silence as he jerks his chin toward the hallway that splits off from the loading bay. "Let's not stand around like targets."

We fall into step, boots crunching over cracked concrete as we move deeper into the belly of the warehouse. This place isn't unfamiliar—we've used it before when shit got too hot or too complicated to bring back to HQ. The bones are solid, the location off-grid, and the interior? Just polished enough to pass for a war room if you squint.

The temporary debrief space is a converted office in the far corner—bare fluorescent lights overhead, a battered table in the center, mismatched chairs, and an old whiteboard still stained with marker ghosts from our last op here. One of the dry erase pens sits in a coffee mug with "World's Okayest Sniper" printed on the side. Matteo's, obviously.

I take the seat at the head of the table without waiting for anyone to offer. Matteo drops the pouch onto the table and leans against the wall behind me, arms folded. Jensen pulls up surveillance feeds on the tablet and drops it in front of me while Eli flops into a chair like it personally offended him.

"He's hooked," Matteo says, eyes tracking mine like he knows exactly how close I am to snapping. "You hit the exact nerve we needed. He wants to trust you. Thinks you're some high-class drug queen looking to move weight."

"Good," I say flatly. "That means we're one step closer to Reyes."

"That also means," Eli cuts in, his tone serious, "you're one step deeper in Cruz's territory. Which makes you a fucking red target if you so much as twitch wrong tomorrow."

"Then I won't twitch wrong," I snap, sharper than I mean to. My voice slices the air, and the silence that follows is taut, brittle.

Jensen watches me with that unreadable expression of his—quiet, careful. Like he's waiting for a bomb to go off.

"Seanna," he says finally, voice low, deliberate. "You sure you're good? You've been... off. Since this morning."

I meet his gaze. "I'm fine."

"Define *'fine'*," Eli mutters from the side, pretending to scroll through his tablet. "Is it the 'slept great, ate breakfast, ready to kick ass' kind of fine? Or the 'didn't sleep, punched a mirror, and now holding it together with caffeine and spite' kind of fine?"

My jaw tightens. I don't answer.

Because the second one is dead-on.

And because I'm not giving them the satisfaction of saying it out loud.

Matteo moves toward the window, peering out through the slats. "No sign of tails," he says. "But I still don't like this. Cruz is a snake, he won't confront you head-on, but get too close and he'll sink his fangs in."

"Let him bite," I mutter, dragging a hand through my hair. "I'll tear his fangs out and shove them down Reyes's throat."

Jensen lets out a low whistle but says nothing. Eli doesn't even try to hide his smirk.

"Graphic," he mutters.

"I'm not here to be delicate," I snap.

Matteo steps away from the window and leans against the edge of the table. His tone shifts—calm, even, but undercut with steel. "Delicate isn't the problem. The problem is what happens if Cruz gets a whiff of the wrong scent off you tomorrow. If he suspects anything—fear, hesitation, lies—you don't walk out of there. None of us do."

"I know," I say, because I do. Every possibility has already played itself out in my head a dozen ways. Best case, Cruz believes I'm the supplier I claim to be and opens the door to Reyes. Worst case? My body gets dumped in a shipping container bound for nowhere. I'm not afraid of either outcome. But I am tired of pretending that's not the truth we're dancing with.

Jensen exhales slowly, like he's weighing how hard to push. "You've got that look in your eyes again. The one that says you haven't slept and your demons are getting mouthy."

"They never shut up," I say, sharper than I mean to. I roll my shoulders, trying to loosen the tension that's been welded there since last night.

Eli doesn't press the issue, but his gaze flicks up from the tablet long enough to clock me with concern—buried beneath sarcasm, sure, but there. Always there.

The silence hangs for a beat too long.

Then Matteo shifts off the wall. "We need to talk about tomorrow."

I nod, grateful for the pivot. "Cruz wants a full commitment. Product volume, drop location, capital—all of it. He's playing like he believes me, but he's still testing. If we show up with a half-assed proposal, he'll bail."

Jensen tosses another folder on the table. "We've got a mock portfolio set up. Cash logs, shell companies, the works. It's convincing. But you'll need to memorize it top to bottom. If he asks even one question you can't answer—"

"He'll slit my throat with that smug little smile," I finish. "Yeah, I know."

"No pressure," Eli mutters. "Just cartel thugs and fake bank statements between you and a shallow grave."

I smile thinly. "Sounds like a Tuesday."

We decide to meet back here tomorrow morning, early, a few hours before the second meet with Cruz. Time to re-check comms, final prep, confirm surveillance, and rehearse contingencies in case shit goes sideways. Which, let's be honest, it will.

But for now, we split.

Matteo heads for his car. Jensen and Eli pile into the SUV they arrived in. Eli stretches with an exaggerated groan like he's shaking off the tension, before lighting a cigarette. Jensen's already dialing someone, probably to double-check one of the narcotics teams.

"I'll catch up with you tomorrow," I call out and they don't question it. I walk off without comment, angling toward the east side exit. My car's parked a block away—always is when we use this place. Too many blind corners for my taste.

We've done what we can today. All that's left is to rest, reset, and hope nobody ends up in a body bag tomorrow.

The air is cooler now, slick with the scent of metal and rain. As I walk into the evening, the gritty wind scraping down the alley, my phone starts buzzing in my palm. I pause mid-step, frown at the screen.

Hydessa.

"If I hide..." she says softly, her voice barely audible, like a secret she's afraid the shadows might overhear.

I close my eyes for half a second, just breathing in the exhaustion, the weight of everything.

"Then I'll seek..." I say, trying not to let too much show through. But Hydessa knows me too well. She pauses.

"Are you okay?" she asks gently, all concern and intuition, like she already knows I'm unraveling by degrees.

"Yeah," I lie with a practiced ease. "Just a lot going on. Don't worry about me."

A beat passes. I shift my weight to lean against a lamppost, pressing the phone tighter to my ear. I can hear waves in the background—she's still on the island.

"How's your investigation going?" I ask, keeping my voice light, trying to redirect her from the minefield I've built under my own feet.

"It's going well," she says, but I can tell she's holding something back. "I have a possible lead."

"That's great!" I say, letting genuine pride leak through. "And have you taken the time to have some fun with a hot guy yet?"

There's a pause. Too long. Something catches in her breath.

She hesitates.

That's all it takes. I smile a little to myself, because that's the sound of guilt. Or... maybe something else.

"Oh my god, you have!" I say, pouncing on the moment like a bloodhound. "Spill the details! Who is he? Is he cute? Tell me everything!"

She doesn't answer immediately.

And that silence is loud.

My smile starts to fade.

"It's... complicated," she finally says, her voice softer now. "I'm not sure it's about having fun. It's more... like a dangerous game, and I'm not sure where it's going."

My chest tightens. Something in her tone needles its way under my skin. I push off the post, walking slowly down the sidewalk, scanning instinctively for anything out of place.

"Are you safe?" I ask, carefully. Not just out of sisterly concern—out of something deeper. A whisper in my gut that refuses to shut up.

"I'm doing everything I can to stay safe," she replies, but there's something in her voice—like she's not telling me everything. I know that tone. I use that tone.

I feel my phone vibrate in my hand, a second buzz low and sharp. A text coming through.

But I don't check it.

"I need you to promise me something," she says suddenly.

"What is it?"

"Be careful. Watch your back. Trust your instincts. Promise me, okay?"

"I promise," I say. And I mean it. But I also know the promise is only half a lie. I can't tell her about Cruz. About the meet. About Rule. About what happened last night. Because if I do, she'll try to protect me. And we both know how that ends.

There's a beat before I say, "And you promise me the same. Don't take unnecessary risks."

"I won't," she lies, just as smoothly.

We chat a few more minutes—lighter things, Organization gossip, some teasing about the new recruits. She makes me laugh, and for a few breaths, I remember what it's like to just be her sister. Not her shield. Not the one holding back a tidal wave of shit with a loaded gun and a bad attitude.

Eventually, we say our goodbyes.

I end the call and the street around me is quiet. Too quiet.

Then I check the message.

UNKNOWN

You only have yourself to blame, darling.

Unknown number. Yet another one. No name. But I don't need it to be signed off. It was Rule or Ruin—hard to say which this time. Not that it fucking matters.

I'm still staring at the screen when my phone starts to ring.

Eli.

I blink. That's... weird. I literally just left him ten minutes ago. He'd barely had time to chain-smoke his cigarette and bitch about surveillance logs.

I swipe to answer. "What now?"

There's noise in the background—Jensen's voice, clipped and sharp, talking to someone else on another line. Probably PD.

"You better get down to the Orchid, boss," Eli says, his voice low, tight.

I freeze.

"We've got a situation."

Chapter 18

Seanna

The scene in front of me is more than a 'situation'. It's a fucking nightmare come to life.

Blood pools like dark lakes across the polished floors, crimson splashes painting a grotesque masterpiece. Bodies litter the club, twisted and sprawled in unnatural positions—Cruz and his creepy lackeys reduced to nothing but broken puppets, their strings cut suddenly. No spray of bullets, no messy firefight. Each of them was executed quickly, efficiently, and methodically. Even the man at the door lies slumped over, surprise still etched permanently on his slack face.

But it's not the violence that freezes me in place, muscles taut and pulse hammering—it's the message scrawled across the wall in blood-red strokes near Cruz's corpse:

YOU WERE WARNED, DARLING

Rage detonates in my chest, molten and wild. I charge forward, instincts screaming to do something, to hunt, to punish—but Eli steps into my path before I get too far. His arms wrap around me, locking me in place.

"Seanna—stop," he says firmly. "You know we can't contaminate the scene, not now."

I struggle in his grip, chest heaving, throat raw with a scream of frustration I don't even realize I'm letting out. He holds firm, his voice low in my ear, steady even as my fury shreds through me like shrapnel.

"I know," he says quietly. "I know what this looks like. But we can't touch anything. Not yet."

I stop fighting. Not because I'm calm. Because I'm shaking too hard to stand.

Matteo arrives seconds later, his boots skidding slightly on a blood-slick tile. Jensen is already here too, his expression grim, scanning the carnage with professional detachment. Matteo takes one look at the scene, at me half-collapsed in Eli's grip, and his expression darkens. But before any of us can speak—

"Darling!"

The voice barks across the room. Ford.

He pushes through the side entrance, a group of agents close behind. He doesn't even glance at the bodies. His eyes are locked on me.

"You and your team. With me. Now."

We follow him out into the alley, silent and stunned.

Once we're out of earshot, Ford turns on us. "You're all on leave. Effective immediately."

"Excuse me?" I snap, stepping forward. "You can't just—"

"I can. And I am." He doesn't yell. He doesn't have to. His voice cuts like glass. "This entire op is now under internal review. Until I say otherwise, you're benched."

"Ford—"

"No. Not this time, Seanna." He points a finger at me. "You show up at the scene of a cartel massacre with a personal message in blood? You think I'm not pulling you off the board?"

I want to argue. To scream. To punch a wall until my hands break. But I don't.

Because I know the worst part isn't being pulled off the mission.

It's knowing *they* got here first.

And they did this for me.

Ford storms away, leaving the rest of us standing in stunned silence. Jensen breaks the quiet first, confusion etched deep into his features. "What the hell happened, Seanna? What does that message even mean?"

I shake my head slowly, exhaustion bleeding through my voice. "Don't worry about it. Just...go home. All of you. Take the break, don't do any digging or investigating—nothing about Reyes or Cruz. Everything needs to be legal, squeaky clean right now. We can't afford any mistakes."

Jensen steps closer, concern clear in his eyes. "Seanna, talk to us. You're not okay. We can see that."

I force a tight smile, my voice carefully even. "I'm fine. I'll be fine. I have a family member on holiday—some tropical island. I might just go join them."

He doesn't look convinced, but he nods anyway. Matteo and Jensen turn away, heading slowly down the alley, their steps heavy and uncertain. Eli hesitates, hanging back, eyes narrowed on mine.

"You were not fine in there," he says softly, voice laced with worry. "At all. Do we need to have someone shadowing you?"

I meet his gaze, swallowing the lump of frustration lodged in my throat. "No, Eli. I'll handle this. Just... trust me. Go home."

He studies me a beat longer, reluctant but finally nodding. "Alright. But call if you need anything. Don't try to carry this alone."

I wait until he's out of sight before letting the brave façade crumble away, sagging against the cold brick wall as the reality settles in—I can't risk them. Not if Rule and Ruin are willing to slaughter an entire club just to send me a message.

Eventually, I push off the wall, forcing myself upright, and walk to my car parked a short distance away. I sink into the driver's seat and sit there in silence, gripping the steering wheel tightly. Months chasing Reyes, countless hours of work, meticulous planning—all thrown aside because of two fucking stalkers.

Frustration and rage boil over, and I punch the steering wheel hard, feeling the sting radiate up my arm. Hot tears blur my vision, a brief moment of weakness that I attribute to exhaustion and raw, overwhelming anger.

Taking a deep breath, I steel myself, allowing the rage to build again, fierce and consuming like a tornado. Grabbing my phone, I furiously type a scathing message to the last number I received a text from:

You fucking assholes think you're untouchable? You're cowards hiding behind your twisted games. Come at me directly if you're brave enough—otherwise, stay the hell out of my way.

The message immediately comes back as undeliverable. My fingers fly over the screen as I try every other number I've received messages from, only to have each attempt bounce back undeliverable.

With a growl of frustration, I throw the phone toward the other side of the car, breathing deeply as I try to regain some semblance of calm. Suddenly, the phone rings, and I scramble to retrieve it from the passenger footwell, pulse hammering with expectation. Maybe it's those bastards.

But then I see it's Mom.

I force myself to exhale slowly, trying to calm myself as I answer the call.

"Hey, sweetheart," Mom's cheerful voice greets me, and I can hear Dad and Papa talking quietly in the background.

"Hey, Mom," I reply, forcing a smile into my voice. "How's Chicago?"

"Busy, as usual," she chuckles lightly. "How's your investigation coming along?"

"Fine," I lie smoothly, projecting ease I don't feel. "Just a few bumps. How about yours?"

"Progressing," she replies casually. "You know how it is, one step forward, two steps sideways."

Dad's voice suddenly joins, warm and steady. "Make sure you're looking after yourself, sweetheart. Are you eating properly?"

"Always," I promise, throat tightening with emotion. "You know I can handle myself."

"We know you can," Papa chimes in affectionately from the background. "But even superheroes need downtime, kid."

"I'll try to remember that," I reply softly, smiling despite the ache in my chest. "You guys stay safe too."

"We love you, sweetheart," Mom says gently. "Don't forget to take a break now and then."

"Love you too. All of you," I whisper, feeling the sting of tears again.

We end the call with soft "I love you's," and I let my head fall back against the seat, the ache of their absence sharper now than ever. Normally, solitude doesn't bother me—but right now, I miss my family fiercely.

With a heavy sigh, I start the car, heading home to my cabin. Maybe a hot shower can wash away some of this stress and drama, but deep down, I doubt it'll make a damn difference.

It's starting to get dark when I get home, and I'm relieved there aren't any twisted gifts waiting for me—because they'd be immediately tossed into the dense forest that backs onto my cabin.

Stepping inside, I slam the door behind me so hard it's a wonder the glass doesn't shatter. Rage and frustration coil tightly inside me, suffocating in their intensity. Shrugging off my jacket, I drop it on the couch, placing my gun alongside it with a heavy thud.

I pour myself a generous glass of whiskey, draining it in one swift, burning swallow without bothering to move from the spot. The warmth does little to ease the bitter fury still clawing at my insides.

With a sigh, I turn and walk down the hall toward my bedroom, hoping sleep might at least dull my anger.

But before I reach the door, someone steps smoothly from the shadows of my bedroom, filling the hallway ahead of me. Even in the fading twilight, I can clearly see the figure's full tactical gear and mask, obscuring every feature.

Rule.

Or maybe Ruin—I haven't seen him yet. I wouldn't put it past them to have matching sinister getups.

A fresh surge of fury floods my veins. I want to launch myself at him, to claw and fight—but I've already tasted Rule's strength. Instead, I pivot quickly, desperate to reach my gun on the couch. My escape route is abruptly blocked by a second figure stepping silently into the hallway, identical gear and mask cutting off any hope of retrieval.

Fuck.

One of them speaks, his voice distorted by a modulator, chilling and detached. "You left us with no choice."

I don't wait—I lunge forward, aiming a brutal strike at the one blocking my path to the couch. My fist connects solidly with his chest, but it's like hitting solid steel. He barely shifts, absorbing the blow easily. Undeterred, I throw a swift kick at his knee, forcing him to sidestep slightly.

The other one—the first who emerged from my bedroom—moves forward, attempting to restrain me from behind. I twist sharply, driving my elbow backward with all my strength. It catches him in the side, eliciting a distorted grunt. Encouraged, I follow up with another strike, this time higher, aiming for his masked face.

He deflects my strike effortlessly, grabbing my wrist and twisting it painfully, forcing a hiss of pain from my lips. The second figure moves in swiftly, catching my other arm before I can lash out again, trapping me securely between them. I fight against their grip, kicking and snarling like a feral animal, but they're too coordinated, too powerful.

"Let me fucking go!" I scream, rage bleeding into every word.

The figure in front steps back slightly, pulling something out from one of his many pockets. The other uses his free hand to hold my jaw in an almost bruising grip. When I see what's in his hand I thrash harder, panic edging into my movements. "No!"

It's too late—the spray feels cold in my nose, almost immediately dulling my senses, limbs turning sluggish against my will.

As darkness creeps into my vision, a distorted voice murmurs, almost soothingly, "This is for your own good, little storm."

Then everything fades into oblivion.

Chapter 19
Rule

I shouldn't be hard, but the moment Seanna decided to take us both on, throwing all of her might into a fight, I swear I have never been more turned on in my life. She is ruthless, a fighter through and through.

My pulse thrums violently, the blood in my veins rushing with the exquisite, chaotic thrill of possessing her fully at last. Seanna Darling. My thoughts coil tightly around her like barbed wire, prickling against my skin. I've always been drawn to darkness, but nothing compares to the perfect storm that is her.

I cradle her in my arms, savoring the warmth and the way her unconscious body molds perfectly against me. Her dark hair cascades softly over my armored forearm, her breathing slow and rhythmic from the sedative Every detail about her is etched into my mind—the curve of her lips, the faint scent of her perfume, the intoxicating darkness that clings to her like an invisible aura. A rush of possessive satisfaction hits me, a dark, twisted triumph whispering through my bones.

"Is everything clear?" I ask Ruin sharply, my voice modulated to an unrecognizable pitch through my mask, but barely disguising the obsessive tension simmering just beneath the surface. I stroke a gloved thumb softly over her cheek, possessiveness swelling through me as I memorize the softness of her skin.

"Almost," Ruin replies, his voice similarly distorted, focused as he moves through the cabin. He wipes down surfaces, packs clothes and personal items, making sure no evidence remains. I watch closely, meticulous as always, ensuring every detail is accounted for. Ruin and I have been friends for a long time—two lonely teens who stumbled across each other in the dark recesses of the web, kindred spirits finding companionship.

I shift Seanna slightly, her head resting against my shoulder now, her delicate frame seeming impossibly fragile in my embrace. But I know better. Beneath that beauty is pure, intoxicating danger. Ruin had found her first, a beautiful black-haired girl who gradually became the object of his dark fascination, discussed fervently during our countless late-night conversations. His obsession slowly bled into me until it became my own—twisted, unhinged, and completely inescapable.

My thoughts darken as I consider Ruin. I can't see his face beneath his mask, but I don't need to. I know him better than anyone. Beneath the friendly facade he presents to the world lies a ruthlessness far more chilling than even my own darkness. Ruin hides his true nature masterfully, the divide so profound that sometimes it's as if he's two entirely different people. I wonder how long it will take for our beautiful girl to see who he truly is—not just the face beneath the mask, but the cold, relentless darkness lurking beneath.

"We can't risk mistakes," I warn him, glancing down at Seanna again, consumed by the need to have her isolated, safe, and completely ours. "No loose ends, Ruin."

"You underestimate me," Ruin replies sharply. "Nothing is ever left to chance."

"What about communication?" I question. "Her job, friends, family—they'll start asking questions."

"She's officially on leave from the DEA," Ruin explains calmly, confidence resonating in his voice. It's a predator's calm, wrapped around him like a cloak. "She warned Max she might go deep undercover. He won't risk interfering. Her friends and team are manageable, but we'll watch them closely."

"And her family?" I continue, my voice tight with obsessive fury at the thought of interference. "Her sister calls regularly. We need to be careful."

"Hydessa will be our biggest concern," Ruin agrees coldly. "We'll keep Seanna compliant during their calls. She'll learn quickly—defiance won't help her here."

"She'll fight us at first," I remark, a dark smile curving beneath my mask.

Ruin chuckles softly, the sound all the more sinister due to the modulator. "Of course she will. The fight in her is what makes her so fucking irresistible. She'll understand soon enough that she's ours. Forever."

We lock gazes, the intensity of our shared obsession crackling like electricity in the air between us. The partnership we've forged through years of friendship is unbreakable, united now in our singular goal—Seanna Darling. She's our storm—unpredictable, fierce, completely unapologetic. She has no idea of the things we'll do now that we have her.

"We need to go," I finally say, my voice low and decisive. "The place is ready, secure. No one will find her there."

Ruin nods in agreement, watching as I shift Seanna gently, ensuring her comfort even in her unconscious state. We move swiftly, and I lead us out, glancing back briefly to confirm our flawless extraction. Once in the car, the drive passes quickly, each mile bringing us closer to our fortress—isolated, hidden from prying eyes.

My mind spins relentlessly with visions of how she'll react upon awakening. The rage, the fire, the struggle—I crave it all, deeply and obsessively. Each thought makes my heart race, desire intensifying until I'm painfully hard beneath my tactical gear. The thought of her fighting against us—against me—sets my nerves ablaze with possessive hunger. I crave her ferocity, the savage rebellion in her spirit. It's intoxicating.

This isn't about breaking her—not exactly. It's about keeping her safe, protecting her even from herself. I know she'll resist, she'll rage, and I relish it. Because her fight, her wild darkness, it's the drug I crave most. And now that I have her, I won't let go. Ever.

I look toward Ruin again, sensing the dangerous edge to his anticipation. "Soon," I assure quietly, my voice chilling even through modulation. "She'll understand she belongs with us."

"Forever," Ruin repeats fervently, glancing at Seanna's peaceful face one more time. "There's no going back now. Not for her, not for us."

She belongs to us now. Completely. Irrevocably. The world can burn for all I care, as long as she remains ours.

"I wouldn't have it any other way."

Chapter 20

Seanna

The moment consciousness slams back into me, rage ignites, hot and furious. I jerk violently, snarling in frustration as thick, unforgiving chains bite painfully into my wrists and ankles, anchored securely to the heavy wrought-iron bed frame beneath me. The bed itself is lavish yet oppressive—black silk sheets cool against my skin, plush velvet pillows in dark jewel tones—emeralds, rubies and sapphires—offering deceptive comfort. The luxury mocks me cruelly as I'm bound like some captured animal.

I force myself to breathe, my eyes scanning my surroundings meticulously. The room is windowless, cloaked entirely in deep shades of burgundy and charcoal—almost exactly matching my preferred style. Against one wall, a large dresser carved from rich mahogany stands imposingly, polished to a dark, reflective sheen, its surface bare except for a single, dim lamp casting faint, eerie illumination across the room. A tall, intricately designed wardrobe looms menacingly nearby, solid and dark like a sentinel guarding its secrets. Even the plush, black leather armchair tucked into the far corner adds to the room's oppressive elegance.

Clever assholes. Clearly, they've paid attention. That realization fuels my anger even more.

My gaze finally locks onto the shadowed figure slouched casually in the armchair. He blends seamlessly with his surroundings, nearly invisible save for the subtle reflective gleam of his glasses over his tactical mask. For a moment, he's so still I think he might be asleep. But then his head tilts slightly, assessing me silently like a coiled snake ready to strike.

"And which asshole are you?" I spit venomously, tugging uselessly against the restraints again, aching to get my hands around his throat.

He chuckles softly, a distorted, darkly amused sound that sends unwelcome, traitorous shivers crawling down my spine. I hate him instantly, hate the way his presence pulls at something twisted and primal inside me, blurring the line between pure hatred and an unsettling spark of lust.

"Ruin," he confirms, voice distorted by his mask yet resonating deep and disturbingly intimate.

"How are your ribs? Hope I cracked a few," I snarl back sharply, clinging fiercely to my defiance.

He leans forward slightly, moving with deliberate, predatory calm. "I'll live," he murmurs smoothly, utterly unbothered. "Though I'd gladly accept as many strikes as necessary if it means keeping you safe."

"Safe?" I scoff incredulously, rage flashing brighter in my eyes. "You ruined everything. You ruined my investigation. I didn't ask for your protection. Didn't want it. So don't pretend you're doing me any fucking favors."

He shifts again. "We warned you, Seanna. You refused to listen and wouldn't stop pushing toward Reyes, despite the warnings. This outcome is your own doing."

I sneer openly, lifting my chin defiantly. "Oh, please. You think chaining me up in some gothic horror fantasy is going to intimidate me into submission? You're even more pathetic than I thought.

Speaking of—are you ever gonna show your fucking face, or are you too chickenshit to let me see exactly who I'm dealing with?"

"We have our reasons," he replies evenly, maddeningly unfazed by my aggression.

"Coward," I hiss, twisting violently again, feeling the unforgiving bite of the restraints against skin. "Only cowards hide behind masks."

"Careful, little storm," he warns softly, danger curling in the deceptive gentleness of his tone. "Push me too far and you might not like the consequences."

"Trust me," I snarl, lips curling into a savage smirk, "whatever you have planned pales in comparison to what I'll do once I get free."

He rises slowly from the chair, shadows clinging possessively as he approaches the bed with confident steps. My pulse races wildly, adrenaline and rage blending dangerously with an inexplicable thrill.

"Promises, promises," he murmurs darkly, voice caressing my nerves like rough silk. "I can't wait to see you try."

I glare, fire blazing in my eyes. "Bring it on, asshole. You'll regret ever messing with me."

"No," he whispers, leaning close enough that his breath brushes against my skin through his mask, sending traitorous tingles down my spine. "You're exactly where you belong, Seanna. With us. Forever."

He lifts a gloved hand, knuckles tracing a gentle, possessive line along my jaw. My muscles tense instantly, instinctively flinching away from the unexpected intimacy. His thumb brushes across my lower lip, coaxing out an involuntary, furious snarl.

"I've wanted to taste these lips for so fucking long," he breathes huskily, the dark hunger in his voice unmistakable.

I lunge fiercely, teeth snapping, only for him to catch my jaw in a firm hold, his gloved fingers pressing into my skin almost hard enough to bruise. "There's my girl," he murmurs reverently. "Fierce, fiery—utterly captivating when you're like this."

His possessive hold, the way he speaks, it does something inside of me. And, though I will refuse it all the way to my grave, part of me doesn't want him to stop. Shameful heat blooms beneath my skin, and I curse inwardly as my body betrays me, responding to his dominance. Fury wars violently with the impulse to lean into the touch.

"You're going to be a good girl for us," he continues. "Eventually, perhaps, you'll earn some freedom—but first, you'll have to prove you deserve it. That you can *behave*."

My rage flares anew, but he merely brushes a final, possessive finger down my cheek.

"Rule will be back soon with food," he says casually, turning to stride toward the door as if we just had a pleasant chat.

I yank against the chains again, cursing him silently as he vanishes through the door, leaving me alone with my seething fury and conflicted emotions.

This isn't over. Not even close.

I don't know how much time passes. It could've been minutes, hours, or even days before the door opens again.

Rule enters quietly, still fully outfitted in his tactical gear, his face obscured by the same dark mask and reflective glasses. But the tray of food in his hands tells me who it is. He moves deliberately, setting the tray down on the bedside table before sitting next to me on the bed, the dark uniform adding an imposing presence despite his calm demeanor. I tense, glaring at him fiercely, ready to tear a chunk out of him.

"Don't bite," he warns gently, amusement in his voice.

I'm tempted, but my stomach growls embarrassingly loud at the scent of the food he brought, betraying my need. Rule lifts a taco—Mexican fish tacos, exactly the kind I love but haven't had in ages. Proof they've watched me far longer than I suspected.

He carefully brings the food to my mouth, feeding me slowly. Begrudgingly, I play along, recalling Ruin's mention of freedom if I behave. *I'll fucking behave until I earn enough slack to stab them.*

"When I first saw you," Rule says softly, "I knew you were special. Your darkness doesn't scare us, Seanna. It's what makes you perfect for us."

"Save the poetry," I snap, glaring up at him.

He nods indulgently, undeterred. "We had to stop you because Reyes was onto you. He'd begun sniffing you out. We couldn't risk losing you to that psycho."

As he feeds me the last bite of the first taco, his gloved fingers brush softly across my lips. The contact triggers a vivid memory from the night before—those same fingers, slick with my own arousal, shoved possessively into my mouth. My cheeks flush hotly, and I quickly look away, embarrassed by my body's treacherous reaction. Rule chuckles knowingly, lifting those same gloved fingers. He tilts his head down before slowly sliding the fabric aside just enough to lick off the taco remnants without me seeing any details of his face. Heat spikes through me, shame and unwanted desire warring fiercely.

"Careful, sweetheart," he whispers, and I can hear the desire even in his modulated voice. "You keep thinking like that, and I won't be able to behave myself."

A brief, dangerous moment flashes through me, and I seriously wonder if I've lost the fucking plot entirely. For just a heartbeat, I don't want him to behave. The realization hits hard, twisting my stomach with shameful desire. He must see the turmoil flickering across my face because he hums.

"Interesting," he murmurs quietly, his tone richly amused and undeniably provocative.

I narrow my eyes, regaining some of my fierce composure. "Don't flatter yourself," I hiss, attempting to mask my internal chaos.

Rule chuckles, low and soft, as he picks up another taco, slowly feeding it to me with care. "You can fight this all you want, Seanna," he says gently, almost soothingly. "But we both know the truth. You're drawn to this—drawn to us—because deep down, your darkness matches ours."

"You're delusional," I mutter bitterly, glaring despite my racing heart.

"Maybe," he concedes easily, his voice still calm and even. "But tell me, how long have you struggled to find someone who truly sees you? Who isn't afraid of the storm inside you? We don't want to tame it—we want to dance in it with you."

I remain stubbornly silent, hating how his words resonate within me. His gloved fingers linger lightly against my lips again as he feeds me the final bite, sending another treacherous jolt of heat through me.

"Think about it," he continues. "We knew exactly how special you were from the first moment we laid eyes on you. We knew we had to protect you—from yourself, from Reyes, from everyone else who would try to dull your edges."

"And chaining me to a bed was your brilliant solution?" I snap, clinging desperately to my anger.

"For now," he says calmly, unwavering. "Until you can see the bigger picture. Until you realize you're safer here than you've ever been out there."

He picks up the empty tray and slowly rises to his feet, towering over me in his intimidating tactical gear. "Rest now, Seanna. You'll need your strength."

"Go to hell," I spit defiantly.

"Sleep tight, little storm," he murmurs, completely unfazed as he strides confidently to the door, closing it firmly behind him and leaving me alone once again with my conflicted thoughts and seething fury.

Silence settles around me again, thick and suffocating. I stare up at the ceiling, the dim lighting painting faint shadows that shift like ghosts along the walls. My body still buzzes from the heat Rule stirred in me—an unwelcome reminder of how easily they can manipulate my responses, how deep they've already gotten under my skin.

What the hell is wrong with me? I'm supposed to be stronger than this. Sharper. Colder. I've survived things that would break most people, clawed my way up in a world that doesn't have patience for weakness. And yet here I am, chained to a bed, humiliated by my own traitorous body, and struggling not to replay the way his fingers brushed my lips—or how I didn't pull away fast enough.

The worst part is that they know. *They fucking know.* Every little flinch, every flush of heat, every second my silence lingers too long—they see it all. They feed off it.

I want to scream. I want to break something. I want my gun, my freedom, my goddamn control back. But most of all, I want revenge. And not the kind that's clean or noble. I want it bloody and brutal. I want them to regret ever thinking they could cage me like some pet.

But I have to be smart. I have to wait. Play their game. Pretend.

Let them think I'm unraveling.

Let them believe they're winning.

Because the moment they slip, the moment one of them underestimates just how far I'm willing to go—I'll make them bleed.

And I'll smile while I do it.

Chapter 21
Seanna

I wake slowly, the edges of sleep peeling back like scabs over a wound—stinging and raw. The restraints dig gently into my wrists and ankles, soft enough to avoid bruising, but firm enough that there's no mistaking the intent behind them.

Same bed. Same silent room. Same fucking sense of being watched.

Because one of them is there—again.

Seated in the same damn armchair tucked into the shadows like he owns the air I breathe. Still as a statue, the low golden light casting sharp lines across the mask covering his face. Just... watching.

I blink hard, jaw tight. "What, is this your new kink? Watching me sleep like a creep in a thriller film?"

No response. Not right away. Just the faint tilt of his head. The shift in his shoulders. Unbothered.

I scoff and let my voice go syrupy-sweet and venom-laced. "Hell, if you're going to be a total freak about it, you may as well crawl in and do whatever the fuck you want to me."

His modulated voice breaks the silence like warm molasses over a knife. Smooth. Sweet. And still so wrong.

"Don't tempt me with things you might regret, little storm."

Ruin.

The rhythm of the voice is too languid to be Rule's. There's a softness to him—honey dipped in something darker. A man who will lull you with charm while planning exactly how he wants to *ruin* you.

I narrow my eyes, voice dry. "So what's the plan now? Keep me tied up until Stockholm Syndrome kicks in?"

He doesn't answer. Just sits there, fingertips steepled like he's contemplating God. Or death. Or me.

"I've got a job," I say flatly, meeting the mask head-on. "One that's going to start asking questions if I don't show."

He finally speaks again, and the calm in his voice makes me want to scream. "Your case was put on hold. After Cruz and his men ended up very, very dead. Reyes is untouchable again, and you? You're benched."

A silence coils between us, sharp and heavy.

"You enjoyed that," I mutter, fury building behind my eyes. "All those men—slaughtered in the name of your little message to me."

Ruin stands slowly, like liquid uncoiling into a weapon. "That was Rule," he says, as if it's a perfectly reasonable explanation. "You didn't do what was asked. You didn't follow his rules. He told you that you would regret going to that meeting."

I let out a sharp laugh. "One guy took out a club full of cartel soldiers? Right. Sure. Sounds legit."

He chuckles. "You don't have to believe it. But you really should be careful how far you push us. You're clever, Seanna. But even clever things break."

He steps toward the bed, slow and deliberate, his boots silent against the floorboards. I can feel the shift in air pressure as he approaches—like the room holds its breath for him.

"If you behave," he says, voice low, "if you learn how to be good for us, then we'll let you off your leash. Give you more freedom."

I narrow my eyes. "Right. That's what this is about, huh? Breaking me down. Making me less of a threat. Less violent. More manageable."

He stops at the end of the bed, head tilting in that unnervingly calm way of his.

"No," he says simply. "It's the opposite."

My breath catches.

"We don't want to change you," he continues, voice like velvet over iron. "Your rage. Your darkness. That hunger to dismantle the world? It's one of the best things about you."

He leans in slightly, his tone dipping into something quieter. Sharper.

"Your soul matches ours, Seanna. In ways you haven't even begun to understand."

I let out a derisive snort. "You really think you have souls?"

"As much as you do." His answer is instant. Unshaken. "And make no mistake—whatever scraps of soul exist between us? They belong to each other. So I'm going to need you to not try to kill either of us for trying to protect you."

The words settle like smoke in the space between us, thick and cloying. I should be recoiling, spitting venom, demanding space—but all I can do is stare, the air stretching taut around my ribs.

I laugh, sharp and bitter. "That's the most romantic thing I've ever heard from a psychopath."

He simply shrugs. "Truth rarely sounds pretty."

I let the silence hang, dragging a breath through clenched teeth as the fury starts to rise again, giving me something solid to hold on to.

I glare, unmoved. "So you don't give a fuck if I want to murder half the world, but suddenly you're concerned I might want to kill *you*?"

His chuckle is smooth and infuriating. "A little murder in your eyes is fine. Fun even. But we need your hands to stay off the weapons. Just for now."

"Great," I snarl. "And what if I just want to piss in peace? Can the hostage at least have bathroom privileges?"

There's a beat of silence.

Then he laughs. Softly at first. Then deeper. Richer.

"I was wondering when you'd bring that up," he says, stepping to the side of the bed. "But you'll have to ask nicely."

I raise a brow. "Are you kidding me right now?"

"Nope." He crosses his arms. "Ask. Sweetly."

I stare him down, teeth gritted. "Can I *please* be allowed to go to the fucking toilet before I decorate this mattress?"

He hums in mock consideration, then steps even closer. One gloved finger trails along my jaw, tapping my bottom lip twice.

"You can do better than that, darling."

I exhale through my nose. Pride shatters like glass in my throat.

"Please," I grind out, trying to force the anger and hatred not to be as transparent in my voice, making it smoother. "May I be allowed to relieve myself like a proper, well-behaved captive?"

He nods, seemingly satisfied. "Much better."

He moves slowly, unlocking the ankle restraints with care—like I'm something fragile he might accidentally shatter. One wrist next, and before I can think about trying anything, his hand wraps tight around mine. Not enough to bruise. Just enough to *remind*.

The strength in his grip is terrifying. Calm. Unshakable.

Then, with his body angled slightly over mine, he leans across and unfastens the final restraint, freeing me. But I don't move. My muscles are too taut, my breath too shallow.

He pulls me upright gently, helping me sit and then stand. His body towers over mine—taller, broader—and he lets the moment hang there, like he's daring me to try something.

I don't.

He turns, walking to the opposite wall and a door I didn't see before. A click sounds, then the door slides open, revealing a hidden bathroom tucked into the corner of the room. Rich, dark marble gleams under recessed lighting. There's a sleek rainfall shower. A deep soaking tub. And, thank fuck, a toilet.

All of it windowless. Of course.

I narrow my eyes at him as I walk into the room. "You *really* went all out for your hostage suite."

He chuckles softly. "Only the best for our Darling."

I shoot him a glare and point to the door. "Out."

He chuckles softly behind the mask and backs out, sliding the door shut behind him.

I move fast. Relieve myself. Scrub my hands. Then I start searching the place like my life depends on it.

Which it might.

The shelves are fully stocked. Some products are mine—stolen from my home. Others are new, unopened, but all my favorite brands. The kind of attention to detail that makes my blood boil.

But one jar catches my eye—heavy glass, expensive, thick. I grab it and test the weight in my hand. Solid. That'll do.

I slide the door open, expecting him to be right outside.

He's not.

Instead, he's back by the bed, his back turned slightly as he smooths out the sheets like he's preparing a fucking hotel room.

Perfect.

I throw the jar with all the force I have. It cuts through the air in a clean arc.

And he *catches it*.

Without completely turning. Without flinching.

The fucker catches it mid-air like it was a feather instead of a weapon.

He tosses it once, twice in his hand, then places it carefully on the nightstand.

I charge him, hoping brute force and rage will be enough.

I'm fast. I'm fueled by adrenaline. But he's faster.

He spins and grabs me mid-run, lifting and slamming me onto the bed with terrifying force. The breath explodes from my lungs. My hands reach for his mask, nails digging—but he catches both wrists, pressing them down against the mattress.

I snarl, thrashing beneath him. He doesn't move. Not an inch.

Worse—he *laughs*. Low. Amused. Dark.

"Still so full of fire," he murmurs, leaning closer. "It's no wonder we can't stay away from you."

I try to buck my hips up, to throw him off. All I succeed in doing is making us grind together.

And *that's* when I feel it.

Heavy. Thick.

He's hard.

My defiance—my fight—it's *turning him on*.

His breath brushes my cheek as he lowers his head.

His body is a cage around mine—solid arms bracketing my head, thighs pressing into mine, heat radiating off him like a second skin.

I writhe beneath him, equal parts fury and something far more dangerous threading through my veins.

"You're enjoying this," I hiss, my voice ragged.

He dips closer. I can't see his eyes behind the mask, but I can feel them—*feel* them devouring me like they already own every breath I take.

"Aren't you?"

I bare my teeth in something that's not even close to a smile. "Oh, totally. Nothing gets me wetter than being manhandled by a masked lunatic. *I'd rather bleed out.*"

He laughs—low, indulgent, and far too pleased. "Let's revisit this blood kink later, little storm. We haven't even gotten to the good parts."

I lunge again, trying to twist free. But he doesn't budge. With little effort, he shifts my wrists so that both are pinned beneath one of his hands, pressed hard against the mattress above my head. The leather of his glove digs lightly into my skin, reminding me how easy it is for him to hold me there.

His free hand trails down my arm, until it reaches my chest. He presses his palm flat just above the swell of my breasts, the contact scorching through the thin fabric of my shirt.

"You keep fighting," he murmurs, voice like silk wrapped around a dagger. "But your body—your breath—it betrays you."

"I *hate* you," I spit, jerking beneath him.

"Good." His gloved fingers slide lower, teasing the edge of my shirt. "Hate keeps things interesting."

His hand grazes the curve of my breast before slipping under my shirt—glove against skin. I jerk, not from fear, but from how *good* it feels. *God, I hate that it feels good.*

His head dips closer, voice low, coaxing. "Rule told me how you responded when he had you like this. All teeth and fury... until your hips started chasing his. You fought him too—until your moans started drowning out your threats."

I freeze. Rage and humiliation crackle down my spine like a live wire.

"He said it turned you on," Ruin continues smoothly, as though discussing the weather. "That even while you were snarling, your thighs were trembling. Your breath caught every time he touched you."

He leans down, and I feel the warmth of his words slip across my skin. "You can keep fighting us if you want. But your body already knows it belongs to us. It's your mind that needs to catch up."

I inhale sharply, chest rising against his.

"Stop trying to deny what you crave," he adds, voice like poison dipped in a glass of honey. "Because eventually, we'll make you beg for it."

And then he shifts.

Not away—*deeper*.

His thigh slips between mine, pinning me open, grinding into the heat that's already begun to pulse traitorously between my legs. My breath stutters.

"Tell me to stop," he says, soft but firm. "And I will."

I glare up at him, lips curled in defiance. "Go to hell."

He leans in, voice brushing the shell of my ear. "That's not a *no*, little storm."

I hate him. I hate him so fucking much.

So why the hell am I soaking through my panties?

And then his mask presses to my throat, like he wants to press his lips there to where my pulse thunders beneath the surface. Just a whisper of heat and breath against skin, but I go still beneath it.

"You want me to stop?" he asks, voice dipped in that honeyed warning. "Say it."

I don't.

Not because I want this.

But because I *don't know* what I want anymore.

He laughs again. Darker this time. He shifts, the thick length of his cock grinding harder against my thigh through the layers between us. It's punishment and promise in one movement, and my breath shudders out in response.

"I could fuck you right here," he says. "Right now. And you'd hate yourself for loving it."

His fingers slide beneath the waistband of my panties, slow and deliberate. He drags them in just a single stroke against my slit. Testing. Savoring.

"You'd scream for me, little storm," he whispers, breath grazing the shell of my ear. "Not for mercy. For *more*."

And the worst part?

He's not wrong.

My body is melting beneath his grip. Burning alive.

It reacts before my brain can catch up—arching, aching, alive under him. And then—just like that—he withdraws, sliding off me in one fluid movement, leaving behind a vacuum of heat and tension.

I sit up too quickly, blood pounding in my ears, fury burning hotter than ever.

He reaches for where the restraints hang and lifts the wrist cuff he'd released earlier. "You're not ready yet," he says simply, like he's explaining something to a child. "You think you are, but your temper still owns you."

"I'm not staying here," I snap, yanking my arm out of reach.

He catches it easily anyway and secures the cuff back around my wrist. Then the other. Not harsh. Not fast. But with finality.

When he steps back, I notice something different.

The chains have been adjusted. A little longer. A little more slack in the links connecting to the headboard. Just enough that I could shift and move freely within the bed—but not enough to make it anywhere beyond that.

My ankles are left free.

"How generous," I mutter, flexing my fingers.

He tilts his head, the movement slow and unreadable. "Consider it an incentive," he says smoothly. "You behave, we reward. Simple. You've earned a little slack—whether you meant to or not."

Satisfied I'm secured once more, he nods once.

"Rule will be back shortly," he tells me. "With food."

I say nothing.

I don't thank him. I don't curse him.

I just lay back slowly, eyes locked on him, watching as he leaves again and closes the door behind him.

The soft click echoes louder than it should.

I stare at the ceiling, wrists aching slightly from the tension, my legs now free. It's not enough to run. Just enough to remind me I can move.

I don't know if it's mercy. Or a mind game. I don't know why it feels like both.

And I *hate* that I'm starting to wonder which one I want it to be.

Chapter 22

Seanna

The oppressive silence shatters when the door swings open again, and my hands clench in irritation as Rule strides casually into the room. Despite the begrudging slack Ruin granted in the chains binding my wrists to the wrought-iron headboard—enough to sit cross-legged and properly glare at my captor—I remain pissed off.

"Wow, room service in a kidnapping?" I mock sweetly, watching him approach with a coffee cup and a paper bag. "How considerate."

Rule chuckles, low and infuriatingly amused. "Consider it a peace offering. We both know how desperately you cling to your caffeine addiction."

I snort, giving the chains a pointed rattle. "Peace offering? You spelled manipulation wrong."

He waves the coffee just within my reach, clearly enjoying my irritation. "Here you go."

Rolling my eyes, I snatch the cup and take a sip, immediately grimacing at the cold liquid. "Seriously? Cold coffee? Are budget cuts hitting kidnappers now too? You can't afford heating?"

He laughs, annoyingly smug. "Did you honestly think we'd trust you with something hot? Give us some credit."

"Oh, don't worry," I snap back, slamming the cup onto the bedside table. "The lack of credit is entirely deliberate."

My attention flickers involuntarily toward the paper bag, and despite my blazing irritation, the familiar scent already has my mouth watering. Cherry cream cheese pastries, my favorite—*damn him straight to hell.*

"Thought I'd tempt you into having a civil conversation," Rule says, deliberately pulling one pastry from the bag and holding it just beyond my immediate reach.

"Bribery is beneath even you," I sneer, though my stomach tightens traitorously. I could hold out, we are trained for situations like this. I could go days without food, refusing every inch they grant out of bitterness, but there is a level of manipulation to this that my training doesn't account for.

"Yet you're clearly tempted," he counters smugly, placing the pastry onto a napkin and sliding it only a fraction toward me yet still out of reach. "Here's the deal. Agree to a temporary truce until after your sister's next call—and the pastries are yours."

My eyes narrow sharply, suspicion and temptation warring inside me. "My sister isn't calling until tomorrow."

"Precisely," he confirms smoothly. "One day. One peaceful day. No fighting, no biting remarks—well, fewer biting remarks—and you get these little indulgences."

"Maybe I don't feel like making a deal," I taunt, arching an eyebrow challengingly.

"In that case," Rule replies casually, picking up the pastry again and moving as if to leave, "perhaps I'll just go make you porridge instead. And I'm sure I can change the future meals to things you like as much as porridge. We know them all."

My lip curls in disgust at the thought, pride clashing with cravings. "Fine," I relent grudgingly. "But once that call comes through, all bets are off."

"Understood," he murmurs, setting the pastry down again and settling onto the end of the bed. "So, are we actually capable of having a conversation, or should I brace for impact?"

I bite back a furious retort, instead focusing pointedly on the pastry, taking a bite that immediately melts on my tongue. A traitorous moan slips past my lips before I can contain it, and I notice Rule shifting subtly. Flustered, I glare at him defensively. "Don't get any ideas. It's just a pastry."

"Clearly," he replies, voice calm but somehow more amused.

I watch him carefully, silently daring him to speak first. The quiet stretches uncomfortably between us as I slowly take bites of the pastry, the taste flooding my senses. *Dammit, these things are heavenly.* When the first pastry is gone he hands me the other. Rule's silence is starting to grate on me, so naturally, I break it first.

"So, is this the part where we braid each other's hair and gossip? Because I forgot my glittery nail polish," I drawl sarcastically, licking a stray cherry glaze off my thumb.

Rule shifts again, the creak of the bed frame a satisfying reminder that my sass is at least hitting some kind of nerve.

"Careful, little storm. Keep it up and I'll think you're starting to like our quality time."

I scoff loudly, leaning forward just enough for the chains to clink pointedly. "You're mistaking my *tolerance* for enjoyment. Don't flatter yourself."

"Wouldn't dream of it," he replies, voice calm, infuriatingly unbothered. "Let's try a topic that won't incite violence. How long have you had a weakness for cherries?"

I narrow my eyes suspiciously, irritation warring with honesty. "Longer than I've had a weakness for putting assholes like you behind bars."

"Ah," he remarks, voice dripping with smug amusement. "A life-long indulgence then."

"You're skating dangerously close to losing the pastry privilege," I warn sharply, trying to stifle the venom in my voice just enough to uphold our temporary truce.

Rule seems completely undeterred, chuckling softly. "Relax. Consider this me learning about the woman beneath the DEA badge and murderous glare."

I laugh sharply, humorlessly. "Please. You kidnapped me. Forgive me if I don't feel like exchanging life stories."

There's silence for a moment, tension hanging heavily in the air before he speaks again. "Fair enough. But perhaps we can at least agree that conversations don't always have to end with threats?"

"Careful," I retort, taking another bite of pastry. "You're talking to someone who's made threats an art form. But for the sake of pastry, I'll humor you. What exactly did you expect—Stockholm syndrome in under 48 hours?"

He gives a short laugh, deep and annoyingly pleasant. "Even I'm not that ambitious. But cooperation, maybe? Even temporary civility could go a long way."

Another bite, another delicious wave hitting my tastebuds, and I let slip another entirely involuntary moan—*fuck, these pastries are too good*. The bedframe creaks again, and I barely resist smirking.

"It's just pastry, remember?" he remarks casually, repeating my earlier line with a hint of teasing.

I swallow hard, eyes narrowing. "The truce covers biting comments, but not outright mocking."

He chuckles again, relaxed despite my icy tone. "Duly noted."

We sit in silence a moment longer, my pastry rapidly disappearing, much to my dismay. Finally, I give a sigh of resignation. "Fine, civil topic it is. How do you even know about these pastries? Did you stalk my bakery, too?"

Rule's voice softens just enough to sound genuinely thoughtful. "We pay attention, little storm. You're worth studying."

The sincerity in his tone startles me slightly, making me pause. I cover it quickly with another bite, but curiosity wins out. "Why me? What exactly makes me 'worth studying'?"

"You really can't see it?" he counters quietly, leaning slightly forward. "You walk through chaos like you own it. You're fearless, angry, uncontainable. It's *intoxicating*."

I blink, temporarily caught off guard, then recover quickly. "That almost sounded like admiration. Dangerous territory, Rule."

"Maybe," he admits calmly. "But danger is half the appeal, wouldn't you say?"

I huff softly, shifting in my chains, deliberately not answering. Instead, I savor the final bite of pastry. "I guess we'll see."

"Indeed we will," he murmurs, his voice heavy with arrogant confidence as he settles back onto the bed, dangerously close.

I roll my eyes, deliberately dragging my tongue slowly across my fingers, savoring the last of the cherry glaze. My gaze locked onto his masked face, daring him to react. Before I can even finish my intentional tease, Rule moves faster than I anticipated, lunging forward aggressively to grab my wrists. He presses them together, securing them both in one of his, his grip tight and unyielding.

My breath hitches as his rough, gloved thumb forcefully drags along my slick fingertip, sending a spike of heat straight down my spine. He leans into me, close enough that his tactical mask brushes my cheekbone, cool and unnervingly intimate.

"You keep tongue-fucking those fingers, little storm, and I'm going to start wondering if you're begging me to put something else in your mouth," he rasps, voice dripping with dark promise.

My heart pounds traitorously at his blunt, heated words, but I force myself to sneer. "Careful, Rule. Your desperation is showing. Who knew a pastry could unravel you so quickly?"

His hand tightens around my wrists, pressing them roughly back against the headboard, chains clinking softly as tension coils tighter between us. "Desperate?" he growls softly, amusement threaded with danger. "You're the one moaning like you're about to climax over a pastry. Keep it up, and I'll make sure your next moan is my name."

"Bold assumption," I retort breathlessly, narrowing my eyes even as my pulse betrays me. "But I've had better offers."

He chuckles darkly, leaning in even closer, his mask grazing the sensitive skin beneath my jaw. "Lie to yourself all you want, Seanna. Your body tells the truth."

I laugh bitterly, trying and failing to pull away from his grip. "You're still delusional I see."

"And you're a terrible liar," he counters, his free hand sliding down to my thigh, the leather of his glove scorching hot against my skin. "Or did you really think I couldn't see how much you enjoyed teasing me?"

My voice shakes slightly as I fight to maintain control. "Maybe I just enjoy seeing you squirm."

"Interesting choice of words," he murmurs, voice impossibly deep, almost hypnotic. His hand drifts higher, dangerously close to where my body is already traitorously responding. "Because squirming is exactly what you're going to be doing soon if you keep pushing."

I swallow hard, fighting the heat rising to my cheeks, the ache building between my thighs. "You talk a big game, Rule. But so far, all you've given me is cold coffee and pastries."

His low, wicked laughter vibrates against my throat. "Oh, darling, if you're craving something hotter, all you have to do is *beg*."

"I'd rather *bite*," I snarl, though my breath betrays how much his touch is affecting me.

"I'm counting on it," he responds smoothly, drawing back just enough to look into my face through his dark lenses. His thumb brushes deliberately over my inner thigh, dragging dangerously close to where I desperately want him and absolutely shouldn't. "Though you might find I bite back even harder."

My head spins, but pride keeps me defiant. "Big talk for a man hiding behind a mask."

"You want the mask off, Seanna?" he taunts, voice dripping with smug dominance. "Earn it."

"And here I thought kidnapping was your twisted form of foreplay," I fire back, trying and failing to steady my racing heart.

He chuckles, his hand slowly sliding higher again, this time pressing between my thighs, his leather-clad fingers firm and bold through the fabric of my panties.

"Oh, darling, you haven't even begun to see twisted yet," he murmurs, his voice dripping with dark intent as he presses harder, dragging a soft, involuntary gasp from my throat.

My pulse surges, heart hammering as I struggle to hold onto my defiance. "You're bluffing," I breathe, my voice betraying the tremor I'm fighting so hard to hide.

He leans even closer, the cold of his mask ghosting across my jaw as his fingers slowly, maddeningly circle the spot that's rapidly becoming my undoing. "Am I?" he rasps, voice low, arrogant. "Or maybe I've already figured you out, little storm. Maybe I know exactly what fantasies keep you awake at night."

My cheeks burn with furious embarrassment even as my hips shift instinctively against his touch. "You don't know shit about what I want," I bite out, desperately grasping onto anger as a lifeline.

"Oh no?" He increases the pressure just enough to have me inhaling sharply, pulse stuttering traitorously. "Then tell me—what is it that gets you off when you're alone in the dark, hmm? What depraved little fantasies make you squirm? What were you thinking during those pretty little shows you put on for us?"

"Go fuck yourself," I hiss, though the words come out breathless and weak, sounding more like a plea than a protest.

He laughs softly, clearly enjoying my struggle. "Not a bad suggestion, but I'd rather fuck *you*. Better yet, I'd rather you admit what you secretly crave."

My defiance surges, but his teasing fingers steal my breath, robbing me of any coherent retort. His touch slows to a torturous pace, lingering right on the brink of pleasure, keeping me aching and desperate. He leans forward again, the cool mask brushing against the hot sensitive skin under my jaw as he takes a deep breath, smelling me.

"Maybe it's something forbidden," he whispers against my throat, gloved fingertips pressing insistently, coaxing my hips to roll involuntarily against him. "Something dark and twisted—like waking up already being fucked, helpless and trapped beneath someone powerful enough to take exactly what he wants. Maybe that's what had you turned on when I woke you the other night. Why you keep pushing us into this predicament right here..."

My breath catches audibly, betraying me completely, heat flushing my skin from head to toe. *Fuck.*

He chuckles triumphantly, stroking more deliberately, confident in his control. "There it is," he murmurs wickedly, voice dripping with satisfaction. "Tell me I'm wrong, Seanna. Tell me you haven't imagined being taken, fucked while you're asleep—waking up with someone already deep inside you, taking you hard, using you exactly as he pleases."

I close my eyes, mortification and desire twisting violently inside me. "Stop," I manage weakly, even though every nerve ending in my traitorous body begs for more.

"Stop?" he echoes mockingly, his tone sugary sweet, his fingers slowing to a torturously teasing pace again, leaving me dangerously close to breaking. "But you're practically begging for it. So tell me the truth—have you ever touched yourself to that fantasy? Imagined surrendering all control, waking up with my cock already inside you, fucking you awake until you're screaming?"

My pulse is wild, betraying any shred of denial I have left. His hand is relentless, fingertips pressing and circling, coaxing out my buried secrets.

"Damn you," I whisper, voice barely audible as I turn my head away, cheeks burning. "Yes."

"Yes, what?" He demands gently, his voice velvet-edged steel, utterly commanding as his fingers slide purposefully lower, expertly building my pleasure. "Say it clearly, Seanna. Tell me exactly what you fantasize about."

I swallow hard, pride finally collapsing beneath his relentless, intoxicating touch. "Yes," I admit breathlessly, embarrassment fighting against the fierce arousal. "I've thought about it—being taken while asleep. Helpless. Used."

"Good fucking girl," he purrs darkly, approval thick in his voice. His fingers withdraw abruptly, leaving me cruelly bereft and trembling. I nearly sob with frustration as he rises to his feet.

"Try to behave yourself today, little storm," he murmurs, smug satisfaction dripping from every word. "I'll be thinking about that fantasy all morning."

The door clicks shut behind him, and I slump against the headboard, heart pounding, body trembling, fury and desperate arousal warring violently within me.

There's no point pretending I'll be able to think clearly now—not with the feel of him still clinging to my skin, and the sick, spiraling realization that a part of me *wants* him to make good on every twisted promise he's made.

Chapter 23

Seanna

Time's a vindictive little bitch when you're chained to a bed with nothing but your own traitorous thoughts for company. Every second stretches and warps like melted taffy—sticky, slow, and so fucking smug about it. I have no idea how long it's been since Rule left me dripping, throbbing, and absolutely goddamn furious. Ten minutes? Ten years? I wouldn't know the difference.

All I know is I'm done.

The silence is deafening. Not peaceful. Not meditative. Just loud in the way only silence can be—echoing every shaky breath I try to steady, amplifying every heartbeat that thuds like a countdown to some inevitable, soul-fucking unraveling.

I yank at the restraints again. Just to hear them rattle. Just to remind myself I'm still *here*, still capable of resistance, even if the chains don't give. I've already counted the links on both sides—fourteen on the left, thirteen on the right. Don't think I haven't noticed the asymmetry. I have. And it pisses me off.

I trace the same small circle on the sheet with my toe like a deranged ballerina on a leash. It's pathetic, but it's movement. Any movement, at this point, feels like defiance.

I should be hunting Reyes right now. I should be on the warpath, dragging that cartel bastard out of whatever snake hole he's hiding in and watching the light drain from his eyes as I make him pay for every name on my list.

But instead?

Instead, I'm here.

Trapped in some fucked-up five-star kidnapping fantasy while two masked lunatics take turns feeding me, edging me, and rewiring my brain like I'm their favorite science experiment with a praise kink.

And the worst part?

It's *working*.

This isn't just kidnapping.

It's fucking *curated captivity*.

A psychological house of mirrors where I'm not just the prisoner—I'm the obsession. The spectacle. The centerpiece.

Every moment feels *intentional*. Every interaction is precision-cut to fit between my ribs and push. Ruin talks like he invented seduction—his words sweet, slow, soaked in molasses and menace. Every syllable feels like a velvet ribbon meant to wrap around my throat and tighten. And Rule? Rule is the opposite. Blunt. Practical. But under that steel edge is a dangerous warmth. The kind of heat that makes you lean closer before you realize the stove is on fire. The kind of man who could break your bones—and then carry you to bed and fuck the pain out of you.

God help me, I must have a kink for masked psychopaths.

Because despite the fact that I want to claw their eyes out, I can't stop reacting. Can't stop *feeling*. Every time they walk into the room, the air changes. My body betrays me. And my mouth? My mouth runs hot and fast, because if I don't spit fire, I might start begging.

I fucking hate them.

I hate that I'm still here. I hate that I'm starting to expect and anticipate the routine—food, chains, emotional whiplash, psychological chess, more chains, then more food and a fresh new round of mindfuckery.

And even worse still?

I hate that a small, twisted part of me is *waiting* for it.

For *them*.

Waiting to hear that door click open. Waiting to see who walks in. Waiting for the next touch, the next taunt, the next round of whatever-the-fuck-this-is. Like some pathetic little lamb, licking her wounds and hoping her wolves come back hungry.

A sick, shadowy part of me wants to know what happens next—not so I can escape, but because I *need* to know. What will they do? What will they say? Will it be Ruin whispering sins in my ear like scripture? Or Rule, rough and deliberate, dragging truths out of me I don't even want to admit to myself?

What does that say about me?

No. I already know what it says. It says maybe I'm just as fucked-up as they are. That maybe all the rage and fire I've used to keep the world at bay... wasn't armor. Maybe it was bait. And now that I've lost every ounce of control, every scrap of power, I'm *cracking*. Not broken. Not yet. But the fractures are spiderwebbing under the surface, and I can feel every single one with every breath I take.

I glance at the door again. I don't mean to. It's a reflex now. A nervous tic. I've started watching it the way animals watch the sky before a storm.

Because I know what comes when it opens.

Everything *shifts*.

The air thickens. My blood kicks up. My body betrays me in the worst, most humiliating ways—every single goddamn time.

I've been edged, fed, restrained, and taunted like some pampered pet who can't decide if she wants to bite or beg. And now I'm alone in this silence, hyper-aware of every place my skin aches. Every throb of need they left me with. Every heartbeat that ticks by without answers or freedom or even the dignity of choice.

I yank the chains again. Harder. Not to escape. Just to *feel* the resistance. To remind myself I'm still in this body. Still pissed. Still dangerous.

The sound is sharp. Final. The chains don't budge.

"Fucking bastards," I mutter to no one. To everyone. To the hidden cameras I *know* are here. Behind the walls. In the vents. Maybe in the goddamn headboard. Who knows with these psychos?

It's another hour—maybe more—before the door creaks open again.

I don't flinch. Don't bother to look up right away. I'm too busy pretending not to give a shit. Too busy trying not to count the thrum of my pulse or the way my thighs instinctively tense in anticipation. But then I catch the scent.

Grilled cheese.

And not just any grilled cheese. *My* grilled cheese. Cheap white bread, slathered in butter, crisped to golden perfection. Gooey, melty cheddar and mozzarella—exactly the way I've made it a thousand times when the world was too heavy and I needed something warm and comforting.

I tense.

My head snaps toward the door like I'm possessed.

One of them steps inside—tactical gear, black mask, gloved hands. Unreadable lenses hiding eyes I swear see straight through me. It could be either of them.

But I know.

Only *one* of them seems to have made feeding me into a personal kink.

"Rule," I say flatly, voice like rust scraping over gravel. I narrow my eyes, not bothering to hide the suspicion burning behind them. "You're really committed to the domestic captor aesthetic, huh?"

He doesn't confirm it. Just steps inside with that same calm, commanding presence and sets the tray down on the bedside table like we're about to have a fucking picnic in hell.

But what's on that tray? That's not just food. That's a calculated weapon. A direct assault on whatever scraps of resistance I've got left.

Grilled. Fucking. Cheese.

The one thing that always hits right when everything else is falling apart. The kind of food you don't just eat—you cling to. A warm, gooey reminder that something can still be simple. Still be good.

Hot. Perfect. Crisped golden on both sides. The smell alone is enough to wreck me—real butter, melting cheese, toasted white bread, just the way I've always made it. My mouth waters before I can stop it.

I snap.

"You shouldn't know this," I bite out. My chest aches, my throat closes up, and I hate how exposed I suddenly feel. "You shouldn't know this is my favorite."

He turns his head, just enough to tilt the mask. "We know everything."

The words shouldn't feel like a caress. But they do.

I grit my teeth so hard it makes my temples throb. My jaw pulses with the effort not to scream. "This isn't kindness," I growl, every syllable a knife. "It's manipulation dressed up in melted cheese."

He doesn't flinch. Doesn't argue. Just lifts half the sandwich, the cheese stretching between the slices in slow, sinful strands. "Does it matter," he says calmly, "if it tastes like both?"

I don't answer.

But my stomach does. Loudly. *Betrayal: level unlocked.*

"Open," he says softly, holding the sandwich just close enough to tempt, not touch.

I stay still. Frozen. Mouth clamped shut. Eyes narrowed.

"You can starve if you want," he continues, voice low and impossibly even. "But you did agree to a truce. *And* you'll still be here. Still be ours. Still be chained and dripping and angry. And you'll still want the next bite even more."

My pride flares, white-hot and violent. Screaming at me to slap the food away. To spit in his face and curse every last thread of control he thinks he has.

But my mouth opens anyway.

And the first bite hits like a fucking memory.

Warmth. Cheese. Bread. Butter.

I chew.

And I *hate* how good it is.

Hate the way my eyes threaten to flutter shut. Hate the way my body forgets for one stupid second that I'm *chained to a bed* and not curled up on my couch with a blanket and bad TV.

He watches every flicker of emotion on my face like it's his favorite show.

"You were crying the first time you made this," he says quietly, like it's a secret he's only just decided to share. "Your hands were shaking. You burned one side. But you made another."

My blood runs cold.

"How—" I choke out.

He lifts the sandwich to my mouth again, not answering.

I shake my head. "How the *fuck* do you know that?"

"We watch," he says simply. "We remember everything."

Rage claws up through my throat, hot and useless. "You're insane."

"No," he says, voice too soft. "We're *devoted*."

And fuck me, there's something in the way he says it that makes my chest hurt.

Another bite. I should resist. But my body doesn't listen anymore.

I hate him just a little more for knowing this version of me. The quiet one. The sad one. The one no one else gets to see.

He feeds me the last bite like it's a ritual, like he's proving something I can't quite name.

And when I swallow, he leans in—just close enough for his voice to slide under my skin.

"We know your rage," he murmurs. "But we also know your softness. Your silence. The parts of you that bleed in the dark where no one else looks."

I turn my face away, jaw tight. "Fuck you."

He doesn't laugh this time. Doesn't tease.

He just says: "Someday, you'll thank us for seeing it all."

Then he moves the plate with the other half of the sandwich to the bedside table and takes the tray as he walks away. Like he hasn't just cracked open a part of me I didn't even realize was exposed.

And this time, when the door shuts behind him—I don't just feel fury.

I feel fear.

Because maybe they *have* read me cover to cover.

And maybe they're not just playing a game.

Maybe they're rewriting my story from the inside out.

Chapter 24
Seanna

I stare at the closed door, the taste of grilled cheese on my tongue. Anger bubbles beneath my skin, restless and sharp-edged. Why the fuck would they even suggest a truce if they're not going to truly take advantage of it? This isn't a ceasefire—it's psychological warfare under the guise of fake kindness. And why the hell does this grilled cheese mean more to me than the cherry and cream cheese pastries?

Both mean they've been watching me closely—too closely—for a long damn time, but the pastries were an indulgence, a treat that I'd given myself freely in happier moments. The grilled cheese, though... it's different. It's a comfort, a crutch I've leaned on in some of my lowest, most vulnerable moments. Times when I was too worn down to be strong. Times I thought no one was watching.

But they were. Fuck, they've always been watching and I never knew.

My chest tightens, and I force down the last of the sandwich, choking on emotions I never invited, memories I never wanted dragged up. I swallow hard, furious at myself for letting this affect me, furious at them for knowing exactly which strings to pull.

It's not long before the door opens again. For a second, I can't tell which one of them it is. He isn't carrying food, but that doesn't automatically mean it's not Rule—he's fucked with me enough times already. Yet, something in the way he moves, the predatory calmness, the quiet assurance of his steps tells me exactly who it is.

Ruin.

Jesus. I'm starting to recognize them without even needing words.

He pauses halfway to the bed, head tilted slightly. I'm sure he is assessing me in that quiet, detached way of his.

"Need to use the bathroom?" His modulated voice is deceptively gentle.

I glare defiantly at his masked face. "If you're feeling generous enough to pretend I still have basic human rights."

He shakes his head slightly, mask unreadable but smugness clear in his tone. "Always so combative, Seanna. It's almost endearing."

I deliberately rattle the chains binding my wrists, my eyes narrowed dangerously. "Glad my captivity amuses you."

He moves closer, each step unhurried. He unlocks my restraints with care, gloved fingers lingering against my wrists, sparking a traitorous heat beneath my rage. I yank my wrists free as soon as the cuffs open.

Standing abruptly, dizziness sweeps over me, and his hands immediately grip my waist, steadying me firmly.

"Don't," I snap, muscles taut as I try to jerk away.

"You keep saying that," he murmurs calmly, tightening his grip in silent warning. "Yet your body always tells a different story."

I hate the heat that rises to my skin. He releases me once he's certain I'm steady, gesturing mockingly toward the sliding bathroom door.

"Make it quick," he instructs, authority sharp beneath the velvet.

Fuming, I step through and slam the sliding door behind me. Fuck quick—I'll take my sweet ass time. After using the toilet, I strip, stepping into the large shower. I luxuriate in the hot water, slowly washing my hair and savoring every rebellious moment.

Eventually, reluctantly, I step out and wrap a towel around my body. I use another to dry my hair. It's only then I realize I have no fresh clothes to change into.

"*Fuck*," I mutter, taking a deep breath and stepping back into the bedroom.

Ruin is lounging arrogantly on the bed, at ease—the asshole. Frustration spikes sharply through me, my jaw aches from clenching it as I stop a few feet from him, fists settling on my hips.

"Where the fuck did you put my clothes?" I demand sharply, glaring.

He hums, amusement darkening his tone. "Maybe I prefer you just like this."

His words slip beneath my skin, sparking an unwanted flush of heat. Gritting my teeth I growl, hating how easily he affects me.

"Careful," he continues, voice like silk-wrapped steel. "Keep looking at me like that, and I might unwrap you myself."

"Fuck you," I snap, eyes narrowing.

He chuckles, dark and rich, the sound scraping over my nerves deliciously. "I think you'd prefer it if I did exactly that. Admit it—you're craving my hands on you."

I scoff, folding my arms tightly to hide how much his words affect me. "Dream on. You're not half as irresistible as you think."

"And you're not nearly as convincing," he counters smoothly, voice dropping to a dangerous murmur. "I've seen the way your body trembles when I'm near, Seanna. You can deny it all you want, but we both know the truth."

My pulse kicks up hard, desire battling with rage.

He's wrong. He has to be.

Except... he's not.

Because I *am* trembling. Because my thighs *are* clenching. Because my skin feels too tight and too hot and too desperate for something I don't want to name.

God, I hate him. I hate how I can smell him, that leather and spice. I hate that I keep replaying the scrape of both of their modulated voices in my head like a song I never asked for.

And most of all—I hate that I want to know what they would do if I *let* either of them touch me again.

No. If I *asked.*

The thought alone makes me burn.

I shift slightly, the towel loosening around my body, clinging to my damp skin like a fucking tease. My nipples harden beneath it, the air brushing them like the faintest whisper of his gloves.

This isn't about weakness.

It's about control.

And if I'm going to be consumed—then fuck it. I'm going to *choose* the flames.

"Do you ever shut up?" I growl, but the words lack bite.

"Only when my mouth is otherwise occupied," he says, voice thick with promise.

The ache in my core pulses harder.

Frustration spikes again—raw and restless and clawing from the inside out. And suddenly, I can't breathe through the pressure.

I rip the towel off and let it fall to the floor.

"*Satisfied now*?" I snap, voice ragged.

And it's *instant.*

He's in front of me, his towering presence sucking the air from the room. I stand my ground, but I feel every inch of my nakedness.

"Very," he murmurs. I can practically feel the heat of his gaze dragging down my body like a claim.

His gloved fingertips graze my bare shoulder, light and unhurried—just enough to make me shiver.

"Are you ready to beg yet, little storm?"

A sharp breath escapes me. My body answers before I do, heat flooding between my thighs, skin prickling with need.

"Fuck it," I whisper savagely, reaching for him on pure impulse, my fingers craving friction, punishment, *something*.

But he captures my wrists instantly, controlling them like he was waiting for the moment I'd break.

"Ah, ah," he tsks softly, mockery rich in his tone. "Do I need to bind your wrists again?"

I glare furiously, chest heaving in a mixture of rage and arousal so thick it threatens to choke me. I want to scream. I want to tear his mask off and bite down on his fucking throat.

But I also want him to shove me to the floor and *ruin* me.

He leans in, his voice a sinful breath against my ear.

"Begging is done on your knees, darling."

My knees buckle. It's involuntary—infuriating. But the burn of surrender isn't weakness. It's *relief.*

I drop, slowly, deliberately, glaring up at him with my chin tilted defiantly. My pulse is a war drum. My thighs are shaking.

But I refuse to look away.

He towers above me like a god made of leather and shadow, watching as if he owns every thought behind my eyes.

Then—only then—he releases my wrists and reaches for his belt.

Every movement is precise. Unhurried. Controlled.

It's a test.

And I don't dare look away.

"Wow," I rasp, forcing a bitter smirk onto my lips, even as arousal claws at my spine. "Is this your idea of foreplay?"

His laugh is a low, indulgent roll of thunder. "Oh, darling," he murmurs, "you haven't even begun to see what I'm capable of."

My smart remark dies the second his hand slips into his waistband and he pulls his cock free.

Jesus. Fucking. Christ.

He's already hard—thick and veiny. But it's not just the size that stops me cold.

It's what's *on* it.

My mouth drops open. My brain stalls.

"What the fuck is *that*?" I blurt.

His laugh this time is dark and amused, like I just played right into his hands.

"That," he purrs, stroking himself lazily, "is a magic cross."

And he's not lying.

Two steel bar piercings cross vertically and horizontally through the head of his cock. Silver balls gleam at the ends, forming an actual fucking *cross* made of metal and sin.

But that's not the part that really unhinges me.

It's the ink.

Bold. Black. Twisting along the shaft in unapologetic, brutal font.

Darling.

I blink. Once. Twice. My voice is sandpaper as I choke out, "You tattooed my name on your dick?"

He strokes himself lazily, like this is just another morning. Like this is normal. "Of course I did," he says, calm and sure. "It belongs to you."

The words hit like a blade slipped under my ribs.

Not because they're sweet. Not because he says it so matter of fact like there is no disputing them. But because I want them to be *true*.

Because the worst part—the part I want to tear out of myself with my bare hands—is how my body *reacts* to them.

A fresh flush rolls over my skin, heat pooling low, my breath hitching even as my spine stiffens in rebellion. I don't want this. I *shouldn't* want this. But want is clawing up my throat anyway.

Ruin shifts closer, his cock heavy and thick in his hand, the tip inches from my mouth. Then he grips my hair—hard. A firm fist at the roots, yanking my head back just enough to assert his control.

"Don't bite," he says, low and dangerous. "Or you'll regret it."

I glare up at him, mouth twisted in a defiant smirk even as his grip burns against my scalp. "Not as much as *you* would," I rasp, voice rough and raw and almost shaking. Not from fear. From the thrill of it. From how fucking unhinged this moment is.

Because this should disgust me. This should humiliate me. This should make me scream and kick and fight my way out of this twisted web he and Rule have spun around me.

But it doesn't.

It *electrifies* me.

There's something feral growing in my chest. Something that feeds on defiance and devours shame. Something that whispers: *If this is the game, then I'm not losing. I'm taking the board with me.*

So I stop pretending. Just for a second.

My hands rise and I slide them up the backs of his thighs. The fabric of his pants is coarse under my palms, the muscle beneath unyielding. I let my nails drag slightly, enough to make him feel it. Enough to show him that if I'm doing this, it's not submission.

It's war.

I hook my hands around his thighs and *drag* him forward, steady and strong, until the head of his cock brushes my lips. My breath hitches against the cool steel of the piercings, my mouth parted.

He tightens his grip in my hair, his other hand twitching slightly at his side. Waiting. Watching.

But I don't give in right away. I let the moment *hang*.

Let him feel the burn of anticipation that he usually forces onto me.

My tongue darts out, slow, dragging across the underside of the head and over one of the piercings.

"You want me to beg?" I whisper, voice hoarse and laced with grit. "You better fucking earn it."

His groan is barely audible—but it's there.

And right now?

I'll take that as a victory.

Chapter 25
Seanna

My tongue traces the steel piercings, swirling slowly around each ball before dragging down the length of his cock. I take my time, teasing, relishing the almost imperceptible shifts in his breathing, the subtle flexing of his thighs beneath my hands.

Because if Ruin wants me on my knees? He's going to fucking feel what that means.

I smirk up at him, dragging my tongue back up his length from base to tip in one slow, deliberate lick. He inhales sharply and I can't help but feel a thrill at the power I suddenly seem to wield over him.

He wants me to fall apart around him. But that's not how this goes.

Not this time.

Not when I'm the one in control of what I do with my mouth.

I swirl my tongue around the piercings again, watching the way his free hand fists at his side, leather squeaking as it strains against his control. But he doesn't stop me. Doesn't pull away. Just watches every movement, breath ragged, groaning again when I lick my tongue around the head, teasing the underside. "You okay up there?" I murmur with saccharine venom, flicking my tongue over the tip again.

His laugh is low. Hoarse. Unstable.

But when he speaks, it's all sharp-edged power. "Be careful, little storm," he rasps, his voice tight with restraint. "You forget who controls whether you can even fucking breathe."

A fresh wave of heat surges between my thighs. *God help me, I like it when he threatens me.* Like this. Like he's fighting his own control harder than I am.

But I don't back down. I press my advantage.

I drag my mouth along the underside of his cock again—slow, hot, wet—and then pull back. Barely touching. Barely there. Just enough for him to need more.

He growls.

"Is that all you've got, darling?" Ruin taunts, voice rough with arousal. "I thought you wanted to make me earn it."

I glance up at him through my lashes, lips curving in a smirk. "Patience is a virtue. Maybe you should try it sometime."

His grip tightens in my hair, just shy of painful. "Cute. But we both know virtue isn't your strong suit."

I let out a low, mocking laugh. "Says the man with a magic cross through his dick. Tell me, does that help you feel closer to God while you're sinning?"

He yanks sharply on my hair. "The only one I worship is you, darling. Now put that smart mouth to better use before I shut you up myself."

Heat floods through me at his words, at the unapologetic dominance in his tone. He's not asking. He's demanding. And fuck, if that doesn't make me want to push him harder, just to see how far he'll go to put me in my place.

"You want me to beg, Ruin? You really think you can make me?" I punctuate my words with little kitten licks, taking my time, savoring the way his cock twitches against my mouth.

"Keep playing with fire," he growls. "And I'll make sure the only thing you're able to do is beg for air."

I laugh huskily, unafraid. "Big words for a man at the mercy of my tongue. What's wrong? Afraid you'll break before I do?"

He uses the fist in my hair to pull my head back. I gaze up at him defiantly, chin tilted, eyes blazing with challenge.

"The only one who will break is you," he promises. "Now put that filthy mouth to better use before I remind you exactly who's in control here."

I lick my lips. "Make me."

Wrong thing to say. Or maybe the most deliciously right thing.

Because in the next breath, he's shoving his cock past my parted lips, filling my mouth in one smooth thrust. I moan around him, the taste of him exploding on my tongue–salt and musk and pure, molten sin.

"Fuck," he groans, the word punched out of him like I just cracked his composure in two.

Good. I want him just as unraveled as I am.

I hollow my cheeks and suck hard, lips stretching obscenely around his girth. He curses again, low and guttural, his hips rocking forward to push himself deeper. The piercings drag along the inside of my mouth and I shiver, the foreign sensation stoking the flames burning me alive.

I bob my head, taking him as deep as I can, reveling in every choked moan and bitten off curse falling from his lips. He's so fucking vocal, each gravelly sound of pleasure sending bolts of liquid heat straight through me. I've never been with a man this responsive and it's intoxicating, knowing I can tear these noises from his throat.

I hum, a vicious little vibration around him, and he jerks.

The sound he makes is fucking obscene—raw, broken, like he's unraveling from the inside out. The noises coming out of him—*God, they shouldn't turn me on as much as they do*. But I want to hear them again. I want to hear what other sounds I can drag out of him. I want to undo him with nothing but my mouth and spite.

I grip the backs of his thighs harder, digging my nails in again just to hear that strangled, guttural noise he makes. It's primal. Wild. Unfiltered.

And then he snaps.

His control shatters.

One second I'm kneeling, the next I'm airborne—lifted effortlessly and *thrown* onto the bed like a ragdoll. I land hard on my back with a gasp, limbs splayed, hair wild across the pillows. And before I can blink, he's *on* me, wrists seized, arms pinned above my head with bruising strength.

"I knew it," I snarl. "You were just fucking with me again. You never planned to—"

"I'm not doing this to tease you," he growls, one hand already reaching for the restraints at the bedposts. "I'm tying you up because I don't trust your hands not to do something *stupid* while I fuck you."

My mouth opens to protest, but he's already binding my wrists. Not roughly. Not violently. But with *finality*.

And then he pulls back to look at me.

Whatever he sees in my face makes him pause. His gloved hand lifts and brushes my hair back from my forehead like I'm something precious. His voice drops to a velvet snarl.

"You think you can push me into losing control? I'm not some itch you scratch and walk away from and go back to pretending you hate us. This was never going to be a quick fuck, Seanna."

He leans in closer, the heat of him sinking into my bones.

"I *can* do quick and hard. I fucking love quick and hard," he breathes against my neck. "But not right now. Not with you. Not for your first time with *me*."

He shifts back, dragging his gloved hands down to my thighs, parting them gently.

"I want you to *feel* everything. I want you to *remember* what it's like to be ruined by me."

I writhe under him, every muscle trembling with unbearable anticipation.

"And you will remember it," he continues, sliding his fingers against the soaked heat between my thighs. "Every inch. Every second. Because after this, you'll never be able to come without thinking of me."

I choke on a moan as two gloved fingers slide inside me—deep, smooth, perfect.

"You're soaked," he breathes. "You've been dripping since the moment you saw my cock. Admit it."

"Go to hell," I gasp, clenching down as he curls those fingers.

"Already there, darling," he growls. "And I'm taking you with me."

Then he pulls his fingers out and replaces them with the heavy, hot head of his cock. He rubs the tip against my entrance, slow and cruel, teasing me with the thickness of him, with the piercings that make me shudder every time they graze my clit.

"Tell me to stop," he says again. Quieter now. More dangerous.

I don't.

Because I don't want him to.

Not anymore.

And then he pushes in.

Slow. Deep. Unforgiving.

"Fuck," I gasp, head tipping back. The stretch is unbearable—thick and full and deliberate—and I cry out, a raw, desperate sound I can't swallow.

He doesn't stop.

He keeps pushing, inch by merciless inch, until he bottoms out and I'm panting, stretched open, throbbing around him.

He doesn't move. Just breathes.

"You feel that?" he murmurs, voice right at my ear. "That's what *devotion* feels like."

And then—*then*—he moves.

Not fast. Not hard. But *slow*.

Each stroke a deliberate, soul-breaking drag that carves me open from the inside out.

Controlled. *Devastating.*

He fucks me like I'm holy and he's desecrating a temple, like each stroke is a goddamn promise that I'll never forget the shape of him. His cock drags against every nerve inside me, igniting fire in places I didn't know could burn. His pace is punishingly slow, deliberate, like he wants to carve himself into my body.

And it's working.

My back arches. My breath breaks. My pride cracks.

Because *fuck*, I've never been fucked like this.

Not worshipped. Not owned.

Ruined.

He moans into my neck, louder than I expected. He curses, praises, whispers filth I didn't know I *needed* to hear.

Every groan, every growled *fuck*, every sharp inhale from the feel of my pussy wrapped around him—it's an aphrodisiac. It's fire on my nerves.

And I'll never tell him.

But I *fucking* love it.

"God, you grip like a fist," he pants. "Like you *need* me."

My hips jerk, helpless beneath him.

"You feel that, darling?" he rasps. "That burn? That stretch? That ache deep in your belly? That's *me*. That's what I wanted. To own this fucking body from the inside out."

My legs shake. My toes curl. My mind starts to blur.

"Say it," he growls. "Say it's mine."

I don't.

I can't.

But he knows.

He *feels* it in every pulse around him.

And when the orgasm hits me, it's violent. Shattering. My spine arches. My body clamps down around him, and I scream—not in fear.

In *want*.

In *need*.

In a goddamn surrender I never planned to give.

He presses his masked face harder into my throat and groans like it's *him* being wrecked.

He keeps going. Keeps fucking me slow. Deep. Maddening.

Until I *can't* breathe. Until all I know is the sound of his voice in my ear and the heavy stretch of him inside me. Until I'm begging without even realizing it.

"Please—"

"Please what?" he snarls, voice fraying at the edges.

"Don't stop."

He growls, his thrusts becoming just a little rougher, a little faster, still dragging out every second like he wants to brand it into my fucking soul.

And then when I'm about to come again—he shudders, curses low and harsh, and spills inside me with a noise that will haunt my dreams forever.

He doesn't collapse.

He *stays*.

Holding himself above me. Still inside me. Watching me come undone.

And when he finally pulls out, it's slow. Intimate. My body clenching around nothing, already missing him like some sick fucking addict.

He doesn't say anything. He doesn't need to.

Because we both know what just happened.

I didn't just lose a fight. I gave in to the war.

And I don't know if I'll survive the next one.

Chapter 26
Ruin

I'm not a good man. Never claimed to be. The kind of darkness inside me doesn't beg for redemption—it demands a throne. And right now, I'm perched in the armchair like I own the fucking air in this room, watching her.

Seanna.

She was utterly silent as I cleaned her up after I fucked her. Not a sound, not a twitch—just quiet compliance that screamed louder than any rage-filled outburst could. Either she's retreating deep into her mind, simply too stunned to react or she's plotting intricate and brutal ways to murder me.

I almost hope it's the latter—her anger is intoxicating, a drug that I'm more than eager to overdose on.

But right now I'll take any time I can get. We've been coming and going without her knowing. Keeping up appearances in our real lives. Pretending nothing's changed. And no one suspects a damn thing. That's the beauty of it. She's here—hidden, restrained, watched—and the world just keeps on spinning.

The door opens with a soft click and Rule steps inside, his gaze sliding from Seanna's naked form beneath the sheet to where I sit brooding in the armchair. He scoffs lightly at the sight of me before moving to set a tray of food on the bedside table. One of his many attempts to worm his way into her good graces. As if pastries and coffee could make her forget she's our captive.

He shifts closer to the bed, looming over her. I don't need to see his face to know the obsessive hunger that must be written there, a perfect mirror to the dark need clawing at my own chest. We are both so utterly consumed by her.

He retrieves something from his tactical pants pocket. A moment later, Seanna's limp body jerks slightly as he sprays a sedative. He then pulls out a compact field kit and strips off his gloves before lifting her limp arm. His fingertips press and probe at the delicate skin there, searching for something.

"She doesn't have an implant," I inform him with a sigh, rising from my seat. "I checked her medical records. She had a bad reaction when she got one with her sister. It's rare, but it happens."

Rule tilts his head at me questioningly. "Then what does she have?"

"Get the bigger kit," I instruct as I step up to the bed.

As he retrieves a larger pouch of medical supplies from the hall, I approach the bed, drinking in the sight of Seanna laid out before me. I peel the sheet back fully, baring her to my greedy eyes. *Fuck, she's perfect. Exquisite.* My cock is already hardening again at the mere sight of her, the memory of her tight walls gripping me.

I part her thighs just as Rule returns, both of us more than competent to perform basic medical tasks thanks to our training. But this is no simple exam.

No, this is pure indulgence. She'll never even know what I'm about to do to her in this vulnerable state. The thought makes me throb.

Reaching into the medical kit, I remove the necessary tools, laying them out neatly beside her. Her body is completely relaxed, pliant thanks to the sedative. It will make this process much easier.

I work swiftly but carefully, and before long I hold up the IUD, studying it clinically. "It actually expired two months ago. The reminders in her calendar all mysteriously disappeared... such a shame."

Rule chuckles darkly, knowingly. "Lucky timing for us then."

"Indeed." I drop the IUD into a biohazard bag and seal it, tossing it aside. My attention is already back on Seanna, drinking in the sight of her splayed out and utterly vulnerable.

"Think she has any idea how tempting she is like this?" Rule muses, his voice thick with hunger as he looms over her.

"No," I reply evenly, stripping off the gloves. "But she will soon enough."

A small trickle of blood seeps out from between her folds, evidence of what we have done. The sight is too tempting–I can't resist. Lifting my mask just enough, I lower my head and slowly drag my tongue through her entrance, lapping at her. The taste of us together mingled with blood is divine, intoxicating.

Groaning softly, I continue eating at her pussy, tongue delving deep to capture every last drop. It's wrong, I know it is, but I can't stop myself. This is the very essence of my obsession–wanting every part of her.

I only stop when the bleeding does, sitting back and readjusting my mask with a satisfied hum.

Rule watches me knowingly, his own arousal clear in the way he shifts. "Should we tell her what you did? That her body is completely unprotected now?"

I consider it for a moment, tracing a fingertip along her hipbone possessively. "No. The revelation will be all the sweeter when it comes."

"Fuck, you're twisted," Rule laughs, shaking his head. But there's no judgment in his tone, only dark amusement and shared understanding.

"And you're not?" I counter with a smirk he can't see. "We're cut from the same cloth, *Rule*. Denying it is pointless."

Rule inclines his head in acknowledgment. "True enough." He slides a hand up Seanna's thigh, squeezing firmly. "It's so tempting to take her like this. She admitted to me she fantasizes about it, being taken in her sleep. But, I suppose we should let her sleep off the procedure."

"For now," I agree, fighting the urge to touch her again. To sink into her warmth and lose myself completely. "But when she wakes, the real fun begins."

We share a loaded glance, the air crackling with anticipation and barely restrained obsession. Our little storm has no idea what's in store for her. But she will.

Oh, she will.

Reluctantly, I pull the sheet back over Seanna's naked form, covering temptation from sight if not from mind. Rule steps back as well, though I can practically feel the hunger rolling off him in waves.

Before we leave, I take a present for her out of my pocket—a black link necklace with an R at each end. I slip it gently over her head, adjusting the length precisely before attaching a small padlock partway between the R's, securing it with a matching little key. One end rests at her throat while the other comes down between her breasts.

I pause to admire the way it sits against her skin. Black on pale, delicate but unmistakably binding. A collar in every way but name.

This isn't just ornamentation.

Satisfied, I unlock the restraints around her wrists, grin darkly to myself behind my mask as Rule chuckles again.

"Sleep well, little storm," I murmur, trailing a finger down her cheek possessively before stepping back.

Rule and I leave the room, deliberately not locking the door behind us.

Chapter 27
Seanna

Consciousness pulls me from dreams that feel more like nightmares. I lie perfectly still for a moment, my instincts prickling, expecting the familiar shadowy presence of Ruin waiting silently in that damned armchair, watching me like his personal twisted form of entertainment.

But as my eyes finally open, the chair sits empty. Strange.

A sharp, sudden cramp sears through my lower abdomen, and I hiss through clenched teeth, annoyed. By my estimate it's right on time, like clockwork. Because clearly, being abducted wasn't inconvenient enough, my uterus decided to join the party. At least the pain is familiar, predictable—it'll fade soon enough.

How could I have been so careless? Letting Ruin slip beneath my defenses, caving to their masked dominance, their arrogant control—it's unacceptable. I'm supposed to be fighting tooth and nail, not succumbing to their twisted fucking games.

Anger sharpening my senses as I sit up, rubbing my temples, only then noticing an unfamiliar weight pressing coolly against my throat. My fingers jerk up to investigate, discovering a thick, smooth chain secured by a small padlock. There's no latch, no weak link. Perfect. Another twisted accessory courtesy of my masked captors. I tug at it futilely, frustration simmering.

It's only then that I realize I'm not chained to the bed.

Suspicion floods through me instantly, slicing sharp and cold through lingering remnants of sleep. I swing my legs from the bed, searching quickly for clothes. I find some of my own—of course—neatly folded inside the large mahogany dresser. *Meticulous bastards.*

Jerking the clothes on as quickly as I can, I silently curse myself. I should've spent every second of my time here plotting an escape instead of playing into their warped little scenario.

Tentatively, I approach the door, gripping the handle with cautious anticipation. It turns effortlessly beneath my palm, swinging silently open into an empty hallway. My heart pounds harder, suspicion tightening my chest. This is too easy, too clean. Like stepping willingly into a trap.

Whatever house we are in isn't small, but I'm sure as fuck not sticking around to play hide-and-seek with my masked abductors. Screw that. All I need is an exit.

My search is brief, driven by desperation. Finally, an unlocked back door opens into darkness that surprises me—I hadn't even realized what time it could be, locked in a windowless room for what felt like days. Judging by the faint, greyish light beginning to creep at the edges of the horizon, it must be sometime in the early morning.

Freedom beckons.

Every instinct screams this is exactly what they want, but I'm too stubborn to ignore the opportunity.

Breaking into a sprint, I rush toward the thick tree line, the sound of my own breath echoing sharply in my ears. It's not until I'm engulfed in shadows that I glance back, suspicion still gnawing viciously at my spine. The house is silent, beautiful, and cruelly calm, yet the unmistakable sensation of being watched prickles coldly along my skin.

Of course I'm being watched. This is their twisted fucking game, after all.

Gritting my teeth, I plunge deeper into the forest, branches scraping mercilessly against my clothes. Direction doesn't matter—distance does. Every hurried step carries me further from the cage they've meticulously crafted for me.

But then, training kicks in.

I force myself to stop.

Crouching low, I steady my breath, dragging in slow, deep lungfuls of air through my nose, letting my body recalibrate. The chill of the early morning air brushes against my skin, but I shove it aside. I focus.

The forest hums around me. Crickets, birds, the rustle of leaves overhead. Life, undisturbed. Somewhere in the distance, I can just make out the faint murmur of water—a stream or river maybe. Could be useful.

I strain harder, tuning out the natural sounds, letting silence stretch over me like armor.

There. Low. Too calculated to be the forest. Beneath everything else—movement.

Not an animal.

Not nature.

Something deliberate.

I'm being hunted.

Because of course I fucking am.

This was never going to be a real opportunity to escape.

It was just another fucking game.

I bolt, heart hammering, ducking through dense brush and weaving between trees thick with shadow. My bare feet thud softly against damp earth, and still, every instinct screams that each step is a countdown. The forest is wild. Untamed.

I feel the wire hit my shin, too thin to see until it's too late. It doesn't trip me—it snaps and something shifts above me. A sudden rustle, then a downpour of dry leaves and forest debris rains down, noisy enough to give away my position. Not intended to harm. Just sound and exposure. Enough to rattle me. Enough to alert them.

Fucking brilliant.

I take off again, moving quickly through trees and underbrush, my pulse hammering in my ears. I hadn't been thinking about traps—I'd been thinking about distance. I was thinking about speed. But they're smarter than that.

A sharp jerk yanks my leg backward mid-stride. I crash to my knees, barely catching myself. Another wire. Thin and low to the ground, tied between two trees. Enough to trip hard— enough to slow me down. To delay. Humiliate.

I scramble up, breath hissing out between my teeth.

The forest is rigged.

"Come on, Seanna. You can do better than that."

The voice is distorted but unmistakable in its tone—confident, crisp, commanding.

I barely make it ten more feet before a branch I duck under triggers something above—rope netting drops from the canopy like a snare. I twist and dive out of the way just in time, heart racing.

Fucking hell. They've built a primal playground.

I veer left, keeping my pace controlled. I find broken branches angled unnaturally, forming a funnel path that leads downhill. A clear route. Too clear. I double back instead, using the underbrush to obscure my movement.

The same voice speaks again, closer this time. "You're making me work harder than I planned. I respect that."

I push forward harder, doubling my efforts to disappear. I climb into a tree and wait—counting every breath, every creak of bark, the sweat sliding down my back.

Hearing a sound further away I drop from the tree and land in a crouch, ignoring the sharp sting in my ankle. I tear through the trees again in the opposite direction, weaving through brush, leaping over fallen logs.

Then pain flares.

I stop and hide in a thick patch of shrubs as a cramp doubles me over with a vicious intensity. I drop down to one knee, dragging air into my lungs like it's made of glass, my arm wrapped around my middle. *Fucking timing. Fucking body.* I breathe through the pain, forcing my muscles to unclench.

"Run faster, darling. You're prettier when you sweat."

My breath stutters. That voice—smooth but sharp, too precise, and too close.

I lunge forward again, weaving through brambles and low-hanging branches. I leave false trails, kick mud in patterns that don't track straight, double back through my own footprints. It's textbook.

And it doesn't matter.

He's better.

"Sloppy," the voice comes again.

Every turn I take, he's just behind it. Every time I think I've bought myself a second of distance, I hear that voice again. Cool. Infuriatingly calm.

Definitely Rule.

I press on, pushing past low branches and thick moss-draped roots. I haven't heard any voice but the one taunting me. No sweet teasing. No coaxing. No purr like velvet over knives.

Where's Ruin?

Is he just being silent? Stalking in the dark like a ghost, savoring the hunt?

Or is it only Rule out here?

The thought unsettles me in ways I don't want to admit.

Another burst of motion—a snap of foliage. I pivot hard, and something smacks into my chest—a harmless but weighted sandbag dangling from a tree. It knocks me back just enough to cost me precious momentum, but it doesn't stop me.

Another trap.

Another fucking reminder that I'm being toyed with.

"Almost had you there."

My stomach twists. Not in fear.

In fury.

Then another cramp hits—not as bad but I still stumble, falling to one knee. I breathe through it, teeth clenched.

"Fuck," I hiss, dragging myself upright again.

Once this is over, I'm going to hunt Reyes down and cut him into pieces simply for existing. For being the excuse behind this whole psychotic shitshow.

This isn't protection.

This is *possession.*

And if I get the chance, I'm going stabby on these bastards first.

Well... maybe I'll leave Ruin's magic cock intact. For a little while.

I move again, slower now. Strategic. My eyes scan every-thing—shadows, soil, subtle shifts in the ground that scream of artificial tampering. I spot one just in time. A snare, half-buried beneath leaves.

I sidestep it and keep going, ducking under a net rigged between two trees. Silent alarms, I bet. Traps designed to let them know where I am. Or maybe just to fuck with me.

Branches snap behind me—closer now. The tension is electric, the air charged. I twist and bolt downhill, slipping through a narrow rocky pass that forces me sideways. A rope snaps around my ankle mid-stride, yanking me upward with brutal force. I slam into the air, wind knocked clean from my lungs.

I hang there, upside down, blood rushing to my head, vision blurring.

"Really?" I mutter to myself, fury boiling. "A fucking snare trap?!"

Footsteps approach slowly. Steady. Calculated.

Rule.

Not rushing. Not panicked.

Because he knows.

He's already won.

And I am going to make him bleed for it.

He steps into view like he owns the forest. Black tactical gear. Mask. Glasses. That whole untouchable, unreadable, arrogant silhouette.

"You're fucking good," he says, voice steady. "But not good enough."

I glare down at him from my upside-down vantage point. "Fuck you."

He tilts his head slightly, considering me like I'm both specimen and prize. "You say that like it's not inevitable."

I snarl, fingers scrambling for the knot at my ankle. My body's already sore, blood thundering in my ears. I twist, swing, reach for the tree bark, something—anything—to give me leverage. He doesn't stop me.

"Go ahead," he sighs. "Let's see what you've got left."

Oh, I'll show him exactly what I've got. Starting with the sharp edge of my rage.

My fingers claw at the knot with frantic determination, and my body swings slightly with every desperate yank. The rope creaks. Bark scrapes my arms. My vision is going hazy now, heat and blood pressure warring under my skin, but I *don't* stop. I *won't*. I'm not going to hang here like his trophy.

I see the glint of the blade too late. And then—*snap.*

The rope gives.

I crash down, the impact knocking every molecule of air from my lungs. Pain explodes in my side as I hit the forest floor hard, rolling once, twice, before I force my body upright.

I stagger to my feet, gasping, legs trembling but obeying. I don't wait. I *launch.* Fury and instinct crackle through me like lightning, and I fly at him, fists already clenched, jaw tight with pain and hate and fire.

Rule doesn't flinch.

He *waits.*

I swing.

He blocks it, easily.

I aim a kick.

He deflects, the movement sharp and clean—but I see the smallest shift in his stance. I made him move. I'll take it.

"Now *that's* the spirit," he says, and there's a quiet, dangerous sort of satisfaction in his voice. "That's the little storm I'm used to. The one that'd fight her own shadow just to prove she could."

I push through the exhaustion dragging at my limbs. Every breath hurts. Every muscle screams. But I shove it down. I throw everything I have at him—punches, kicks, feints. I *fight*. Not for freedom, not anymore. For spite. For the satisfaction of knowing that I made him *work* for it.

He taunts me between blocks and dodges, his voice laced with amusement, like he's watching his favorite gladiator bleed for him.

"You're getting sloppy," he says as I swing again. "Tired."

I miss—overextend—and he grabs my wrist, twisting it hard enough to make me cry out. I twist, using the momentum to throw an elbow toward his face.

But he's *faster*.

He ducks and shoves me back. I hit the ground with a thud, skidding on damp leaves, arms up already, bracing for more.

And he *gives* me more.

He's on me before I can fully rise, straddling my hips, knees pinning mine, weight anchoring me like a vice. His knife flashes silver in the low light as he presses the flat of the blade to my throat—cold and unflinching. His other hand grabs my wrists, slamming them into the soft earth above my head and pinning them there.

Breathless, I glare up at him, chest heaving. My heartbeat pounds so violently I swear he can feel it through the grip on my wrists.

I should be fighting harder.

I should be spitting blood and curses and venom.

Instead, my thighs clench involuntarily.

Again.

What the *fuck* is wrong with me?

My body doesn't seem to know the difference between threat and thrill anymore—not when it comes to them.

And Rule? I'm sure he fucking knows it.

He probably fucking *feeds* off it.

He hums low, and the sound vibrates through my body like a dark promise. The blade shifts, pressing deeper against the sensitive skin of my throat. Not cutting, just threatening. A whisper of danger, sharp and intimate.

My breath hitches.

His head cocks slightly, like he's savoring it.

"I'll scream," I grit out, voice strained but defiant. "I'll scream loud enough the whole fucking forest will hear."

He leans in closer, and the blade follows—still flush to my skin, making every inhale feel like it could be the last.

"Go ahead," he murmurs. "Scream for me."

My lips part, fury and humiliation mixing in my throat like acid.

"But if you're going to make noise," he continues, calm and deliberate, "don't lie about what it's really for."

I freeze.

"Don't pretend it's fear when I know you're soaked through your goddamn underwear," he says, voice like a scalpel—precise, cutting, true. "You want to scream?"

The knife shifts again, lower now, trailing with purpose down the center of my chest, barely grazing cloth, just enough to make me tense beneath him.

"Go on, little storm, scream for me," he breathes, close enough I feel the heat of it. "*Beg* for me."

My heart slams against my ribs.

He's waiting.

Poised.

Ready to rip the truth from my throat one way or another.

And the worst part?

My silence *isn't* denial.

It's shame tangled in want, and fury wrapped in the kind of arousal that should never fucking exist—but *does*.

God help me, it *does*.

Chapter 28
Rule

She thinks she hates this.

But her body tells me otherwise.

The tremble in her thighs. The flush blooming across her chest where her top dips just low enough for me to see the heat rising. The subtle grind of her hips beneath mine—slow, searching, betraying her need like it's instinct.

She's fighting it. Of course she is.

She always does.

That's why she's so fucking *perfect*.

Ruin had his fun last night. We've both been obsessed with her for years. She's the only thing in this world dark enough, *wild* enough to match us blow for blow. The kind of woman who doesn't leash her demons—she takes them dancing.

And fuck, we love her for it.

When she hit the tree line earlier, I watched her bolt from the back door on the security feeds like she actually had a shot. Like the forest wasn't already mapped out with more cameras than trees and nearly as many traps. Ruin chuckled in my earpiece as she disappeared into the shadows, letting me take the lead this time.

"She's fast," he'd said. "But not faster than you."

He's watching now, no doubt—silent, still, drinking in every second of this.

But I've got her.

Our little storm.

Pinned beneath me with her wrists held tight to the forest floor and my knife at her throat. Her chest rises in rapid, shallow bursts, skin flushed and glowing in the faint morning light breaking through the canopy. She's furious. She's humiliated. She's *aroused*—and trying to pretend she isn't.

She thinks no one's ever satisfied her because no one could keep up with her.

She was wrong.

She just needed someone to *take* control.

Someone who could strip it from her, tear her down until all that's left is instinct. Need. Surrender. Me. Or Ruin. Preferably both.

"You fight like hell," I murmur, my voice low and even, letting the blade tease a whisper lower between her collarbones. "But you've never really been chased before, have you?"

She squirms. Not to get away. Not really.

It's subtle. Her hips arch just enough to brush against the pressure of my body. Just enough to chase friction where I know she's aching.

"You want to scream?" I press. "Then fucking scream. Scream because you want me to break you."

She goes still—every breath, every muscle coiled like she's balancing on the edge of a cliff.

I press down slightly more with the knife—not enough to hurt her. Just enough to remind her I could.

"I'm going to make you admit it," I whisper near her ear. "That no one else could ever do this to you. That no one's ever *earned* the right to hear you scream."

My grip on her wrists tightens.

She can't run now.

She can barely breathe.

And I won't let her lie to herself for much longer.

She doesn't realize how fucking beautiful she was out there.

Running through the forest like she had a prayer. Sweat clinging to her skin, breath ragged, clothes clinging to every curve like a second skin. She hit every trap like she was being tested by the gods—and kept going. Even when the leaves rained down on her head. Even when that wire yanked her legs out from under her. Even when the snare dragged her kicking into the air.

She never broke.

She just burned hotter.

And I nearly came in my fucking pants watching her.

She was art in motion—rage and desperation wrapped in skin that begs to be bruised, claimed, *owned*.

My cock is rock hard now, straining against the unforgiving fabric of my pants, pressed against the cradle of her hips. She feels it. I know she does. Her lashes flicker. Her hips shift again—almost imperceptible—but it's there. She's aching. Wet. Wound tight.

She's trying so hard not to want this.

But her body's already sold her out.

I know exactly what she needs.

But she's not getting it.

Not yet.

Not until she screams for it.

Not until she *begs*.

I let the knife trail along the curve of her jaw, slow, reverent—like I'm memorizing her by touch. Her breath catches. Her back arches just slightly, barely perceptible, like she's leaning into the danger.

Needing it.

I drag the blade lower, tracing the line of her throat down to her chest, just above the swell of her breasts. She shivers—not in fear. Not entirely. It's something darker. Deeper. Hungrier.

She wants me to break her.

Wants me to pierce the surface and dig underneath the armor she wears like a second skin.

I press the knife gently against the side of her ribs, not hard enough to draw blood, just enough to make her *feel* it.

Her breath stutters again.

And her eyes—fuck, her eyes—they flash not with fear but *need*. Like she's wondering what it would feel like if I did sink the blade into her flesh. If maybe pain is the only thing sharp enough to cut through the chaos in her chest. If it would drown out the war between pride and want.

"You want it, don't you?" I whisper, my voice low and brutal. "The pain. The pressure. Something to override the noise in that pretty little head of yours."

She doesn't answer.

But her pulse flutters wildly at her throat. Her skin flushes deeper where the cold steel kisses her.

She's so close to cracking. So close to giving in.

But I need the words. Need her to *admit* it.

She's aching. Needy. Desperate.

And still trying to wear that mask of defiance like it's not cracking beneath the weight of her own desire.

"I could fuck you right now," I murmur, voice like gravel and fire. "Right here. With you pinned down, filthy and furious, just how I like you."

Her jaw tenses. Her eyes flare.

But her hips shift again—seeking friction.

"I could bury myself in you so deep you forget your own name," I continue, dragging the knife lower, just above her waistband. "And I *will*. But not until you *ask* for it."

She glares at me, lips trembling between a curse and a cry.

I lean in, breath hot at her ear. "Scream for me."

The blade presses in—not cutting, but threatening again.

"Beg for me to break you."

I feel her pulse rabbit-fast beneath my hand. See the war behind her eyes.

She wants to deny me.

Wants to hold on to that last shred of control.

But it's slipping.

Chapter 29
Seanna

No. No. No.

I repeat the word like a shield, like it'll hold the line as Rule presses in, his blade dragging slow and deliberate over my skin. But my body—the traitorous bitch—is already arching toward the threat.

His voice snakes through me, low and level. *Scream for me. Beg for me to break you.*

I should spit in his face. Snarl something violent and sharp. Fight until my body gives out.

But instead, my thighs tighten. My breath catches.

And the heat between my legs pulses like a fucking metronome, synced perfectly to every shift of the blade.

God. Fucking. Dammit.

This isn't me. I don't give in. I don't *beg*.

But he isn't backing off.

And that edge… that cold steel sliding across my chest, down my ribs, lower—taunting—has my thoughts spiraling into a molten mess. The way he moves like this is inevitable. Like my resistance is just the warm-up act.

The burn in my wrists from his grip. The throb between my legs. The sting in my lungs as I try to hold back the sound clawing its way up my throat.

I'm unraveling and he knows it.

The worst part? I don't even know if I want to stop it anymore. I'm tired of resisting.

"I hate you," I whisper, breathless, the words trembling.

He doesn't respond. Doesn't flinch. Just tilts his head slightly, blade brushing across my stomach like a calculation. Like he's measuring how close he is to cracking me open.

And fuck, I *hate* that he's close.

Because I *feel* it.

The weight of him straddling me, solid and unyielding. The hard, unforgiving ridge of his cock pressing into my lower stomach through the layers of our clothes—and it's not subtle. He's thick and hard and *ready*. My hips shift again without permission, and that's when I know:

My pussy is a traitorous fucking bitch.

She doesn't care about the humiliation. She doesn't care about the mask or the knife. She wants that goddamn cock. She wants to be bent over and taken—*used* until the fight bleeds out of me in moans and broken cries. She wants him to make me *beg*. To make me *weep* for it.

And I hate that I want it too.

This isn't supposed to happen.

I've spent my life building walls and sharpening edges, making sure no one could get close enough to even *touch* me. But Rule doesn't knock on doors. He *carves through them*.

I clench my jaw, trying to breathe around the ache inside me. Rage and heat war for dominance, and still, that blade traces the lines of my body like he already knows what the answer will be.

I jerk against his grip.

Not hard enough to break it though I doubt I even could. Just enough to say, *I'm still here.*

His hold tightens.

"You want to fight," he says quietly, calm as steel. "And you think that means you're still in control."

I grit my teeth.

I can't see his eyes behind those reflective lenses. Can't read a thing from that blank, armored mask. But his presence is every-where—pressing into me from all sides.

He's already inside. Not physically, not yet. But close. Too fucking close.

And every second I spend fighting myself is another second he *wins*.

I feel the slick heat between my thighs. The way my body keeps subtly grinding against him—seeking friction, chasing what it *needs*. Every inch of me is trembling, pulsing, aching. My pride is burning out like a dying star, and all that's left is a desperate want.

I want to bite him. I want to scream. I want to rip free and murder him.

But more than all of that?

I want to submit. I want him to *destroy* me.

Control yourself, Seanna.

But I can't. Not fully. Not when he's this close. Not when I can *feel* how hard he is—feel the tension in his thighs, the pressure of his hips, the way he holds his position like a king above his prize.

"Still holding on?" he murmurs, blade grazing the underside of my breast—light, taunting. "Even when your body's already given you up?"

My back arches before I can stop it. My wrists pull hard against his grip. I hate the sound that slips from my throat—it's not a protest.

It's a *whimper*.

"Fuck you," I snap, desperate to reclaim something—*anything*—of myself.

His head tilts.

"You will," he says, calm and controlled. "But not until you *ask*."

And that? That breaks something loose.

Not my will. Not completely.

But the wall between resistance and *need* crumbles, brick by crumbling brick.

His blade drags lower—not cutting. Hovering. Waiting.

"You want the pain," he murmurs. "You want someone to take everything you're carrying and rip it away. You want to *feel* something stronger than guilt or anger or control."

I don't say no. But I *can't* say yes either.

So I stay silent, my entire body screaming louder than any words ever could.

He waits. Quiet and still.

And I feel myself falling into the space he's carved out for me—this cage, this moment, this fucking *need*.

I'm done pretending I don't want it.

I'm done pretending I don't want them, *him*.

My voice scrapes up from the back of my throat, raw and reluctant. "Please."

One word. One betrayal. One truth too ugly to hide.

Rule stills above me. The knife pauses just below my ribs, his body tensing as though that one word hit harder than any punch I'd landed in the fight.

His voice comes low, almost a whisper. "Say it again."

I grit my teeth, shame and heat choking me. My pride's bleeding out somewhere between my thighs, and still—it pulses.

"Please," I force out again, quieter. More desperate.

"Please what?" he demands, calm as steel, the edge of control still in his voice even as the pressure in his body coils tighter. "Say it, Seanna. Beg me."

"Fuck you," I hiss—but it's broken now, the venom hollow. "Please... fuck me. Just—do it already."

He waits.

And the stillness strangles.

"Please," I whisper again, voice cracking. "Please, Rule. I need it. I need you. I need—"

My throat closes. I can't say it. But it's already there, in my voice, in my body. Everything inside me is unraveling.

He hums, satisfied.

The knife vanishes from my skin, set gently on the forest floor beside us. His weight shifts, just long enough for him to reach into one of the deep side pockets of his pants.

I barely have time to breathe before there is rope unfurling like a viper in his hand. He doesn't hesitate.

He binds my wrists together, tight and sure. Firm with no give. Then he pulls a steel spike from another pocket and drives it into the forest floor. Pinning the rope into the dirt, anchoring me in place.

I tug once, instinctively. There's no escape.

Only then does he pick the knife back up.

He leans over me slowly, that maddening calm still clinging to every motion. The blade kisses my hip first—pressing just beneath the waistband of my pants.

Then it *slices*.

The sound of fabric tearing is obscene in the quiet between us. He cuts slowly, methodically, and occasionally—deliberately—slices through skin.

Little lines of red bloom across my thighs, my stomach, my ribs. Not deep..

But intentional.

He doesn't just cut—he carves. Slow drags. Crosshatches. A series of shallow, deliberate slashes that sting and burn, every one a punctuation mark to my surrender.

My body arches without permission. Heat floods my core. The pain stings, electric and sharp—but it only drives the hunger deeper.

He drags the flat of the blade through one of the lines, collecting blood on the edge.

Then he brings it to my lips.

"Taste yourself," he commands.

I glare. But my mouth opens.

The metal touches my tongue. I taste copper and heat and something primal. It causes my breath to shudder.

He lowers the blade and presses his thumb to one of the shallow wounds, smearing the blood across my stomach in slow, reverent streaks.

"War paint," he murmurs. "You wear it well."

He paints me with my blood. My body becomes his canvas. Long strokes down my ribs. A smear between my breasts. He presses a hand to the small of my stomach and slides it up, leaving a crimson trail behind.

And then lower. Between my thighs. His fingers dip into the slick heat already pooling there, mixing it with the blood. He smears that up my inner thighs and across my stomach, painting words with his fingers, like a signature.

By the time he sets the knife aside again, my body is a live wire. I'm drenched. Aching. Writhing.

He kneels between my thighs, unbuckling his pants.

And then I see it.

Two steel barbells pierce across his cock. His cock is thick and flushed, heavy in his hand. And of course it's pierced. Of course his dick is accessorized like Ruin's.

My breath catches, eyes flicking down.

And yes. There it is. Tattooed in bold, black ink. *Darling.*

I choke on a sound. A strangled, disbelieving laugh. *Does every part of them belong to me now? Is that the point?*

He lines himself up, and I feel the slick head of his cock drag through my folds—cool steel bumping against hypersensitive flesh.

My whole body locks up.

He thrusts in—hard. Savage. Unrelenting.

The stretch is brutal. Pain lances up my spine, white-hot and blinding.

Fuck. Of course my uterus decides to be a bitch and join the party. The cramp screams—but so does the pleasure.

It twists together, blurs the lines. Pleasure and pain folding into something I can't name.

He's thick. Hard. Piercings grinding inside me, dragging against every nerve. My mouth opens in a silent cry.

"Feel that?" he growls, voice tight now, no longer calm. "That's me. Every fucking inch of me. Right where I belong."

And then he starts to move.

Each thrust is a demand. A punishment. A reward.

My wrists strain. My thighs tremble. The sharp pain deep inside me adds to it all—makes me more raw, more desperate, more alive than I've ever fucking been.

He fucks me like he's snapping my spine in half with every thrust. *And I take it.*

I scream. I moan. I sob his name.

Tears blur my vision. I don't know if I'm crying because it hurts or because it doesn't hurt enough.

I beg. Not because I want mercy. Because I need more.

"Please—harder—faster—please—"

He growls and obeys, slamming into me with savage force. Every stroke is dizzying, maddening. I can't breathe. I can't think.

My back arches off the forest floor. My body convulses around him.

"Please, Rule—I can't—I—"

But I can. I want to. I need to.

His hand drags up my ribs—slow, possessive—then wraps around my throat, cutting off every gasp of air I'm not using to beg him with. The pressure is perfect—tight, unyielding—and it pushes me to the edge of delirium.

His other hand presses down on my lower abdomen—right where the ache is deepest. The dull pain flares sharp again beneath his palm, throbbing, insistent.

He thrusts deeper—each angle hitting that one spot inside me, the one only they seem able to find. That maddening, impossible place that makes my vision blur and my hips jerk, desperate and wild.

The pressure builds. Deep. Tight. Spinning.

And just when I think I might survive it—

I clamp down. Hard.

My body contracts so violently it forces him out.

And then I gush.

It sprays the ground beneath me—hot, wet, blinding.

"Fuck yes," he snarls, reaching down and rubbing my clit hard and fast, coaxing the climax to new hights, dragging the pleasure out of me.

My body convulses. I sob his name, because it's too much. I'm breaking apart at the seams.

He presses harder, working me through it.

"Good fucking girl," he growls. "Making a mess for me."

And just as my body begins to still, he grips his cock and slides it back to my entrance.

Then thrusts back in. Deep and hard.

He keeps fucking me through the aftershocks, through the wreckage, through the whimpers.

My body's limp beneath him, hypersensitive and raw. But he doesn't stop. Doesn't falter.

His cock grinds against every swollen nerve, the drag of his piercings making my breath hitch with each thrust.

The second climax rises slow—less violent, but no less consuming. A heavy, molten ache that builds and builds until I'm crying out beneath him again.

"Please—please, I'm—"

It breaks.

My pussy clenches around him, tight and trembling. The wave crashes through me, dragging him down with me.

He groans—deep and rough—and his hips jerk once, twice—then they still as his cock pulses.

Hot, thick release spills inside me.

He stays buried deep, panting harshly, body braced over mine.

And I can feel it all. The twitch of him. The heat. The burn.

And even though he has pretty much destroyed me—I want *more*.

Chapter 30

Seanna

There has to be something magic about their dicks.

And no, I'm not talking about the piercings—though let's be real, the steel crosses and barbells probably qualify as dark fucking runes at this point.

No. It's something else. Something cursed. Something *wrong*. Because every time either of them is inside me, my brain turns to soup and my spine forgets how to function. I'm not a stupid girl. I'm not weak. I lead a goddamn DEA task force. I've interrogated men twice my size and watched them piss themselves when I smiled. I take down predators for a living—ruthless, slick assholes who think power makes them untouchable.

And I've *never* needed a man to fuck me.

When I have sex, it's on *my* terms. I scratch the itch, I climb on top, I get off—maybe—and then I walk away because the poor bastard is usually halfway to tears just trying to keep up. Most of them don't even get that far.

So *how—how* the fuck did I end up here?

In the arms of one of the two masked psychopaths who stalked me, kidnapped me, sabotaged my investigation, and derailed the takedown of Javier fucking Reyes. One of them hunted me through a forest rigged with traps and branded my body with my own blood. The other didn't need blood to brand me—he used devotion like a weapon, fucked me with reverence so dark it felt holy, until my body couldn't tell the difference between worship and war.

And the worst part?

I let them.

Hell—I begged for it.

The shame simmers under my skin, sticky and raw, but it doesn't drown out the need. It doesn't cancel the high of being taken apart with such precision that I forgot where I ended and they began. They've hardwired me with arousal. Rewritten my tolerance for pain. Hijacked my brain chemistry and made submission feel like *relief.*

And maybe it should bother me more that I'm not screaming in rebellion right now. That I'm not biting Rule's fucking neck as he carries me back toward the house I tried to escape from just hours ago.

But no. My traitorous, aching, blood-streaked body is *nestled* in his arms, curled instinctively toward his chest like it's safe there. Like I'm not being dragged back into the lion's den by the same beast who choked me until I shattered and then fucked me through every aftershock.

I should be plotting to murder these men slowly and creatively. I should be focused on clawing my way out of this mindfuck long enough to regroup, reload, and hunt Reyes to the ends of the fucking earth.

But instead?

I'm watching the tree canopy blur overhead while Rule's hand supports the base of my spine like I'm made of porcelain instead of rage. My pulse is a slow, hypnotized thud. My thighs are still trembling. And despite everything—despite *everything*—I don't try to wriggle free.

And the masks? I should care more about the masks. I should be demanding names, peeling back layers, memorizing every detail for the revenge I *swore* I'd carve into their skin.

But the truth?

I've spent so long in the shadows myself, wearing masks the organization gave us, that theirs don't even faze me.

Maybe that's the real problem.

The mask is something I respect.

I've worn one too many times myself.

My half-skull mask hiding my face, the hood of my jacket up, a blade strapped down the inside of my thigh while I creep into places no one should know I'm in. When I'm on jobs for the Organization—ones that don't show up in the DEA's pretty little database—I become something else entirely. A shadow. A ghost. A storm no one sees coming.

And they know that. They've *watched* me be that.

So maybe that's why I haven't been clawing at theirs more. Maybe that's why I haven't been trying to tear off their masks with bloody fingernails and demanding to know who they are. Because some part of me understands the power in anonymity.

Maybe that's why I'm not fighting as much as I should.

To see what's underneath. To demand names or identities or truths.

Because they already know *me*.

They've said it. Whispered it. *Proven* it in every cruel, calculated move they've made.

I know they've watched me for years. Know they've memorized the way I walk, the way I fight, the way I run my tongue over my teeth when I'm debating between cutting a man's Achilles or just dropping him with a bullet.

But who the fuck are *they*?

Are they part of my everyday life?

People I see at work? On the street? At the goddamn café down the block where I used to get those cherry pastries they somehow knew I loved?

Or are they just ghosts—observers with obsession issues and a god complex—who've watched me from a distance for far too long?

They say they want Reyes in the ground. That I was going to get myself killed. So they *had* to interfere.

But why?

Why did it matter to them?

How did they even *know* he was targeting me? That I was getting close enough to be a threat?

And why risk blowing my entire case—*my entire life*—just to get in the way?

I should be thinking clearer than this. Plotting my next move. Getting answers. Setting fires.

But all I can do is stare ahead numbly as Rule carries me into the house like I'm something breakable. Like he hasn't already fucked the fight out of me on the forest floor. Like he didn't stretch me open and destroy me—*twice*.

Because of course the bastard hadn't been satisfied with just one round. No. He'd stayed inside me, still hard, still *there*, his magic cock dragging slow and deep like he was etching himself into my fucking soul. He didn't rush. Didn't pull out. Just rocked into me with that same unbearable control until the *asshole got a second wind* and fucked me again. Right there in the dirt, while I was still shivering from the first round.

And now?

Now he's carrying me through the house like I weigh nothing. Like I'm not still leaking his cum down my thigh. As though I'm not splattered with dried blood and humiliation and goddamn *need*.

The sun's up now. Full and bright and mocking.

I don't know what time it is anymore, but I know it's long past dawn. I know I should feel shame. Fury. Something sharp enough to cut through the haze still thick in my veins.

But all I feel is hollow.

No—*raw*.

Because everything hurts. My thighs. My wrists. My pride. And still, my body remembers every second of it.

Rule carries me straight back to the room they've kept me in and heads directly into the bathroom attached to it.

It's too pristine. Sleek, polished, dark marble that gleams like it's mocking me. Now I'm going to be bleeding all over those pretty surfaces.

Rule sets me down on the counter like I'm something precious. As though I won't immediately try to slit his throat if I ever get my hands free and a knife in them.

He doesn't speak. Just steadies me with one firm gloved hand on my thigh, the other ghosting along my waist as he makes sure I don't fall.

As if I could fall *more* than I already have.

Once he's sure I'm not about to topple over, he unties my wrists before turning his back to me and moves toward the shower. As if this is normal and all just part of the fucking routine now.

And maybe it is.

Maybe that's what terrifies me most.

That even after everything—after blood and blades and forest soil smeared across my back while he fucked me until I forgot how to breathe—part of me wants him to come back.

Part of me wants him to touch me again. Wants both of them to touch me.

Part of me wants to see what happens next.

And *that*?

That's the part I don't know how to kill.

The shower hisses to life, steam beginning to curl into the air as Rule turns the handle. The sound is almost soothing—enough to lull me into some false sense of calm after being completely and thoroughly wrecked in a goddamn forest.

But it doesn't last.

Because a moment later, the shrill ring of a phone cuts through the air like a bullet.

My spine snaps straight.

Rule freezes. His head turns slightly toward the sound, his whole body coiling with instant alertness. Then, slowly, he turns the water back off. The sudden silence makes the ringing feel even louder, sharper, more intrusive.

He steps back toward me with deliberate calm, reaching into one of his deep pockets. I see the glint of a familiar screen as he pulls it out.

My phone.

The fucker has *my* phone.

The ringtone grows louder now it's not buried in his pocket, while he is gripping it in his gloved fist like a goddamn leash. His thumb ghosts over the edge of the screen, but he doesn't look at it. He looks at *me.*

Tilts his head.

Like a predator debating whether to play with its prey or sink its teeth in.

Then he speaks—low, steady, dangerous.

"Be a good girl, Seanna," he murmurs. "And remember our agreement."

That tone—it's not a suggestion. It's a fucking threat wrapped in velvet. My stomach twists. The fucking truce. I hadn't even thought about it when I ran earlier.

He extends the phone to me slowly, deliberately, like a test.

I don't hesitate. I take it with shaking fingers, my pulse a thunderstorm beneath my skin. The screen lights up with Hydessa's name.

My throat tightens.

Rule doesn't step away.

Instead, he plants both fists on the counter to either side of me, caging me in without even touching me. His body towers over mine, every inch of him heat and pressure and power. I can't move. Can't breathe.

Swallowing past the lump in my throat, I accept the call.

It clicks through, and I don't even get a full second before her voice comes through—soft, tentative, familiar.

"If I hide..." Hydessa whispers.

I swallow the lump in my throat. My lips move on autopilot, voice low, cracked, but steady.

"Then I'll seek..." I whisper back.

God, just hearing her voice almost breaks something in me.

Her sigh on the line is like a warm breeze, brushing against the jagged edges of my nerves.

"You okay?" she asks.

The question cuts. I want to say no. Want to scream *I'm chained in hell and I don't know who I am anymore and everything's on fire inside me and I think I might like it*—but my mouth won't cooperate.

I stare up at Rule's mask, his breath just barely audible above me, his arms braced like he owns this fucking space.

I swallow hard, forcing something that *might* pass for a laugh out of my throat.. "I was about to ask you the same thing."

My voice sounds almost normal. *Almost.*

But I don't answer her question.

And neither does she.

Typical.

We sit in silence, this heavy, awful silence full of everything we aren't saying.

Then I break it.

"Please make sure you're being careful," I say, the words a brittle whisper. "Look after yourself first. What you're doing there comes second, remember?"

My voice cracks a little at the end.

And Rule's breath flares against my skin.

The silence on the other end turns heavy. I know what Hydessa's thinking. She knows me. She knows I *don't* say things like that. I'm the one who charges in head-first, tells her to run toward the fire, to not waste time worrying.

But now I'm here, wrapped in invisible barbed wire, and all I want is for her to be safe.

She doesn't press. Not yet. But I can hear it. The tension tightening her voice, the inhale before the question—

I beat her to it.

"I'm sorry," I say, cutting her off before she can dig. "I have to go. I love you."

There's a beat.

"I love you too," she says, and then the line goes dead.

Silence falls again.

The screen goes black.

And I just sit there.

My hair a mess, the faint streaks of blood still smeared on my thighs, the necklace locked around my neck, and not sure what the fuck I'm doing anymore.

Rule straightens slowly, gaze still fixed on me through those unreadable lenses.

The phone slides from my fingers to the counter, and I feel like I've been gutted.

Because I didn't say the code words.

I could've.

But I *didn't*.

And I'm not sure if it's because I couldn't find the right moment—

Or because part of me *didn't want out*.

Rule leans down just slightly, his breath ghosting the shell of my ear.

"Good girl," he murmurs.

And I swear to God, if I weren't still trembling from everything he had done to me—I'd punch him in the fucking throat.

Chapter 31

Seanna

I don't need help walking.

Try telling that to Rule—who lifts me off the counter like I'm some broken doll and carries me toward the shower as if I didn't just survive being hunted through a goddamn trap-laced forest and fucked into the soil like a prize-winning mare.

"Put me down," I growl, shoving weakly at his chest. "I'm not glass."

"No," he agrees calmly, stepping into the bathroom with that maddening steadiness of his. "But you're bleeding and dehydrated. So for once, try not being so fucking strong."

That shouldn't make my breath catch.

It shouldn't make something ugly twist in my chest either.

But it does.

The bastard sets me down carefully in the oversized shower stall, the tiles cold against my feet, steam already curling around us in lazy spirals. Then he steps back, but not far. Just enough to lean against the wall on the other side of the glass and cross his arms, black mask fixed on my naked body like I'm a specimen in his private collection.

I glare at him. "You're not staying."

"You want to fall face-first into ceramic and bleed out?" he asks mildly. "Didn't think so."

Arrogant son of a—

I step under the water.

And I let it hit me—hot and unrelenting. It stings against the welts, the shallow cuts, the bruises that are already blooming purple across my thighs and ribs. But I stand there anyway, fists clenched at my sides, trying not to collapse under the heat or his gaze.

I don't ask him to leave again.

Because I know he won't.

Because a small, sick part of me doesn't want him to.

I grab the soap and start scrubbing, harder than I need to. Like maybe I can scrape off the layers of Rule and Ruin still clinging to my skin. But no matter how raw I make myself, I still feel them there. Their hands. Their voices. Their fucking breath in my ear.

When I'm finished, I shut the water off and step out, dripping wet and exhausted.

Rule's already waiting with a towel. *Of course he is.*

I snatch it from him—but his hand doesn't let go. He holds it firm.

"Let me," he says, quieter now. "Just this once."

I want to scream at him. Tell him to fuck off. That I'm not his pet, not his responsibility, not his anything.

But the towel in his hand is soft. And I'm so goddamn tired.

So I let him.

He kneels and starts at my ankles, drying me with slow, deliberate strokes. Up my calves. Over my thighs. He doesn't rush. Doesn't leer. Just touches me like he has every right to. Like this is penance. Or prayer.

"Why do you care?" I ask suddenly, voice brittle and sharp with accusation. "Why any of this?"

Rule stills, the towel held loosely in his hands, his body tense, every muscle suddenly rigid beneath his tactical gear. "Because we've watched you for a very long time, Seanna. Longer than you can imagine."

I narrow my eyes, feeling a chill climb slowly up my spine. "How long?"

"Long enough," he murmurs, his voice softer now, almost distant. "Ruin found you first, years before we even met. It's not my place to tell his story, but he showed you to me. I was fifteen, just a fucked-up kid with too much anger and not enough purpose. And then I saw you through a video feed—footage he'd hacked into—and suddenly, you became all the purpose I needed."

My pulse quickens, breath catching in my chest. "What the hell does that even mean?"

"It means we've watched every part of your life unfold," he continues. "The way you fight, the way you bleed, the way you hide every vulnerability behind rage and strength. We've watched you pace your cabin late at night when sleep wouldn't come. Seen you train until your knuckles bled because you'd rather hurt than break."

"I know how long it takes you to lace your boots in the morning when you're pissed off. I know you leave your cabin exactly two minutes early on Thursdays because you always drop by your sister's cabin to make sure she is safe. I know you grind your teeth if anyone talks over you. You clench your left fist tighter than your right when you lie. And you make grilled cheese when you're feeling low."

My throat tightens.

"I know," he breathes, pressing the towel to my collarbone, "that when you wear your hair in a braid, it's because you're trying to look more put together than you feel. I know you buy cherry pastries when you want a treat, and I know you eat the cream cheese out of the center first. I know that the sound of a lighter flick makes you flinch. I know where every scar on your body came from."

His voice drops even lower.

"And I know you pretend not to want to be owned. But you do. You want someone to see through every shield you wear and still choose you. You want someone to take the control away, just long enough for you to remember how to breathe."

My heart's slamming in my chest now.

"I care, we both care," he murmurs, leaning in slightly, "because we've been inside your life longer than you realize. Not just a shadow, not just a name. We were there. Every time you thought you were being watched—you were. Every time you felt like someone had been inside your cabin—someone had. It was us."

I swallow hard, trying to breathe.

His voice grows quieter, deeper. "And we watched you bury your friend last year—Jessica. The one who went through DEA training with you. Watched you stand by her grave in the rain, fists clenched so tight I thought your bones would break, all because Reyes' drugs stole her from you."

Pain lashes through me, sudden and raw, slicing open memories I've tried desperately to keep buried. "Stop it."

"No," he says firmly, standing to his full hight. "You asked, so now you get the truth. You consumed us, little storm. Ruin first, and then me. You became our obsession, our fixation—something fierce and unstoppable. We've watched you burn through life, leaving destruction in your wake, and instead of turning away, we found ourselves wanting to step closer. Wanting to feel the heat firsthand, knowing full well it might destroy us."

I'm breathing harder now, chest heaving as something dark and tangled coils tightly within me. "Why do you both call me that?" I ask, my voice quieter than I intend but steady.

His head tilts slightly, considering me. The stillness in him is more unnerving than any movement could ever be. "Little storm?" he repeats, as though savoring the words.

I nod, my heart aching beneath the weight of everything he's revealing. He steps closer. My heart slams violently against my ribs, but I refuse to flinch.

"Because," he murmurs, voice silk and smoke, "you've swept through our lives like thunder and lightning. Unpredictable. Fierce. Impossible to control."

He circles me slowly, and I shiver despite myself. I sense him behind me, his presence brushing my skin like an invisible force. The heat radiating from him, the whisper of his mask against my hair, intensifies my awareness of how dangerously close he is.

"But storms are also beautiful," he continues softly. "Terrifyingly so. They are untamed power, captivating chaos."

A shudder rakes through me—not fear, but something else, something darker and deeper. His gloved fingers trace the curve of my shoulder, barely touching, sending electricity jolting through every nerve.

"So we watched you," he says. "We waited. We saw you set your sights on Reyes. Tried to predict your moves. But deep down, we knew storms can't truly be tamed. They can only be admired—or feared."

I turn my head slightly, desperate to catch a glimpse beyond his mask. "And you?" I ask, voice barely above a whisper. "Do you admire the storm, or fear it?"

He pauses for a moment, his proximity suffocating, his touch tantalizingly withheld. "Both," he admits, the single word wrapping around me like velvet bindings. "And perhaps that's exactly why you're irresistible. Taking you was like capturing lightning in a bottle—thrilling, impossible, bound to burn us if we aren't careful."

My breath hitches as he finally steps back into view. My pulse thundering in my ears.

"Now you know," he says quietly, and for the first time, there is something in his voice that might be vulnerability. "Does the truth change anything?"

I stare at him, anger and longing warring violently inside me. My voice emerges raw, betraying every conflict I feel. "It changes everything—and nothing at all."

I say it without thinking, without even caring that I'm still standing there naked, steam curling from my skin, water clinging to my body like grief I can't wipe away. I don't care anymore. There's nothing left to hide. Nothing Rule hasn't already seen, nothing he doesn't already fucking know.

So I ask a question that's been plaguing me.

"How did you do it?" My voice is quieter now, but laced with a sharp edge. "Cruz. The club. All of them. You took them out by yourself. That wasn't chaos—it was surgical. They were cartel soldiers. On alert. Guarding one of Reyes' top men. And you walked in like it was nothing."

He doesn't answer right away. Just stands there, still as shadow, the towel hanging limply in his hand like he's waiting for something he can't name.

"It wasn't nothing," he says eventually. "But it was easy."

My stomach twists. "How? It was broad daylight. Not club hours. There weren't even patrons there to hide behind. Just Cruz and his men. Locked down. Private. No reason to expect anyone."

His voice is flat. Distant.

"Porque sabían a quién servían."

The words roll off his tongue like smoke.

And I freeze.

Because I know what that means.

Because I speak enough Spanish to recognize the quiet weight behind them.

Because they knew who they served.

My eyes narrow. My heart kicks up. "What did you just say?"

Rule tilts his head slightly, like he hadn't meant to say it aloud.

"I said I walked in," he replies instead.

"No." I take a step forward. My voice sharpens. My chest heaves with the effort of trying to contain the storm building inside me. "No more cryptic bullshit. How did you just walk in? How did they let you get that close with a weapon? And then not a single one of them raised a fucking gun?"

He looks at me for a long time.

Then he says it.

"Because they would never raise a weapon to Reyes' son."

The air leaves my lungs like a punch. The room tilts. My knees threaten to buckle.

"What... what did you say?"

He doesn't flinch. Doesn't look away.

"My real name is Kingston Reyes."

It hits like a gunshot straight to my spine.

And then I move.

I launch at him, fury snapping through me like a live wire. I swing, and he catches my wrist. I twist, kick, claw, screaming without sound. My whole body fights him like it's the only thing left keeping me from shattering.

"You bastard! You fucking lying, manipulative, stalking piece of shit!"

He grabs both my wrists and shoves me back against the wall, water still dripping from my skin. I don't care. I bare my teeth like an animal, thrashing.

"You're just like him," I snarl. "You think the world owes you. You think you can take whatever you want just because your name is Reyes! You think you can watch me, take me, fuck with my life—and what? That makes you better than your father?"

"Don't," he growls, his voice sharp and guttural. "Don't you fucking *dare* compare me to him."

I spit the words like acid. "Why not? You use power and fear. You stalked me, drugged me, kidnapped me. You played God and called it obsession. If that's not a Reyes move, then what the hell is it?"

"I'm not him!" he snaps, voice like thunder now, echoing off the tiles. "Everything he built, I want to tear apart with my bare fucking hands. Every brick, every drop of blood that funded his empire—I want it gone, burned to ashes. Because of what it cost people like you. Because of what it cost *me*."

"Then show me your face," I demand. My voice breaks, my hands trembling even as I try to wrest them from his grip. "If you're not him, then take off the fucking mask. Look me in the eye. Prove it."

His hold tightens. He doesn't move.

Silence.

The refusal is louder than a confession.

"You can't," I whisper, devastated. "Because you're still hiding. Because you're still him."

His jaw clenches behind the black tactical mask. "I'm not my father, Seanna. But I'll never show you my face if the only reason you want to see it is to look for the monster you think I am. You already know the face beneath this mask—but right now, you're not in the right frame of mind to remember that. And the face I wear? It's not my father's. It's not carved by power or fear. It's the face of someone who chose to fight against everything he built. Someone who has already bled trying to undo the legacy I was born into. And deep down, you know that. You've seen it—you just don't realize it yet."

My throat thickens with grief, rage, betrayal.

I shove him again. This time with everything I have.

And this time he lets me go.

I don't say another word.

I just wrap the towel around me, turn my back to him, and walk away.

But my knees are shaking.

And my world is already burning.

Chapter 32
Ruin

She didn't eat.

Not the lunch. Not the dinner.

I wasn't home when Rule tried—had my own mess to deal with on the outside—but when I finally stepped through the door, he was waiting in the hall like he'd aged ten years in my absence. His voice was low and careful when he told me like he thought I'd be pissed.

I wasn't.

Not really.

He said she just stared at the tray, then turned her back and wrapped herself tighter in one of those oversized shirts she always wears when she's trying to convince herself she's safe. Like fabric and defiance are armor enough. Like comfort can't be turned into a weapon if you know how to wield it right.

He's lucky she didn't throw the plate in his face.

I think she wanted to.

I could hear it in his voice—how much it wounded him. He hides it, but I know him. I know what it does to him when she won't even look at him. He can handle violence. Fury. Screaming.

But silence?

Silence is a blade between his ribs.

He can deal with knives and bullets and blood, but he can't stomach her silence.

Still, it won't last.

Her rage burns hot and fast—wildfire that consumes everything in its path. But fire doesn't last forever. Not even hers. It'll smolder. It'll shrink down to embers. And then it'll shift. It always does. Because that's what makes her dangerous.

Rule left after that to take care of his own errands, but really I think he needed a moment's distance.

So, I wait until she's asleep before I go in.

It's almost a ritual now—the way I sit in this armchair, silent, breathing her in from across the room. The way I watch the lines of her body beneath the sheets. The way I catalogue the small things. The twitch in her thigh. The way she curls her fingers near her face. The slow, even rhythm of her breath.

I watch her like she's something sacred.

Like she's mine.

Because she is.

Her lips are parted. Her lashes tremble with whatever images dance behind her eyes. I wonder if she dreams of us. I hope she does. I hope she wakes up soaked in it, dazed and desperate, craving what only we can give.

She looks fragile like this.

She isn't. But fuck, it's a good illusion.

I want to touch her. I want to crawl into that bed and stretch her open again, press my mouth to the bruises we left and make her cry out my name in a tone that isn't rage but surrender.

The truce between her and Rule is already ash. The moment he told her who he was—Kingston Reyes—the fragile line holding her tolerance in place snapped. I knew it would. I heard when she screamed like she wanted to rip the Reyes name straight out of his throat. And I get it. I do. That rage? That explosion? It was beautiful.

And I can't even blame her for it. I saw it coming the second Rule started slipping deeper into his obsession for her. But I understand why he did it.

Because I couldn't have held that secret much longer either.

But it doesn't bode well.

Not for when she finds out the rest.

I've spent years watching her through screens, through stolen surveillance, through audio files that I played on repeat until I could recite every inflection in her voice like a psalm. I memorized the rhythm of her footsteps before I ever heard them in person. I know her better than she knows herself.

And now?

Now she's here. Warm. Breathing. Close enough to touch.

I don't want to go back to distance. I don't want to return to cold monitors and silent worship. I want this. Her. All of it.

The part of me that still pretends to be a good man—that thin layer of restraint I only wear when I have to—it's screaming at me to go slow. To give her time. Space. A chance to adjust.

But the rest of me?

The part that's been starved for her?

That part wants to *devour* her.

How will she react when she finds out the rest? When she learns how deep this goes? When she finally understands who I am underneath the mask... and how long I've loved her?

Because make no mistake.

I do love her.

Not the sweet, forgiving kind. Not the kind that builds houses or reads poetry.

No. Mine is the kind of love that chains itself to her soul and whispers in the dark.

The kind that watches her sleep like a goddamn altar and takes pictures. That breathes in the scent of her skin, counts every eyelash, and imagines the sounds she'll make when she finally lets herself be ours, fully and without fear.

And now that she's here?

I don't ever want to let her go.

Even if she hates me for it. Even if she tries to run again.

Because obsession this deep doesn't fade.

And whether she knows it yet or not—Seanna Darling belongs to us.

She always has.

She paired her oversized shirt with a pair of panties, as though that could form some sort of shield between her and me.

It can't.

Her defiance is beautiful, but futile.

I rise from the armchair in the corner, every step toward her a deliberate surrender to obsession. Even if she hates us right now, she can't erase what she told us. What she admitted in that thick moment of weakness, when words filled with need spilled from her lips like confession.

She told us her fantasy. She confessed it like it would never come back to bite her. Like admitting it out loud didn't make it real.

To be taken. In sleep. No pretense. No permission.

And now? Now she's asleep in one of those shirts like a lamb in its own soft wool, dreaming she's safe.

She isn't.

The sheets are low, the shirt barely covering her thighs. I drag it down gently, revealing the pale curves of her hips, the band of her panties thin against her skin. I spread her thighs and kneel between them, sliding the panties aside. Not off. Just enough to bare her. Just enough to remind her body it belongs to me before her mind even wakes.

My cock is already hard. Has been since I stepped in the room. Since I saw her curled up like a gift she doesn't remember wrapping. The two steel barbells piercing the head throb with every beat of my pulse, a subtle weight and pressure I've learned to savor. I grip myself, line up, and push in.

The piercings drag across her entrance, the sensation sharp and perfect, her slick heat clutching around me like a fist. She doesn't wake. Not yet.

She sighs in her sleep, body instinctively parting for me. Like she knows, like her body knows, even in her sleep.

I move in her, slow and steady, dragging my cock out just enough to feel the barbells catch and pull before sinking back in with a groan. Again. And again. A handful of careful, measured thrusts—each one a claim, each one coaxing her body deeper into instinct before consciousness catches up. The steel piercings press against her walls in all the right places, making my restraint fray at the edges. I fuck her slowly, deeply, the barbells tugging just enough to drive me insane. Every drag out makes her walls twitch. Every push back in forces them deeper.

She's so tight around me, her body still mostly slack with sleep even as I move inside her. Each thrust is a revelation, a dark promise. My obsessive thoughts spiral as I fuck into her slowly, savoring every clench of her walls. She has no idea what we've done. That she is completely unprotected now, ripe and ready.

The knowledge makes me throb harder inside her, a primal surge of possessive need. I want to fill her up, paint her insides with my cum until it takes root. Until she's swollen with my child. The fantasy consumes me as I roll my hips, burying myself as deep as I can go.

My thrusts become slightly harder, more deliberate. Each push drives me deeper, the steel piercings dragging against her most sensitive spots. Her body responds instinctively, even in sleep—muscles clenching, hips shifting subtly to take me deeper.

A soft moan escapes her lips and she begins to stir, consciousness seeping back in. Her brow furrows in sleepy confusion, body tensing slightly beneath mine.

Her breath starts to shift. The rhythm changes. Her fingers twitch.

She wakes as a cry of pleasure leaves her beautiful lips, with me buried deep inside her.

Her body tenses as consciousness floods back, her muscles instinctively clenching around me. The moment she realizes she's being fucked, a soft protest rises in her throat.

"Rule?" she mumbles, confusion and lingering anger threading through her voice. "What are you—"

"Try again, darling," I purr, my voice low and dangerous.

She goes completely still. Recognition floods her eyes as she realizes it's me inside her. The anger shifts, transforms—becomes something darker, more primal.

"Ruin," she breathes, and it sounds like a curse and a prayer.

Her hips roll against me, no longer resisting. "Don't stop," she whispers, voice raw. "Fuck me. Please. Make me forget it all, just for a moment."

I growl, something feral and possessive breaking loose inside me. It doesn't want to be gentle. It fills me with pure, unrestrained need.

I grip her hips and start to move—harder. Faster. Each thrust a violent claim, the steel piercings dragging against her most sensitive spots. She arches beneath me, crying out as I fuck her with a ruthlessness she's never seen from me.

I brace a hand above her head and keep the other locked around her thigh, pinning it up so I can thrust deeper, harder, pounding her into the mattress with the force of everything I've held back for too fucking long.

She doesn't ask for tenderness. She doesn't beg me to slow. She doesn't flinch or cry.

She *takes it.*

Takes *me.*

And fuck, I swear I've never seen anything more beautiful than the way her body surrenders even as her eyes burn like they want to murder me. She's still pissed. Still furious about Rule's reveal. But right now? That fury is all tangled up in lust, all mixed into the haze of me slamming into her, dragging the sound of my name from her throat like it's been trapped there all along.

"More," she gasps, nails clawing at the sheets as I drive my hips forward with brutal precision. "Fuck—don't stop. Don't you *dare* stop."

I don't.

Because I know what she needs.

Not comfort. Not apologies. She needs to be *wrecked.* She needs the truth rewritten on her skin.

And I do it with every filthy, obsessive thrust.

One of her hands rises, reaching blindly for my face, but I don't let her unmask me. I catch her wrist, pin it to the mattress.

"Not yet," I whisper. "You're not ready."

Not ready for what I look like. For who I *am* underneath the armor and devotion and years of watching her life unfold like prophecy.

I roll my hips deeper, harder, making her breath hitch. I feel her start to shake beneath me, that telltale tension tightening her, her orgasm building fast and feral. Her pussy clamps down on me with each thrust, fluttering tight, and the sound she makes when I thrust in again—fuck, it's *divine.*

I lean down, my mask brushing against the sweat-slick curve of her cheek, the lenses of my tactical glasses close enough to reflect her wrecked expression as I bury my cock deeper than she's ever taken me before.

Her moan is ragged, broken, *perfect.*

I keep fucking her like that—unrelenting. My full weight behind every thrust, the piercings rubbing across every nerve ending inside her. I feel her break apart again and again beneath me. Her cunt tightens around me like she's trying to trap me inside, and maybe that's what I want too—because I'm not going anywhere.

I want her bred and fucked open. I want her soaked in us, wrecked and shaking and so thoroughly claimed by us that the thought of anyone else makes her *sick.*

I pull out just long enough to flip her onto her stomach, drag her hips back, and slam into her again. She screams into the pillow and it's not from pain—it's from *release.*

Because no one fucks her like this but us.

No one worships and destroys her in the same breath like we do.

The wet sound of my cock fucking into her echoes through the room as I lose myself in the rhythm of her. She's soaked and pulsing, her body greedy for every inch I give her.

And when her third orgasm crashes through her, her whole body seizing, I press in and *stay* there—cock throbbing deep, stretching her wide, grinding down as I groan and spill deeply inside her.

She gasps at the heat. At the *depth.*

And I hold there. Buried to the hilt.

I don't speak. I just breathe.

Heavy and ragged against her skin as she trembles underneath me.

Because this moment means everything.

And I don't care if she hates us tomorrow.

Because tonight, her body told the truth.

That it belongs to us.

Chapter 33
Seanna

He's watching me again.

Same armchair. Same posture. Same silent stare like I'm a painting he keeps trying to memorize in case I disappear.

As though he didn't wake me last night with his cock already buried deep inside me. As though he didn't fuck me until my body melted into the mattress and I couldn't remember why I hated them.

As though he didn't leave me raw, shaking, and wide-eyed in the dark.

But now? Now he just sits there like the model of fucking restraint while I stir under the covers, pretending I didn't notice the way my thighs are still sticky from him.

I don't give him the satisfaction of a hello.

I throw the blanket off and swing my legs over the edge of the bed, head pounding, body sore, mouth dry. My oversized shirt clings to my skin and smells faintly like sweat and him, which only pisses me off more.

Ruin's voice breaks the quiet. Low. Even. Like I haven't been fantasizing about driving a knife through his ribcage since I opened my eyes.

"Rule told you because he had to." His tone is quiet, like he's being reasonable. "It was time. Even if it's not the whole truth yet."

I snort. "Not the whole truth?" I shoot him a glare sharp enough to draw blood. "What does it matter if it's the *whole* truth? You think hiding the fact that he's Reyes' little prince isn't *just slightly* relevant?"

"He's not hiding anymore," Ruin answers carefully, voice still modulated beneath the mask. "He knew it would cost him something. He told you anyway."

"Yeah," I mutter, standing and shoving my fingers through my hair. "Because nothing says trust like kidnapping and then revealing that you're cartel fucking royalty."

Ruin watches me, silent for a beat. Then he leans forward slightly, arms on his knees. "You would've found out eventually."

"That supposed to make it better?" I ask flatly, walking to the dresser and yanking out a fresh shirt and clean underwear. "Newsflash, I don't feel *grateful*."

He doesn't flinch. Doesn't rise to the bait.

"He still hasn't told you everything," he says, voice low and honest. "Neither have I. But this... this was a start."

I stare at him for a long moment, then shake my head. "You know what I hate most?" I ask quietly. "You fuckers think that because you know me—because you've *watched* me—I'm going to roll over and play nice once the truth starts dripping out."

"You don't roll over," Ruin replies calmly. "You bare your teeth and tear out throats."

"Damn right," I snap, turning away from him and storming into the bathroom. I shut the door harder than necessary, but not hard enough to break anything. Not yet.

I stay in there longer than I need to. Take care of business. Wash my face. Avoid looking at myself in the mirror.

I throw on the shirt and underwear I grabbed—still oversized, still one of mine they brought from home, but this one doesn't reek of memories just yet. I grab a hair tie, twist my hair into a bun. When I come back out, the room's empty. Ruin's gone.

Good.

I sink onto the edge of the bed slowly, hands braced on my thighs, staring at the floor like it's supposed to hold some kind of fucking answer. My chest tightens. Not with grief. Not with fear.

With the kind of rage that smolders quietly and poisons you from the inside.

I hate that they think they know me. I hate that they *do*.

And most of all? I hate that part of me is still listening. Still curious. Still *waiting* for the next goddamn shoe to drop like I don't already know I'm barefoot in a fucking minefield.

They haven't shown me their faces.

They haven't told me the rest.

And I haven't burned the place down yet.

Which might be the most terrifying part of all.

The rest of the day drags.

Rule tries. Of course he does. He steps just inside the door at breakfast with a plate and what I assume is cold coffee. Simply waits with that stupid patience of his, standing there like some kind of wounded dog.

I simply turn away.

At lunch, I finally accept the food, because hunger trumps pride and I'm not stupid. I take the plate and water from his hands before telling him to get out, and I eat in silence. The food is good. Of course it is. The asshole probably made it himself, like feeding me will make me forgive him.

It doesn't.

I eat everything. And I don't say a word.

Dinner is the same. Except this time when he steps in, I have a scowl already in place.

"Seanna—"

"Don't." I snatch the plate from his hand. "You had your moment of honesty. Congrats. Gold star. Don't think for one fucking second it bought you anything."

His jaw clenches and I can tell he wants to say more—but he doesn't.

Smart.

I point him out the door again. Eat. Stew. Let the rage cool just enough to be bearable.

I pace the room once. Twice. My muscles ache with the need to hit something, scream, *fight*. But the rage doesn't boil anymore. It broods. Smolders. Lingers like a storm just waiting for someone stupid enough to step outside.

When I go into the bathroom again I catch my reflection in the mirror—hair a mess, face pale, eyes sharp and wild.

Still me.

Just... more cracked than I'd like to admit.

Eventually, I peel myself off the edge of the storm and force myself into the shower. Not because I want to feel clean—God knows that ship has sailed—but because my skin feels tight, like it's trying to crawl away from my bones. Like if I don't do something, I'll lose whatever grip I've got left.

Hot water. Steam. Silence.

None of it helps.

I scrub until my skin is raw, until I can't smell them anymore—except I *can*. Still there. Still underneath everything.

When I step out, the mirror's fogged, the room thick with heat, but nothing's changed. I towel off, throw on another one of the shirts they packed from my drawer.

Later, Ruin returns.

I know it's him because he isn't moving like a kicked puppy. He just opens the door and walks in like it's his right.

"Do you have a fucking death wish?" I snap, already standing, body coiled tight.

He closes the door behind him without a word.

"I gave you space," he says calmly, voice still filtered through the modulator. "All day. You've had time to think."

I narrow my eyes, arms crossed. "And you decided now was the moment to get brave?"

He tilts his head slightly, like he's studying me—measuring the amount of fury left in my bones.

"You're not as angry as you were."

"Maybe I'm just better at hiding it," I shoot back, taking a step toward him. "Or maybe I'm just saving it for the right moment."

He doesn't flinch. Doesn't move. Just keeps staring through that mask like it sees straight through me.

"You're right to be pissed," he says eventually. "You deserved the truth sooner. But if Rule had told you from the start, you never would've listened. You would've run. And I wasn't about to lose you over your own fucking pride."

My lip curls. "Don't talk to me about pride like it's some flaw. You of all people don't get to lecture me."

His gloved hands flex slightly at his sides, like he wants to reach for me but knows better. "You think I'm here to lecture you?"

"Then why *are* you here?" I demand, stepping in close. "To explain? To justify the lies? To make another speech about how this is for my own good?"

"No," he says. "I'm here because I couldn't stay away any longer."

My breath catches.

He closes the distance in one slow step, towering over me like some specter of obsession that's been haunting my dreams. I hate how the sight of either of them does something to me. How it pulls heat low in my stomach despite everything. Despite *him*.

"Get out," I whisper, not backing down even as my voice betrays me.

He lifts a hand but doesn't touch me, just hovers it near my jaw. "Tell me you don't want to understand. That you don't want to know the rest. And I'll leave."

I say nothing. I can't. Because the truth is—I *do* want to know. Every dark, twisted secret they're still hiding. Every fucked-up reason they think I belong to them. Every mask. Every name. Every motive.

But I'm not giving him that. Not yet.

"I don't forgive you," I say instead.

"I'm not asking you to."

"And I'm not yours."

His voice drops low. "Yes, you are."

My skin prickles. I hate that he's right.

Hate that I'm not throwing a punch. Hate that I'm letting him stand this close. Hate that my body remembers the way he touched me like he knew it better than I do.

His voice softens. "We've both done fucked-up things, Seanna. You're not clean. You never wanted to be. And that's why this works. Because Rule and I—we don't want the sanitized version of you."

He shifts even closer now, like he's daring me to swing. Like he *wants* it. My pulse jumps, but I don't move. I don't give ground. I just stare up at him like I'm willing him to combust under the weight of everything I haven't said yet.

But he doesn't burn.

"I knew who you were before I ever saw you," Ruin says quietly. "Before I saw your face. Before I ever heard your voice. Your name was already carved into my fucking head."

That stills me.

He continues.

"I was young. A teenager. Too young to be feeling what I felt for someone I hadn't even laid eyes on. But it didn't matter. Because the second I knew you existed, it was already over for me."

My stomach twists.

"I watched everything," he says, softer now. "Every move. Every breath you gave to the world. And it wasn't enough. It was *never* enough. I needed more. I've always needed more."

He tilts his head again, and for the first time, there's something fraying around the edges of his calm. Something dangerous.

"It got worse with time. My obsession grew deeper, sicker. I stopped pretending it was anything else. I stopped fighting it. And when Rule finally saw you too?" He gives a slow exhale. "We *knew* we were in this obsession together. Because no one else would ever fucking understand what you are."

I swallow hard, something thick rising in my chest that I *refuse* to call emotion.

"I would kill for you, Seanna," Ruin says, voice low and lethal now. "I have. I will again if I have to."

My breath stalls.

"I'd burn down cities if it meant keeping you out of someone else's hands. I'd flood streets in blood and sleep like a baby next to you. There is no world where I let you go. No version of me that ever fucking stops."

My heart is thundering now. Not from fear. Not exactly.

From the terrifying pull of hearing someone say the thing you didn't even realize you've always craved.

"I'd burn down the goddamn world for you," he finishes, voice a gravel-sharp whisper behind the mask. "And I wouldn't feel a single fucking ounce of guilt."

Silence pulses between us.

I hate him. I want to touch him. I want to run. I want to *stay*.

My jaw clenches, hands curled into fists. "You're insane."

His head dips. "I know."

"You're unhinged."

"Yes."

"I'm still not yours."

He laughs quietly—low, dark, reverent. "That's the funniest lie you've ever told."

And then he does the thing I *don't* expect.

He turns.

He walks toward the door like he didn't just tear himself open at my feet. Like he didn't just admit something that would make most people scream.

But before he leaves, he pauses, hand on the knob.

"You'll know everything soon. And when you do? You'll understand why this was never going to end any other way."

The door clicks shut behind him.

And I'm left with silence. But it's not a peaceful silence. The kind of silence that comes after a detonation—when the world still feels like it's ringing and you're waiting to see if the building is going to collapse or hold.

I stare at the door like it might open again. Like he might take it back. Or come back and finish what he started.

I'm shaking. Not visibly. Not enough for someone else to see.

But I feel it. Under my skin. In the pit of my stomach.

I sink onto the edge of the bed slowly, chest tight, thoughts spiraling.

Because I should hate him. But I don't.

And he was right about one thing.

It was a lie.

Chapter 34
Seanna

The armchair is empty again.

And I don't fucking trust it.

Last time it was empty, I thought—stupidly—that maybe they'd let up. Maybe the obsession had quieted. Maybe I wasn't being watched every second like some lab rat in heat. And then I opened that door and ran, thinking I could outpace them.

Only to be hunted through their goddamn trap-rigged forest by Rule like prey.

So no. I'm not buying it. For *whatever* reason the chair is empty. It's probably just bait.

I stare at it, muscles tense, every inch of me humming with unease. My mind won't shut the fuck up. Not after everything they've told me. Not after everything I've felt.

Their confessions claw under my skin and build a nest. The kind you can't burn out. The kind that eats you from the inside.

I'm not this person, or at least, I wasn't. I was rage and vengeance. I was the woman who built her career on gutting predators and walking out clean. And now?

Now my gut twists when I think about what might be behind their masks, about wanting them to crawl between my legs while I sleep. I dream about their hands and wake up soaking wet, caught between hatred and hunger.

My obsession used to be taking Reyes down. It was my everything. But now?

Now I'm obsessed with *them*.

And I hate it.

Fuck, I should still be fighting this. I should be attacking the next asshole who walks through the door, seizing a vehicle, and getting the hell out of here, not thinking about the twisted thrill of another primal chase through their fucked-up playground. But their confessions have wormed beneath my defenses, gnawed at my resolve, and left me uncertain of everything I thought I knew about myself.

But instead, I'm still here sitting in this goddamn cage. I keep thinking about their hands. Their voices. The truth buried under all that armor. The confessions that carved deeper than any blade ever could.

I'm not this fucking woman. I'm unraveling. Piece by piece. And I don't know how to stop it.

The door opens without warning—of course it does—and Rule walks in with a tray of scrambled eggs and a mug. He sets it down gently, then steps back—calm, back to the cool, controlled persona from before. Yesterday's raw vulnerability might as well have never happened.

Suspicion gnaws at me, but I eat, grateful for the quiet reprieve even though it won't last long. I pick at the food slowly, eyes flicking toward the mug. It's hot but not boiling when I finally take a sip—fresh coffee. That pisses me off more than if it had been cold. He didn't just bring me food. He made sure it would be good. And of course, he watches.

Rule crosses his arms, voice smooth like steel wrapped in silk. "Still haven't decided whether to stab me or fuck me again, have you?"

I don't even blink. "Not mutually exclusive."

He huffs a low breath through his mask—amused, maybe. "I figured if I brought hot coffee, I might not get stabbed today."

I arch a brow and take a slow sip, letting the silence stretch. "Bribery and sarcasm. Impressive. Trying a new strategy?"

He leans against the wall like he's settling in. "I've got layers. You just keep peeling them off with your claws."

I snort. "Cute. Bet you practiced that one."

"Only in my head," he says, tone shifting—sharper now, more pointed. "Must have been absolute torture—no constant flow of coffee for days. Surprised you're still functional."

I arch a brow, lifting the mug again with deliberate slowness. "You have no idea how close to death you've been keeping me."

He hums. "Oh, I think I have some idea."

I set the mug down harder than necessary, the ceramic hitting the table sharply. "Trust me, if coffee withdrawal was my biggest problem, I'd consider myself lucky."

He pushes off the wall, stepping closer with ease. "That's the thing about torture—it's all about perspective."

I rise from the bed, closing the distance between us, refusing to back down. "You're one twisted bastard, you know that?"

He leans forward just enough to make my heart skip, his breath ghosting over my cheek. "That's why we get along so well."

I growl. "You really don't know when to shut up."

"You don't want me quiet, little storm. You want me honest. You just hate that you're starting to believe me," he says as he steps back.

I narrow my eyes. "Careful. You're mistaking my tolerance for trust."

He tilts his head, just slightly. "No. I'm counting on the fact that you know the difference."

Before I can respond, he calmly turns away, collects the tray from the table, and leaves without another word.

The quiet doesn't last.

Maybe an hour passes. Maybe less. I lose track of time staring at the walls like they're supposed to give me answers. My pulse has finally settled into something approaching normal and my coffee is long gone.

Then the door opens.

Rule steps inside, but there's something different about his posture—like he's braced for impact. My phone is in his outstretched hand. Ringing.

Every nerve in my body goes still.

The last time I saw my phone was right before he dropped the bomb. Kingston fucking Reyes. That name has been ringing in my head like a curse ever since. Anger flares like a whipcrack—instant, burning.

But I don't move.

Not until he reaches me and places it in my hand, slow and precise, like he knows it might explode.

I don't thank him.

I don't speak.

My eyes lock on the device. The screen is glowing. Hydessa.

I stare at that screen for exactly one breath. Then I answer.

"Hey, sis," I say softly, injecting warmth I don't feel. The words taste wrong. They're not ours. They're never ours.

And I know she hears it immediately.

There's a pause on the other end of the line. A beat of silence I feel in my bones.

Then Hydessa responds, voice low and careful. "Hey, sis."

I don't look at Rule. I don't give him anything. I just keep my gaze fixed on the far wall, I focus on Hydessa, as though that's safer than acknowledging the six-foot fucking asshole standing beside me.

"How's the investigation going?" I ask, forcing cheer into my tone. I sound upbeat. Relaxed. Like I'm not currently sending out a silent scream.

"We got the bad guys," she says gently. "We always get them, remember?"

I force a hum of agreement, even though it cuts like a blade. I shift my weight on the bed, one leg folded under me, the phone pressed just a little closer to my ear, like proximity might make this less unbearable.

"I'm glad," I whisper. My fingers tighten around the phone. "I have to go, sis."

I hear her inhale. Sharp. My chest aches.

"I love you, Seanna," she says quickly, voice cracking right through the center of me.

"Love you too," I whisper back—and I end the call before I can fall apart.

***

Rule

She hands me back the phone with that fake-ass smile she's perfected so well—lips curled like everything's fine, like I didn't just witness the subtle tremble in her fingers or the stiffness in her shoulders.

But I see through it.

She can't lie to me, not really. I've watched her too long, studied every twitch in her jaw, every micro-expression she thinks she hides behind those sharp eyes. That smile doesn't fool me, not for a fucking second.

I hum low in my throat and slide the phone back into the pocket of my utility pants, letting the silence stretch just long enough to needle her nerves.

Then I move.

She growls the second I grab her arm and I don't bother explaining as I secure it back into the shackle bolted to the bed frame. She snarls and tries to claw at my face, her nails aiming for the gap beneath my mask. It's a fast swipe, well-placed. But I'm faster, snatching the hand midair and securing it to the bed frame too. The cuffs snap shut with a familiar metallic bite. It's not tight enough to cut off circulation. Just tight enough to remind her she's not calling the shots.

I don't flinch. Just stand at the edge of her fury and let it burn.

"I'm not stupid," I say simply. Cool. Detached. Unbothered.

Her glare could burn holes in walls.

"Don't worry, Seanna," I murmur. "You'll be punished for that."

She screams. Loud. Raw. Frustration and fury all twisted together into something sharp enough to flay.

I don't give her the satisfaction of a reaction.

I turn, stepping through the door. Shutting it behind me with a soft click.

Her voice keeps going. Screams trailing after me down the dim hallway like smoke from a fire I'm pretending not to smell. But I don't stop. I don't slow. I know she'll burn herself out eventually.

She always does.

My boots echo down the narrow corridor, steady despite the chaos behind me. I pass the stairs, duck into the main room—dark wood, colder air, reinforced everything—and finally breathe.

Then I reach up and peel the mask from my face.

The air hits cooler now. It always does after wearing it too long.

I pull my burner phone from my pocket and pull up the contact I need. It's practically the only name this phone knows.

He answers on the first ring. Doesn't speak, just hums.

Someone's near him.

"We have to move again," I say. "Her sister knows. This location is now compromised."

He responds with a darker hum. One I know too well.

Then his voice, quieter than mine and twice as deadly.

"Make it happen."

The line clicks off, and I don't waste a second.

Her phone is still warm in my pocket when I pull it out again. The screen is blank now—silent, innocent—but I know better. Hydessa knows. Which means others might soon, too. It's compromised. Contaminated. A liability.

I snap it in half.

The screen cracks with a satisfying crunch. Then I pry out the SIM, crush it under my boot, and toss the remains into the fireplace. One flick of my lighter and it's gone. No signal. No trail. No chance.

Then I move.

Every step is clockwork—methodical, precise. I clean the house top to bottom, scrubbing surfaces, wiping prints, burning anything with a trace of us. The dishes. The linens. Even the fucking doorknobs. It all gets cleaned and erased.

Anything we can't take or clean? Torched.

By the time I'm done, this place looks like we were never here. A ghost house. A blank slate.

Ruin's equipment is next—his high-end surveillance gear, servers, laptops, signal jammers. It all goes into two reinforced cases, which I load carefully into the back of the SUV. I double-check it, then lock it all down tight.

One task left.

I head back down the hallway—slow, controlled. Her room is quiet now, but I don't trust it. Not with her. Quiet with her could mean she's sharpening something.

When I open the door, she's sitting on the bed, arms still cuffed. Her legs are pulled tight to her chest like she's waiting. Like she knew I'd come.

And she's *ready*.

The second I step into range, she kicks. Hard. Right at my ribs.

I block it, but it still lands with enough force to remind me how fucking lethal she is even chained.

"Feisty," I mutter, catching her ankle, twisting and pulling to send her backward against the mattress.

She snarls, scrambling, swinging her other foot out, this time she goes for my face.

Her entire body is fighting now, a last stand.

I'm sure this sudden resurgence of anger is about that name. That fucking name that I hate. Kingston Reyes. It's like poison. I knew it would burn.

It's why I don't use that name.

I didn't choose it. That bastard did. That alone makes it toxic. I prefer the one I picked for myself.

Ruin's the same. He picked his own name, but not out of spite. He just wanted to disappear.

He went so far as to wipe us from every system that matters. Altered documents. Faked images. Scrambled facial recognition.

Our birth names? Dead and buried to anyone not family. The world doesn't get them. It gets what we became.

I move fast.

I drop my weight onto the bed, pinning her legs with my body. Her fists thrash, teeth bared, hair wild around her face like some mythic creature in chains. Beautiful. Terrifying.

Ours.

"Enough," I growl, yanking the small black canister from my pocket.

She sees it too late.

I press the nozzle under her nose and fire a burst of vapor.

She thrashes once more—violently. Then again. Then slower.

Her breathing hitches. Her limbs falter.

And then she slumps.

Her head lolls slightly to the side, lips parted, lashes fluttering as the sedative pulls her under.

I sit there for a beat, letting my own pulse come down. Then I release the restraints from her wrists. Her skin is warm, sweat-damp from the struggle, her breath slow and even.

With haste, I grab all the final things we need.

Clothes. Toiletries. The few items we brought from her cabin I shove into a bag. When everything's packed, I scoop her up into my arms. She fits there too well.

Her oversized shirt clings to her skin. Her bare legs dangle slightly, one arm curled against my chest as though even in unconsciousness she hasn't fully let go.

I carry her out of the house and to the SUV and lay her carefully across the back seat, strapping her in gently. My gloved hand brushes a lock of hair from her cheek before I close the door.

Then I slide behind the wheel, start the engine, and drive.

Chapter 35

Seanna

Consciousness creeps in slowly, gentle and deceptive, easing me back into reality like it's afraid to jolt me awake too quickly. A quiet groan slips past my lips, body sluggish, heavy like I'm swimming through molasses. Whatever sedative Rule used still lingers, dulling my edges, but not enough to mask the ache echoing deep within my bones. I stretch instinctively, only to feel familiar resistance—the cool leather cuffs wrapped around my wrists.

My eyes flutter open, vision blurred at first, but slowly sharpening, taking in my newest prison from where I'm secured to yet another new bed.

Another cage. Another goddamn room.

Except this room... this room isn't just a cage.

It's a goddamn temple built to worship everything they seem to think I embody.

And fuck if it doesn't scream their particular brand of obsession louder than ever.

If the other room felt tailored to me, this one fits like a goddamn glove.

It's beautiful in a way that makes my stomach twist. Dark and seductive—an offering, a shrine built from sin. The bed beneath me is massive, its headboard a luxurious slab of plush black velvet that begs to be touched. The silk sheets tangled around my body are burgundy, rich and bold, sliding over my skin like warm whispers. If decadence had a bedroom, this would be it.

There's a faint scent in the air—something dark and expensive. Leather and something spiced. Maybe sandalwood. Or clove. Whatever it is, it smells like them. Like power dressed in sin. The lighting is low. Soft golden pools of light warming only the edges of the room, casting long shadows that seem to move if I stare too long.

And it pisses me off because they know me so fucking well.

Testing the cuffs gently, I find I've got just enough slack to shift and sit up slightly, propping myself against the velvet headboard. The softness teases my skin, and I push down the absurd urge to rub my face against it like a fucking cat. It feels far too comfortable for a cage.

I shift again, slower this time, letting my bare feet brush against the sheets. The silk slips between my toes like it's trying to seduce me. My stomach turns. I fucking hate how good it feels. Every inch of this room is a trap—soft and scented and beautiful, designed to lull me, to convince me this is where I belong. Like if they make it tempting enough, I'll stop fighting. Like comfort can undo the fury.

My gaze sweeps across the room, sharp and assessing. Gray walls, dark enough to be soothing yet oppressive, adorned with minimalist art that feels too carefully chosen—black and white scenes hinting at stormy skies and shadowed forests. Dark, sleek furniture in shades of gray and black sits polished and impeccable, every angle deliberate, every surface spotless.

My heart stutters when I see the black velvet armchair tucked in the corner. Empty for now, but I know better. He'll be sitting there soon enough, watching.

Every detail of this room screams control, possession, and intimate knowledge of exactly who I am beneath all my armor. It's meticulous. Crafted. Designed to pull at threads I didn't even know were unraveling until now.

I shove away the discomfort that coils through my chest, refusing to acknowledge the creeping heat beneath the anger. Their twisted truths and hidden identities still linger in my thoughts, taunting me. They've stolen more than my freedom; they've seeped into my blood, rewired my fucking soul, and left me craving things I despise myself for.

And then my eyes catch on the nightstand beside me.

On the vase filled with black roses.

My jaw tightens, eyes narrowing dangerously. The flowers are stunning—flawless ebony blooms spilling artfully over the rim.

Lucky for those masked bastards they're not here, because the heavy crystal vase holding those roses would look perfect shattered against their skulls.

The door is closed, and I assume locked. I'm alone, but I'm not stupid enough to believe they aren't watching.

They're always watching.

Time passes.

Slow. Uneventful. Suffocating.

Eventually, the tension threading my spine loosens. The rage doesn't leave, not fully, but it simmers low and quiet, like embers waiting for dry kindling. My head lolls back against the velvet headboard, and I let my eyes close, just for a second. Just to rest. Just to breathe.

Sleep drags me back under like a riptide.

I don't dream.

Or maybe I do—dark things that curl like smoke, soft touches and sharp edges, masked shadows whispering things I'm too afraid to want.

But when I jolt awake, there's no more pretending.

They're here.

One of them sits in the black velvet armchair, legs spread, gloved fingers steepled beneath his chin like he's been there all along, watching me sleep like I'm some fascinating, dangerous thing under glass.

The other leans against the far wall, arms crossed over his chest, posture loose but unreadable. His mask gleams faintly in the low light, his silhouette cut from shadow. Casual. Lethal.

My body stiffens instantly.

I blink hard, heart thundering once before slamming itself into a wall of rage. "Jesus fucking Christ," I snap, voice hoarse. "You ever consider knocking before you decide to creep-watch me like a pair of serial killers?"

Neither of them moves.

I scan them both, my pulse pounding behind my eyes. Rule is the same—cool, steady—but Ruin? There's a stillness to him that unnerves me more than anything. He doesn't even twitch. Like he's carved out of something colder than bone. And yet... I swear I can feel the heat of his attention pinning me to the mattress.

Ruin is the one who speaks. Calm. Measured. Like I didn't just accuse him of being a psychopath with a voyeurism kink. Which, let's face it, I'm pretty certain he is at this point.

"That was very stupid of you."

I glare at him. "You'll have to be more specific. I do a lot of stupid shit these days. Mostly because of *you two*."

"You shouldn't have told Hydessa," he clarifies. His tone isn't angry. It's colder than that—flat, controlled, and edged with something dangerous beneath the surface.

I scoff, yanking against the cuffs even though I know it's pointless. "Yeah? Well, it was *stupid of you* to take me in the first place."

He doesn't show any reaction. Just sits there in that throne-like chair like judgment incarnate. Watching. Measuring.

"I should be out there," I growl, heat bubbling under my skin. "Hunting Javier. Stopping him from hurting anyone else. Instead, I'm stuck here like some twisted fucking pet while people die."

And I can't even say his last name anymore—not now. Not after learning Rule carries it too. *Reyes.* That word used to burn like gasoline on my tongue, used to ignite me with purpose. But now I can't force it past my lips anymore, not when it tastes like betrayal. Now it feels like a noose I didn't see tightening.

It belongs to both the monster I have been hunting and the man who held me like he could rewrite my bones. They share the same blood, the same name, and suddenly, everything I thought was black and white starts bleeding into shades I hate myself for seeing.

Rule pushes off the wall, arms dropping to his sides. "You need to trust us."

"You're kidding, right?" I snarl. "Trust you?"

He steps closer, tone deceptively calm. "Sometimes you don't have to do everything yourself, Seanna. We already have a plan for Javier."

That stops me. Not because I believe him—but because the audacity is fucking unreal.

But then the fire roars back, hotter than ever. "It's too late now. You've wasted time I didn't have. Max will find me. He's the best hacker we've got. He'll burn this whole place down to bring me back."

Ruin laughs.

Not amused. Not gentle.

Dark. Low. Almost pitying.

"Max is good," he says. "I'll give him that."

I roll my eyes, scoffing loud enough to echo. "I've known Max my whole life. The man's a fucking legend in cyber intelligence. You're just a psycho in a mask."

I lift my chin. "He's more than good. He's the best. You seriously think he won't find me?"

Ruin chuckles low in his throat, the sound scraping against something inside me. "He's not better than me."

My eyes narrow. "You wish."

"I don't have to wish." His voice is calm, but his eyes behind the mask feel too focused. Too precise. "I *know*."

I scoff again. "Please."

Ruin leans forward in the chair slightly, like he's about to tell me a secret I won't survive. "Because Max taught me everything I know."

That hits like a gut punch.

I stare at him, lips parting—but nothing comes out. I blink, heart stalling in my chest.

"What?"

His voice is quieter now. Not mocking. Not cruel. Just final.

"My name is Huxley Vaughn," he says.

My stomach drops.

No.

No, that can't be right.

"Vaughn?" I whisper, the name tasting foreign in my mouth despite how many times I've said it in passing. Max's full name—Max Vaughn. My parents' best friend.

My fucking godfather.

Ruin—Huxley—nods once. Just once. Like he knows what that name means to me. Like he's been waiting for the moment it would detonate inside me.

"No," I breathe, shaking my head. "No fucking way."

Rule says nothing. Just watches me like he's waiting to see which direction the shrapnel flies first.

"You're lying," I hiss. "You're just saying that to fuck with me."

"I'm not," Huxley says calmly. "Max Vaughn is my father."

Chapter 36
Seanna

"No," I whisper, like denial alone can make it untrue. "You're lying."

The name echoes—louder inside my skull than in the room. *Vaughn.* It shouldn't shake me this hard. Shouldn't feel like someone's kicked a hole straight through my stomach. But it does.

Because that name *means* something. It means Max. It means safety. It means childhood memories of being told not to touch the encrypted drives on his desk. It means *trust.*

And now it means *this*?

I stare at Ruin—Huxley—like if I glare hard enough, maybe the mask will crack. Maybe this whole fucking fantasy will dissolve and leave me with a version of reality that makes sense.

"Max never said anything," I snap, voice rising sharp and raw. "Not once. Not even a hint."

Except... that's not true.

The memory punches through the haze like a knife between ribs—just last week, he *had* let something slip. Not much. Barely a whisper. But it was there. A shadow in his eyes. A quiet nod. A line about keeping people hidden to protect them. I'd brushed it off at the time, assumed it was just his usual cryptic bullshit. But now? Now it clicks. Now it burns.

"No one *could* know." Ruin's voice doesn't waver. "Not after what almost happened to my mother."

That stills me.

"What happened to her?" I ask slowly.

Ruin leans forward slightly, elbows resting on his knees. "She was targeted before I was even born. Max told me it was because of his work. Because he got too close to something someone wanted buried. He doesn't talk about the details. Only that he spent months with her in hiding. After that, he moved us constantly. Never the same place twice. Never told anyone. Not even your parents."

I try to breathe, but there's something thick in my chest now. Something that tastes like betrayal and grief, old and fresh all at once.

"He didn't want us to be found," Ruin says. "Didn't want *me* to be found. He always said the safest secret is the one no one even knows exists. He kept me off the grid. No birth records. No schools. No friends. Just training. Constant relocation."

My pulse stutters.

"Max doesn't trust anyone around his family," Ruin continues, voice softening just a fraction beneath the harsh modulation. "He couldn't afford to. But he did tell me stories. When I was little, he'd come home late some nights, sit on the edge of my bed, and tell me what I thought were bedtime stories. But they weren't fairy tales—they were real people, hidden in plain sight. He'd tell me about your parents. About Agent Alexandra Darling and the two men who loved her enough to tear the world apart."

I swallow hard, my throat dry, a lump forming as I try to picture Max—stoic, guarded Max—sharing anything so intimate, so personal.

"He started telling me about these beautiful twin girls," Ruin continues, and something twists low in my stomach at the tone in his voice—soft, almost reverent. "Hydessa, quiet and steady. And

Seanna—the black-haired girl with a spirit of fire, the little storm of a girl who fought every rule, who burned bright and fierce. Even before I ever saw your face, even before I knew what you looked like, you were already seared into my mind. You'd wormed your way into a part of me I couldn't rip out even if I tried."

My breath stalls, throat tightening. I can feel Rule watching us, silent and still as stone, but I can't look away from Ruin.

"He didn't know he was planting seeds," Ruin continues. "But every story Max told wormed its way into my bones. Especially yours. Because of those stories I knew you. Seanna, the storm. The untamed fire. The fearless girl who laughed when most people would scream."

My chest aches, something heavy settling into the hollow space carved by his words.

"How did Rule get involved?" I manage, voice quieter than I want it to be.

Ruin looks at Rule for a moment. "We were teenagers. Bored, too smart for our own good, both with access to places on the dark net we shouldn't have had. We met in a chat room—two kids from entirely different worlds. He had his own darkness. His own secrets. But we connected and became friends. And then..." He pauses, taking a slow breath, looking back at me. "Then, eventually, I told him about you."

My pulse spikes painfully, fists clenching against the cuffs.

"You became our shared obsession," he says softly. "At first, it was distant—just surveillance. Watching. Tracking. Learning every detail we could gather. But that wasn't enough. We needed more." His voice tightens. "We worked towards inserting ourselves into your life, carefully, subtly. Closer and closer without you even knowing.

Until it felt normal to have us nearby, watching from within arm's reach."

I swallow hard, feeling like the walls are closing in, like the room itself is pressing against my lungs.

"You lived with Max," I say, piecing it together slowly, like assembling shards of broken glass. "How—?"

"Max was barely ever home," he answers quietly. "So sneaking out wasn't hard at first. And by the time I moved out, I was already an adult. He hated it—thought I was risking everything by stepping into the open."

I nod slowly, processing each revelation like a series of blows I can't dodge. "If you had joined the organization, it would have been a big deal. You'd have been a legacy. That matters."

Ruin's voice dips lower, threaded with quiet intensity. "That's exactly why I'm not part of the organization. Besides, it would be a little hard to avoid Max if I ended up working in the same place he did."

Rule finally breaks his silence, shifting slightly from his place against the wall. His voice is calm, controlled, but with a dark undercurrent that makes my heart skip. "Taking you wasn't the original plan. We were going to do things slowly. Carefully. Earn your trust, make you see we weren't your enemies. But then you set yourself on a mission to take out Javier."

I raise my chin, ignoring the tightening ache in my chest. "Javier needed to be stopped. You, of all people, should understand that."

Rule exhales slowly, and his mask gleams in the dim light. "I understood better than anyone, Seanna. Even when you targeted Javier directly, we weren't intending to rush things. But you were too fucking good at what you do. You kept working your way closer, relentlessly dismantling his operation piece by piece, until one night

I overheard him talking about you with his men. At first, he wasn't overly concerned—just another agent thinking she could rattle his cage. But when you pulled Diego into your web, and then set your sights on Cruz, Javier decided you were too dangerous to let live."

My pulse quickens, fury and fear tangling sharply beneath my ribs. "So what, you thought kidnapping me was the best solution?"

"It was the only solution," Ruin answers quietly, his voice hardening with conviction. "We weren't going to let Javier have you. Not after everything—not after how deeply you'd embedded yourself in both our lives, even from a distance. We knew exactly what Javier would do if he caught you first."

My stomach twists, nausea rising bitterly at the realization. I'd known it was dangerous. I'd known I was painting a target on myself, but hearing it confirmed so plainly...

"Letting Hydessa know you've been taken has only put you at risk." Rule continues, his voice low, careful. "Someone could track your location simply by your family trying to find you. Javier has eyes everywhere."

Frustration simmers beneath my skin. "So what? I'm supposed to stay locked up here indefinitely?"

"No." Ruin stands abruptly, moving toward me, his presence filling the room with quiet intensity. I tense instinctively as he reaches for the cuffs, but all he does is unlock them, the restraints falling away, leaving my wrists free. He steps back, giving me space. "You're not a captive here, Seanna. Not anymore. But Javier won't stop until you're dead, and we're begging you—don't leave. Don't put yourself at risk when we're already working to take him out."

My wrists feel strange without the cuffs, lighter but then my heart is still heavy with the weight of the moment. I look between the two men, caught between resentment, confusion, and something dangerously close to trust. Their words circle in my head, relentless, digging into every crack I thought I'd sealed shut. They're not just trying to keep me locked away. They're trying to keep me alive.

I lick my lips slowly, voice softer now. "Do I get to see your faces, then?"

Rule laughs, a low sound edged with dark amusement, while Ruin hums—a quiet, thoughtful sound.

"Yes," Ruin answers eventually. "But not right now."

I narrow my eyes slightly, suspicion rising again, but before I can speak, he steps closer. Close enough that I can feel the warmth of his body standing so close to the bed, even through the layers of black.

His gloved hand rises slowly, and I flinch—just barely—before freezing as he brushes a strand of hair away from my face. His touch is gentle. Unexpected. The leather cool against my skin. It's not possessive. Not harsh. Just... tender. Reverent, even.

My breath hitches.

My brain screams at me not to soften. Not to feel. But I find myself tilting into his touch, aching for something I don't dare name. It's so stupid. So dangerous. But in this moment, I want more than I should. Crave more than I'm willing to admit.

"I know you want to see our faces," he murmurs, thumb ghosting near my cheekbone, "but I want you to see what's beneath all this first. Prove you can be a good girl. That you understand... what matters is what we feel together. What we make you feel."

His voice is low, intimate. It crawls under my skin, coils around my spine.

I should shove him away. But I don't.

Because part of me—the part I've been trying to kill for days—wants to believe him. Wants to see what's underneath.

His hand lingers for a moment longer, thumb tracing just beneath my jaw before falling away. But the imprint of his touch remains, ghostlike and impossibly vivid.

He studies me quietly, then adds, softer this time, almost hesitant—

"I became obsessed with you before I ever saw your face. The girl in the stories. The storm Max described. The fire no one could put out. That's who I fell for first. And maybe... maybe we're hoping, just a little, that soon you might start to feel the same before seeing ours."

The ache in my chest blooms outward, confusion and heat crashing together in my ribs. I hate that they're inside me like this, clawing through everything I thought I was.

But I don't move.

I don't tell them to leave.

Because deep down, part of me doesn't want to.

Chapter 37
Seanna

Ruin steps back, a single calculated retreat that leaves space between us—space I immediately intend to violate.

I rise from the bed slowly, the silk sheets dragging against my skin like a lover's whisper, my gaze locked on him like a predator testing the fence. My legs feel steady beneath me. Strong. Every muscle in my body aches, but it's the kind of ache I've learned to savor. A reminder that I survived. That I'm still standing. Still me.

I take a single step forward.

Then another.

Close enough that I can hear the faint change in his breath. I lift my hand—slowly, deliberately—and press my fingertips to his chest. Testing. Teasing.

He doesn't stop me.

My fingers trail higher, ghosting along the edge of his shoulder, then across his collarbone through the fabric of his shirt. My nails graze lightly. Not enough to scratch. Just enough to say *I could*.

"I'm not sure I can control my hands," I murmur, voice dripping mock innocence. "They've been so... crazy lately. Reckless. Just begging for a reason to misbehave."

Rule's voice cuts in—calm, amused. "Should I bind them then?"

I don't turn toward him. I let the corner of my mouth twitch up into a slow, wicked grin. "Might be the only responsible option."

"I'll take that as consent," he replies—and then he's gone, like a shadow slipping away.

I keep my focus on Ruin, still trailing my hand across his chest. "Think I should be worried?"

"No," he says, low and certain. "But he's going to make you behave."

I drag my palm down his chest and flick my fingers against his belt. "That's adorable. You still think I can be tamed."

He doesn't respond for a moment. Just lifts his gloved hands to the hem of my oversized shirt, slow and deliberate. Then his voice drops to that dark, dangerous place that always lands somewhere low in my stomach.

"You were always meant to be ours, little storm. So we're just taking what's already mine," he murmurs. "From now on, you don't wear something like this unless you want it taken off. So let me take care of it."

And he strips me.

I don't flinch. I don't cover myself. I stand there like a fucking goddess demanding worship, head high, daring him to make it something it's not. The shirt falls to the floor in a whisper. He crouches, fingers catching the waistband of my panties, and drags them down with reverent slowness.

I step out of them with zero hesitation, not a single nerve flinching. Because this isn't submission. This is me giving them the storm.

He rises, then turns and moves to the armchair, lowering himself into it with languid confidence. He spreads his legs, reclines like he's watching his favorite show come back for another brutal season.

And then Rule returns, he's carrying two lengths of rope—soft, black, the kind that looks too elegant for what it's about to do. He doesn't speak. Just approaches in that calm, unhurried gait like he already owns the room. Owns *me*. I arch a brow, watching him like a cat approaching a mouse that doesn't know it's already fucked.

He steps behind me.

The air shifts the second he's close. My breath catches—more out of anticipation than nerves—but I don't give him the satisfaction of seeing it. I keep my chin high, my posture proud, even as he gently gathers my wrists behind my back.

The rope brushes my skin—cool and unnervingly sensual—and he starts binding my arms with deliberate grace. His movements are slow, patient. Like he's enjoying this way too much.

"Careful," I murmur, smirking. "Start tying me up too pretty and I might start thinking you're in love."

"I am," Rule says softly, and fuck him for saying it like a damn fact.

His fingers tighten the first knot. Firm. Sure. My wrists are locked behind me, but I don't feel caged. I feel... present. Focused. Hyper-aware of every place the rope touches, of the way he works me like a canvas he's been dying to paint.

He moves higher, looping up my arms and then across my shoulders and chest, sculpting the rope over my breasts with the kind of attention that should be illegal. The rope presses in—snug, never harsh. It forces me to stand taller. Straighter. Like my body isn't mine anymore, but some rare fucking artifact he's decided to display.

"You're doing beautifully," Rule murmurs, his voice like velvet. "I knew you would."

The praise slips over my skin like a warm palm, low and smooth and maddeningly effective. My breath hitches—just once. It's not fear. It's the heat uncoiling slow and thick inside me, pooling lower with every pass of that rope, every brush of his knuckles against bare skin as he pulls, tugs, knots.

He loops again around the swell of my breasts, binding them tight enough to make them sit high and proud, the rope sinking into the soft flesh. A soft gasp escapes before I can swallow it. I tilt my chin higher in response, pretending like the way my nipples harden under the ropes isn't a betrayal.

He notices.

Of course he does.

Rule slides his hand between the tensioned ropes and my chest, his fingers brushing just beneath one aching peak, barely grazing it—just enough to make me tremble. Enough to make my thighs twitch together.

"You're so responsive," he says softly, reverently, like I'm some finely-tuned instrument he's tuning by touch alone. "It's beautiful."

Behind him, Ruin is watching everything like he's fucking starving. I glance toward him and see him sprawled in the armchair, one gloved hand casually wrapped around the thick length of his cock. He strokes slowly, like he's savoring the tension between us as much as I am.

The sight shoots a bolt of heat straight through me.

Possessive, obsessive, unrelenting bastard—and even though I can't see his face the way he looks at me, it makes me feel like I'm prey and sanctuary and everything he's ever wanted. Makes my knees threaten to buckle.

Rule keeps working. The rope moves down my torso in elegant, winding paths. It coils under my ribs, frames the curve of my waist, crosses and winds its way across my stomach in a lattice of firm touches. Every knot feels like a kiss. Every tug, a command.

My breathing has gone shallow. Not panicked—aroused. Hyper-aware. The rope is like a second skin now. One that hugs all the parts of me most men are too afraid to even look at directly.

"You feel that?" Rule asks quietly, looping a fresh strand between my thighs.

I nod once, lips parted as the pressure builds where I'm already wet and throbbing. The rope presses against the lips of my pussy, tight and teasing, brushing the aching spot that's been throbbing for attention since the moment his voice said *I'll take that as consent.*

"Good girl," he says, tightening the tension with one practiced pull.

Fuck. That praise again.

It shouldn't work. It shouldn't *do* anything. But I can't lie to myself anymore—not with the way my body clenches when he says it. Not with the way I'm practically grinding on the rope now, thighs flexing involuntarily just to feel more.

I steal another glance at Ruin. His hand moves a little faster. He's just watching. Possessing. His whole body like a shadow carved into the chair.

I want him to touch me. I want him to *join* this. To *ruin* me while Rule builds me into art.

"I'm going to finish binding your thighs next, then we're going to put that sharp little tongue to better use," Rule murmurs, voice silk-wrapped steel as he tightens the rope between my thighs just enough to make me shiver. "You're going to get on your knees and choke on both our cocks—until your throat's as wrecked as your cunt's about to be."

God, the way he says it—like a promise, like a threat. Like he's already halfway down my throat.

My breath stutters and I swear I feel Ruin's hot gaze from the chair like a physical touch. I don't need to look to know he's stroking himself harder now.

Rule's hands trail over the rope framing my hips, sliding between my legs, fingers brushing my entrance where I'm already soaked. I gasp, muscles twitching, hips trying to roll, but the bindings hold me in place—perfect, inescapable tension.

"You feel that?" he whispers, dragging his fingers slowly through the wetness. "That's from us. From being watched. From being tied. From knowing exactly what we're about to do to you."

He stands and leans in closer, his mask brushing my jaw and his breath hot against my ear.

"We're going to fuck you together, Seanna," he growls. "And you're going to take everything we give you. Every inch. Every brutal thrust. Every fucking drop. Until your pussy is so wrecked and full, you can't tell whose cum is leaking out of you."

I moan—low and filthy—because fuck, I want it. I hate how much I want it. But I do. My whole body's burning for it, every nerve ending wired for overload.

"You think you're strong?" Rule continues, pressing one palm flat against my belly as he reaches around with the other to tug the rope just slightly between my legs again. "We're going to break you in the best fucking way. And when we're done, you won't *want* to be strong. You'll *beg* to stay like that—on your knees, dripping with us."

I feel my legs weaken.

My breath comes in shallow pulls now, the ache between my thighs sharp and relentless, my nipples tight between the rope as my body writhes against its bindings. I glance again toward Ruin, I can't fucking help it. He's still watching like I'm his religion, one hand pumping slow and steady, the other resting on the arm of the chair like he's reigning in the monster inside him—for now.

But his voice breaks through the tension—low, dark, hungry.

"She's going to look so fucking pretty with both our cocks shoved down her throat," Ruin growls. "Her eyes all glassy, her spit dripping, taking it like the fierce little goddess she is—our perfect addiction."

A sound escapes me—a choked-off needy whimper that tastes like heat and shame and *yes*.

Rule chuckles beside me, dark and delighted. "That's the sound I wanted."

He presses his fingers back against my pussy, slipping one inside just to feel how ready I already am.

"Fuck," he murmurs. "You're already soaked for us. Needy little thing."

He pulls back, running his hands down the ropes that bind me—like he's checking his work. Like I'm a piece of art he's about to defile.

And all I can think about—*need*—is to be wrecked so completely I forget how to say no.

Chapter 38
Seanna

The ropes hold me.

Not harshly. Not cruelly. But absolutely. Like their only purpose is to keep me upright so I don't melt into the floor under the weight of everything Rule just promised to do to me.

And I want it. God help me, I want it all.

The space between my thighs throbs with need. The rope tight against my pussy presses in just right—relentless and teasing. Every breath makes it rub against my already slick folds, and I'm losing the war with my pride. Because even though I'm standing tall, even though I'm biting back whimpers and holding on to my fire, I know they see it.

They feel it.

Rule steps in front of me now, one gloved hand sliding along the length of the rope binding my chest. He stops when his fingers reach the valley between my breasts, brushing over the sensitive skin with maddening slowness.

"On your knees," he says, his voice so cool and calm, a contrast to the rapid drum of my heart.

I hesitate. Not out of resistance. Not even out of pride.

Out of anticipation.

But then I drop.

The floor is hard and cold against my knees as they hit with a muted thud. The rope around my thighs pulls tight, controlling the width of my stance. There's no modesty in this—I'm kneeling, bare, bound, open. And Ruin lets out a dark sound from the chair that makes my nipples pebble even harder.

Rule slides his thumb possessively over my cheek. His gloved fingers curling under my jaw, lifting my face toward him.

"Look at me," he says.

He doesn't need to raise his voice. The command slides down my spine like smoke. I lift my gaze, and he hums in pleasure at the sight—like seeing me there, bound and open, is the final piece of some puzzle only he understands.

Then he unzips his pants slowly, freeing his cock—thick, heavy, pierced. I've never had him in my mouth before, and the sight of him now makes heat punch low in my stomach.

"Open," he orders.

I obey.

He presses in slow at first, filling my mouth in one long, possessive glide. The burn is instant. The stretch, deliberate. The piercings scrape against my tongue and the roof of my mouth—foreign, heavy, fucking perfect.

He holds me there. Doesn't move. Just watches me breathe around him. Watches me submit.

Then he moves.

His hips snap forward, and I gag, the head of his cock punching into the back of my throat. My eyes water. My lungs scream. But I don't pull away—I fucking *lean* into it.

He drags back slowly, the ridged metal scraping like a threat, then slams forward again. My throat convulses, spit spills down my chin, and the rope behind my back creaks with the strain of my restraint.

I flick my tongue along his underside between thrusts—every barbell, every ridge, every soft hiss of breath I can drag from him. He groans low, the sound primal, his fingers tightening around my jaw.

His breath stutters, his fingers tightening against my jaw in warning—or appreciation.

He pulls back.

"Switch," he says darkly.

Ruin steps forward, his cock already hard and glistening with precum. He strokes it once, then guides it to my mouth. There's a tenderness in the way he brushes his knuckles against my jaw first—a silent question. I part my lips in answer.

He pushes in, slower than Rule, but just as firm. The weight of him, the different piercings, the stretch, the taste—different. Deeper. His rhythm is slower, less brutal—but no less claiming.

"You're fucking addictive," he murmurs, voice like gravel and reverence.

I moan around him.

He rolls his hips deeper, forcing air from my lungs and shame from my body. There's no room for either anymore. Just them. Just the rhythm.

I swirl my tongue around the head, tasting him, teasing the piercings. He groans, thrusts a little deeper, letting his breath shudder through clenched teeth.

Then he pulls back.

Rule takes me again. His thrusts are harder now, more desperate, like the sight of Ruin using my mouth has stirred something primal. The piercings in his cock strike against the back of my tongue and drag on every exit.

They switch again.

And again.

I flick my tongue over each of them every time they press to my lips. Teasing. Worshipping. Demanding more. Their tastes blur together—dark, hot, endless.

My mouth is stretched, aching, flooded with their taste. My throat is raw, my jaw sore, but I take them both, again and again, until my lips are swollen. There is spit dripping down my chin, and my lungs are screaming for breath I refuse to ask for.

Everything else disappears. My mind goes blank.

The next several minutes blur into a rhythm of dominance and possession. They switch every time one of them gets too close, dragging my mouth from one cock to the other like it's the most natural thing in the world. Rule brutal. Ruin controlled. Both hungry. Both relentless.

Time bends. My throat is their altar—shared, worshipped, wrecked. And I take it all because I want to, because this is mine. They don't just switch—they orbit, a force of nature with me at the center, held together by rope, heat, and the kind of obsession that can't be faked.

Tears stream down my cheeks. My spit coats my chest, my chin, the ropes—but I don't stop. I don't want to.

Rule finally pulls me up by the rope at my chest, breath ragged. Ruin catches me before I can sway. Lifts me like something sacred. My body is boneless, trembling, but I don't feel weak—I feel *claimed*. Their hands are reverent, but there's nothing gentle about the hunger burning in the air.

They lay me on the bed like I'm something breakable.

But something they fully intend to break.

Ruin slides in behind me, his body warm and heavy as he spoons against my back. The bed dips beneath us. I feel the hardness of his cock pressing between my cheeks before he reaches past me—grabbing the little packet Rule passes him with steady fingers.

The sound of the packet tearing is sharp. Then, he brushes his masked face against my shoulder in some sort of imitation of a kiss.

Before he spreads my cheeks and I feel the coolness of lube on his gloved fingers. He pushes one finger in.

Slow. Measured. Unavoidable.

The stretch burns beautifully. Then comes the second. Stretching me further, coaxing breathless little gasps from my throat. And the third. I whimper, breath catching on the edge of a moan as he fucks my ass open with his fingers. The ropes dig into my thighs as I push back against him, desperate for more friction, more fill.

"You ready?" he murmurs.

"God, yes."

His response is a gloved hand wrapping around my throat from behind—tight enough to still my breath, not enough to choke it out. Not yet.

His mouth brushes the shell of my ear, voice low and lethal. "Let's make this clear, little storm—we are your gods now. And it's only us you'll ever worship again."

The words brand themselves into me—hot and permanent and final.

Then Ruin pushes in.

Inch by thick, stretching, unrelenting inch.

The first push burns—deep and delicious—ripping a strangled cry from my throat, but I don't pull away—I take it. I fucking *feel* every ridge of his cock, every cold brush of the piercings as they drag over my nerves and light them up.

I tip my head back against his shoulder, mouth parted, gasping. My ass tightens around him instinctively, trembling with every slow glide forward.

He groans.

He holds me, one arm moving to wrap under my ribs as he sinks deeper, slower, until he's seated fully inside me.

And then Rule is in front of me again.

His hand lifts and shifts my thigh, opening me wider, moving the rope away from my clit and around my thigh to keep it higher. He doesn't rush—no, he watches. *Watches* as Ruin holds me still from behind, cock dragging, pushing in and out of my ass. Watches the way my body stretches around him, how my tits rise and fall with every labored breath.

And when Rule finally lines up with my pussy it's a different kind of ache. I whimper at the first press of him. And then he pushes in.

Slow at first. Deliberate. But unrelenting. He doesn't stop until I'm split open, completely full—Ruin in my ass, Rule in my pussy, both of them stretching me past the edge of anything I thought I could take.

"Fuck," I choke, shaking. "Oh, *fuck*—"

Rule's gloved hand wraps around my throat. Not tight. Not yet. Just resting. Waiting. Claiming.

Then they start to move.

Ruin rocks forward as Rule pulls back. Then Rule thrusts as Ruin withdraws. Their rhythm is slow at first, deliberate—like they're syncing with each other through the conduit of *me*. Their cocks grind into me in perfect opposition, stretching me to the brink and then dragging me back again.

I'm moaning, begging, gone.

Each thrust stokes the fire higher, hotter. Rule's cock drags along my soaked walls, his piercings hitting every sensitive nerve ending inside me, while Ruin's girth stretches me wide, his piercings grinding against places I didn't know existed.

The air is thick with sweat and filth and heat.

Ruin reaches around, two fingers finding my clit. He circles it firmly—no teasing, no patience—and my vision blurs.

I break.

My orgasm slams through me, sudden and savage, making me scream as my body convulses. They don't stop. If anything, they fuck me *harder*—using the slick, the clench, the chaos.

Rule's thrusts become frantic, his breath coming fast, his hand tightening on my throat until the lack of air turns everything to white-hot static. The pressure mounts again, and I feel him shift his angle, pressing down on the spot above my clit with terrifying accuracy. The tension shifts.

"Come again," he snarls into my ear.

And I do. I don't even have a choice.

The climax tears through me like a live wire, every muscle spasming.

My pussy squeezes them both so hard until they can't keep their rhythm anymore. Until they can't stay inside me. And then I feel it: the dam inside me snapping.

A gush of liquid erupts from between my thighs, and I scream again, not from pain or even pleasure—but from sheer *release*. From the fact that they did this to me, and I wanted every second.

The harsh pulsing of my climax hasn't even subsided before they're thrusting back inside me again. My body jerks, helpless in their grip. My mouth opens around a sob, but no sound comes out—just broken air and the feeling of *too much*.

"Please," I choke. "I can't—"

"Yes, you fucking can," Rule growls, tightening his grip on my throat. "You were made for this. For us."

They keep going. Hard. Brutal. Devouring.

My muscles cramp, my arms tremble inside the ropes, and my brain *blanks*.

Another orgasm builds fast. *Violent*. My clit is on fire. My body isn't mine anymore—it's theirs. Held. Used. Worshipped.

Rule comes first, buried deep, grinding into me with a groan that sounds like victory as it tears me apart. His hips still, cock twitching, spilling heat inside me as his breath stutters in my ear.

Then he slips out, and the absence is sharp. But Ruin is already pulling out and moving me.

He grabs a pillow—shoves it beneath my hips in one swift motion. The change in angle lifts my ass, puts me on display, and drives my bound arms deeper into the mattress behind me. It arches my chest up, tightens the ropes across my back, and sends a new wave of strain through my shoulders. My tits rise with every breath, nipples peaked and exposed as my body is contorted and offered up.

Then his gloved hands wrap around my thighs—and *force* them wider.

The grip is punishing. His fingers dig into the soft flesh like he owns it, bruising me without apology. Pain and pleasure blur. I cry out, but not in protest—because it only makes me wetter.

I'm open now. Stretched. Helpless.

And he fucking *loves* it.

Ruin kneels between my legs and doesn't waste another second. He lines up, the head of his cock pressing against my entrance, still slick from the wreckage Rule left behind.

Then he sinks into me.

Slow. Deep. Unforgiving.

The piercings drag along my inner walls, catching every nerve. My back arches harder against the ropes, my arms screaming with tension, but I can't move. Can't reach. Can't take control.

I'm *his*. And he knows it.

His rhythm is brutal in its restraint. Each stroke calculated. Each thrust a study in control. He drives in deep and pulls out just far enough to make my breath hitch—then does it again. And again. And *again*.

It's maddening.

Every time I get close—every time my body starts to tremble, my pussy starts to clench, my breath starts to break—he slows down. Edges away. Leaves me clawing at nothing.

"Fuck—please," I gasp, trying to rock my hips. But the ropes won't let me. My legs are spread, my wrists are useless, my voice is the only weapon I have left—and it's barely holding.

He doesn't answer.

Just shifts slightly. Hits that fucking spot. Then backs off again.

"Ruin—please—I need to come," I sob, tears slipping from the corners of my eyes. My thighs tremble under his grip, already sore from how wide he's forced them. "Let me. *Let me*—please—"

His gloved palm presses low on my belly, right above my clit, trapping me. Holding me still.

"Beg louder," he says, voice low, even. Unmoved. "You want it that badly? *Beg like it's mine to give.*"

I'm falling apart.

"Please," I cry. "Please, Ruin—I'm begging. I need to come. I *need* it—fuck, please—"

And he gives it to me.

He slams in deep—hard, precise, merciless. Again, and again until everything inside me explodes. The orgasm rips through me like a blade, sharp and savage, every nerve igniting under the weight of his cock and his control and the brutal, overwhelming pressure between my legs.

I scream. I *convulse*.

My pussy clenches around him in wild, pulsing waves. My chest is heaving, the ropes pulling tight as I writhe. I feel him shudder, feel when he comes with a snarl. He buries himself deep, cock pulsing as he fills me—thick, hot, and endless. His hands hold me open, locked wide around my trembling thighs. My vision goes white.

And I fall.

Down, down, down.

Into the kind of ruin that tastes like worship.

And I *belong* to it.

Chapter 39

Seanna

Morning comes slow, dragging light across my skin like it's afraid to wake me. It feels strange to be in a room with a window after spending days in a room without.

My body aches, sore in all the ways that remind me I was used—thoroughly, savagely, obsessively—by both of them last night. I only vaguely remember the aftermath. The gentler side of monsters. The way they'd cleaned me up, massaged the knots out of my trembling legs. Rule tending to the rope-burned cuts he'd given me when he chased me through the trees like prey, his hands steady and careful now, almost reverent.

I remember warmth. Steady pressure. Their voices low, murmured things I didn't quite catch. Fingers brushing sweat-damp hair back from my temple. The softness of a cloth between my thighs. Then nothing.

Now, the room is empty. No armchair sentinel. No masked men. No restraints.

I blink at my wrists. No rope. No cuffs. Just the familiar sting of bruises and the dull burn of used muscles. I stretch, slow and lazy, testing the boundaries of this unexpected freedom.

Then I do what any sane person in a new house would do.

I snoop.

I kick the covers off and push upright. My legs threaten mutiny, but I ignore it. First things first: clothes. If I'm going to wander through whatever curated hellscape they've dumped me in now, I might as well be dressed.

Dragging myself to the tall dresser, I yank open the top drawer—only to pause.

What greets me isn't some borrowed T-shirt or folded sweatpants.

It's *the* lingerie.

Not tucked away in the gift box this time. No. It's folded. Placed deliberately. Like it belongs here. Like *I* belong here.

The same set they left on my bed when they were still just shadows in my periphery. When I was still pretending they didn't exist. Still pretending I wasn't unraveling.

I scoff under my breath, fingers brushing the familiar blend of leather and lace again. Of course they brought it here. Of course they unpacked it for me. Probably laid it out with reverent hands while whispering to each other about how perfect I'll look in it.

So just to be a contradictory bitch, I put it on.

No ceremony. No performance.

I step into it like armor.

Then I find and pull on one of the long oversized shirts of mine from another drawer—soft, black, worn thin at the edges because I've had it forever. I bypass all the *brand new* clothes surrounding it purely because of Ruin's words.

My bare legs protest every step with a satisfying ache. The hallway outside the bedroom is just as quiet, lined with sleek grey walls and dark wood trim, modern but cozy. Two doors stand closed across from me. One has the sound of a shower muffled but unmistakable.

Tempting.

God, it's so fucking tempting to barge in, to catch one of them off-guard and ruin their carefully orchestrated mask of control. To get the answers before I have earned them. But I stop myself. That would feel like cheating. After everything they told me... their confessions, their truths—the faces and names still hidden—I won't cheapen them.

If that's one of their rooms, then logic says the second door belongs to the other.

My fingers twitch with curiosity, but I keep moving, further down the hall and into the heart of the house.

It's massive. Open. Every line, every corner drenched in indulgence, like someone took my subconscious, wrung it out, and decorated with it. Black velvet furniture. Smoky gray walls. Blood-red accents. If I ever made a Pinterest board it would look exactly like this.

Of course it would.

They've studied me for years. Obsessed. Watched. They've been inside my mind, my records, my patterns. They probably know the exact brand of eyeliner I use and which of my bras I secretly think I look best in. So yeah. Of course they knew what kind of house I would love.

Of course they got it right.

Of course they built this world out of everything I've ever wanted, everything I never said aloud. It makes my stomach turn and twist and ache all at once.

I move through each room slowly, taking it all in. A sitting room with black silk curtains and a fireplace. A hidden nook with floor-to-ceiling bookshelves and a plush reading chair that practically begs to swallow me whole.

I wander through to the kitchen, fingers grazing the cool marble of the counter. The fridge is unnecessarily stocked. The shelves are arranged with a terrifying precision. The pantry is next—dark, deep, full of everything from imported oils to obscure spice blends. I'm halfway through opening one of the lower cabinets inside the pantry when—

"If you wanted a tour," a voice murmurs behind me, lazy and low, "you could've just asked."

I don't jump. I don't freeze. I turn slowly, already rolling my eyes because I don't need to see him to know exactly who it is.

Rule.

There's something in the way he speaks today—less edge, more velvet. It's disarming. Infuriating.

"I didn't realize snooping required an appointment," I reply.

He leans against the doorframe like he owns the damn air in the room, mask still in place, modulated voice unmistakably amused. "Fair point."

"I knew you'd come find me eventually," I add, turning back to the pantry casually. "You two always do."

He chuckles softly, the sound low and unhurried as his footsteps draw closer. "I was going to make you some more pastries."

That gets my attention. I turn to face him again, raising a brow. "Cherry cream cheese?"

His mask tilts slightly in acknowledgment. "Of course."

I shrug, pretending I'm not already imagining the buttery layers and sweet filling. "And here I thought you were going to punish me for wandering."

He steps closer, hands tucked behind his back. "I still might."

Then, softer—almost like a tease veiled in something more vulnerable—"But if you'd like to help make them... that would be even better."

I narrow my eyes. "What, no threat? No forced compliance or bribes with caffeine this time?"

"You're not bound," he reminds me quietly. "You're choosing."

I hate how that lands in me. Soft. Undeniably real.

I look at him fully now, leaning just enough to let my mouth twist into something between a smirk and a dare. "Fine. But if they don't come out perfect, I'm blaming you. And I want extra glaze this time."

He chuckles. "Noted."

I let the silence stretch between us, just for a second longer than comfort allows, then move past him and back into the kitchen proper. My skin prickles with awareness of his proximity. But I don't flinch when he brushes against me after he follows me. I don't pull away.

I pull my hair up into a lazy knot as Rule moves around the kitchen like he's done it a hundred times. Efficient. Confident. Silent when he needs to be, and deliberate when he doesn't. It's unnerving how domestic it looks on him. Like the same hands that tied me to a bed, that chased me through the forest like prey, could also know exactly where to find the vanilla extract and the right size mixing bowl.

I hop up onto the edge of the counter, watching him prep ingredients. "So," I say, voice casual as I dangle my legs off the edge, "this your new plan? Seduce me with carbs?"

He pauses just long enough to glance at me—head cocked, expression unreadable beneath the mask. "You moaned last time I gave you these. Figured I'd play to your weaknesses."

"That was appreciation," I say, lifting my chin. "Not seduction. There's a difference."

"Mm." He slides the cream cheese onto the counter, the sound of foil crinkling under his gloved fingers. "Sounded a lot like foreplay to me."

I narrow my eyes. "You're just pissed I licked the last of it off my fingers and didn't offer you a taste."

"Not pissed," he replies smoothly. "Impressed you managed to make pastries obscene without even trying."

I grin. "I'm talented like that."

He nudges a cutting board toward me, along with a knife that gleams under the kitchen light like a dare. "Want to chop the cherries or just keep staring at me like you're plotting something?"

I slide off the counter with exaggerated grace and grab the blade, running my finger along the flat edge before giving him a slow, arched look. "Wow. Trusting me with a knife already? I'm touched."

His stance doesn't shift, but I can tell I've caught his attention. The tilt of his head, the way his gloved hands pause just slightly above the bowl of sugar. He's waiting.

I smirk, lifting the blade and turning it slightly so it glints. "You sure you want to be that close? I'm unpredictable. Unstable. Probably holding a grudge or two."

"Only two?" he murmurs, voice edged in amusement.

"For now," I say sweetly. "But you're really underestimating the damage a serrated edge can do."

He finally steps closer, close enough that I feel the heat of him, the weight of him—not threatening, just inevitable.

"If I thought you'd try to stab me," he says, calm and matter-of-fact, "I wouldn't have given you a knife."

I raise my brow. "So what—you *want* me armed?"

His voice dips lower, the kind of low that knows exactly where to settle in your chest. "I want you exactly like this. Sharp. Dangerous. Honest."

The last word lands heavy, harder than it should.

I blink, just once. Then I shake my head, huffing out a dry laugh as I slice the first cherry clean in half. "You're either incredibly confident or profoundly stupid."

"Both," he replies, going back to his preparations. "Depending on the day."

"Today's looking like a stupid day," I mutter, but there's no real heat behind it.

I keep chopping, the blade rhythmic against the board. He doesn't flinch. He doesn't watch my hands. He just moves beside me like he trusts that I won't drive the knife straight into his ribs.

That, more than anything, unsettles me.

Because part of me wishes he *wouldn't* trust me.

And part of me... doesn't hate that he does.

But because of that my mind chooses that moment to remind me of all the facts I *do* know.

I finish chopping the last of the cherries and slide the board toward him with a little more force than necessary. "Here," I say flatly. "I didn't poison them, if that's what you were hoping for."

I lean against the counter, arms folded. I should stop. Should leave this quiet little truce in one piece. But that's not who I am. I don't do peace. I do sabotage—especially when things feel too easy. Too safe. Too *good*.

He doesn't rise to the bait. Just scoops the fruit into the bowl and starts folding it into the mixture like I haven't been inching toward combustion.

So I strike where it hurts.

"You know, I still can't get over it," I say casually. "The way you touched me last night, the way you spoke. And the whole time, your last name is Reyes."

His movements pause—just barely—but it's enough.

"Javier's son," I press, voice curling into something sharp. "The heir. Groomed since birth to inherit the throne. Tell me, Rule—how does it feel knowing your legacy is built on bodies and blood and trafficking girls and drugs?"

He doesn't look at me.

He doesn't have to.

His knuckles tighten over the whisk, the leather making soft sounds as his grip tightens. For a moment, the only sound is the low hum of the oven preheating behind us.

Then—soft, low, controlled—he says, "You think I don't know what he is?"

I lift my chin, defiant. "Do you?"

He turns toward me fully, and even through the mask, his presence is searing. His voice is razor-edged and hollow. "I've spent every fucking year of my life knowing exactly what he is."

There's something dangerous and trembling underneath the words, something deeper than the smooth confidence he usually wears like armor.

He sets the whisk down with too much care.

"My mother was a possession to him. A body to fuck. A name to own. He paraded her like a queen at events, then hit her hard enough behind closed doors to make her teeth rattle. I was seven the first time I tried to stop him." His breath hitches slightly, but he swallows it down. "He backhanded me so hard I saw stars. Told me if I ever stepped between them again, he'd make me disappear."

I blink, stunned—but I don't speak. I let him bleed.

"She tried to leave once," he continues, voice quieter now. "Tried to take me and my brother and sister with her. We got as far as a safehouse in Cartagena. It didn't last twenty-four hours. His men found us. Dragged her back by her hair. Beat the maid who helped us until she couldn't walk."

He steps back slightly, giving himself space to breathe, and I realize—he's not just recounting it. He's *still* there. In every word. Every detail.

"And now," he says, a bitter laugh caught in his throat, "he's arranging for my sister—my *baby sister*—to marry a monster. A man at least twice her age who runs a rival cartel in Michoacán. She's twenty. He wants to 'secure the alliance'—his words."

My stomach twists.

"She cried to me," he says, like a confession. "Begged me not to let it happen. And I promised I wouldn't. So I'm not. I already have a plan in place to get her out. She just doesn't know it yet. But he'll never touch her again. That bastard won't use her like he used the rest of us."

I can feel his gaze, it pins me, sharp and aching.

"I'm not him," he says lowly. "The name Kingston Reyes is the only fucking thing I have in common with that monster. That's not who I am. And if you really *see* me the way you act like you do—you should *know* that."

The silence between us stretches thick and tense.

I cross my arms tighter, trying to shield the way his words hit me. But I don't back down. I can't.

"How do I know that?" I ask quietly. Not biting now—just honest. Wounded. "Right now... all I know about you is that he's your father."

He doesn't flinch. Doesn't lash out or retreat.

Instead, Rule steps closer.

Slowly. Intentionally.

He takes my hands in his—gloved, warm, steady—and lifts them gently, placing them at the edges of his mask. His voice is a low, steady rumble, more vulnerable than I've ever heard it.

"You do," he says. "Because you *do* know me."

I freeze, hands hovering just beneath his jaw. And it's insane—because only a few days ago, I was clawing at this very mask, trying to rip it off in a blind fury. Now he's letting me. Voluntarily. Like this moment—this offering—is sacred.

I stare up at him, breath caught in my throat.

My fingers curl slightly around the edge of the material, but I don't pull. Not yet.

I don't know if it's mercy or fear or something else entirely, but I hold still. Because this? This isn't about control anymore.

This is trust.

And that terrifies me more than any cartel heir ever could.

And he notices.

Of course he fucking does.

He tilts his head, voice dark with soft amusement. "What's wrong, princess?" he murmurs, that familiar rasp rolling over me like velvet and barbed wire. "Scared of what you'll find?"

My breath hitches.

Not at the words.

At the *nickname*.

Princess.

Only one person ever called me that like it meant something both teasing and reverent. Only one man made it sound like both a dare and a promise every time it left his mouth.

No. Fucking. Way.

Without thinking, I move.

I slide the glasses from his face first. Beneath them, his eyes are already watching me—sharp, calculating, heartbreakingly familiar.

Then I reach up and pull the mask off, slow and deliberate. My fingers tremble, just slightly.

And there he is.

Bodhi.

The smug, too-charming organization operative I've been sparring with for *years*. The same Bodhi I pinned to the mats only a week ago—*pinned*, like I'd actually overpowered him.

Bull. Shit.

I step back, reeling, heart pounding in my chest like it's trying to claw its way out.

"You—" I choke out, eyes narrowing to slits. "You absolute bastard. I *pinned* you. You *let* me win."

He shrugs, totally unbothered, like I didn't just uncover a goddamn bombshell. "You needed the ego boost."

"I should shoot you," I mutter, fury and confusion tangling in my throat. "I should've *known*. You were always there, always watching, and I *still* didn't fucking see you."

His lips twitch like he's fighting a smirk. "That's kind of the point, Seanna."

"You're stronger than you ever let on," I accuse, voice rising.

He nods once. "Yeah."

"You're faster."

"Obviously."

"You're *infuriating*."

"And yet," he murmurs, stepping back into my space, voice a dangerous hum, "you never could keep your eyes off me."

I open my mouth to snarl something else—but I don't get the chance.

He kisses me.

Not tentative.

Not questioning.

Like he's been waiting for this since the moment we met—since before I even *knew* who he was.

His mouth claims mine with heat and hunger, all rough edges and suppressed obsession. It's not soft. It's not sweet. But it *is* honest.

And worse?

I kiss him back.

For one hot, burning second, I let myself sink into it—let his hand slide to the back of my neck, let his body press close until there's nothing but heat and fury and the electric *crack* of connection that should never have happened.

And when I finally pull away, breathing hard, I don't slap him.

I don't scream.

I just stare at him and say—

"...Still can't believe you *let* me win."

He grins, flushed and feral. "You gonna punish me for it, princess?"

Oh, I will.

Just not in the way he thinks.

Chapter 40

Seanna

His kiss is rough and consuming, like he's trying to brand himself into my mouth—like he's daring me to forget who he is and remember only how he tastes.

I shove at his chest mid-kiss, not because I want him to stop but because I hate how much I don't want him to stop. "I hate you," I breathe, lips brushing his with every syllable.

"You hate a lot of things," he murmurs, voice dark and amused as he trails his mouth down the curve of my neck. "Doesn't stop you from wrapping your legs around them."

My fingers tangle in the front of his shirt. "Fuck you."

He grins against my skin, low and unbothered. "You already did."

That earns him a bite—sharp, just below his jaw. He hisses through his teeth and presses harder against me, thigh slotting between mine like he owns the space. Maybe he does.

He tastes like sugar and indulgence, and I hate how much I melt into it.

"You're still such a smug asshole."

He hums, dragging his nose along my collarbone. "You're still letting me touch you."

"Temporary lapse in judgment."

"Sure," he says, voice dipping into something deeper, "just like the way you moaned last night. Just like how you begged."

"I didn't—"

"You begged, Seanna. Don't lie to me. Don't lie to *yourself*."

God. I want to hit him. I want to kiss him harder.

I settle for digging my nails into his shoulder.

He growls low in his chest, hands sliding beneath the hem of the oversized shirt I threw on this morning.

He leans in again, lips brushing my ear. "You remember what Ruin said?"

I do.

Too well.

"If you wear something like this," Rule murmurs, fingers sliding up the hem, "then be prepared for one of us to strip it off you."

I snort, but my voice cracks when I speak. "You're so fucking obsessed."

"And you're still standing here," he replies, "waiting for me to do it."

"Weren't you making pastries?"

"You don't care about the pastry," he says, voice low, teasing. "You only ever cared about the filling."

I feel his hands gather the shirt. He lifts it—slow, measured—like he wants to memorize every inch of skin as it's revealed. Up my ribs. Over my arms. And gone.

Then he freezes.

His eyes roam over the lingerie like he's seeing something he was never supposed to. His breath catches, and everything in him stills.

"Fuck me," he says under his breath.

I tilt my head, smug. "Already did."

His gaze snaps back to mine, heat flickering wild behind it.

Then he moves.

He grabs me by the hips and lifts me like I weigh nothing, setting me down on the cold marble countertop. I hiss through my teeth—the shock of it stealing my breath—but he's already stepping in close, his body heat chasing away the sting of cold.

His gloved hands settle on my thighs—but only for a moment.

He peels off the gloves one at a time. Slow. Deliberate. The sound of the leather sliding off is practically pornographic.

He tosses them aside.

Then his bare hands—warm, rough, *real*—slide up my thighs with reverent precision, tugging me to the edge and spreading me open just enough to make me feel utterly exposed. I'm forced to brace my hands behind me on the marble counter to not fall back.

He doesn't strip the lingerie off me.

Instead, he drags two fingers beneath the thin strip of lace covering my pussy, hooking the fabric to the side with almost obscene care—*because he wants to see me wearing it while he wrecks me.*

He drags his thumb lightly across my exposed folds, humming under his breath like he's already savoring me.

And then he reaches for the bowl.

The one filled with cherry cream cheese filling.

I blink at him, breath hitching as he dips two fingers into the mixture—cool and pale pink, thick and sweet.

"You like it messy," he murmurs, gaze locked on me. "Don't you?"

I don't get the chance to answer.

Because he drops to his knees.

The room feels suddenly too quiet, too heavy.

Then he paints a line of pastry filling across the inside of my thigh—slow, obscenely slow.

The contrast is instant. Cool cream cheese filling on heated skin. I bite my lip to keep from making a sound.

He leans in, tongue sliding along the trail he made—licking it off like I'm dessert he's been waiting far too long to taste.

"You taste better than the filling," he says between licks, voice thick and low, lips brushing against my inner thigh.

I open my mouth, maybe to insult him, maybe to moan, but then he does it again. Another line. Another slow, decadent drag of his tongue that leaves me shaking.

His hands spread my thighs even further, holding me open for him. My lingerie still half-twisted to the side, lace biting into my hips. And then he's there—mouth on me, tongue parting me, licking into me with slow, devastating precision.

"Fuck," I whisper, head tilting back, eyes fluttering shut as heat floods every inch of my body.

He groans against me, tongue working deeper, slower. Then faster. Like he's trying to map me from the inside out. Like my pleasure is the only thing that matters.

When he drags two fingers back through the bowl and pushes them inside me—sweet and slick and devastating—I nearly fall back on the counter.

He moves them in and out slowly, curling them perfectly against that spot that makes my whole body tighten.

I move a hand to fist his hair, tugging. "God, Rule—"

"I told you," he growls against my soaked, swollen clit, "you only like the filling."

And then he doubles down.

He *eats* me with a desperation that borders on madness. Like he's starving. Like he's waited *years* for this moment and he's going to *savor every goddamn second*. His tongue flicks over my clit again and again, and when I gasp, he moans into me like my pleasure fuels him.

My thighs clamp around his head and he doesn't pull away. He grips my hips tighter, anchoring me to his mouth, fucking me with his tongue, grinding his mouth against me like he needs it as much as I do until I'm spiraling.

When I come, it's not gentle. It's brutal. Messy.

It rips through me like a detonation—sharp, wild, wrung from someplace deeper than I want to admit exists.

And he doesn't stop.

He licks me through it, slow and thorough, collecting every drop like it's owed to him, savoring every broken sound I make.

I'm still gasping when he finally pulls back and stands, his mouth and chin are glistening mess of pastry filling and me.

He wipes his fingers across his lips—but doesn't bother cleaning the rest.

Instead, he presses his fingers—slick with filling and my own arousal—against my mouth.

"Open, princess," he says, voice low and dark and unbearably satisfied.

And like the broken, fucked-up thing I am, I do.

I open my mouth, and he shoves his fingers between my lips, deep, curling them against my tongue.

The taste of me and sugar floods my senses at once—sweet and obscene and inescapable.

His thumb traces the edge of my jaw as he watches me suck them clean, his breathing heavy, almost ragged.

"Good girl," he murmurs, voice like sin and promise.

I glare at him over the mess of his fingers, but I don't pull away.

Because somehow—*fuck*—I want more.

I drag my teeth lightly over his fingers before letting them slip from my mouth, slowly, seductively. His hand drops away, but his gaze doesn't.

It clings.

Like he's still tasting me just by looking.

I smirk, wiping the corner of my mouth with the back of my hand. "Hope you got your fill. Would hate to think I left you hungry."

His mouth twitches, a dark grin threatening. "Little storm, I'll never get my fill of you."

I roll my eyes, but my skin burns all the same as I slide off the counter.

He steps closer again, knuckles grazing my bare hip where the lingerie's still bunched and askew. His touch is deceptively light, almost casual.

"Didn't think you'd actually wear it," he murmurs, voice rougher now, more honest. His eyes drag over every piece of exposed lace, every inch of black that still clings to me. "Figured you'd burn it. Or strangle me with it."

"I considered it," I say breezily, even as my chest tightens under the weight of his stare. "But then I figured... might as well make you suffer."

He chuckles low in his throat, hand sliding higher, fingertips skimming just under the waistband where the lace bites into my skin. "You call this suffering?"

"You look pretty fucking wrecked to me," I shoot back, voice saccharine. "Face of a man about two seconds away from begging."

"Begging's not my style." He leans in, lips brushing my ear again, a shiver dragging down my spine. "Taking is."

God, he says it like a promise. Like a threat dressed in silk.

I shove his chest again—not hard enough to move him, just hard enough to make a point. "I need a shower. And *you* now officially owe me pastries."

He grabs my wrist before I can step fully away, thumb stroking the inside lightly, almost idly. "Is that a fact?"

"And coffee," I add sweetly, cocking my head. "Hot. Strong. Two sugars. You now owe me both."

He doesn't let go immediately. He just looks at me like he's memorizing this moment, like if he lets it slip away too fast it'll turn to smoke in his hands.

"You're a demanding little thing, you know that?" he murmurs, thumb brushing over the pulse hammering against my skin.

I yank my hand free with a smirk. "And you're a hungry little thing, so we're even."

He laughs low, dark, and wrecked—and I don't wait for him to say anything else.

I pivot on bare feet, purposefully swaying my hips in the ruined lingerie as I walk back down the hall toward my bedroom. I flip him off without breaking stride, heading for the hallway with every ounce of dignity I can scrape together—which isn't easy, considering I'm half-dressed, sticky, and very obviously wrecked by his mouth.

"Better be fresh pastries," I call over my shoulder. "Or I'm starting a rebellion."

"Princess," he calls back, voice warm with threat and affection in equal measure, "you *are* the rebellion."

I don't turn around.

I just smile to myself, wicked and satisfied, and disappear into the shadows of the hallway.

Chapter 41

Seanna

I push open the door to what seems to be *my* bedroom with a lazy swing of my hand, muscles still buzzing with the aftershocks of Rule's mouth on me.

The room is a goddamn dream—or a nightmare, depending on how you look at it.

Dark, modern, seductive. Big enough to fit half of my cabin inside it. Burgundy silk sheets still tangled at the foot of the bed like an invitation I'm pretending I don't see. Every inch of it curated, crafted.

For me.

I blow out a slow, measured breath and make a beeline for the two doors I haven't opened yet, tucked side by side along the far wall. One has to be the bathroom. The other... no clue. Storage, maybe. Weapons closet. Secret trapdoor to hell. Knowing them? All three.

I grab the handle on the first door and swing it open.

And freeze.

It's not a closet. It's *a closet.*

A walk-in the same size of the fucking wardrobe room at the organization. And it's filled. Wall to wall. Floor to ceiling. Clothes—*mine.* Or, at least, everything I would have picked for myself if I had unlimited money and no goddamn conscience. Rows of black leather jackets, sleek dark jeans, ripped shirts, moody dresses in stormy shades of gray and blood-red. Boots, combat and heeled. Statement jewelry glinting under the soft recessed lights.

And there, tucked between it all, a few familiar items.

My ratty hoodie from the cabin. My favorite worn-out jeans with the split seam at the pocket. My first black leather jacket I spent six months saving up for.

I take a stumbling step back, chest tight, a tidal wave of *too much* rolling over me.

They didn't just guess.

They *knew*.

They studied me so closely they could rebuild me from memory if they had to.

I slam the door shut harder than necessary and lean my forehead against it, squeezing my eyes shut, forcing a deep, slow breath into my lungs. It doesn't help. The reality still slams into me like a freight train:

They *built* this world around me.

And part of me—*the most traitorous part*—wants to step inside that closet, run my fingers across every hem, every leather jacket, and *belong*.

I shove the thought down so hard it almost chokes me and push off the door, marching toward the second door.

The bathroom is exactly what I expect: more dark decadence. Black marble countertops, gray tiled floors that gleam under soft recessed lights, burgundy towels folded with military precision. The shower is a glass-walled monstrosity, big enough for two—or three. The air smells faintly of sandalwood and something sharper underneath. Something that smells like *them*.

I cross to the counter, hands bracing the cool stone, and lift my gaze to the mirror.

And stop.

My reflection stares back at me: hair a wild mess, cheeks flushed, eyes still heavy-lidded from pleasure and exhaustion. A dark bruise is beginning to bloom low on my throat where Rule's hand wrapped around it last night. I look wrecked. I look wild.

I look *theirs*.

My throat tightens against the truth of it.

I drop my gaze, desperate for a distraction—and find it.

The counter is lined with products. Neatly, carefully. All my usual brands. All the things I love and use without even thinking. My lotion. My makeup. Even the specific brand of fucking eyeliner I hoard like a dragon.

Another hit, square to the chest.

My hands curl into fists against the marble, knuckles aching white.

I lift my head slowly, ready to snarl at my own reflection—But my breath catches in my throat.

Because in the mirror, behind me, is *Ruin*.

Silent. Still.

I know it's him, because he is still masked. Still gloved. Still dressed in his perpetual black like a goddamn shadow that refuses to let me go.

He's standing just inside the door, arms folded, watching me with that devastating, brutal patience that always feels like it's peeling my skin back one layer at a time.

My pulse jackhammers in my throat.

I don't turn. I don't move.

I refuse. If he wants something—*he can fucking come get it.*

My muscles lock stubbornly, a silent dare in the set of my shoulders. I see his reflection—see the way he stands there, still as a storm just before it breaks. Waiting. Watching.

But I won't be the first to move. *Not this time.*

The seconds stretch, brittle and sharp, vibrating with too much meaning.

The tension between us hums, a livewire under my skin, sparking with every shallow breath I take.

I keep my chin high, my back stiff, my fists clenched white against the cool marble counter. I tell myself I'm not trembling. That the buzz under my skin is rage. Not anticipation.

And then—he moves.

Slow. Unhurried. Each step a deliberate act of control. A reminder that he doesn't have to chase me anymore.

I'm already caught.

I watch him come closer through the mirror, the reflection sharpening with every step until he's right behind me—so close that the heat of his body prickles against the nearly bare skin the lingerie barely covers.

Still, he doesn't touch me.

Instead, he cages me in—one hand braced on the marble either side of me, his body hemming me against the counter like he's building a prison out of his own limbs. A prison I'm not sure I want to escape.

My chest rises and falls faster, lips parting around breath that suddenly feels too thick, too heavy to drag down.

I can't see his eyes behind the glasses. But I *feel* his gaze like a caress. We stare at each other, reflections locked. Neither speaking. Neither surrendering.

The air between us practically vibrates—dense, electric. I swear I can hear my own pulse pounding in my ears.

Finally—*finally*—he speaks.

Low. Raw. A voice like gravel and reverence braided into one devastating thing.

"You have no idea," he murmurs, breath hot against my neck, "what you do to me."

I blink once—slowly—but I don't look away.

I *can't.*

He leans in closer, his mask brushing the stray strands of my hair, his chest brushing the curve of my back in a contact so light it feels almost imagined. But it isn't. It's real. Every atom between us charged and aching.

"You standing there..." His voice scrapes lower, rougher. "Wearing that fucking lingerie we bought for you. So still, so proud. So fucking defiant."

His hands move. At last. Sliding up the outside of my thighs—slow and reverent, like he's memorizing every inch of skin, every sharp line and soft curve.

"You're beautiful," he breathes, voice breaking like it costs him something vital. His fingers trace the curve of my hips, skating over the delicate lace that cuts into my skin. "You're *ours*. You're *mine*."

The possessiveness in that word doesn't scare me.

It *brands* me.

I shudder under his touch, a helpless tremor running through me that no amount of willpower can suppress. Heat floods my skin in waves, drowning every rational thought I still have left.

"I look at you," he breathes, "and I wonder how the fuck I ever thought I could stay away."

His hands trail higher—up over my waist, my ribs—dragging lightly over the faint bruises and rope-burns they left etched into me like a map of ownership. His touch is achingly careful now. Tender. Worshipful.

"You were born for this," he rasps against my skin, his breath ghosting over the sensitive spot beneath my ear. "Born to drive us insane. To bring us to our fucking knees."

One hand cups my breast through the thin lace—fingers rolling my nipple between them with almost cruel precision—while the other slips lower. Fingertips finding the scrap of lace between my thighs and shifting it aside with devastating ease.

Two fingers press against my slick entrance—teasing, testing. I gasp, clutching the edge of the counter, knuckles bone-white against the marble to stay upright.

He watches me through the mirror. Watches every flicker of my expression, every desperate twitch of my thighs. Sees *everything* I'm trying not to give him.

He watches my face as his fingers circle—once, twice—then slip inside me with a slow, deliberate thrust.

Stretching. Curling.

My mouth falls open in a soft, broken moan I can't swallow down fast enough.

He groans low against my neck like my sound fuels him.

"You feel it too," he rasps, his breath skating across my throat. "The way you fit around me. The way you fucking *melt* for me without even trying."

His fingers pump slow, curling just right with every thrust, coaxing a tremor up my thighs, a helpless twitch in my hips.

And still—still he holds back.

The tension thickens. Grows almost unbearable. I can feel him waiting for something. Expecting something.

Finally—he speaks again. This time softer.

"Now that you know," he says, almost a whisper, "that it was Bodhi behind Rule's mask..." He pauses, like he needs to force the next words out. "Does it change anything, Seanna?"

The question lodges under my ribs like a blade, cuts me open. Lays me bare.

I open my mouth—close it again.

Because fuck, I don't know. Because *yes*—it should change everything. And *no*—it changes nothing at all.

I don't answer. I can't. Not yet. Not when my chest is cracked open and my heart's slamming against my ribs like it's trying to escape.

Not when I can still feel the steady, relentless press of his fingers inside me, the way he's holding me together and tearing me apart all at once.

All I feel is this hollow, aching need to know him.

All of him.

And so, my hands lift—shaking, hesitant. I reach behind me.

The pressure inside me coils tighter, sharp and relentless, spiraling upward like a wire pulled too tight.

He doesn't flinch. Doesn't stop me. Just keeps fingering me—slow and relentless—and then he shifts his hand.

The heel of his palm grinds against my clit with devastating pressure, a slow, brutal friction that drags a desperate sound from deep inside me. It's not gentle. It's not teasing. It's pure fucking intent. A dark, deliberate claim meant to tear me apart while I still stand here, helpless and shaking and staring into the mirror like our reflections might splinter under the weight of it.

A whimper breaks loose, wrecked and helpless, my hips rocking into his hand despite every shred of pride left clinging to my bones.

Still, my fingers find the edges of his glasses. I slip them off—slow, careful—feeling them leave his face with a soft scrape. I drop them onto the counter with a tiny, final sound.

And then—I meet his eyes.

I'm so close I can barely breathe, barely stand. The world narrows to nothing but the slide of his fingers, the throb building between my legs, and the devastation waiting in his gaze.

Dark brown. Sharp. Steady. *So goddamn familiar it rips the breath from my lungs.*

Recognition slams into me like a freight train.

Those eyes—those eyes I've trusted on ops, trusted in fights, trusted to watch my six when I didn't trust anyone else. Those eyes belong to one man. One name.

I reach up again and curl my fingers under the edge of his mask. My pulse pounds so hard I swear he can feel it in every part of my body.

Slowly—deliberately—I peel it away.

Every nerve ending in my body screams for release, trembling at the edge, the need clawing up my spine like a living thing.

The mask falls to the counter beside the glasses with a whisper of fabric.

And there he is.

Matteo.

My breath hitches. My heart fucking stops.

And just as my mind shatters into jagged pieces of disbelief and recognition—his fingers hit that spot inside me—pressing, curling—dragging a shuddering, broken moan from my lips.

The orgasm tears through me without warning, violent and raw, all sharp edges and devastating force, clawing up my spine with a violence that rips the air from my lungs.

I can't look away.

I can't breathe.

All I can do is *fall.*

The pleasure crashes over me in waves, brutal and unstoppable, my body convulsing helplessly around his fingers as I cling to his gaze like it's the only thing anchoring me to this world.

"Matteo," I gasp—wrecked, raw, desperate—his name tumbling out like it's the only thing left keeping me upright.

Not Ruin. Not Huxley. *Matteo.*

The man I've trusted my life with more times than I can count. The man I thought I knew better than anyone.

He watches me fall apart around his fingers—watches every second of my undoing—with those same dark, wild, *familiar* eyes. Jaw tight. Breath shaking. A storm barely held in check.

And when I shudder—panting, clenching helplessly around him, my hands scrambling at the marble for something, anything to hold onto—he leans down, mouth brushing the shell of my ear, voice guttural and wrecked and irrevocably *his.*

"You were always mine, little storm," he whispers, every word searing into my skin like a brand. "You just didn't know it yet."

Chapter 42
Ruin

She's trembling against the counter, still panting from the force of her orgasm, her knuckles white where they're braced against the marble. And fuck, she's beautiful like this—shattered and furious and mine.

Her body is still clenching helplessly around my fingers when I drag them from her slowly, savoring the way she shudders at the loss. I bring them to my mouth, licking her taste from my glove like a man starved.

But the haze barely lifts before the storm comes roaring back.

"You," she rasps, voice shaky but sharpening fast. "You were with me. The whole time. On my team. Helping me hunt Javier."

I watch her, chest heaving, hair wild, lingerie twisted and clinging to her flushed skin. My beautiful little hurricane.

She turns and shoves at my chest—weakly, but enough to make her anger clear. "How the fuck could you be that close and never tell me?"

I catch her wrists—not to restrain, just to steady her. "Seanna—"

"No!" she snaps, ripping free and pacing away, her arms crossing tight over her chest like she's trying to hold herself together. "You watched me bleed. You let me trust you—and still, you lied."

I move slowly, hands out in surrender, voice rough from holding too much back. "It wasn't supposed to happen like this."

She spins on me, eyes blazing. "Wasn't supposed to happen? What, Matteo?"

The way she says my name—like it's poison and a prayer all at once—cuts straight to the bone.

I shake my head, throat tight. "When we first infiltrated your life, it was just about getting close. Watching from inside your circle. Becoming important to you."

Her laugh is bitter, broken. "Congratulations. Mission accomplished."

"We would've told you," I rasp. "Eventually. But your hunt for Javier—it sped everything up."

She freezes, a ripple passing through her.

I press on, needing her to hear it. "Rule heard his father's threat against you. After that, slow wasn't an option anymore. Protecting you became everything."

She trembles, and for the first time since I touched her, it isn't from lust. It's from the weight of everything she's been forced to carry.

"You made it impossible for me to hate you," she whispers, like the words wound her to say them.

God, I feel that in my fucking bones.

She turns her face away, scrubbing a hand across her mouth like she can erase the truth. "You were there for everything. After every op. Every late night. Every time I thought I was alone—you were there."

I cross to her, slow and sure, desperate to close the distance she keeps trying to put between us.

"I never stopped watching your back," I say low, the words cracking raw in my chest. "Even when you didn't know it. Especially then."

She lets out a broken sound, somewhere between a laugh and a sob. "You know what kills me?"

I shake my head, helpless.

"You were *inside* my life," she whispers. "Right there beside me. Day after day. Sitting next to me in briefings, fighting beside me in the field. Laughing with me after the missions when I let myself believe the world wasn't so broken."

I flinch inwardly.

I know she didn't have this harsh reaction to Bodhi. I listened. But Bodhi... he showed up when necessary, for missions with the organization and afternoon training where he could place himself in her path. But me? I was there nearly every day. I lived in the trenches with her. I sat beside her for hours, shoulder to shoulder, breathing the same air, pretending like every moment wasn't slicing me open because I couldn't have her the way I needed to. I was the one bleeding with her. Drinking with her. Watching her try to stitch herself back together while I barely held myself in one piece.

I lived in the spaces between her breaths.

And fuck if it didn't destroy me every single goddamn day.

"It gutted me," I rasp, dragging the words from somewhere deeper than my ribs, "what was worse was watching you at those clubs after missions. Celebrating. Laughing. Dancing with boys who didn't even know how to touch you. Watching them try—and knowing they'd never satisfy you the way I could. The way we could."

Her shoulders hitch slightly, her hands tightening against her sides as if she's trying to hold herself together.

"Every time you smiled at them," I say, softer now, "every time you let yourself believe for one second that they could see you the way I do—it tore me apart."

Her breath catches, but she doesn't move away.

"You deserved better," I whisper, taking another step forward, close enough now that I can feel the heat radiating off her skin. "And every goddamn night, I dreamed about giving it to you."

Her chin lifts, defiant and trembling. "And yet you lied to me."

"I lied to protect you," I say, rough and breaking. "I lied because I didn't know how to be close to you without wanting to destroy the world for you."

She swallows hard.

I step even closer, my hand lifting to brush her jaw with a touch so reverent it feels like prayer. "But, I wasn't lying the other day," I murmur, voice thick with everything I've never been able to say. "I've wanted to taste your lips for so fucking long."

Her breath stutters.

And then I kiss her.

Not rough. Not brutal.

A kiss so slow, so desperate, it feels like I'm trying to memorize the shape of her mouth against mine—like I'm trying to stitch something broken back together with nothing but touch and breath and the hollowed-out pieces of everything I never said. A kiss born from years of silent wanting, from restraint worn down to rust and ruin. From the silent obsession in every stolen glance, every unspoken word. A kiss heavy with all the promises I never dared to make aloud.

A kiss that tastes like regret and hope twisted into something unbearable.

I pour it all into her—the mistakes, the obsession, the devotion that's carved me open and hollowed me out until only she remained inside me. Everything I am. Everything I could never be without her. I give it to her now like an offering, knowing it will never be enough to fix what I've broken.

I kiss her like she's oxygen and I've been drowning for years.

My hand skims her side with aching reverence, tracing the curve of her waist, the trembling tension under her skin. My fingers brush over the lingerie we bought for her—the fragile black lace clinging to her like a second skin, like a brand burned into her for no one but us.

And still—still—I want more. Not just her body. Her trust. Her fury. Her broken, beautiful heart.

Even if I know I'll never deserve it.

She stiffens slightly, pulling back just enough to breathe. Her forehead rests against mine, breaths mingling between us.

"I don't know how to forgive you," she whispers.

"I don't expect you to," I murmur back. "But you should know... it was never a game."

She shakes her head slowly, a few stray tears slipping free.

"You broke everything I thought was safe," she says, voice cracking open under the weight of it.

I close my eyes briefly, feeling her words rip straight through me. Because she's right. I didn't just break her trust—I shattered the foundation she built her entire life on. I tore apart the belief that her instincts, her choices, could protect her. I made her doubt the one thing she was supposed to be able to trust—herself.

"I know," I rasp, my voice thick. "I was supposed to be the safe one. The one you didn't have to question. The one standing beside you when everything else went to hell."

Her eyes shine with something furious and betrayed, something that cuts deeper than any blade ever could.

"You *were*," she says bitterly. "You were the steady one. The one I didn't second-guess. You were the ground under my feet when everything else was burning—and you let me lean on you while you lied."

Her words crack something open inside me. A wound I know I'll never stitch closed again.

"You made me believe I could trust you," she whispers, voice splintering. "And now... now I don't know if I can trust anything."

"I know," I breathe against her skin. "But I swear to you, Seanna... I was yours long before you ever knew."

Another trembling breath leaves her, shaky and uneven.

Her eyes close for a second, her whole body folding in on itself like she's trying to hold together the broken pieces.

I just stand there, breathing with her, feeling the crack in the world we built between us.

God, if I could take it back. If I could undo every lie stitched into the seams of us.

But I can't.

And somehow, she's still standing.

She pulls back a little more, steel finding its way back into her spine.

"I need a fucking shower," she mutters, voice rough, brittle around the edges.

I smile softly, brushing my knuckle along the lace at her hip. "Want some help?"

She scoffs, fire sparking back to life in her gaze. "Get the fuck out, Matteo. I know damn well if you step into that shower, I'm getting railed against the glass."

I chuckle low, dark, and wrecked, backing away with my hands raised in mock surrender. But fuck, the image carves itself into my skull like a brand I'll never scrape off.

"Would that really be so bad?" I throw back, voice rasping with promise.

She flips me off, and it's the most beautiful fucking thing I've ever seen.

I move to the door, pausing just outside it to rake one last hungry look down her body—memorizing the rage, the heartbreak, the goddamn *fire* that makes her who she is.

"We will be waiting in the living room, little storm," I promise, voice thick with everything I can't say. "Don't be long."

She slams the door in my face.

And for a long moment, I stand there, leaning against it. Breathing her in.

And knowing—knowing with a hollow, aching certainty—that I will never want anything the way I want her.

Even if it costs me everything.

Chapter 43

Seanna

The water scalds my skin, but I don't turn it down.

I brace my palms against the cool marble of the shower wall, letting the punishing heat burn away the aftershocks still coiled in my body—the soreness, the betrayal, the desperate ache I can't seem to scrub clean.

It doesn't work.

It never does.

I tilt my head back, closing my eyes as the spray beats against my throat, the bruises there a testament to how easily I'd unraveled for them. How easily I still could.

Even now, with the truth lying between us like a smoking crater, part of me aches for them. Part of me still fits too easily against their hands, their mouths, their voices low and reverent in the dark.

And worse?

Part of me feels something almost akin to admiration simmering under the rage.

A begrudging respect for how thoroughly they infiltrated my life. How carefully they threaded themselves through every inch of it until I couldn't tell where they ended and I began.

I should have seen it sooner.

I should have paid more fucking attention—the looks I now realize were more frequent than anyone else's. The emotions behind them I missed, too busy chasing my demons, too busy burning myself alive trying to save the world.

They weren't hiding as well as I thought.

Not really.

Looking back, I can see it now. The way Matteo's gaze lingered after every mission debrief. The way he never let anyone get too close before putting a bullet in them. The way Bodhi never let anyone else sit between us at HQ if he could help it. And the times he offered to spar with me just to touch me. The way both of them stood just close enough, just constant enough, like satellites that never drifted out of orbit.

It wasn't just professionalism. It wasn't just friendship. It was this. Obsession. Quiet. Meticulous. All-consuming.

They had stitched themselves into my life so seamlessly that I never thought to question it.

And maybe that's the worst part. That I didn't notice.

I was too focused on the darkness.

Too focused on tearing down every corrupt bastard who preyed on the innocent, too obsessed with embracing the fire inside me to notice the two men who had already lit the match.

I missed it.

I missed *them*.

I press my forehead to the tile and breathe hard, trying not to drown in my own hindsight.

It's so much easier to be angry. So much easier to drown in betrayal. But even in the wreckage, there's a jagged, brutal admiration chewing its way through my bones.

Because *fuck*, they did it. They infiltrated my life, my defenses, my heart—piece by patient, merciless piece.

God. I let them in. I never saw it coming, and I don't know if I regret it.

Get it together, Seanna.

After what feels like forever, I finally drag myself out, toweling off mechanically. I pull on a pair of black cotton shorts and a tank top from the collection of clothes that they brought from the cabin—simple, familiar—armor against the vulnerability still bleeding out of me.

I don't bother with makeup. Don't bother looking in the mirror. I already know what I'd see.

When I open the door to the bedroom, the house is unnervingly quiet. No looming shadows. No waiting threats.

Just the faint murmur of voices down the hall.

I follow it.

My bare feet are silent against the hardwood as I move toward the open living room. They're there—the two of them.

Rule. Ruin.

Bodhi. Matteo.

Kingston. Huxley.

The names snarl in my head, none of them fitting, all of them too fucking real. I've known them separately for years. Bodhi—the cocky operator, slipping in and out of my missions at the Organization, always lurking at the edges like smoke. Matteo—the one who sat beside me almost every goddamn day. The steady hand in the middle of the chaos. The one who stayed late sometimes at the office after missions, buying me shitty vending machine coffee when the world got too heavy.

And now— Ruin and Rule. Masks. Violence. Obsession.

I've never known them as Kingston and Huxley. And maybe that's why it's almost easy to shove those names aside. To pretend the weight of their bloodlines aren't bleeding out all over my skin.

Because standing here now—watching them—those names mean nothing.

They're just... *them.*

Two men from two parts of my life that were never supposed to meet. Never supposed to fit together like this—quiet, casual, comfortable.

Talking like they didn't just rip my world apart with their bare hands.

The smell of coffee hooks into me before anything else.

Rich. Sharp. Exactly how I take it.

There's a plate on the coffee table. Pastries. Cherry cream cheese. Of course.

Rule doesn't even glance back when he speaks, but his voice slides across the room like a hand around my throat. "They're still warm, princess."

I freeze.

Fingers tightening in the hem of my tank. Breath snagging somewhere too deep to pull free.

I don't know what the hell to call them in my head anymore. I don't know how to step into this room without feeling like I'm walking into a war I've already lost.

But the coffee smells good.

And I'm not the kind of girl who runs from a battlefield.

Not even one I never had a chance of winning.

So I lift my chin, square my shoulders, and step forward.

Because if they think I'm going to crumble now—if they think for one second I'll break easier just because they finally ripped their masks off—they don't fucking know me at all.

I cross the room, the smell of coffee thick in the air, the pastries still steaming slightly on the plate. They don't move as I approach, just glance at me with a casual, almost lazy awareness that I still feel like a physical touch.

I grab the coffee first—priorities—and take a long sip, letting the bitter heat burn its way down my throat. Exactly the way I like it.

I don't sit right away. I stand for a moment by the edge of the coffee table, mug in hand, staring at the two men sprawled across the black velvet couch like they own the fucking air in the room.

Maybe they do.

Ruin is in his usual position, forearms resting on his knees, his head tipped slightly to the side like he's trying to read my mind. Rule sits straighter, arms thrown over the back of the couch, looking at me like he's already plotting ten moves ahead. The masks are now gone. The names are stripped away. Only the bones are left: *Bodhi. Matteo. Obsession.*

And me? I'm the battlefield they bled for.

The plate of pastries sits between us like a peace offering. Cherry cream cheese, just like he promised. They even glazed them a little heavier this time. I should laugh. I should throw the fucking plate at them. Instead, I pick one up, break off a piece, and pop it into my mouth.

It's good. Too good. A decadent little betrayal of my own anger. Of course they'd know how to weaponize pastry against me.

I chew slowly, eyes never leaving theirs, feeling the heat of their gazes burn hotter with every second of silence I let stretch between us.

"Coffee's good," I say finally, voice light, almost bored.

Rule's mouth curves into a slow, knowing smirk. "You're welcome, princess."

My fingers tighten around the mug at the nickname—but I don't correct him. Not this time.

Instead, I sink onto the armchair opposite them, folding one leg over the other. Deliberate. Calm. Unbothered. I won't give them the satisfaction of seeing how raw I still am under the skin.

"So, we've established you two have been planning this for a long time," I say, picking invisible lint off my tank top.

Neither of them deny it.

"Years," Matteo agrees, voice low, steady.

I shrug, feigning indifference. "You did your homework. Congratulations. Top marks for stalking and sabotage."

A flash of something dark moves through Bodhi's eyes, but he reins it in fast.

"It wasn't just stalking," he says quietly.

"No," I agree, tilting my head. "It was infiltration."

The word hangs between us, sharp and clinical. It should taste like ash. It doesn't. It tastes like truth. And something dangerously close to understanding.

I take another slow sip of coffee, letting the heat roll through me.

"Did you ever think," I murmur, voice cool, "that maybe you didn't have to work so hard?"

Matteo leans forward slightly, muscles tight under his black shirt. "What do you mean?"

I meet his gaze head-on, no flinching, no apology.

"You didn't have to orchestrate every detail. You didn't have to puppet-string my whole fucking life to get me close."

I set the mug down carefully on the table between us, the ceramic making a soft clink against the marble.

"You just had to ask."

Their silence is a tangible thing. It wraps around me, heavy and stunned and vibrating with something raw.

"You think we could have saved years of stalking?" Bodhi says at last, voice rough.

I smile, slow and a little cruel. "No. Not the versions of you I knew then. You weren't ready."

I let the truth sink in before I continue, my voice softening only a fraction:

"But maybe... maybe if you'd asked even a month ago, I would've said yes."

The confession costs me something. It digs in under my ribs and twists.

Matteo's hands clench into fists against his knees. Bodhi's jaw ticks, a muscle feathering along the sharp line of it.

"You're saying," Bodhi says slowly, "you're not running."

I snort. "Running? From *you*?"

I lean back, letting my head tip lazily against the chair.

"You think a little betrayal's gonna send me scattering?"

Matteo's mouth curves into something small and wild. Not a smile exactly—something darker.

"You're fucking magnificent," he says under his breath, almost like he didn't mean to let it slip.

I let it slide. Mostly because it feels... good. *Dangerously good.* And I'm not about to admit to how much the newly discovered praise kink will work for them.

But I don't let the moment stretch too long. I don't give them the satisfaction of thinking I've gone soft.

Instead, I tilt my head slightly, studying them both under the lazy drag of my lashes.

"You know," I say, voice casual, almost sweet, "you never did tell me where the villain names came from."

Bodhi's mouth quirks. Matteo's jaw ticks once, a flash of something between amusement and resignation crossing his face.

"You mean *Rule* and *Ruin*?" Matteo asks, voice dry.

I nod, picking up the coffee and sipping it, watching them over the rim like a cat playing with two very stupid mice.

"Rule was easy," Bodhi says with a smirk. "It's a bastardization of my real name. *Kingston.* King. Rule. Reign. Control."

His eyes glint wickedly. "Figured if I wasn't allowed to have a crown, I'd take the fucking throne anyway."

I hum low in my throat, not hiding my amusement. "Little dramatic, don't you think?"

His smirk deepens. "You're one to talk, princess."

I flip him off without missing a beat and turn my attention to Matteo.

"And *Ruin*?" I ask, voice dipping sharper. "That's a whole different flavor of fucked-up."

Matteo doesn't smile. Doesn't blink.

"It's not complicated," he says, voice low and matter-of-fact. "Even when I was a kid... I knew one thing for sure."

He leans forward, resting his elbows on his knees, gaze locking with mine.

"If anything or anyone ever got between me and you—" His voice drops, dark and quiet. "I would ruin them. Ruin *everything*."

The honesty in it burns hotter than any lie ever could.

No apology. No shame. Just a simple, brutal truth.

And fuck me, part of me wants to throw my coffee at his face for saying it so plainly. And part of me—God help me—wants to straddle him for it.

I set my mug down a little harder than necessary on the table, the sound sharp in the charged silence.

"Of course," I murmur, fingers tapping against the ceramic. "Of course you picked your own damn destiny."

He just watches me, silent, steady. Like there's no universe where he regrets it. Like he would choose it again. Every fucking time.

And maybe he would.

Maybe he already has.

I lean back in the chair, folding my arms loosely across my chest.

"Fine," I say. "You've got your dark little fairytale titles sorted."

I let the words linger just long enough to cut before I strike where it matters.

"What about Javier?"

The amusement vanishes from both their faces in an instant.

Good.

I press harder, voice going low and cold.

"What's the plan? What are you going to do to him?"

They exchange a glance—quick, practiced, silent. The kind of look that tells me whatever their answer is, it's already written in blood.

But Bodhi—no, *Rule*—is the one who answers, voice slow and careful.

"Patience, princess," he says, almost gently. "The plan's still in motion."

I narrow my eyes. "I'm not asking for a full play-by-play. I just want to know *something*."

Matteo—*Ruin*—shakes his head once, final.

"It's better if you don't. Not yet."

"You're not protecting me," I snap.

"No," Matteo agrees, standing slowly, stretching his shoulders with a casual roll that makes every muscle under his shirt shift. "We're protecting the plan."

He steps closer, slow and easy, like he's circling prey he already knows can't outrun him.

"And," Bodhi adds lazily, following suit, "we can keep you... *distracted*... while you wait."

My stomach knots, heat flashing low in my abdomen even as my jaw tightens in defiance.

I push up from the chair, slow and deliberate, facing them square.

"You think pastries and a quick fuck are going to keep me from demanding answers?"

Bodhi's mouth curves—not into a grin this time, but something darker. He steps closer, voice a low, lazy rasp that brushes against my skin like smoke.

"I'm pretty sure," he says, gaze dragging down my body with shameless hunger, "we can both agree when we fuck it isn't *quick*."

I snort under my breath but don't rise to the bait. Not this time.

Instead, I fold my arms and level them both with a flat look.

"Fine," I say. "You don't want to tell me about Javier yet. Then you'd better find another way to keep yourselves useful."

Matteo's mouth twitches, that small little twist again.

"We thought you might say that," he says smoothly.

Before I can ask what the hell that means, he gestures behind him with a lazy tilt of his head.

"Come on, little storm. Let's show you what else we built for you."

I narrow my eyes suspiciously but follow as they move toward a set of double doors tucked discreetly off another hallway on the other side of the living room.

Matteo opens them with a flourish, stepping aside so I can see inside first.

The breath catches in my throat.

It's a sparring room.

Fully fucking equipped.

Sleek dark mats cover the floors, punching bags hang heavy from reinforced beams, weapon racks gleam against the far wall, mirrors lining one side like a brutal confession. The entire space smells like leather, steel, and adrenaline. Like violence waiting to happen.

"You built me a fight room?"

"Built *us* one," Bodhi corrects. "You needed an outlet. So we gave you one."

I cross my arms. "How thoughtful. You plan to throw yourselves at my fists until I calm down?"

Matteo's voice is low, unreadable. "If that's what it takes."

The silence that follows hums with a different kind of violence. My hands twitch at my sides. It's been too long since I hit something for the fun of it.

I tilt my head slowly. "And if I win?"

"You won't," Bodhi says smoothly.

"You *want* to lose," I counter.

Matteo steps into my space, close but not crowding. His voice brushes against me like a challenge wrapped in silk.

"We want to earn our place again. However you make us do it."

My pulse stutters, then catches fire.

I don't answer.

I just smile—a slow, dangerous baring of teeth—and step onto the mat.

If they want forgiveness, they're going to have to bleed for it.

And God help them, I'm in the mood to make them.

Chapter 44

Seanna

The mat is cool under my bare feet. The air isn't. It's charged—hot and electric with the promise of violence.

Matteo cracks his neck to one side while Bodhi circles behind me, smug, and already radiating too much heat.

"Rules?" I ask, voice dry. "Or are we going full chaos today?"

"One-on-one," Matteo replies, stretching his shoulders, slow and deliberate. "Only one of us engages at a time. No interference. No pile-ons. Unless you ask nicely."

I roll my eyes. "Cute. And what's the wager?"

Bodhi steps forward, smirking. "You lose? Twenty-four hours. No complaints. No fighting us on decisions. You keep that sharp mouth shut and *wait*."

"And if I win?"

Matteo's eyes narrow just slightly. "Then we do it your way. For twenty-four hours, you call the shots."

"Deal," I say without hesitation.

Bodhi moves first.

I barely have time to register his forward lunge before I duck and twist, slipping past him with a grin.

"You move slower when you're trying to impress me," I taunt.

He spins, and this time he's faster—more brutal. I block the elbow, redirect the follow-up punch, but he grabs my wrist and twists, shoving me backward toward the edge of the mat.

I recover quick, swinging my leg up and landing a sharp heel against his side. He grunts, but it only fuels him.

"You call that a kick?" he growls, charging again. "Your left was better last week."

"You *liked* my left last week," I snarl, driving my shoulder into his chest.

He catches me, grips me around the waist, and I'm airborne for a second before I twist out of his hold midair and land in a low crouch. My tank top rides up. His eyes drop.

"I know what you're staring at," I snap.

"I'm appreciating the view," he says—and lunges again.

This time when we collide, his hand tangles in the hem of my shirt. He uses the motion to spin me, but I drop down and wrench free, the fabric ripping as I twist out of his grip. I feel it tear over my ribs.

"Oops," he mutters with zero remorse.

"Next one of you that tries to rip something is getting kneed in the dick," I promise.

I don't even get to finish my breath before Matteo's hands are on me.

No warning. He just comes in low and fast—slamming into my side like a freight train, spinning me across the mat. I crash shoulder-first, barely catching myself before I eat the floor.

"Cheap shot," I hiss, pushing to my feet.

"Adapt," Matteo says, stalking toward me like he's already inside my next move.

I launch at him—fast and vicious—but he grabs my arm mid-swing, redirects me with a smooth pivot, and slams my back into the mirror wall.

"Fuck off," I growl, twisting in his grip.

"Only if you say please."

He grins—too smug, too sharp—and I snap.

I grab the front of his shirt in both fists and yank. The sound of it tearing is sharp and satisfying.

Except it doesn't go how I want.

He freezes for half a beat… then lets out a low, dangerous laugh as he steps back and strips the rest of it off himself. It's slow and deliberate, revealing smooth muscle, scars, and those tattoos I always pretended I hadn't noticed crawling up his ribs during ops.

Shit.

I hate how fucking good he looks. Hate how my breath catches even though I *knew* it would. Hate how the bastard knows it, too.

"Feeling better now?" he asks, tossing the ruined shirt aside.

I don't answer. I lunge instead.

We clash again—harder now. He catches my kick with a knee, absorbs the impact, spins me by the hips and slams me chest-first into the mirror. His hand grabs my tank at the back and yanks it up high enough to expose my bare skin underneath.

I'm reminded that I have no bra on. No panties. Just sweat-slick cotton and attitude.

I manage to twist before I lose my shirt, shove Matteo off me, and spin fast enough to catch Bodhi with an elbow to the ribs.

Bodhi laughs. *Laughs.*

"You're getting sloppy," he murmurs, grabbing my wrist. "Thought you were better than this."

"I *am* better than this," I snap, twisting out of his grip and landing a solid knee between his legs.

He grunts, staggers back a step—but recovers fast.

"Warned you," I say, teeth bared.

"You *did*," he growls—and then he's right back on me.

He lunges low, trying to sweep my leg, but I pivot fast and catch his shoulder, using the momentum to swing behind him. My hand grabs the back of his shirt, fist twisting in the fabric as I pull.

"Payback," I snarl—and *rip*.

His shirt tears up the middle, splitting open in my grip. I shove it off his shoulders and throw it to the side.

Fuck.

All I can see is ink.

I've never seen him without a shirt, even sparring at the organization he had a shirt on. His back—*all* of it—is tattooed. Shoulder to waist, spine to ribs. A solid canvas of black and gray, sharp lines and winding chaos that moves like smoke across muscle and scar. There's a serpent coiled around a dagger. A storm cloud shattering over a cracked crown. Wings—*ripped*, not spread.

I forget to breathe.

God. Fucking. Damn it.

I hesitate. *Half a second.*

Just long enough.

Matteo is behind me again before I can blink.

His hand snakes around my waist—tight, possessive—and his other grips the hem of my tank top and *yanks* it up over my head in one fluid motion. It's just *gone*.

"Shit—" I gasp, trying to twist out of his grip.

Too late.

My arms are tangled in the cotton for a beat too long, leaving me exposed—bare from the waist up, breathing hard, sweat-slick skin pressed to his chest as he holds me still.

Bodhi laughs, the sound low and brutal as he turns back toward me.

"Aw, princess," he purrs, eyes dragging down over my now-bared chest. "You hesitated. Never hesitate in a fight."

"Fuck *you*," I growl, struggling in Matteo's hold—but the way his hand slides down, gripping the waistband of my shorts while Bodhi prowls forward?

It's not a fight anymore.

It's a war.

And I'm losing.

And God, part of me wants to.

But it doesn't stop me.

I slam my heel down onto Matteo's foot, twist at the same time, and break free with a grunt—dropping low and sweeping his leg hard.

He crashes onto his back, cursing.

"You think I'll roll over just because my tits are out?" I snarl, chest rising with every breath.

Bodhi grins like the devil. "No," he says, circling. "We're counting on you fighting harder."

I rush him.

We collide mid-mat, limbs locking, muscles straining, sweat and skin sliding against each other. He grabs me around the waist, tries to lift—I twist, slam my elbow into his ribs, and bring us both down in a messy tangle.

He's under me for a second—just long enough for me to straddle his hips and grind down with enough force to make him groan.

"You're slipping," I hiss, hand sliding across his throat in a mock choke. "Getting soft on me?"

He snarls—*snarls*—and the next second, we're flipping again.

His grip tangles in my hair, yanks me back just enough to expose my throat as he pins me under him, breath hot and ragged over my mouth.

"You really think you're winning?" he pants, dragging his hips tight to mine. "*This* is you losing."

"Then fuck—" I twist hard enough to throw him off, only for Matteo to step in, catching me mid-lurch, slamming me sideways against the mirror again with enough force to rattle it.

"You're gonna break the glass," I rasp, struggling against his hold.

"We'll replace it," he growls into my neck.

His hand slides up my ribs, fingers catching the underside of my breast with bruising intent, and I *bite* him—right at the edge of his jaw.

I slam my heel back into his shin and twist out of his grip with a snarl. He grunts, but lets me go.

Good.

I spin fast, fist already cocked, and throw a punch at Bodhi the second he lunges. He dodges—barely—but I follow with a knee aimed straight for his ribs. He catches it mid-air, grunting as we crash to the mat together in a tangle of limbs and sweat.

We roll. Hard. He tries to pin me. I bite his shoulder.

"Fuck—" he hisses, grabbing both my wrists and forcing them to the mat above my head as he straddles my hips.

"You done?" he pants, chest heaving.

"Not even close," I growl—and bring my head forward hard enough to *crack* against his.

He flinches back just long enough for me to reverse us.

Now I'm on top again.

My bare chest brushes against his sweat-slick one as I hold his wrists down and snarl into his face.

"You were always too fucking cocky."

His smile is blood and lust and savagery.

Matteo growls low from behind. "My turn."

I barely have time to shift before he's there—*ripping* me off Bodhi like a fucking ragdoll and throwing me onto the mat. I hit hard. My body bounces once, air knocked from my lungs.

Then his body crashes down over mine. All heat and weight and muscle.

"Don't—" I start, breath ragged.

His hand wraps around my throat.

Not choking. Not cutting off air. Just *claiming*.

"Fight me," he says.

I do.

We roll again—his hips between my thighs, my nails clawing down his back, my teeth bared before he crushes his mouth to mine.

It's not a kiss. It's violence and claiming.

Teeth. Tongue. Bruising pressure. His other hand yanks my shorts down past my thighs in jerky, brutal tugs. I kick at him, twist, snarl—*wanting* the fight. Demanding it.

And he gives it.

Bodhi's suddenly there—his hands joining Matteo's, helping to tear the shorts the rest of the way off until I'm completely naked.

Matteo's grip shifts *hard* as he flips me over and shoves me down.

Palms slap the mat. Knees scrape. I catch myself on all fours, breath heaving, body slick with sweat.

"Stay down," he growls, chest pressing into my back as his hand fists in my hair and yanks my head up.

"Make me," I snarl.

He laughs, low and ruined, then drags the head of his cock along my slick folds, slow just to piss me off—just to make me tremble in spite of myself.

"You're soaked," he mutters like a fucking accusation as he starts pushing inside me.

"You're delusional."

But the second I say it, he slams into me—hard.

That first thrust nearly folds me in half. The weight of him, the sudden burn—*and the piercings, those fucking piercings*—drag a raw sound from my throat.

My arms buckle and I collapse to my forearms, a gasp tearing loose as his cock fills me, thick and brutal and so goddamn deep I swear I see stars.

"Fuck," I choke out, hips jerking.

He doesn't give me time to recover. Doesn't pull back gently. Just drives in again, rougher, and the piercings scrape my inner walls with every thrust like it's branding me inside out.

Again. Again. And again.

My fingers claw at the mat for purchase. My breath stutters. My body betrays me with every wet, harsh slap of skin on skin echoing off the walls. The sounds leaving my throat are obscene.

And then Bodhi moves into my line of sight.

Bare chest gleaming, rising and falling with ragged breath. His hand fists his cock as he watches Matteo fuck me from behind—watching me collapse a little more with every thrust.

"You look fucking feral," he says, stepping in front of me.

I bare my teeth but don't stop him when he drags the tip of his own pierced cock across my lips.

"Open up," he says, voice dangerously calm.

I glare up at him from under sweat-drenched lashes—but I open.

I don't just open. I suck him in *hard*, my teeth scraping against his length just to remind him I can *bite*.

He hisses through his teeth, head tipping back.

Behind me, Matteo groans—his hands bruising at my hips, dragging me back into each thrust with a punishing rhythm.

I moan around Bodhi's cock, and the vibration makes him swear, his piercings glide over my tongue as I take him in. Smooth. Heavy. Fucking *filthy*.

"Fuck, she *likes* it," Matteo pants behind me.

"She wants to come like this, don't you, little storm," Bodhi growls, hand threading into my hair.

He rocks hard into my mouth just as Matteo thrusts deeper from behind, and the stretch—front and back—makes my arms tremble beneath me.

I don't stop.

I *can't* stop.

Not when they're using my body like a battlefield. Not when I *asked* for this with every punch, every insult, every twist of resistance I threw in their faces.

Matteo leans forward, one hand wrapping tight around my throat from behind, his chest flush with my back as he fucks me harder.

Bodhi groans, head tilting down as he looks into my eyes.

"Good fucking girl," he snarls.

I growl around his cock in answer.

I'm not giving in.

I'm giving *everything*.

Every thrust from Matteo slams me forward into Bodhi's cock, and every time I try to pull back, Matteo yanks me right back down his length like I'm a toy built to be used between them.

"Still think you were winning?" Matteo growls into my ear, his voice savage. He pulls me up enough to arch my spine and make the next thrust hit even *deeper*. "Still think this is *your* fight?"

Bodhi's hand tightens in my hair too, guiding my mouth up and down his cock, pushing deep into my throat, making me gag.

"She won't say it," Bodhi pants. "Even now. She's too fucking proud."

"She'll say it," Matteo growls, grinding in deep and holding there, his cock pulsing inside me. "She knows who won."

I moan around Bodhi's length, my body burning, every nerve ending stretched to its breaking point. Sweat slicks my skin. My thighs tremble. My hands dig into the mat so hard my nails hurt.

"Say it," Matteo snarls, snapping his hips forward.

I choke on a breath, on Bodhi, on the *need* crawling through my veins like poison.

"Say we won the wager."

I shake my head, lips parting around Bodhi's cock as I gasp for air, broken but defiant.

"Say you're ours," Bodhi says, voice razor-sharp. "Say you lost."

Another thrust. Another slam of bodies. Another pull of hair.

And then Matteo's other hand slips between my legs, rubbing ruthless circles over my clit as he drives into me from behind.

I jerk violently, the pleasure too much, too sharp, my body a livewire about to explode.

"You want to come?" he demands. "Say it."

I fight it. I swear I do.

But my body's already folding. Already tightening. Already fucking *breaking*.

Matteo bites at my shoulder, growling into my skin. "Say we won, little storm. Say it, or we don't let you come."

My moan turns guttural, helpless. Bodhi drags his cock free from my mouth and grips my jaw tight, forcing my eyes to meet his.

"You lost," he says, breath harsh. "Now admit it."

I snarl. I shake. I *burn*.

But it slips out anyway—choked, shattered, gutted.

"You... fucking... won."

"Louder," Matteo demands, slamming into me again, fingers moving faster over my clit.

"I said you *won*," I cry out, voice raw.

And then I break.

I come with a scream, body clenching violently around Matteo's cock, my thighs shaking as my vision whites out from the force of it. It hits like a detonation—hot, filthy, brutal.

Behind me, Matteo fights against the tightness of my body, his thrusts stuttering, and he growls deep in his chest as he spills inside me.

Bodhi strokes himself once, twice—his breath coming in short, ragged bursts—then snarls low in his throat.

His grip tightens in my hair.

Without warning, he jerks my head back—*hard*—forcing my spine to arch further and my mouth to fall open in a gasp. My eyes flick up to meet his again, and he *holds* me there, trembling with it, chest rising like he's barely holding himself back.

"Fucking *look* at me," he growls.

I do.

Because I want to see it.

Because I want to *watch* him fall apart over me while my thighs are still shaking from the brutal rhythm Matteo fucked me through just moments ago—our combined releases dripping down my thighs, marking me from the inside out.

Bodhi's hand works his cock with a brutal rhythm—wet, fast, hungry—and then he *breaks*.

He groans through clenched teeth, a deep sound that barely sounds human as he comes—thick, hot, and *everywhere*. My throat, my breasts, my collarbone, mixing with the sweat that coats every inch of my skin.

His hand stays tangled in my hair, anchoring me. Holding me in place like a possession, like a *prize*.

He watches me with dark, wild eyes—his lips parted, his breath caught somewhere between awe and exhaustion.

When he's done, his thumb drags across my jaw as he murmurs, "You were made for us."

And I'm still shaking.

Still panting.

Still braced on all fours in the middle of the mat, sweat-drenched and wrecked, lips swollen, thighs and chest slick and dripping with both of them.

"I hope," I gasp finally, voice hoarse and full of venom, "you enjoy your twenty-four hours, assholes."

Bodhi chuckles darkly and drops to his knees in front of me, brushing a kiss against my temple.

"Princess," he murmurs, dragging the word out like a kiss, "you gave them to us."

Matteo presses his mouth to my shoulder, voice still ragged.

"And we're going to savor *every* second."

Chapter 45

Seanna

My skin still stings. My thighs ache. My throat's raw from growling curses and choking on cock, and there are streaks of Bodhi's release drying on my breasts.

So, obviously, I head for the bathroom.

The hallway is too quiet as I walk, bare feet whispering against hardwood. My calves tremble slightly, and the skin of my inner thighs is tacky with sweat and dried arousal. I smell like sex and violence.

I'm still naked. And I don't care.

Let them look.

Let them fucking watch.

I earned this walk. Every bruise on my hips, every scratch on my ribs, every ache between my thighs was paid for with sweat and the kind of surrender that always ends in teeth and claw marks. I'm covered in their come, their sweat, and I don't cover a damn thing as I walk.

Because I'm not ashamed of what they did to me.

I'm just not sure what it means that I *wanted* it.

The bathroom door creaks as I push it open. It's the one in my new bedroom—the room too perfectly tailored to not be unnerving. Steam still lingers faintly from my earlier self-scorching rinse, curling around the black marble like ghosted breath. The mirror's fogged at the edges, distorting the woman inside it until she barely looks like me at all. A blur of skin and shadows and things I'm not ready to face.

I step up to the shower, fingers reaching for the faucet.

Then I hear it. Boots hit the floor behind me.

Then the soft sound of fabric peeling from skin.

I don't turn around. I don't have to.

"I said I was taking a shower," I say over my shoulder, voice dry.

"I know," Matteo answers simply. "I'm not letting you do it alone."

Not a question. Not a demand.

Just Matteo being... Matteo.

I don't argue. Not this time.

I step into the shower as the water kicks on, cranking the temperature up until it scalds. It feels good. Real. A bite I can control. It cuts through the haze still clinging to my limbs and brings me back to my body. Behind me, Matteo steps in, bare now except for the scars and ink carved into his skin.

He doesn't reach for me right away.

He grabs a washcloth instead.

Wets it. Lathers it.

Then kneels.

He starts at my ankles working his way up, the cloth warm and sudsy against sore skin. His hands are careful. Strong. Reverent in a way that makes my skin itch—not because I want him to stop, but because I don't know what the hell to do with this.

I'm used to violence.

I'm used to men who fuck like they're trying to prove something and then disappear before the sheets cool.

But Matteo?

He washes me like he's *praying*.

Like the act itself means something more than just soap and water and skin.

His fingers glide over the bruises on my calves, the dried streaks on my thighs. He doesn't speak, doesn't leer, doesn't flinch. He just presses a kiss to a scrape on my knee like it's instinct.

And that... that does something to me I'm not ready to unpack.

Then he washes between my thighs.

No hesitation.

He slides the cloth between my legs, parting me with firm, patient hands, cleaning me with the kind of care I've never been given after being fucked. No teasing. No filthy comments. No rush to shove his fingers in just because he can.

When he stands, he keeps going—arms, shoulders, collarbone. The cloth moves to my breasts, slow and methodical. He wipes away the crusted streaks of Bodhi's release, the grit of sweat and lust from every violent second of our fight.

Like it matters.

Like *I* matter.

His breath is quiet. The heat of his body is steady. The cloth slips down over my sternum, across the curve of one breast, then the other. No grope. No lingering. Just intention.

He moves behind me again, hair already damp from the steam. His hand lifts. Fingers drag through my hair once, twice, then slowly start to lather shampoo into it with strong fingers, massaging my scalp gently.

"You don't have to," I mutter. My voice is rougher than I expected.

"I know," he says again, quiet.

Then nothing. Just the sound of water and the motion of his hands in my hair.

I close my eyes.

Just for a second.

And that's when it happens.

I think of Hydessa.

A sharp, uninvited image—her face scrunched in worry, her voice cracking on the other end of the line as I said the wrong words to her.

Hey sis, I said. She knew. I could hear it in her breathing. Could feel her panic the second I hung up.

God. She must be spiraling by now. Calling everyone. Searching every contact she can trust. Probably not sleeping. Probably blaming herself.

My chest tightens.

And the worst part? Matteo is right.

Not that I'll admit it out loud.

It was *stupid* to let her know something was wrong. And I know I can't even warn her now without it risking my location. All I can do is hope this ends soon.

Hope she holds on.

Hope she doesn't come looking.

"You okay?" Matteo murmurs from behind me, voice low.

I stiffen. "Yeah."

He doesn't call me on it. Just rinses the shampoo from my hair, his fingers massaging the base of my skull until the tension in my shoulders starts to loosen. Until my muscles remember how to unclench.

"I could get used to this," I mutter, the words slipping out before I can catch them.

He goes still. Then lets out a breath.

"I hope you do."

The silence after that is thick. Not uncomfortable. Just full. Brimming with all the things we haven't said.

He turns off the water. Reaches for a towel. Wraps it around me before I can even move.

Then he dries me. Carefully. Like I might break if he rubs too hard. Like my skin is glass and he's learned how to handle it without cracking it.

I let him help me into a tank and a pair of my soft lounge pants—the kind I used to wear when I still had a normal life. When I still had mornings with vending machine coffee and busted surveillance gear and office banter with Matteo that wasn't soaked in obsession.

He towels off my hair next, messy and uncoordinated. I pull a face before taking the towel and doing it myself.

"That's not drying," I mutter. "That's abuse."

He snorts. "You want a salon experience?"

"I want to not look like I got electrocuted."

He leans in and presses a kiss to my temple. "You always look dangerous."

I roll my eyes and shove him lightly toward the door.

When we step into the living room, Bodhi's already there—showered, barefoot, shirtless, a smear of sauce on his chest and a wooden spoon hanging from his mouth as he adjusts a burner.

"You good?" he asks without turning.

"She's vertical," Matteo answers from behind me, voice dry.

"Barely," I mutter, eyeing the tattoos on Bodhi's back again..

Bodhi turns with a grin, waving the spoon like a weapon. "Then sit your wrecked ass down and eat."

I narrow my eyes again but obey, flopping onto the couch. Matteo follows, his thigh pressed to mine. I don't lean into him—not yet—but I don't pull away either. He's close but not crowding me. Just steady.

Goddamn fortress of a man.

Bodhi brings me a plate a minute later. Pasta. Creamy. Garlicky. The kind of comfort food I didn't ask for but definitely want. He hands me a mug next. Coffee.

Exactly the way I like it.

"You're ridiculous," I tell him as I take it.

"You'll get used to it," he says, dropping onto the other side of me, taking up too much space and not caring in the slightest.

He leans over to grab the remote and flicks through menus.

"Pick your poison," he says.

I blink and glance between them.

They're serious.

"You're actually giving me a choice?"

Matteo smirks. "Within reason."

"No serial killers," Bodhi adds. "You get weirdly into those."

I lift a brow. "You two kidnapped me and staged an obsessive infiltration that took literal years. And you think *I'm* the weird one?"

Bodhi raises both hands. "Hey, I didn't say we weren't weird. I said we have limits."

I scroll through the options. For a second, I consider picking something soft. Something gentle. But no. That's not where I am.

"Put on something violent," I say. "Explosions. Gunfights. Broken noses. Catharsis."

They don't argue. Just queue up a gritty action thriller with a woman covered in blood on the cover. Perfect.

As it starts, I dig into the food. It's good. Too good.

Of course it is. The pasta is perfectly cooked—rich, creamy, edged with heat and garlic and some kind of smoky spice that makes my tongue curl.

Everything they do is too good.

Too *much*.

I drink the coffee. I let my legs stretch out, draping over Matteo's lap. He adjusts slightly to accommodate me, hands warm as they rest loosely on my calves. His thumbs sweep once—soft, absent-minded—over a bruise he left.

Bodhi's arm is stretched across the couch behind me. Not quite touching, but close enough that every breath pulls me deeper into the heat of his body. I can feel the occasional twitch of his muscles as he laughs at the screen or adjusts his position, like he's reminding me he's there without actually crowding me.

They're not pressing.

But they're not backing off, either.

They're *surrounding*.

And God help me, part of me likes it.

The movie pours violence across the screen, blood spatter and grit and gunmetal carnage that somehow calms the roar in my bones.

I should pull away from them.

Should draw the line back where it was—back where I thought I could keep them in their boxes. Rule. Ruin. Matteo. Bodhi. Stalker. Liar. Friend. Threat.

But right now?

Right now, I'm still aching. I'm still bleeding in ways that aren't visible.

And there's something about being *here*, between them, caught in the gravity of two men who fought to break me just to prove I belonged to them—something about it that lets me breathe.

They didn't win me. Not yet.

But they have *this*.

This moment. This night.

They have the bruises on my skin, the taste of my surrender still clinging to us, the ache they left between my legs that somehow feels like more than just sex.

I settle a little deeper into the couch, my head tilting just enough to rest against Bodhi's shoulder. Not fully. Just enough to feel the thrum of his pulse against my temple.

Bodhi shifts slightly, letting his fingers trace the barest touch down the outside of my arm. Just once.

They say nothing.

And that silence—that stillness—is louder than anything.

Because they're letting me choose. For now.

And maybe—for one fucking night—I can sit between them and just *be*.

Not as the agent. Not as the target.

Just... me.

And if that version of me is twisted, bruised, and too tired to keep snarling?

Then fine, I'll take it.

The movie plays on. The heroine screams into the void, shotgun smoking. Everything burns.

And I sit between two men who already burned everything else to the ground just to keep me here.

Just breathing.

And maybe—for now—that's enough.

Chapter 46
Rule

She falls asleep twenty minutes into the second movie. Somewhere between the third explosion and the antihero's last betrayal, she gave in.

Matteo had glanced over when her head started to tip toward my shoulder. I gave him a look and he stretched out on the couch and pretended not to keep checking on her every few minutes.

But I didn't pretend.

I watched every breath.

Because I wanted this.

This moment.

This surrender she didn't mean to give.

Her lashes didn't flutter. Her hands twitched once, a little aftershock of exhaustion maybe. The tank top she wore rode up just enough to show the marks low on her ribs. Our marks. Her body was still wrecked from the fight-turned-fuck we dragged her through. And she fell asleep anyway.

With us.

She never relaxes like this. Not fully.

The movie's still playing in the background—gunshots, sirens, shattered glass echoing across the sound system. But her breathing stays soft. Steady. She's deep under now.

She fought so hard not to relax tonight.

But she still fell asleep between us.

Because part of her—some buried, feral part—*trusts* us now.

She'd never admit it. She'd claw us to ribbons before she'd say it out loud. But it's there. In the way she let her guard down long enough to sleep without a blade tucked under her pillow.

Now she's soft. Quiet. Open.

And I can't stop looking.

The credits roll.

Matteo stretches, mutters something about going to check the perimeter. He gives me a pointed look, but doesn't say anything.

He knows.

We don't need to speak it out loud anymore.

When the door clicks shut behind him, I move.

Careful. Slow.

She doesn't stir when I lift her. Her body curls instinctively into mine, head tucked under my chin, breath warm against my throat. She smells like vanilla and something uniquely her.

She's heavier than she looks—muscle and tension packed into every inch of her frame. But in my arms, she feels small. Breakable.

I nudge the door to her bedroom open with my foot and bring her inside. The bed's too big for just her. We made sure of that. Black velvet headboard. Burgundy silk sheets. Fit for a queen. Or a conqueror.

I lay her down carefully, adjusting the pillow beneath her head. Her tank rides up again as she settles. I smooth it down without thought. My thumb catches the edge of a bruise peeking out above her waistband.

Fucking beautiful.

She looks perfect like this.

I stand over her for too long, watching the slow rise and fall of her chest. Looking down at the girl who has carved her name into my every waking thought.

The girl I would tear my father's kingdom down for.

The girl I plan to rebuild the world around.

Seanna *fucking* Darling.

I sit on the edge of the bed, hand trailing up the outside of her thigh—light, slow. I don't want to wake her. Not yet. Not for this.

I shift over her slowly, lowering myself until my body is half over hers—just enough to cage her. Feel her.

One hand brushes her hip, then the band of her pants.

Then lower.

She's warm there, soft.

I press against her through the fabric, slow and testing. Before I slip my hand into her pants, until I find the heat I knew would be waiting. She's wet already. Maybe from a dream. Maybe from the lingering touch of everything we did to her today.

I stroke her slowly, watching her face. Her brows twitch. A soft sound escapes her throat.

Still, she doesn't wake.

I slide my hand out and drag the pants down her hips, inch by inch, until she's bare beneath me.

Her legs shift slightly, thighs parting just enough to make room for me.

My cock's already hard. Has been for the past twenty minutes, if I'm honest. Watching her sleep does something feral to me. Ancient. Territorial.

I nudge her legs further apart gently. Sliding between them, and fuck—I've been good. Patient. Careful.

But I'm not built for restraint.

Not with her.

Not when she's lying here like this—her scent in my lungs, her pulse steady and soft, her mouth just barely parted.

My hands settle on either side of her. My hips rock forward.

The first push is everything. Hot. Tight. So fucking *right* I nearly lose my mind.

I sink into her slowly, inch by inch, until I'm buried inside her. Balls-deep. Caged by the heat of her and the weight of every fantasy I've ever tried to choke down.

And she doesn't wake, not all the way.

Just breathes different. A soft hitch. Her brows pull slightly. Her mouth parts.

She sighs, and God help me, it sounds like my name.

I stay still inside her, savoring the stretch, the heat, the instinctive way her body clenches around me even in sleep.

Like she knows.

She's going to carry my child.

It's instinct and expectation.

It's blood-deep and bone-engraved—something my father drilled into me before I even knew what sex was.

Legacy. Bloodline. Heir.

But it won't be his name the child takes. No.

It'll be hers.

Darling.

God, yes.

That name—sharp as glass and twice as dangerous—already sounds better in my mouth than Reyes ever did.

Let them carry her name. I'll fucking change mine, if I have to. Legally. Publicly. I'll burn the Reyes line to ash if it means building something with hers.

I move inside her slow and deep. Grinding at that perfect angle that makes her gasp even in unconsciousness.

"Good girl," I whisper eventually, brushing hair from her cheek. "You know who's inside you, don't you."

Her body answers before she does.

Clenching. Gripping. Pulling me deeper.

"You take me so well, princess," I murmur, voice rough. "You're made for this. For *me*. For *us*."

This is different. It's ritual and reverence.

"I don't want to just come inside you. I want to stay there. Sink so deep I leave a part of me behind."

Because Seanna *Darling* is the only woman I've ever wanted to put a child in.

She shifts under me, hips rolling just slightly, her breath catching as my piercing drags over that spot that always makes her gasp when she's awake.

She still doesn't know.

Still fucks us like she's untouchable. Like she's safe.

Like we haven't already stacked the odds in our favor.

She's close. Even now.

Even unconscious. Her body *wants* it.

My grip tightens. My thrusts deepen.

And that's when I say it. The thing I never let myself say out loud.

"You're going to have our baby, little storm. We'll breed you so deep you'll still feel us when you close your eyes. You'll drip with us for days."

I don't care if it's mine or Ruin's. We're already in her blood. Her bones. There's no pulling us out now.

But the thought of it? Her belly growing round with one of us buried deep inside her, the curve of it—that's enough to make my cock throb.

I fuck her harder now. Not punishing. Just *deliberate.*

Every thrust a claim.

Every grind a promise.

"I want to watch you grow round with our child. Want to see your belly swell while I fuck you from behind—still dripping with need even when you're full."

My hand slides to her stomach, palm resting over the space that could hold it. That could hold *us.*

"You'll be perfect," I breathe. "So fucking perfect. You'd glow."

Her head turns into the pillow, lips parting in a soft whimper as her body shudders around me. Thighs twitching around me.

She moans. A soft sound. Broken. Raw.

And it's mine. All of it is mine.

I fuck her slow, steady, deep. No rush. No pounding. Just a relentless, claiming pressure—like every thrust is another line carved into her soul that says *mine, mine, mine.*

Her body tightens around me.

She gasps and wakes. Eyes fluttering open—blurry, confused. She looks up at me, dazed.

And still, she doesn't fight. Not really.

Just blinks up at me like she already knows how this ends, like she dreamed it already.

My hand moves to her cheek. I press a kiss to her lips. Soft. Gentle.

"You feel that, princess? That's what happens when you're ours. When your body begs to keep every drop."

Her legs tighten around my hips. Her body gives the answer for her.

And I fuck her like I'm building a future with every thrust.

Like she's already carrying it.

Like she was *meant* for it.

She chokes on a gasp, a breathy cry breaking loose from her throat as she clenches tight around me.

It starts slow—then *hits*. Her orgasm crashes through her in a shuddering wave, her hips jerking as she comes on my cock, clenching hard.

And then I break.

I come inside her with a growl, cock pulsing deep, spilling everything into that perfect, warm body like I've been waiting my whole life to do it.

My hand slides to her lower stomach again, palm spread wide, holding her still as I empty myself inside her.

Every drop. Every *fucking* drop. Right where it belongs.

I stay there for a long moment.

Inside her.

Breathing her.

Worshiping her.

Chapter 47

Seanna

I'm already tired of waiting.

Twenty-two hours and change into this forced ceasefire, and my skin feels like it's crawling. The silence is too loud. I pace the living room like a caged animal, back and forth across the black velvet rug.

And I'm fucking done.

I've burned through three cups of coffee already. Tried to nap. Tried to breathe. Tried not to think about Javier Reyes and how close I was to putting him in a federal lock up.

Didn't work.

I got dressed in black tactical pants and tank, even laced up some sinfully soft boots. Now all I can do is move.

Bodhi's on the couch, lounging like a smug asshole, watching me pace like I'm his favorite form of entertainment. One hand draped lazily over the backrest, the other tapping a slow, infuriating rhythm against his thigh. He hasn't said a word in ten minutes. Doesn't need to. His smirk says it all.

Matteo leans against the far wall, arms crossed, black shirt stretching taut across his chest, mouth twitching every time I spin on my heel with a little more venom.

"Something on your mind, little storm?" Bodhi drawls finally.

I stop mid-step, stare at him, deadpan. "You mean besides the part where I'm still technically your hostage and we're apparently on a fucking spa retreat instead of hunting the man who traffics girls and drugs?"

He lifts one shoulder, unbothered. "You look hot when you're filled with rage."

"Do you want your teeth kicked in?"

"Not opposed."

Matteo snorts. I spin on him.

"And you. You just gonna lean there and brood, or are you planning to unlock the fucking door?"

His gaze slides over me, slow and deliberate. "If I unlock the door, what exactly do you think you're going to do?"

"I'm going to find Javier. I'm going to make him bleed, throw him in a deep dark federal hole. Then I'm going to burn what's left."

A beat of silence.

Then Bodhi says, "So, just another Tuesday."

I roll my eyes so hard it gives me whiplash and drop into the armchair like it insulted me personally. "You two said twenty-four hours. I gave you twenty-three. Don't make me regret the generosity."

"Wasn't generosity," Matteo says. "It was a bargain. You lost. This is the fallout."

"Yeah? Well I'm done playing." I lean forward, elbows braced on my knees, voice low and sharp. "So unless the next sentence out of your mouth is a name, location, or set of coordinates—get out of my way."

They exchange a look.

That silent communication that makes me want to throw something at them both.

Bodhi leans forward, resting his forearms on his thighs. "You want him. We understand that. But the second you step out that door without a plan—without control—he wins."

Matteo's voice follows, quieter but firmer. "We're not letting that happen."

I go still.

Because for all their violence and all their obsession... they're not wrong.

But that doesn't mean I'm patient.

Bodhi stretches, catlike, then stands slowly. "All right, princess. You want out so bad?"

I tilt my head, watching him with narrowed eyes.

He gestures toward the far window—the one that looks out over the tree line, the dark slash of forest beyond. "Then go."

I blink, looking between them. "Excuse me?"

Matteo's voice is soft, amused. "You heard him. You want to hunt Javier so badly? Then run for the gate."

My stomach tightens. "Gate?"

"Perimeter gate," Bodhi supplies. "Back side of the property. About a mile through the trees. You want out? You want a shot at handling Javier your way? Run. Make it to the gate, and we'll consider your terms."

"That's it?" I ask, squinting.

Bodhi grins wider. "That's it. You reach the gate, you win."

Matteo leans forward, his voice smooth as silk. "And because I'm such a nice guy, if you win, I'll even help you hunt down Javier."

"Generous," I murmur.

"Hell," Bodhi adds, cocking his head, "if you make it to that gate, maybe I'll throw in my help too. Maybe we adjust the plan. It wouldn't take much as his son to draw him somewhere private. Somewhere... intimate."

I scoff. "Just like that?"

Matteo shrugs and smiles like a man who knows exactly how deep the water is—and doesn't care if we both drown. "We're men of our word."

"And if I lose?"

Bodhi's smile doesn't waver. "Then you stay. You trust the plan we already have in place."

I think for a second. Calculate. I've run with Matteo before. DEA training courses. Urban assault simulations. I know how fast he is. How precise.

Bodhi's different. Less technical. More brutal. He doesn't run—he hunts. I still have the bruises from the last time he chased me through a forest, mask gleaming in the half-light.

But it's not semidark this time.

It's the middle of the fucking day.

I stare at them.

My heart is already starting to pick up speed, adrenaline whispering through my veins like it recognizes this game and wants to play. But I'm not stupid.

And I'm not going in unarmed.

Not if I play this right.

"I want a knife," I say flatly.

Matteo's brow lifts. "A knife?"

"It's only fair, Bodhi had one last time," I shoot back. "This time, I get one too."

His mouth twitches. "And if I say no?"

I smile slow, wicked. "Then I'll make do with your bones, sweetheart."

Bodhi barks a laugh. "Give the girl a blade, Matteo. Let's see what she does with it."

Matteo walks down the hallway and then returns with a sheathed combat blade with a gleaming black hilt and leather holster. It's smaller than theirs, like he had it specially made for me.

He doesn't hand it to me.

He stalks close, then carefully straps the holster around my hips, tucking it under my shirt. His fingers linger—just long enough to press the handle against my spine and lean in.

His voice is a whisper against my ear, calm and cool. "Try not to stab yourself."

I just grin. "Try not to cry when I win."

Bodhi nods toward the back of the house again, where the forest waits like a living thing. "Come on then. We'll give you a ten-second head start."

"How generous," I murmur, already moving toward the doors.

Matteo follows, pacing me like a shadow.

Ten seconds to outrun two men who have spent the last several years learning exactly how I breathe.

The woods stretch in front of me—dappled light, thick under-growth, narrow paths and gnarled roots. One mile. One gate.

If I make it, I win.

If I don't... I know exactly what kind of punishment waits.

And part of me—some vicious, twisted part—wants to lose just to feel it. But another part just wants the hiding to be over.

Every muscle in my body is coiled, heart already hammering. I glance once over my shoulder.

Matteo and Bodhi stand side by side.

Predators. Waiting.

"Ten seconds," Matteo repeats, smiling sweetly, eyes locked on mine. "Then we come for you. Use it wisely."

The wind shifts and I run.

The forest is a blur of green and brown and shadow. The sun painting the ground in jagged slashes of light. My breath burns in my lungs as I leap over a fallen log and duck under a low branch. I can only hope that they didn't plant any traps in this forest like they did in the other.

Then I hear it.

Somewhere behind me, I hear the countdown.

"Five," Bodhi calls, too calm.

"Four," Matteo's voice now—low and dark and already promising something worse.

"Three."

I don't look back.

"Two."

My heart pounds.

"One."

They don't shout. They don't laugh. There's no noise at all.

But I know.

They're coming.

I don't pace myself. There's no point, not with them behind me.

My chest pounds as I veer left, up a narrow path where the underbrush is thicker. My legs are already protesting, but I don't slow. I can't.

Bodhi calls behind me, sing-song and wicked: "Run, little storm. Let's see if you learned anything."

I ignore him. Push harder. Every step tears at my calves, my lungs, but I force my body to comply. One mile. I can do one fucking mile.

Branches whip against my arms. Sunlight flickers in and out. I keep low, fast, weaving between the trees, picking the fastest line through the terrain like it's second nature.

Because it is.

Because I've done this before—obstacle runs, field drills, adrenaline-soaked missions.

Bodhi laughs again. Loud, wild. The crunch of leaves underfoot tells me he's moving fast—but I expect that. I *remember* that. The way he chased me last time, how he gave me a lead and still cut me down like a shadow with teeth.

But it's not Bodhi that makes my blood run colder.

It's Matteo.

He hasn't made a sound. Not one goddamn noise.

I catch glimpses of him through the trees. Cutting off paths. Herding me.

Like he already knows where I'm going before I do.

"Fuck off, Matteo," I hiss between gasps, shoving through a thicket of branches.

No answer, of course not.

He wants me off balance.

He wants me afraid.

But I'm not afraid. I'm *turned on.*

Something snaps to my left—sharp, deliberate—and I drop to my knees on instinct, rolling into the underbrush. A body crashes through the space I just vacated. Bodhi.

Too slow this time.

"Clever girl," he pants, spinning mid-sprint.

I snarl and take off again, darting deeper into the woods. I zigzag, change elevation, sprint hard for a wide ridge I spot ahead. It'll give me height. Line of sight. Control.

A flash of movement to my right.

Too fast. Too smooth.

Matteo.

Of course it's fucking Matteo.

I curse under my breath and cut hard left, bounding over a fallen log and skidding down a shallow ravine. My thighs burn from the angle. My lungs scream. But I don't stop. I can't.

Bodhi explodes out of the brush ahead of me with a grin like the devil and lunges. I duck just in time, feel the brush of his fingers in my hair, and twist under his arm. I pull out the knife just in case.

"Keep running, princess!" he calls out, breathless and gleeful. "I'm getting hard just watching you."

"Too slow," I growl, dodging left, ducking under another branch. I tighten my grip on the knife hilt.

I push harder, slicing through the trees with sharp, controlled bursts of speed. I don't waste time looking back. I *know* they're there. I *feel* them.

I can do this.

The path narrows. I leap over a small stream, half-slip on a slick rock, recover just in time to avoid eating dirt. My pulse thrums in my throat. Sweat slicks my spine.

I spot the glint of metal through the trees—maybe a fence post, maybe the gate.

It's close. So close.

A branch snaps to my right.

I spin mid-stride, knife raised—but there's no one there.

Then something slams into me from the side.

Matteo.

We hit the ground rolling hard, a mess of limbs and dirt and breathless curses. My elbow drives into his ribs, the knife flashing upward, but he catches my wrist in one practiced move and pins it to the ground as we come to a stop.

He doesn't speak at first. Just stares at me, eyes glittering, un-readable.

Then his hand finds the chain at my throat—the one I'd basically forgotten about until now—and he yanks.

The chain tightens like a choker, a noose, cutting off my breath with a sharp, strangled sound. My body jerks in his hold, eyes wide, lungs screaming.

His voice is low, rasping, lethal. "You really think I've shown you everything I am?"

I tense beneath him, suddenly and terribly aware that this isn't the same Matteo I trained with. This is the one who's always been lurking beneath the surface. The predator beneath the polish. And I've underestimated him.

He loosens the chain just enough to keep me from blacking out.

He leans down, breath hot against my jaw.

"Your mistake," he says, each word a slow cut, "was thinking I'm the nice one."

Then Bodhi's there too, kneeling beside us, eyes wild with adrenaline.

"You make it to the gate?" he asks, catching his breath. "No?"

He grins.

"Then I guess that means you belong to us again."

Chapter 48

Seanna

I twist beneath Matteo, every muscle screaming protest—but it's not fear that lights me up inside. It's fire. It's hunger. His grip on the chain doesn't falter. Neither does the sharp gleam in his eyes. I can't breathe properly—only in tight, shallow gasps—but it doesn't stop the slick pulse of heat between my thighs.

"You planning to choke me out or fuck me?" I snarl.

His mouth curves into something dangerous. "Why not both?"

His eyes lock on mine, then drift to where the hilt protrudes from my curled fingers. He doesn't rush. Doesn't threaten. He just *takes*. Two fingers slide between mine, prying them open with maddening slowness until he's palming the knife like he always meant to reclaim it.

"I said try not to stab yourself," he murmurs, almost amused. "Didn't say you'd keep it."

I snarl. "Give it back."

Instead, he presses the cool metal flat against the curve of my breast. I freeze. Not in fear—never that—but anticipation. My pulse roars.

"You want to play with knives, little storm?" His voice is low, coaxing. "Let's play."

The blade traces the curve, slow and shallow, parting skin with a delicate, deliberate graze that beads crimson. It's not deep—barely more than a scratch—but it *burns*, a thin line of pain blooming into heat that pulses straight to my core.

My breath shudders.

"You bleed pretty," Matteo murmurs. "Wonder if your blood tastes as good as your come."

Then he *leans down*. Tongue flicking out, he licks the line of blood from my skin, slow and savoring, like he's sampling something forbidden. Like he's starving.

And then—the knife bites again, adding another sting to the other breast. Sharp and deliberate.

My breath hitches. Once again it isn't deep. Just enough to let blood rise in a delicate line beneath the steel.

He watches it bead. Watches me.

Then he leans in. Licks the blood from my skin again like it's wine.

Bodhi groans low behind him. "God, you're so fucking twisted."

"Don't act surprised," Matteo says, not looking away from me. "Besides, she likes it." His voice drops to a whisper. "Don't you?"

I breathe hard. Glaring. Wanting.

He shifts backward, sliding between my legs, then flicks open another thin cut just above the waistline of my pants. Sharp enough to send another jolt to my pussy. I gasp, body jerking, thighs clenching.

He drags the blade just below the first line, slow and surgical. Another sting. Another shimmer of crimson blooming in its wake. I flinch—but the pain sharpens everything. Makes me wetter. I hiss through my teeth. Bodhi watches, mesmerized.

Matteo leans down and presses his tongue to the blood, licking a clean stripe along the parallel lines like they belong to him. The bastard *groans*.

"You taste like violence," he whispers against my skin. "Like fucking war."

I shudder. My core is hot and aching with need.

Bodhi laughs low, head tilting as he drags his gaze down my body. "God, you're fucking beautiful like this. Filthy and defiant." He slides his hand between my thighs, presses the heel of his palm against the soaked crotch of my pants. "You're soaked, little storm."

I arch against Matteo's hold just to spite them both, but there's no denying it. I hate how wet I already am. I've been wet since the first breathless sprint through the trees. Since their eyes locked on me like prey. Since I knew they'd chase. And catch. And ruin.

Matteo jerks the chain once more, sharp and claiming, as he moves to the side.

Bodhi's already taking his place and unfastening my pants, tugging them down my legs with a grunt and a wicked grin. His hands are rough, greedy, dragging the soaked fabric away and baring me to the cool air.

"No panties?" he murmurs. "You came out here *begging* to lose."

"Shut up," I snap.

But Bodhi just laughs again and leans forward, pressing a kiss to the inside of my thigh—hot, open-mouthed, biting just enough to make me gasp.

"Fuck, she's so wet already," he growls. "You like the game, don't you? You *love* losing."

"Shut the fuck up," I grit, trying to close my legs—but his hands are there, spreading them wide, holding me open.

"Tell us," Matteo says, reaching down to slide a finger along my wet entrance, pushing it just inside, teasing, "what do you want, *little storm?*"

My body betrays me.

I moan.

Low. Desperate.

Bodhi laughs again, louder this time, and bites at the swell of my breast—enough to sting, enough to bruise. Matteo adds another finger at the same time and I cry out, not in pain—but in *need*.

"Say it," Matteo urges, voice like silk dragged across a blade. "Say you want us, say you're ours."

"No," I pant, writhing under them both. "I want—"

But then Bodhi thrusts two fingers inside me alongside Matteo's without warning, and my sentence dies in a moan. Matteo tightens the chain again—just enough to steal the air and make my vision starburst white.

My world becomes sensation: the dirt under my back, the bite of cold metal, the heat of their hands, the way they both crook their fingers just right.

"Not going to last long, princess," Bodhi says, grinning down at me. "I can already feel you tightening around my fucking fingers."

He's right. I'm already close.

And that pisses me off more than anything.

My back arches off the forest floor as their fingers work in tandem, dragging slick, obscene sounds from my pussy while my throat strains under the chain still tight around it. Matteo's watching me like a wolf watching prey weaken.

"You want to come?" he asks softly. "Beg."

I snarl up at him, even as my body bucks against their hold. "Fuck. You."

Bodhi chuckles and twists his fingers deeper, rougher. "Already working on it, princess."

They remove their fingers without warning. I cry out—desperate, angry—but it only earns me a sharp slap to my now empty pussy. The sound echoes in the trees. The sting is immediate, dizzying.

"You don't come until we let you," Matteo says, voice pure command, even as he lets go of the chain. "Understand?"

I nod once, sharp and furious.

"Good girl."

Bodhi moves first, shifting up to straddle my chest with a knee either side of my ribs. His cock—thick, flushed, pierced—is already in his hand. He strokes it once, then taps the head against my lips.

"Open," he says.

I don't.

"You want this to stop, just say so. If not, then open that pretty mouth."

I bare my teeth but open my mouth. He slides in, slow and claiming, until I'm choking again, my jaw aching, my throat stretched.

Matteo kneels between my legs now, pushing my thighs up and out. He takes a moment to brush his own pierced cock against my entrance, before lining himself up.

"Breathe," Bodhi murmurs, just before Matteo thrusts into me.

I choke on Bodhi's cock.

Matteo doesn't ease in. Doesn't give me time.

He fucks me with the same intensity he stalked me with—every thrust deep and measured, timed to each ragged breath I try to draw around Bodhi's cock.

"God, you feel like fire," Matteo groans, pounding into me. "So fucking tight."

I moan around the thickness in my mouth. My body is undone—split open, used. I should hate it.

But I've never wanted anything more.

Bodhi holds my head still, both hands in my hair now, rocking his hips with a snarl. "You look so fucking pretty gagged on my cock, princess."

He pulls out for just a second—just long enough for me to gasp air—and then pushes back in, deeper. Harder.

Matteo's thrusts are savage now. His hands grip my hips so hard I know I'll bruise, and I want him to. I want every mark. Every ache.

"Fuck," Bodhi groans. "She's shaking already."

"You should feel how tight she is," Matteo mutters, voice ragged. "She's *gripping* me."

I try to glare, but Bodhi is already pushing deeper.

I feel my orgasm building—dark and deep and *devastating*.

Matteo's fingers find my clit, pinching hard, cruel and perfect.

"Come for us, Seanna," he demands. "Come on my cock while you choke on his."

I scream around Bodhi's cock, the sound high and wrecked. My body convulses, wave after wave rolling through me until I'm shaking, muscles locking, the orgasm dragging me under like a riptide.

Matteo groans, still pounding into me. Then his rhythm falters. He jerks forward once, twice, and I feel the hot flood of his release inside me.

I'm still dazed—trembling and gasping—when Bodhi takes his place. His cock is slick with spit and need.

And he doesn't wait.

He slams into me, fast and unforgiving, eyes locked on mine.

"You're ours," he growls. "You were always *fucking* ours."

I moan, back arching. His cock hits deeper, sharper, the metal of his piercings dragging against something *perfect*.

"Say it," he hisses.

"Fuck you," I gasp.

He grins. "*Say it*."

I want to fight. God, I do. But it's slipping through my fingers. My defiance. My logic. My fucking breath.

Every inch of me is burning.

My mouth opens on a gasp—part rage, part surrender.

But I know the truth deep down.

"Yours," I choke out. Voice wrecked. Eyes wild. "I'm—fucking—*yours*."

Bodhi's snarl is animal. Pure possession.

He slams in harder, until my vision whites out again, until I'm clawing at the dirt, until my second orgasm tears violently through me.

Bodhi follows with a loud, broken groan, hips jerking as he spills inside me.

When it's over, we're a tangled mess of limbs and sweat and come and dirt.

For a long moment, there's just the sound of panting. Wind threading through the trees. The faint shift of leaves above us like the forest itself is catching its breath.

I blink up at the sky, my body wrecked—core pulsing, thighs trembling, throat raw, and a warm, slick mess dripping between my legs.

Then reality decides to be a bitch.

"Ow," I mutter, voice wrecked. "Everything fucking hurts."

Bodhi laughs. A hoarse, satisfied sound as he slumps beside me, one hand dragging through his hair, the other lazily resting across my thigh like he's claiming the territory all over again.

"Didn't hear you complaining a minute ago," he says, smug.

I roll my eyes. Or try to. "That's because I was too busy choking on your cock."

"Poetry," Matteo murmurs behind me. His hands are already moving—wiping sweat and dirt from my face, gentle now in the way that always throws me off balance. "Hold still."

He grabs my pants, crumpled and ruined in the dirt, and shakes them out. They're stiff with soil, torn a little at the hip, and damp with more than just sweat.

I glare down at them as Bodhi tugs me upright with a hand under each arm, then brushes a few leaves from my hair.

Matteo crouches to help me step into my pants, holding them steady while I wobble like a newborn deer. My legs still don't work right. The fabric drags up my thighs, catching on grit and the wet stickiness of come clings between my legs.

It's *awful.*

I groan, face twisting. "Oh my *God.* That's disgusting."

Bodhi snorts behind me. "That's what happens when you let two men fill you like a fucking cream donut."

"Don't ever say that again," I growl.

"Cream... filled... donut," he says slowly, delighting in every syllable.

I shoot him a death glare over my shoulder as Matteo pulls the waistband over my hips. I flinch when it tugs against the fresh cuts. He carefully sheathes the knife in the holster at my back again.

"You okay?" he asks, voice low now. The one he saves for damage control. "You look so annoyed. Is that the pants or the losing?"

I narrow my eyes. "Yes."

Bodhi's laughter is wicked. "She's still got fight. I'm proud of her."

"I *will* stab you," I mutter.

Matteo chuckles low, brushing dirt from my shoulder as we start walking back toward the house, like it'll make any of this better. "You say that like it's not exactly why I love you."

I freeze mid-step. Just one heartbeat. One sharp intake of breath.

But he keeps walking, like he didn't just drop that word like a loaded gun between us.

Bodhi arches a brow and grins. "Well *that's* one way to ruin the afterglow."

"I hate both of you," I mutter.

"I *love* that you said that right after he said he loved you," Bodhi calls over his shoulder.

"I swear to God—"

"By the way, you're walking like a drunk baby deer after a gang-bang in the woods."

"I will *bite* you before I stab you," I say, limping after him.

He tosses a grin over his shoulder. "That's not the threat you think it is."

I scoff, but I'm too busy trying not to wince at the way my pants cling. Every step is uncomfortable. The material sticks in all the wrong places, tugging against swollen skin and fresh bruises, and I can *feel* their come leaking from my pussy. It's obscene. And frustrating. And distractingly hot.

We eventually reach the back door to the house, Bodhi ahead, Matteo brushing his fingers lightly down my spine as I stumble across the threshold.

Bodhi freezes in front of me, two steps inside. I don't notice until I slam into the back of him.

Behind me, Matteo tenses. His hand lifts off my back.

Then, quietly, just above a breath: "*Fuck.*"

I blink past Bodhi's shoulder.

Men.

Four of them. No—five. All armed.

I freeze.

One of them is leaning against the kitchen counter with a glass of what looks like whiskey in his hand. He's flanked by another with a gun held loosely at his side.

"Well," the man says. "You've been busy, *hijo*."

Bodhi doesn't move. Doesn't breathe.

Then, with a voice that sounds suddenly *emotionless*, he murmurs—

"Papá."

Chapter 49

Seanna

"Well don't just stand in the doorway," Javier Reyes drawls, voice rich with casual menace, like a king hosting a dinner party in the middle of a war zone. "Come inside."

His tone is smooth—cultured even—but there's something underneath it. Something sharp and coiled. Like a serpent. He's older than the last surveillance image we had, but age hasn't softened him. His suit was tailored to perfection, all charcoal silk and crisp white lines, his salt-and-pepper hair slicked back from a face carved from control and charm.

I step forward automatically, tension crawling down my spine. Bodhi's still in front of me, Matteo a half-step behind. I feel the press of his hand against my lower back—subtle, anchoring—but it doesn't stop the flare of fury beginning to ignite behind my eyes.

My gaze cuts to the man beside Javier.

Marcus Vega.

The same man we ID'd from the surveillance footage. Javier's favorite little lapdog. Errand boy.

Fucking perfect.

Javier wanders further into the open living area like he owns the place. His fingers trail idly across the edge of the kitchen counter as he takes a sip of his whiskey, eyes sweeping the space like he's judging the decor. Or maybe measuring how much blood it'll take to stain the floors.

"I've been trying to reach you for days," he says idly, not even looking at us. "Imagine my surprise when I had to *search* for you. And what do I find? A little house. Tucked away like a secret."

He pauses as he hears Matteo's breath catch behind me.

Javier's dark eyes slide to him.

"You look... familiar." He studies Matteo for a beat, eyes narrowing slightly. "Have we met?"

Matteo doesn't respond.

But it doesn't matter. Because Javier's already bored. Already moving on.

His attention lands on me.

And just like that, the entire room shifts.

He draws his gun.

There's no dramatic wind-up, no threat shouted in advance. Just the cold press of metal against the side of my head before I even finish a breath.

"Now *you* I recognize," he says, almost gently. "And I have to admit—I'm a little concerned. Why would my son be playing house with a DEA agent?"

His voice softens into a mockery of surprise. "Unless... he didn't know."

He cocks the gun. I don't flinch.

"Give me one good reason not to kill you."

I open my mouth, venom already curled on my tongue—but Bodhi beats me to it.

"She might be pregnant with my heir."

The words slice through the tension like a fucking guillotine. The gun doesn't move, but Javier's gaze flicks toward his son. Bodhi doesn't blink. Doesn't back down. He might as well have carved those words in blood.

I freeze.

What the actual fuck—my gaze dart to Bodhi, sharp enough to draw blood, but he looks dead serious. Like he's *sure.*

Like it's *true.*

My stomach twists. I know it's not possible—*I have an IUD, you absolute lunatic.* But then Matteo shifts closer behind me, his body brushing mine.

He *knows* something.

"Sorry, little storm. We removed the IUD," he murmurs, barely a breath and only loud enough for my ears.

And now I want to strangle both of them.

The fucking assholes. No, I'm going to kill them. I'm going to stab them in *very* creative ways.

I grind my teeth so hard my jaw aches.

Looking back to the snake in the room, I see the shift in his focus. The calculation. The possibility.

Legacy.

Fucking hell.

I could *see* it in his face—the moment the scales tipped. The moment I became less of a threat and more of a pawn.

Javier chuckles, low and dangerous, but he doesn't lower the gun. "Now *that*... changes things."

He steps back, smiling as if we're all just sitting down to brunch, but his gaze didn't soften. If anything, it sharpened.

"If that's the case," he murmured, almost indulgent now. "Maybe I won't shoot you in the face today. Maybe keeping you close is exactly what I need."

His smile didn't reach his eyes.

"To keep my son in line."

Bodhi steps forward. "You're not taking her."

Javier doesn't even glance at him. Just moves.

The back of the pistol cracks against Bodhi's cheekbone so fast it sounds like a firecracker.

The sound echoes—sharp, brutal, final.

Bodhi staggers back a step, blood blooming where the metal splits his skin, and for half a breath I see red. I *move.*

But I don't make it far.

Marcus is already there, stepping in smoothly, the cold steel of his own gun now pressed against the base of my throat. His eyes are dead calm, glacier-blue and unforgiving, like he's not looking at a person—just a problem to be neutralized.

"Don't," he says simply.

Javier turns back toward me, smug now. "Good girl," he purrs. "Let's go."

I don't have a choice. Marcus forces me forward, the gun never leaving my skin, his grip a vice around my arm. I stumble across the cold tiles and out through the open front door, still half-expecting Bodhi or Matteo to charge after me. But they don't.

I don't hear anything. Not a word. Not a single step.

The betrayal festers like rot.

Outside, the afternoon air slaps my skin. Two black SUVs near the treeline, the other men climbing in the lead car.

Marcus shoves me into the back of the second one.

The layout catches me off guard. There are three rear facing seats facing the three forward facing. I'm dumped into the rear-facing row, no restraints, but that doesn't matter.

Javier slides in after me, cool and unhurried, taking one of the forward-facing seats across from me. Marcus drops into another forward seat, gun in hand, barrel resting casually against his thigh but aimed squarely at my chest.

Another man climbs into the front seat, wordless, engine rumbling to life. The other SUV pulls out ahead of us, taking point.

I don't scream. I don't cry. I don't bang on the fucking glass.

There's no point.

The trees peel past, and every inch of my body vibrates with rage. I can't see Bodhi or Matteo. They're not following. They're not fucking *coming*.

"You know," Javier says, voice low and conversational, "I always imagined my son would disappoint me, but this? Hiding in the woods. Bedding a fed. Playing house with the enemy." He clucks his tongue. "You're a very pretty mistake, Seanna. I'll give him that."

My glare could strip paint.

"I wonder—" his eyes cut back to me "—did you seduce him before or after he forgot who he belonged to?"

I let the fury burn, deep and quiet. I don't rise to it.

He exhales slowly, as if the weight of the world rests on his shoulders. "I should've known something was wrong when Kingston stopped answering my calls. He's always been difficult. But this?" His eyes narrow, voice dropping to a razor's edge. "This is a betrayal."

A pause.

"I can forgive betrayal from an outsider. A woman with pretty eyes and a badge tucked under her bed. What I don't understand..." He leans forward slightly, voice almost gentle. "Is why *he* didn't put a bullet in your head the moment he found out who you really were."

I don't blink. I don't breathe.

"I have to assume he knows," Javier murmurs. "Which means he chose this. Chose *you*." His head tilts just slightly. "You must be very special."

Then the corner of his mouth twitches—not a smile. Something uglier. "Or maybe you're just very good at lying with your legs open."

The gun aimed at me stays steady.

But my hands curl into fists.

Then—*pop*.

A sharp sound. Clean. Precise.

The SUV lurches violently left. Tires screech as the vehicle bucks, nose jerking toward the ditch.

"What the fuck—" the driver shouts as I hear the front tire shred, rubber flailing like black ribbons.

Everything spins.

Javier's hand slaps against the ceiling to brace himself, the world tilts. We're heading straight for a thick pine trunk. The world tilts as the car jerks to a stop.

And then—*bang*.

Gunfire. Inside the car.

The sting at my neck comes fast, white-hot, and I flinch, thinking—*he shot me*. My body braces for collapse.

But I'm still breathing.

I twist, heart hammering, just in time to see Marcus lower the barrel—smoke curling from the muzzle. The driver slumps forward against the wheel, blood spraying across the dash.

He shot *past* me.

Distant gunshots crack through the trees, echoing wild and sharp like the woods just caught fire with bullets.

Javier curses in Spanish and reaches for the door handle. It flies open, and wind rushes in as he stumbles out.

I lunge.

Fury snaps through me like lightning, and I *move*, leaping out of the car after him.

My fist collides with his face just as he twists around.

There's a satisfying crunch. Javier reels back, stunned, blood spraying from his split lip—but he recovers fast. Too fast. He's raising his gun again—

But Marcus is already between us, blocking my path, his weapon shifting—but not toward me.

"Mátala!" Javier bellows, voice ragged, rage slashing through every syllable. "Kill her!"

Marcus... looks at him.

Then looks at the tree line.

Bodhi and Matteo are emerging slowly from the woods like phantoms, both armed, both calm in that lethal, *final* way that makes the air go still.

Bodhi's face is carved from ice. Cold rage.

Javier snarls, blood on his teeth, and snaps his arm up toward me. His finger pulls the trigger with deadly intent.

Click.

Nothing.

The empty, hollow sound rings louder than any gunshot.

His expression fractures.

He looks at the gun. Then at Marcus.

And in that moment, I see it.

Betrayal.

Pure. Guttural. Soul-deep.

He stares at Marcus like the world just cracked open beneath him, disbelief etched in every furious line of his face. As if all his power has just been ripped from his hands—and handed to someone else.

"You—" he chokes, voice strangled.

Marcus doesn't flinch. Doesn't speak. He just holds Javier's gaze with that same dead calm as before.

Bodhi steps forward, slow and deliberate, barrel still trained steady on the man who made him.

Marcus' head dips toward Bodhi and he says: "Long live the king."

Javier freezes.

I don't breathe. My pulse hammers like a war drum.

"You said you wanted him in the ground," I snap, turning toward them, my fury like a blade between my ribs. "So *are you going to shoot him*? Or was that just another fucking lie?!"

Bodhi doesn't blink. "I do want him dead," he says, voice low and razor-sharp. "But that honor was never going to be mine."

Matteo steps up beside him, eyes never leaving Javier. "It was always going to be yours, Seanna."

My gaze snaps to him. I blink. The words hit harder than I expect.

"What?" I rasp, the fury choking a little on something else—something deeper.

"Our gift to you," Matteo says.

Bodhi nods, slow and solemn. "He dies by your hand, Seanna. That was always the plan."

My breath catches, caught somewhere between disbelief and something sharp and aching.

I look at them—both of them. My stalkers. My captors. My monsters.

My kings.

And I realize I fucking love those assholes too.

I reach behind me slowly, fingers curling around the hilt of the blade Matteo strapped there earlier.

The moment my hand closes around it, something in me *shifts*.

I draw the knife free with one smooth, practiced motion.

Javier watches me, panting, blood at the corner of his mouth. His eyes widen—not with fear, no, he's too much of a narcissist for that—but with dawning comprehension.

He knows. He sees it now. The inevitability.

He's staring at his executioner.

I take one step forward.

He raises his chin like a king refusing to kneel. But his lip is bleeding, his gun is empty, and his legacy is slipping through his fingers like dust.

"I should've killed you when I had the chance," he sneers.

I smile, slow and vicious. "Yeah. You really fucking should have."

He snarls and lunges, but he's too slow, too off-balance.

And I don't hesitate.

I slam the knife into him, just under the ribcage—angled upward, clean and brutal. His breath catches. His eyes go wide.

I don't stop, jerking it out before thrusting it back in.

Then I twist. *Just like my parents always taught me.*

He chokes on blood, tries to reach for me, but I shove him back. He stumbles, crashing to his knees, one hand clutching the wound. The other reaching blindly—for help, for power, for a name that used to mean something.

Bodhi and Matteo don't move.

Marcus doesn't move.

This is *mine*.

I kick him in the face.

Hard.

Bone cracks under the heel of my boot—his nose or his cheek or both, I don't fucking care. His head snaps backward, blood spraying like crushed cherries.

He crumples further, mouth slack, eyes dazed.

I stand over him, chest heaving, the knife still warm in my hand.

The silence that follows is *thick*. Holy. Heavy in the way all endings are.

Then Matteo steps closer, slow and steady. He doesn't say a word—just reaches out and brushes a smear of blood from my cheek with the pad of his thumb. His touch is soft. Reverent.

Bodhi exhales like he's been holding his breath for years. "Fucking finally."

I look down at Javier Reyes—the king who built empires on blood and fear.

And I don't feel guilt.

I feel *free*.

Chapter 50
Seanna

Marcus took care of everything.

The cars. The bodies. The blood spatter threading through the dirt like a broken vein.

It turns out he was never Javier's errand boy.

Not really.

He was Bodhi's. Or, more accurately, an *ally*. An embedded ghost who'd been working quietly for years to dismantle Reyes' empire from the inside—cutting off its limbs one by one until the body collapsed under its own weight. They had even turned Navarro.

The plan I hadn't been trusted with.

The one they kept telling me to *wait* for.

And now? According to all of them—Marcus, Bodhi, Matteo—*Kingston Reyes* is dead.

Buried alongside his father.

The cartel?

Shattered.

It won't survive the week.

The pieces are already falling.

We'd fallen into bed sometime after. Still bloody. Still wrecked. Still too wired to sleep and too exhausted to speak. Every muscle in my body screamed, but I didn't care. Not when I finally had control again. Not when Javier Reyes was cold and silent beneath a blanket of pine needles and dirt.

I don't remember who fell asleep first.

Doesn't matter.

Sleep came for me like a drug, pulling me under hard and fast.

I don't know how long I'm out.

But I jolt awake with a hand on my shoulder—soft, careful.

My breath catches.

My eyes snap open.

Hydessa.

Her face is inches from mine, cast in an eerie neon glow. One side tinted red. The other green. Her expression is urgent. Pale. A little wild. Her dark hair is tangled, her mouth parted like she's halfway between a whisper and a scream.

And that's when I see them.

Two figures—one on each side of the bed.

Still as statues.

Each wearing a glowing neon mask—one red, one green.

Each holding a knife to the throats of the men I love.

Matteo jolts awake.

His hand flies up—almost catches the wrist of the man holding the knife at his throat—but the blade doesn't move. It just presses harder.

Bodhi comes to a half-second later, blinking up at the ceiling, then glancing down at the blade beside his neck like it's an inconvenience.

Matteo snarls low, voice rough and venom-laced. "How the *fuck* do people keep getting past my security?"

The red mask tilts toward him, and the voice that comes out is modulated—cold, robotic, with just enough edge to make my spine stiffen.

"Because your security is a *joke*," he says dryly. "Even a five-year-old could hack that system. Honestly, I expected better."

Matteo's glare could set bone on fire.

Hydessa clears her throat, her hand still lightly pressed to my shoulder. "So..." she says, slow and deliberate, eyes flicking between the masked men and the half-naked chaos of the bed, "you need rescuing or...?"

Her gaze lands on Bodhi and lingers. I know that look.

She *recognizes* him.

Of course she fucking does. She knows him from the organization. But she's not saying anything. Not yet.

I sit up slowly, rubbing a hand across my face. "I'm good," I mutter. "Don't need rescuing."

Hydessa arches a brow. "You sure? Because from where I'm standing it looks like you lost an argument with a knife."

"We've moved past the bloodletting," I mutter. "Mostly."

Bodhi shifts under the knife, stretching lazily like a jungle cat. "Wouldn't say no to a coffee, though."

"Shut up," Matteo growls.

Hydessa snorts and flicks her eyes back to me. "Well, in that case," she says, voice suddenly more clipped, "maybe get up. Fix your hair. Wipe the sex off your face."

I blink at her. "Why?"

She gives me a long, weighted look. "Because our parents are about ten minutes behind us."

My soul leaves my body.

"And Uncle Max," she adds sweetly.

Jesus. *Fucking. Christ.*

The masked intruders vanish like smoke—as quickly as they arrived. Just a final, glitchy "Upgrade your firewalls, moron," tossed over a shoulder in that same modulated tone.

Then one blink, and they're gone—slipping back into the shadows like a shared hallucination. Hydessa rolls her eyes like this is somehow *normal* and mutters something about cloak-and-dagger freaks needing to schedule their chaos before she disappears out the door too.

Matteo flips off the air they vacated with a murderous grunt. "I *hate* people."

"You're not allowed to talk about security ever again," I mutter, yanking on a hoodie over my dirty shirt and frantically dragging my fingers through my hair. "Ever."

Bodhi somehow finds and shrugs into a fresh t-shirt like we're late for brunch, not dealing with the fallout of abduction and cartel war. "So what you're saying is, we don't have time for a shower orgy?"

I glare at him.

Matteo's already at the mirror. "We have under three minutes to look less like we just had a cartel execution preceded by feral sex in the woods."

"Then you better move fast, *Ruin*," I snap, hopping into pants with more frustration than grace.

By the time we scramble toward the front door, we're still rumpled, but not bleeding. Mostly clothed. Not actively fucking.

So, progress.

I can hear the rumble of tires—engines cutting off, doors slamming.

My stomach flips.

Fuck.

I throw open the door and step outside just in time to see *them*.

My parents.

Armed. Angry. Dangerous.

Dad's got a sidearm on his hip, Papa has a gleaming knife drawn, Mom's got her gun plus a crossbody harness—which I *know* has at least two knives in it—and they all look seconds away from declaring a personal war zone.

Uncle Max is with them. It's the first time I've ever seen him with a gun.

They're storming toward the house like they're ready to breach and clear.

I throw my hands up and march forward quickly.

"I'm okay. I'm fine," I say loudly. "Everybody calm the fuck down."

They all stop.

They all give me the exact same look.

A mixture of exasperation, disbelief, and sheer parental rage barely held in check.

Then—I hear the footsteps behind me.

I don't have to turn. I know who they are.

Bodhi's the first to step into view.

Mom squints, and then her mouth opens in shock. "*Bodhi?*"

Shit.

Uncle Max is a half-step behind her. His face shifts instantly from confusion to shock to something far more rattled. His eyes widen.

"Huxley??"

Everything halts.

All eyes land on *Matteo*—still brushing dirt from his sleeves, hair a mess, shirt half-tucked.

He looks up.

Then shrugs faintly. "Hey, Dad."

A beat.

"I can explain."

Epilogue

Seanna

Love was never in the plan.

I told myself that from the beginning. I wasn't the kind of woman who got love stories—I was the cautionary tale girls whispered about behind closed doors. Too sharp, too wild, too willing to chase monsters through bloodstained streets and call it foreplay. I hunted the worst men alive, dismantled empires, and let my rage burn hot enough to cauterize the parts of me that still believed in things like fate.

But apparently, fate has a fucked-up sense of humor.

In the aftermath, the Reyes Empire collapsed like wet paper. With Javier dead, and "Kingston" officially burned from the world's records, there was nothing left but ghosts and ashes. Max and the organization swept up the limbs the guys hadn't already severed—quiet, precise, irreversible.

As for the DEA? They cleared me within a week. Apparently, a cartel kingpin wiping out his own men is a bureaucrat's wet dream. Cruz's murder—along with every single one of his men—was pinned directly on Reyes, with ballistics, doctored footage, and enough digital breadcrumbs to feed an entire task force. None of it traced back to me. Or Bodhi. Or Matteo.

Funny how easy things fall into place when the right people rewrite the story.

And Max? Uncle Max told me, days later, that when I'd asked him about the flowers early on—those first haunting red petals of the Rhododendron left as a warning—it reminded him of his wife. Matteo's mother. Just for a moment. Then he dismissed the thought as sleep-deprived paranoia.

I should've known then.

I went back to work. Filed my reports. Sat through the final debrief with internal affairs. Smiled my polite little smile when the director shook my hand like I hadn't spent the last weeks being stalked, hunted, fucked, and nearly executed.

Javier Reyes and his line were gone. And with the cartel in pieces, the threat was neutralized.

They called it victory.

The night the case was officially closed, Jensen, Eli, and Matteo dragged me out for drinks. It was tradition. Whiskey. Sarcasm. False cheer. But this time felt different.

I tossed back my whiskey neat, and then Matteo grabbed my wrist and pulled me onto the dance floor. His hand found my waist like it belonged there. I let him lead.

He moved like he already knew every inch of me. Like he wasn't asking, just taking what he wanted. Like I was his—publicly, privately, always. I didn't fight him.

Not when I caught the glint in Jensen's eyes. The half-smile Eli shot our way. Like they knew. Like maybe they always had. Like I was the last one to figure it out.

And maybe I was.

Maybe I'd spent so long convincing myself I was immune to the whole twisted idea of love that I hadn't noticed it creeping in. I'd always said if someone wanted me, they'd have to be obsessed.

Dangerous. Willing to break bones just to keep me. Turns out I'd manifested two of them.

Another hand found my waist. Another heat pressed into my spine.

Bodhi.

Of course it was fucking Bodhi.

I didn't even turn. Didn't need to. I felt him smile against my neck.

I just leaned back into him as Matteo's hand slid lower and the three of us moved like a single dark pulse.

I thought I'd never find a love like my parents.

Turns out, it found me first.

It carved its way in with knives and masks and bloodstained devotion.

It ruined me beautifully.

And I let it rule my body.

Because I'm not built for soft. I'm not built for safe. I'm not built for fairy tales.

But I am built for war.

And somehow, without meaning to, I found the kind of love that doesn't beg to be tamed. The kind that sharpens its teeth beside mine. That doesn't ask me to shrink or soften, but drags me deeper into the dark and says *more*. A love that doesn't just survive the blood and fire—but *thrives* in it.

So no—I didn't get a fairy tale.

I got something better.

THE END

FOR NOW

...

Keep an eye out for an invitation to a
Darling Family Christmas

Author's Note

I hope that you enjoyed seek me darling!

The darling family will return all together for one last get together. You will get to see the whole family interact without worrying about spoilers.

You will also be getting a novella for Max, timing dependent on my schedule.

I would like to say thank you to my husband for always supporting me and putting up with my random obsessive personality that gets me totally lost in my writing etc. and also helping to answer all the questions that would land me on a federal watch list... If I'm already on it though, hey there, how you doing?

I want to thank my amazing team which has grown so much over the last two years of publishing. All of you are amazing and thank you so much.

And lastly thank you to you, my readers, for picking up this book and taking a chance it, and me, I completely appreciate it and you.

xx

Maree Rose

About the Author

Maree is an indie author who, although she has been writing most of her life, never thought she would ever get something published, which is now why she published this herself. She has always been an avid reader since a young age after roaming through book exchanges with her mum when she was just starting to read serious big girl books.

Maree lives on the East Coast of Australia with her wonderful husband, her son, and her two gorgeous squishy british bulldogs.

When she is not writing, she is working in a financial career (for something completely different to the creative side) or she is working on her photography (which is just as hot as her books).

Stalk Me

Please feel free to stalk me.
Like metaphorically, not literally of course!

Also By

SHATTERED WORLD

Shattered Safety Duet:
Untouchable & Unbreakable
Shattered Memories Duet:
Unforgettable & Unstoppable

DARLING WORLD

hunt me darling
hide me darling
seek me darling

DEAD DEVIL'S WORLD

Dead Devil's Night
Dead Devil's Playground (COMING SOON)

WHISPERS OF WICKED FAE

The Wild Hunt

STANDALONES

Home Sweet Home
Pose For Me
The Darkest Gift
All We Want

9 781764 066105